To Carrie + J.
thank you
friend
M.

WARDER

Dominic
Verwey

SAMARITAN OF THE SAHARA

Not by might, nor by power, but by my spirit, saith the
Lord of hosts.
Zech 4:6

2005

A DROMEDARIS BOOK

Copyright © 2005 Marie Warder
Published by **DROMEDARIS BOOKS**
Library and Archives Canada Cataloguing in Publication
Warder, Marie
Dominic Verwey : Samaritan of the Sahara / Marie Warder.
(Stories from South Africa ; no. 5)
ISBN 0-9733625-0-2 (set)
I. Title. II. Series.
PS8645.A74D64 2005   C813'.6   C2005-905262-7

Cover art:
"Africa". A painting by Leigh van der Schyff.
"Wildflower" Rapier courtesy of James "The Just"
Amazonia Enterprises
"My Honour Is My Life"
www.jamesthejust.com
The author gratefully acknowledges the inestimable contribution of Bruce
van der Schyff, Luis Wiechers, Keith Bridgefoot and Erin Potts.

Other Acknowledgments: My sincere thanks, in no special order, to Clay
and Mary Otto, Josie Cooper, Rowan Reynolds and Shaun Warder, for
their invaluable assistance. I could not have done this without them.
Dromedaris Books
Box 82 Stn Main
Delta, B.C
V4K 1V0
info@dromedarisbooks.com
Tel: (604) 948-0866
Fax: (604) 948-0867
www.dromedarisbooks.com
Printed in the USA

To order additional copies, please contact us.
BookSurge, LLC
www.booksurge.com
1-866-308-6235
orders@booksurge.com

Another novel in the Stories from South Africa series
By the author of '*When you know that you know that you know!
or The redemption of Benjamin Ashton*'
Dominic Verwey: Samaritan of the Sahara
Marie Warder

The Beauclaire saga continues…

Marie Warder

Dominic Verwey

SAMARITAN OF THE SAHARA

***

*In the stockade of an outlaw band in the Sahara desert, Doctor
Dominic Verwey is introduced to the Bedouin chief as '***Sahbena el-
Hakim***'—my friend, the doctor. But he would very shortly thereafter
earn a second name; that of '***Hamid Pasha***'—protector and leader
of his people, 'refuge of the refugee and sanctuary of the oppressed'.
His main purpose is to settle a score with the unprincipled Arab,
Abdel Sharia, who incarcerates innocent men in his labour camps and
enslaves beautiful women in his harem…*

In the introduction to this book, readers who loved the
people whose stories they followed in '***When you know that you
know that you know!***' will readily recognize such characters
as Uncle Ash (Benjamin Ashton) and a few of his friends from
his Nelspruit days—Fallah (Peter Crawford, the priest) both
Richard and Trudy Evans (the doctor, and his wife) as well as
Stella and her biologist husband, Paul Verwey—as Antoinette
Spencer Crawford, determined to put the record straight, takes
up the cudgels on behalf of the notorious ***El-Hakim*** (Uncle
Dominic), whose grandson, Stephen, she wishes to marry…

A DROMEDARIS BOOK

Dominic
Verwey

SAMARITAN OF
THE SAHARA

Other novels in Marie Warder's "Stories from South Africa" Fiction Series

When you know that you know that you know! ISBN 0-921966-09-1
or
The redemption of Benjamin Ashton
Under the Southern Cross, an awesome awakening amid the orange blossom on a South African Citrus Farm.

Set amid orange groves in the lovely town of Nelspruit, South Africa—among 'Bougainvilleas, Flame trees, Jacarandas and Poinsettias; Scarlet Flamboyant and Bottle Brush, yellow Bird of Paradise, crimson Erythrina, salmon, rose pink and white Oleander, interspersed by a riot of the sky blue, Duranta'—the air is heavy with the perfume of orange blossom in this well-written novel with an unusual plot, unusual complications and an unusual conclusion. It is the story of a successful young American, one of the wealthiest men in the world, who travels to South Africa where, going in search of his brother, he finds God—and, in so doing, finds himself! To say more would be to spoil for our readers what should prove to be a captivating read.

Storm Water—ISBN 0-921966-05-9
In exchange for giving him a son, the proud and fascinating Count Louis de Maupassant offers wealth and an elevated position in society.

This historical novel about South Africa, set in the very early days of the Cape of Good Hope, transports the reader to a distant, romantic past—to the adventurous days of the Dutch East India Company, when the Colony was young.

With no remorse…ISBN 0-921966-03-2
An extraordinary narrative of daring and courage, of sacrificial love and rock-solid loyalty is, at the same time, a tale of suspicion and jealousy; of devilish cunning and despicable treachery.

During World War 11, Joshua Naudé, a young South African agronomist, is sent on a clearly defined mission to the strategic island of Malta. His gentle, plucky but frail wife, Anna, accompanies him. Not long after their arrival on the island, they are joined by Joshua's devastatingly good-looking airman brother and, through him, they become acquainted with beautiful and captivating Stephanie Velez; a ruthless charmer of volatile Latin temperament.

Tarnished Idols—0-921966-07-5
"No mortal is perfect enough to be idolized." Around this proven adage, Marie Warder has woven a gripping tale—a story in which pure love and flaming passion are interchanged with venomous envy and bitter hatred.

In convincing manner, the writer relates the story from the point of view of Paul Jansen, the man who sincerely loves the beautiful Jeanne, but can never be more than a brother to her. The reason? Jeanne already worships another man—an idol with 'feet of clay'. Her initial adoration and later struggle against this 'idol' make for an intensely moving story, sensitively recorded.

EXTRACT

From *"When you know that you know that you know! or The redemption of Benjamin Ashton"*—"Stories from South Africa", *Dromedaris books*, April 2005.

"I feel as if I'd like to resort to a disguise," Benjamin Ashton confessed. "And I'm dreading the hearing on Monday!"

"Why?" Paul Verwey wanted to know. "You've got nothing to worry about. The very fact that the Attorney General has decreed that it should be held here, and not in some other place like Witbank, or Standerton—or even further away, in Bethlehem—is a good sign. Someone's watching over you, pal. Amy-Lee has already gone a long way towards getting you off the hook, and you should just be grateful that public opinion is so much in your favour. There is a saying that most people are fascinated by a charming rogue…and, although you're very far from being one, you could, for all you know, willy-nilly, nolens volens, already be in the 'charming daredevil' category by now!" He grinned at Ben. "A mystery man in the opinion of the masses!

"Why, I ask again? Why be embarrassed? You know you're not a rogue, and even if you ever were, so what? You certainly aren't one any longer. If Amy-Lee can forgive you, just forgive yourself now. I do know from experience, however, that there are bigots in every group." *He shrugged his shoulders resignedly. "My father-in-law was one, but I hope he's changed…… He could never be reconciled to the fact that we have what you might call a 'swashbuckler' in our family, and that we all just roll with the punches!"*

He examined Ben's face quizzically. "You probably think I'm taking your problem too lightly. Perhaps I am!" He chuckled with amused affection. "Have you ever heard of the notorious **'Samaritan of the Sahara'?**"

"One of my childhood heroes!"

"And mine," said Paul. "None other than my Uncle Dominic! Known in Egypt as 'El-Hakim', the doctor. More correctly, among the Gyppos, as the daring 'Sahhena el-Hakim'—'My friend the doctor'!"

"And he's your uncle?...I can't believe it! I had forgotten that he was a South African?"

"Well, he is."

"Now that Peter has become a priest, I think he doesn't consider it expedient to be too openly enthusiastic, but I suspect that he secretly still retains that boyhood admiration for a man who, for the sake of others less fortunate, took the most unbelievable risks. It has been said of Uncle Dominic that he was utterly fearless!...I think I'd rather say that he was utterly selfless. I think that's why Dick Evans is so selfless....I've never known any other man except El-Hakim—and perhaps, Peter—physician, priest or otherwise, to go that extra mile so readily for others!"......

"So you have known Dick and Peter for quite a while?"

"Since I was nine. We were all there together that summer, and kept up our friendship..... But I expect you know that..."

"I do....But all this is utterly compelling! Amazing!" Ben was quite carried away......... "After we had heard the grownups discuss them, our imaginations were fired, and my brother and I sometimes pretended that we were the Verwey brothers. Jamie always wanted to play Dominic, and I was Philip, the heroic younger brother!....

....."What a story that is! Someone should write a book about them!"

"Perhaps someone will...some day....!" *

"And why was Mr. Morgan so especially disapproving?"

"He was a personal friend of Dominic's nemesis, Sir Humphrey Talbot. But now I must go!" Paul rose and started down the steps. *"I hope I've succeeded in taking your mind off your problems, for a bit!"*

***

(*Twenty-two years later, it would fall to Antoinette Spencer Crawford, the daughter of Fallah and Marina Crawford, to tell the story, while recuperating at *Bentleigh*, the home of her brother's godparents, from a fever contracted as a missionary in Central Africa.)

PEOPLE WHO FEATURED IN:

W*hen you know that you know that you know! or The redemption of Benjamin Ashton"*

IN THE UNITED STATES:
The Ashton family:

Benjamin (Ash), Amy-Lee and their children—James (Jamie, or James Ashton the Fourth), Eugenie (Zhaynie) and Albert Jordan.

Ferguson, the chauffeur.

Deceased: James (Jamie)—James Ashton the Third. Founder of a centre for black children and their mothers near in Bethlehem, South Africa, where he died after falling from a windmill he was repairing.

The Crawfords: Now living at *Bentleigh* with the Ashtons.

The Rev. Doctor Peter (Fallah), Marina, and their children: Antoinette (Tony) Gregory, Isobel (Izzie) and Benjamin.

IN SOUTH AFRICA
The Verwey family

Dr. Paul and Stella Verwey and their son, Dominic—who run the citrus farm, *Beauclaire,* established by Benjamin Ashton near Nelspruit.

Dr. Dominic Verwey—*El-Hakim* (Uncle Dominic)

Dr. Stephen Verwey (his grandson)

Dr. Philip Verwey—brother of *El-Hakim*

<u>The Mostert family</u>

Albert (Bert) and Isobel—Marina Crawford's parents, and grandparents of Antoinette (Tony) Gregory and Isobel (Izzie).

Also Aunt Minnie de Beer, great friend of the late James Ashton the third. Now a patron of the Ashton's youngest child, Albert Jordan (mostly just known as Jordan.)

THE DROMEDARIS CONCEPT

Dromedary: *Camelus Dromedarius*: a one-humped camel. Camels are commonly regarded as carriers—of both people and merchandise. ***Dromedaris*** was also the name of a ship which took our ancestors to South Africa in 1652. Our mandate, in the 'Dromedaris concept', is to bring a different kind of merchandise from South Africa to the rest of the world....Our books, written by acclaimed expatriate authors.

For Sam. My friend, the doctor.

INTRODUCTION

For months after I first began to try and write the story as it had been told to me (reluctantly and with a marked degree of self-effacement, I might add!) by Uncle Dominic (*El-Hakim*) himself, and encouraged by other more enthusiastic people—like his grandson (my beloved Stephen), Uncle Ash and Aunt Amy-Lee, Uncle Dick and Uncle Paul—I had a strong feeling that Fallah was not pleased about my doing so. I reckoned it was because, as a priest and man of God, Fallah could not reconcile himself with some of things *El-Hakim* did. Thus, because Fallah is one of the two people I love best in the whole world (Stephen being the other), and I never, ever want to displease him, I knew I would have to tackle him on this score.

I hoped to find both the opportunity and the courage to do so, because of something Uncle Ash said while Uncle Dick and Aunt Trudy were here recently, on a visit from South Africa. Uncle Ash had been questioning Uncle Dick on the subject of Uncle Dominic, because he had once been told by Uncle Paul, who is Uncle Dominic's nephew, that it was on account of *El-Hakim* and his brother, Philip, that he, Uncle Dick had wanted to be a doctor. Uncle Dick struck a chord in Fallah, I think, by telling us—and thus reminding Fallah—of how much fun the two of them had derived, when they were children in Natal, from playing at being the notorious Verwey brothers. A wry, reminiscent grin on Uncle Ash's face, at that, caused me to wonder whether it was because he was thinking of how he and his brother, Jamie, had played the very same pretend game on the other side of the world....Or perhaps he could not help recalling how the citrus inspector, biologist Paul Verwey (Uncle Paul, had talked nineteen-to-the dozen about *El-Hakim*, one stressful day in Nelspruit more than twenty years ago, to try and keep him, Uncle Ash, from dwelling on his impending court hearing.

Having just read what I've written, I realize that this must be very confusing to anyone who does not know that, in South Africa, it is common practice to call any close friend of the family, and also any grown-up whose name one doesn't know, 'Uncle' or 'Auntie'. So perhaps I'd better start over and sort out some of the relationships.

To begin with, none of the above is a relative at all, but I guard very closely the fact that Fallah is not my 'father' by birth. And when anyone dares to say, in my presence, that he adopted my brother Greg and me, I immediately take exception. Fallah, whose real name is the Reverend Doctor Peter Crawford, may have adopted Greggie; but he did not adopt me! I adopted him! He is the only father Greg and I have ever known, and long before he and my mother got married, he was my 'Fallah', which was the only way I could pronounce that word. I was just three when my birth father, Gregory Spencer—of whom I have no memory at all, because he was away so much—was killed, fighting in Angola, and I must have heard someone in our home refer to this priest as 'Father'; so I somehow assumed that he was mine! Greggie and I are now both 'Crawfords', like our half-brother, Benjamin, and our half-sister, Isobel Jillian Crawford.

Our Benjamin has been named for Uncle Ash, whose

proper name is Benjamin Ashton, and we all now live in Uncle Ash's beautiful, enormous house called *Bentleigh* which is on Long Island. My sister, Isobel, (who hates being called "Izzie") has the names of our grandmother, Isobel Mostert, who still lives in Nelspruit, South Africa, and Jillian—the girl to whom Fallah was engaged, long before he met my mother. (Jill was killed just a few weeks before their wedding.) Izzie is lucky to have Fallah's red hair, but, instead of his freckles—which I love—she has that porcelain complexion that many redheads are blessed with, and eyes of the most incredible, almost turquoise colour.

Now, as I should have explained, Uncle Dick Evans is the doctor who brought all four of us Crawfords into the world, and Aunt Trudy is his wife. It was because of Uncle Dick that Fallah went to be the rector of Saint Margaret's church in Nelspruit, South Africa, and that's where the two of them became best friends with Uncle Ash. And that's how our family later came to be living in America, at *Bentleigh* with the Ashtons—Uncle Ash and Aunt Amy-Lee.

From the time I was three, I wanted nothing more out of life than to have Fallah for my real father. In fact, I wanted to own him...father or no father! I only felt safe when I had him somewhere in sight, and to have had to wait two-and a-half years for the two of them—my mother, Marina, and Fallah—to get round to marrying each other, was torture. The trouble was that my mother, as much as she loved Fallah, had taken a vow that Greggie was not going to be allowed to grow up in South Africa, in case he also someday became what she constantly still refers to as 'cannon fodder', like my birth father. It took a promise that we would emigrate before my brother was old enough to be eligible for conscription, to make her say 'yes'!

I don't remember this, but I am told that, when I could

not have Fallah where I could see him, Aunt Amy-Lee Ashton was the next best thing. I adored her, and actually thought that she was a fairy princess. Well, she's gorgeous enough to be one...even now! And I still adore her. She and Uncle Ash are very, very rich, and they have this mansion in the States, and apparently I once asked her to grant a wish that my mom and Fallah would get together. In time—not by wishing, but by Fallah praying about it—the Ashtons invited us to come and live with them. Of course, we could not come right away. It is not easy to get to live in America. It took a long time and, in the interim, Fallah studied and obtained his doctorate, and then Uncle Ash set up this place for us here in *Bentleigh*, where Fallah counsels troubled people, when he is not lecturing or preaching somewhere else. He is very much in demand to lead 'missions', among other things.

Sometimes Uncle Ash takes time off from running a stupendous international conglomerate, to go with Fallah, and he often leads 'retreats' on his own. Fallah says that Uncle Ash would make a great priest, but he, Uncle Ash, only smiles and says he will, if and when he feels 'called'. In the meantime, he ministers 'in the market place' to his staff, wherever they may be, in many places around the world, and to some of the wealthiest—but often unhappiest—people he does business with.

So it seems to me that he and Aunt Amy-Lee do okay with just what they are doing, anyway. No matter where he has to travel, he will not go without her, and whenever possible, their children have gone, too. All of us, me included, have been taken to school and brought home every day by Ferguson, the chauffeur, and once home, we've obviously never lacked for playmates.

It's really neat the way the Ashtons accommodate so many

people at *Bentleigh*. They have remodelled the mansion in such a way that we Crawfords have a complete suite, almost like a separate cottage, and there are two smaller suites like ours, for friends, missionaries on furlough, or others who need to make a fairly prolonged stay in New York. (Strange how, when you have younger siblings in your family, you pick up their slang. Like 'neat' and 'cool'. They don't 'dig' many of my expressions, however. When I once said I was feeling quite 'gay' they nearly had a fit!)

As I have said, there are the four of us Crawfords, and the Ashtons have three children. Their eldest son is called James Michael—'James Ashton the Fourth'. The Michael is for his maternal grandfather, Michael Marsh (Aunt Amy-Lee's father), and my sister, Izzie, just about swoons if Jamie as much as looks at her. He went away to Harvard just over two years ago, and it's quite pathetic to see how she blossoms whenever he comes home, and starts to wilt the moment he leaves! Actually, I can understand why, because his father is a knockout, and he looks just like him!

There is another Ashton boy, his full name is Albert Jordan but he has never been called anything but just 'Jordan', and, at seventeen, he is already as tall as his father and his brother. His first name is for my grandfather, Bert Mostert, and you would have to know the whole story about Uncle Ash's brother, the 'James Ashton the third' about whom I have spoken, and a dear old lady they call 'Aunt Minnie', who lives in Bethlehem, in the Orange Free State, South Africa, to know where that second name comes from. When Aunt Minnie's husband, Uncle Charlie de Beer, died a few years ago, we were not surprised to learn that Jordan is the De Beers' sole heir. Whenever he can get to South Africa, he invariably heads straight for Bethlehem.

The middle Ashton child is called Eugenie. (Pronounced like 'Zhaynie'). She is very, very beautiful. Just as nice as her mother is, but, strangely enough, is not one of the 'blonde' Ashtons. They say she looks more like the Beauclaires of Louisiana, and her hair—which is as long and shiny as her mother's—is as black as the poetic 'raven's wing'. She has her father's devastating smile and his intense blue eyes, though.... Now, there's another case of 'love at first sight'!

Last year, Uncle Paul Verwey and his wife, Stella, were here from South Africa for two months. (Aunt Stella has the unfortunate, and dubious distinction, of being the daughter of the very same Valentine Morgan, aide to *El-Hakim's* nemesis, Sir Humphrey Talbot, who, for a long time refused to allow his daughter to marry Uncle Paul). They also live in the Nelspruit district, with their son, another Dominic, and run the citrus farm at Beauclaire Estates.

Once every year the Ashtons go back and stay in the house Uncle Ash built there in the 1970's, and which has, of course, had to be enlarged over the years, to accommodate the children. In all that time, Dominic (not to be confused with *Uncle* Dominic, the doctor whose story I mean to tell), and Eugenie hardly saw each other. During this last visit to America, however, when the Verweys brought Dominic with them, it was as though they, Zhaynie and Dominic, had been struck by lightning! What will come of that, I don't know. I can't begin to imagine how Eugenie's family will feel about her marrying and going to live in South Africa—especially at a time when people are leaving there in droves! It's like my parents' story in reverse!

There was a great deal of talk about the notorious Doctor Dominic, of 'Sahara' fame, while the Verweys were here. Uncle

Paul Verwey (who, while being 'Doctor' Verwey, is not a medical doctor) and Uncle Dick Evans (who is), were part of the three-man admiration society, and Uncle Ash, rapidly became the fourth, after also having my Stephen's adored *El-Hakim—the Doctor Dominic*—and his wife (who is a real princess, believe it or not!) as house guests for those two months last year. I think that Uncle Ash could really relate to *El-Hakim* because his own past history has been similar, in some ways but not all. In many ways, although they are in no way related, and despite the age difference, they even look alike, and I can easily picture Doctor Dominic long ago, with golden hair like Uncle Ash's...

What a magnificent looking man *El-Hakim* still is! Although he had grown up on a farm in the Eastern Free State, he and his grandson, Stephen, speak with that same, distinctive Natal accent as Fallah and Uncle Dick Evans, and I noticed at once the beautiful hands that my Doctor Stephen has clearly inherited! Ever since they returned to South Africa, Uncle Ash has consistently declared, as he had already done for the umpteenth time before that, that someone should write a 'decent' book about the 'Samaritan of the Sahara', and that's what I am now trying to do—for reasons of my own...!

By the way, Uncle Ash says I should mention, because he did not know until Uncle Paul came to inspect his orange trees for red scale, that 'Verwey' is pronounced '*Firvay*'.

To get back to what I was saying, when I started out, I had this strong feeling that Fallah was not pleased about my embarking on *El-Hakim's* story, even when I pointed out that it would help to pass the time. I thought that he disapproved—until I overheard him, as I was approaching the Ashtons' library, where Uncle Ash said I could work. I heard him saying to Uncle

Ash: "I am really concerned about Antoinette, Benjamin. You know how dear she is to me and I can't help thinking that I should never have allowed her to go to Burundi, in the first place. The Congo was the limit!...She is an excellent nurse and could readily have found a position at Addington in Durban, in Nelspruit, or even right here in New York. Maybe she wasn't meant to be a missionary! And I am troubled that she might have done that for my sake!"

"That's nonsense, Pete, and you, of all people, must know that!" I then heard Uncle Ash respond. "Few would ever suspect that Tony is not your own flesh and blood, because she is so like you, and so very obviously your favourite!...She knows she doesn't have to do anything to make you love her any more than you already do.—Do you remember what you wrote on the card you left for me after my court hearing all those years ago?...I still have it, and I recall your words clearly....'*My prayer for you is that God will give you the grace to hear and recognize that voice always, and the grace to respond and obey it when you do.*'... Can't you just trust in the fact that she was given the 'grace to respond and obey!' "

"You're right, Ash," Fallah said slowly, "but Stephen Verwey will have it that these tropical things take time, and he was adamant about her resting a great deal until she has regained her strength. I agonize about her sitting at that computer until the small hours!...She definitely doesn't look well, to me!"

"Pete!" Uncle Ash protested. "Surely you can't be so blind! What ails Tony now, is not a tropical fever....It's love-sickness! No one knows the symptoms—or the pain of it—better than I!...If you ask me, her current problem isn't anything she contracted while in swamps and jungles....She caught it in Pietermaritzburg—and the root cause of it is young Doctor Stephen Verwey!"

'*Oh, Stephen, Stephen,*' I was crying in my heart as I listened. '*He knows, and he's so right!*' I remained just out of sight, and stood there so very quietly that I was able to hear Fallah's sharp intake of breath.

"Good heavens, Ash! Is that why she spends most of her time writing about his grandfather?...That never occurred to me!...Do you think she wants to plead his case with people who misjudge him too readily?...Someone like me, for instance?"

'*Why should I have to choose between the two people I love best in the world?*' I demanded of my heart.

"That's exactly what I do think!...Maybe, knowing my history, and how you could find it in your heart not to condemn me," Uncle Ash told my father, "she wants to have a shot at telling the whole Sahara story....What's more, doesn't that give her the most wonderful excuse for staying in close touch with the family? Whether it is by phone, fax or email, she needs to interview *El-Hakim* at greater length than she was able to do when he was here.

"I know that makes you very unhappy, Padre, but I have to be as frank with you now, as you have had to be with me, in the past.—How much of this is actually due to unwarranted disapproval of all young Doctor Stephen's family...because of the man who could yet be Tony's grandfather-in-law? I think you are simply, albeit subconsciously, jealous of any other men she might have in her life!

"How can you truthfully say that it is not so, when you know as well as I do that, in the first place, you don't want her going so far away from you again...and, in the second, it's hard to have to face the fact that you can't be number one in her life forever? Do you want her to have to choose between keeping you happy, and being happy herself? In any case, without your blessing she'll never be happy anywhere! You're also as scared to contemplate her living back in South Africa, as Marina was to have Greggie remain there! You're terrified that she won't be safe!"

I, Antoinette (Tony) Spencer Crawford, hated it when Buthelezi's Zulus and Mandela's ANC were slaughtering each other, and when thousands died in the South African townships every night, because that was a terrible tragedy for the country and for its people. But the violence did not frighten me! I had probably seen worse in Burundi and the Congo. Right now I do not care about anything except wanting to be with Stephen—now, and when he goes off to obey his 'call' once more—and how hard it will be to leave Fallah and all the beloved ones here! I do not want to write about *El-Hakim* to impress anyone....I only want to set the record straight because I love his grandson. I sincerely love him, and I adore Fallah. I want my children to know, someday, how wonderful the menfolk, and all the people in their lives are now, and have been in the past. At the same time, I hope I may succeed in telling the story dispassionately, so that people can judge for themselves...!

So, while I am getting my strength back, waiting for the day I can marry my Stephen and go back to South Africa again, I apply myself assiduously to my manuscript; loving every minute of it, and falling more and more in love with *El-Hakim* with every word I write. Sometimes he and my dearest Stephen become almost fused into one person, in my thoughts, and I find myself developing such a passionate affection for the rest of his family that it now seems as though I have known Princess Thérèse, Doctor Philip and the rest of them, all my life. How amazing it will be to become a part of that family!

Here then for them, with my love, is their story...

THE STORY OF DOMINIC VERWEY

Sahhena el-Hakim...my friend, the doctor.

Samaritan of the Sahara

PART ONE

CHAPTER ONE
PROLOGUE

Dominic Verwey narrowed his eyes against the sharp, perpendicular rays of the early morning Egyptian sun. The expression on his face was one of mixed concern and disbelief.

"It's impossible, Philip. What on earth could have become of her?"

Philip's only response was an eloquent shrug.

Alone on the balcony, the two brothers faced one another in silence. Dominic, the older of the two, an exceptionally good-looking giant of a man, was clearly still half asleep and hardly in a fit state to grasp what his brother had just told him. He blinked, rubbed his eyes repeatedly, and kept drawing his fingers through his thick, blond hair as though this would restore him to full consciousness. He was clad in wrinkled pyjamas that would have put the rainbow to shame. His younger brother, on the other hand, already appeared cool and well dressed, in an immaculate, white linen tropical suit. Philip's lean, handsome young face bore ill-disguised signs of impatience.

Behind him, in the distance, rose the great dome of the Mosque of Mohamed Ali, and from the minarets sharply silhouetted against the fiery red ball of the rising sun, the voice of the muezzin could be heard. The crowding buildings of Cairo lay stretched out on every side, shrouded under a heavy cloud of smoke.

Suddenly Dominic was wide-awake....If Philip spoke the truth! "What were you doing in Lydia's bedroom, to begin with?" he demanded. "And you're up disgustingly early!"

"I told you!" Philip replied, with some annoyance. "But you're uncommonly obtuse this morning, Dom....She asked me yesterday, when we were still on the ship, if I would accompany her to the Gezira Club. That English colonel invited all of us to go riding there with him. Surely you must remember that! When you said it wouldn't be possible for you to go, Lydia asked me—as I have said—because she did not want to go alone."

"I do remember now," Dominic acknowledged, "but that still doesn't tell me why you had to go to her room."

"I'm waiting to explain, but you won't give me a chance to finish." Philip sighed with exasperation. "By the time we checked in here at the hotel last night, I was so tired that I went straight to my room, and consequently did not find an opportunity to ask her when and where I should meet her. I really did not want to hang around in riding breeches all morning, in this heat, so I got up and dressed myself early, in something light, and knocked at her door to wake her. I must have kept knocking for nearly five minutes and when she did not respond, I opened her door—which, to my surprise was not locked—and went inside. There was no one in the room and it was obvious that her bed had not been slept in!"

"Perhaps she was also up early, made her own bed, and went for a swim," Dominic suggested.

"I thought of that," Philip informed him, "but the chambermaid assures me that there is no sign of luggage, all the cupboards in her room are empty and..."—he hesitated uncertainly—"she was last seen by the *dragoman* (interpreter)... at two o'clock this morning!"

"What? Where was she at that hour of...?"

"She was seen getting into a car...but that's not all..."

"What do you mean...that's not all?"

Philip surveyed his brother sympathetically. "Lydia wasn't alone, Dom....She was with that pale-skinned Arab who disembarked with us in Alexandria yesterday.—The sheik Mohammed Ahmed!"

Dominic's deep blue eyes glinted dangerously, and for the first time in his life, Philip wondered if his brother would strike him, because he clenched his fists as he confronted him furiously. Then, suddenly, his attitude changed.

"I don't believe it, Philip—do you hear me? I don't believe it! Lydia would never do something like that! I'm going to dress myself, immediately, and then I shall go and make my own inquiries!"

With that he stormed back into his bedroom and frantically began to pull clothing from the chest-of-drawers in which he had placed it less than twelve hours before.

(ii)

Philip had never really liked his brother's fiancée. Lydia—Dominic's alluring girl friend—was just a little too much aware of her own attractions for his liking. In addition, she was far too fickle to deserve the love of a man like Dominic, who perhaps, like many other such powerful males, had been drawn to her mainly by that innocent, deceptively delicate look, because he felt naturally protective towards a cute little creature like that.

Dominic had very recently passed his finals at the University of Edinburgh and, as a specialist in tropical diseases, a brilliant future awaited him. Philip secretly held the opinion that his prospective little sister-in-law, with her shallowness and flighty bohemian, almost hedonistic habits, would prove to be an obstacle in the path of his success, but he had never, in any way, made his brother aware of those sentiments. If Dominic—his idol, his childhood hero—had deemed the Medusa, herself, to be essential to his perfect happiness, he would have sanctioned the choice. He, Philip, had tried to be unfailingly friendly...kindness itself...towards the girl, while she seemed to go out of her way to make him feel like a green, clumsy schoolboy—except when she wanted something from him!

On the ship she had, in his opinion, behaved particularly badly. Three months before, when he had arrived in Britain to attend his brother's convocation at the university, it had been a great shock to find Dominic engaged to Lydia Scott-Brady. It had been an additional disappointment to learn that she was to accompany them on the homeward trip. He and Dominic had talked for so long about the sea voyage they would some day undertake together. From the time, he, Philip, reached his teens, 'Some day, when I turn eighteen, and leave school...!' had become a sort of mantra.

Finally that long-awaited eighteenth birthday had come, but the voyage had to be further postponed as Dom continued his studies, spending time working at a number of centres for disease control—in Brussels, Geneva and Johannesburg— before returning to Edinburgh. Now Dominic was well on the way to thirty, he, Philip, now in his early twenties, and that dream would never quite be realized.—Not with Lydia around! Perhaps life was just like that!...You longed for something so fervently that, when the day came for you finally to get it, it was not one bit as you had pictured it.

He was convinced that his brother—who was hardly the

most experienced man in the world when it came to women—
had not, thus far, enjoyed the trip very much, either. Lydia,
with her porcelain-doll beauty, was far too popular and flirted
shamelessly. With Dominic's glittering sapphire securely
on her left hand, it was unnecessary to keep putting herself
out too much for him, and she was thus free to exercise her
charms, unhindered, on the other passengers. A chill ran up
Philip's spine as he recalled, with vivid clarity, the look in the
calculating dark eyes of Mohammed Ahmed when he had first
caught sight of the blonde beauty. It had been the unblinking,
venomous stare of a cobra.

When they had arrived in Alexandria the day before, it
had been a relief to see what he hoped was the last of the Arab.
'Two days in Cairo,' he had promised himself, 'and then we'll
be permanently rid of the Middle-Eastern menace!' When the
invitation to go riding with the colonel had been extended
to Lydia, and Dominic, who was seemingly too blind to see
what was going on before his eyes, had declined to accompany
them—because he preferred to go and discuss some medical
condition with a fellow specialist in the city—Philip knew,
with a sinking heart that he would once again have to be the
chaperone.

…And now what?

One day of their visit already over, more or less, and here
he sat, entirely alone and bored out of his wits, in one of the
most expensive suites in the most expensive hotel in Cairo,
and the situation was worse than ever! Dominic was visibly
unhappier than he had been at any stage of the trip so far.

The door handle turned, and Philip looked up expectantly.
To his relief, it was his brother who entered. Dominic walked
with slow, heavy tread.

"Hullo, Phil," he said flatly, and flung his powerful frame

into the nearest easy chair. He wiped his damp forehead with his handkerchief. "Phew! Have you ever known such heat! Even Durban in summer is cool by comparison!"

For a while Philip said nothing, but he was finally moved to ask: "What about Lydia? Have you found out anything?"

His brother shook his head. There was another long silence as Dominic tried to compose himself. He was obviously exhausted and his face was ashen under the deep tan.

By now Philip was seething with anger. How dared any woman treat his gentle, softhearted brother in such a fashion? If he had been able to grab hold of Lydia, at that moment, he would surely have throttled her. His own fists were clenched this time, as he sprang up and strode over towards Dominic.

"The trouble with Lydia," he growled, thin-lipped, "is that she has seen too many films! In that empty head of hers she probably finds something terribly romantic about the very word 'sheik'! And what are they, after all...? A filthy, half-breed, low lot...!"

"Please, Phil," Dominic, ever the charitable one, said quietly, holding up his hand. "Mohammed Ahmed is probably quite as proud of his ancestry as you and I, and, in addition, he's very wealthy. Among Mohammedans, the term 'sheik' is an expression of respect!"

"You can skip the protestations, and forget all the noble sentiments!" Philip came back at him impatiently. "Who the heck are you trying to convince?...Rather tell me what you plan to do about this? You're surely not going to allow Lydia to wreck your entire holiday!"

Dominic rose from his seat and stretched himself to his full six-foot-four inches. He looked down at his tempestuous young brother and said calmly: "I'm going to look for her, of course!"

"What!" Philip was momentarily speechless. He could not believe his own ears. "You're going to look for her?—And where, I ask you?" He grabbed Dominic by the arm and the rage in his voice subsided. There was a measure of compassion in his voice, as he pleaded with him. "Oh, please, Dom, don't go and humiliate yourself. You can't give the girl that satisfaction!—Not after the way she has betrayed you!"

Now it was once more Dominic's turn to be angry. "Is *that* what you think? No, my dear Philip. You are mistaken!... Lydia would never betray anyone. She's far too honourable!...If she left the hotel with Mohammed Ahmed—and all evidence points to that—it was not of her own free will....The man must have abducted her!"

Philip was so flabbergasted that he could only gape, open-mouthed, at him. He wanted to argue, at first, but the sharp words died on his lips. Dominic was either the world's greatest fool—or saint! He found it difficult to see wrong in anyone. Philip lowered his hands with a sigh of hopelessness. He did not want to quarrel with his brother. The poor man was already unhappy enough. Philip sighed again. He had no other choice than to submit.

"Very well. Then we'd better start looking!"

(iii)

By the time the brothers were due to leave on the following day they were no nearer a solution to the mystery. The tour guide had knocked on their door several times to remind them that the other members of the group were already gathered on the sidewalk, ready to depart. The bus which would take them back to Alexandria was expected at any minute.

Dominic paced back and forth like a caged lion. "I'm not

leaving without her, Philip! Man, I tell you, *I can't*! The most dreadful things might have happened to her already!"

Even Philip, who had his own opinions on the subject, had to acknowledge this possibility. No matter how fed-up he was with the whole situation, he could understand how Dom must be feeling. They had notified the police, consulted the South African Consul and combed a great part of Cairo. In vain! Lydia had disappeared without a trace!

There was one thing about which Dominic was concerned above all else. The sheik Mohammed Ahmed was evidently very wealthy, and very important, if the priceless jewels he so openly displayed on board ship were taken into consideration—and the *dragoman* was convinced that Lydia and her abductor had left the hotel in a Rolls Royce. But neither the police, nor the countless Bedouin desert dwellers, whom they had questioned with the aid of the interpreter, had ever heard of such a man.

Again there was a knock at the door, and the anxious voice of the guide reached them from the passage. "It grows late, *Effendi*!...We must leave *now* or you will miss the boat!"

Perspiration beaded Dominic's forehead. "The police here seem to be useless, Phil. They will not search for her, I feel sure. Much less find her....I *cannot* go!"

"*Effendi...*?" The voice was growing impatient.

Dominic, who was habitually patience itself, jerked the door open. "For Pete's sake, man, stop this hammering!... Go and tell the people that only the young gentleman will be going with you!...I shall come later—with friends!"...He made a threatening movement. "Go!...ISHMA YELLA!...Be off with you!"

He bellowed so loudly that the other man, a slight, delicate looking fellow, almost fell over with fright.

"Good, *Effendi*...good...I shall tell them!" The guide

backed away slowly, with one eye on the young giant, bowing with almost every step he took, but, once around the corner, he took off like a frightened rabbit.

Once again the brothers looked at one another searchingly. Dominic strong and determined.—Phillip, shorter, leaner, hardly more than a lad; yet equally determined.

"If you're staying, Dom, I'm staying, too!"

"You can't, little brother. I dare not allow that. We don't have visas to stay here any longer. The moment the ship leaves without us, and we are missed, someone is bound to start looking for us....You must go home while there is still time!"

Philip rested his hand on his brother's shoulder. His words were hardly audible. "Go *home*?...Where is my home?...I have no one in the world, except you, Dom, and wherever you are, that is where my home is!"

There was a long silence, and when Dominic finally spoke, his voice was husky. "You are a good brother, Philip. I should very much like to have you with me!"

"Well then..." Philip felt a trifle embarrassed and his practical words were calculated to cover the embarrassment. "Let's make ready to leave. It's clear that we can't waste too much time, here!"

CHAPTER TWO

Ａnd that is how it came about that Dominic and Philip Verwey stayed behind in Egypt. There are many stories in existence about these two and their adventures, but there are only two people able to relate the story in all its detail, and those are the brothers themselves. The Bedouin love to exchange tales, when they lie around their campfires at night, but, as Doctor Dominic says, personally, they add on a bit here and leave out something there, until eventually no one can tell truth from fable.

For two weeks the Verwey brothers remained just beyond the reach of the law. They kept themselves hidden during the day and only ventured to continue the search after dark. While they had money, the adventure was reasonably exciting, but at the start of the third week, Dominic began to feel anxious. They dared not go near a bank to cash a cheque and the food situation was becoming critical.

Despite the disdain they had expressed, concerning the local police force, they could never enter a shop with any confidence, much less risk passing a cheque with Dominic's signature on it. Very likely the police never gave them a single thought but, inexperienced fugitives that they were then, the mere glimpse of the black tunic and trousers and the red fez was enough to induce cold shivers.

"How can we ever hope to find work? How can we as much as dream of *beginning* to look?" Philip asked more than once. "Our Arabic...or Egyptian...or whatever they speak is less than pathetic—even with the aid of the dictionary!"

That was when Dominic, reluctant but desperate, came up with a plan.—The first of many. He would make out a traveller's cheque, and then they would steal whatever they needed and leave the cheque in its place. They were able to try that with amazing success in several places, until they began to run out of cheques.

"Let me take a turn tonight," Philip offered, at the end of the second week. "You're very conspicuous you know, Doctor Verwey. With your height and fair hair, you stick out like a sore thumb. There is a measure of consolation in the number of foreign troops who are still here, even though the war ended more than three years ago, but I doubt if they march around too often, dressed the way we are!...I'm not comfortable after seeing that headline about the mysterious foreigner who has been scattering Thomas Cooke cheques around.—Perhaps I could pass for an Italian or some other nationality," he offered helpfully.

Dominic glared at him. "Don't you dare!" he cautioned. "Don't even think of it! It's kind of you, but it's bad enough that I, who have always prided myself on being such a god-fearing guy, could set my kid brother such a poor example! Every time I do this, I think of the Ten Commandments and I cringe—until I remind myself of why we're doing this! We *have* to find Lydia—and soon!

"I think I can get away with this, one more time, but after that we'll have to find jobs—or turn ourselves in. I haven't yet reached the stage where I can take *anything*, let alone money, without the consolation that I am at least paying it back..."

"Nor can I." Philip suddenly began to laugh. "And what sort of work should we actually begin to look for? My qualifications consist of a matriculation certificate, ten months into studying for a science degree, and the two stripes I earned in the army!...Yours?...How good is a medical specialist at scrubbing floors or peeling potatoes?"

"You'll see," Dominic promised, also exploding with mirth. "I'll find work...I'll earn us some money—even if I have to go out into the desert and extract teeth!"

His face suddenly brightened. "The *desert*!" he mused. "You know, Phil, that's not a bad idea. It's high time we moved on! You're right about our never being really safe in the city, and it's becoming obvious that we are not likely to find out anything here. Lydia might very well be held captive in the desert, rather than here.....In any case, I think we've exhausted every clue and possibility. Every one of them has only led us to a dead-end..."

Philip considered this and had to agree. He was actually quite keen to see something of the desert before the holiday was over. "We have wasted too much time here already.... Incidentally..." he grinned, "which establishment do you propose to rob tonight, Al Capone?"

Dominic took the last of his change out of his pocket, spread it out on his palm and counted his money. Then he said airily: "Tonight I'm going to show you how cunning I've become. I'm going to march boldly into Shepherd's Hotel and get some money—right under the noses of people who know me!"

***

Philip would later tell that it seemed as though he waited a lifetime in that dark doorway near the hotel. The slightest noise, he readily confesses, almost made him pass out. At long last he was able to recognize the blond head and broad shoulders of his brother, and by that time, his muscles were so tense that it ached to relax them. He waited until Dominic came right up to him before he ventured to whisper anxiously, "Did you get it?"

Dominic nodded affirmatively but said nothing. He was panting, and in the light of a passing car his face was harrowed. Philip had never seen him like that before. It was obvious that he had received a great shock.

"What is it, Dom?" Philip tugged at his sleeve when he did not reply. "Tell me, man! What happened?"

The older Verwey could hardly rely on his voice. "Come!" he said shortly. "Let's get out of here!"

About a mile from the hotel, they were fortunate to find a taxi to take them in an easterly direction, past the great Citadel of Saladin and beyond, to where they alighted in front of a Greek grocery store, above which they had taken lodgings. All the while Dominic had been sitting beside Philip as though turned to stone, but by the time they reached their destination he had pulled himself together. He had his feelings well under control—for good!

Under the naked light bulb in their room Philip studied his brother's face closely and came to a surprising conclusion. There was something in his countenance that had not been there previously. A coldness that was like steel, and a tightness of his jaw that boded ill for anyone who dared to interfere with him. Gone was that kindly curling up of the corners of his mouth. The laughter lines around his eyes had become grooves of bitterness!

Dominic stretched out his arm and, with admirable self-control, gave the letter he was clutching, to Philip.

"Read it!" he muttered grimly, his voice icy. "We've been wasting our time!—Just as you predicted!"

Philip took the letter.

Perplexed, he drew it from the envelope, without comment, and the words scrawled on it danced like flames before his eyes.

"*Dear Dominic,*" he read, " *I am not a woman who should ever make promises. I always find them too difficult to keep. Forgive me, but I can't give Ahmed up.*

"*Please advise the captain that I shall not be returning to the ship. Hope this note reaches you in time.—Lydia*"

"Isn't that strange," Philip observed reflectively. "We must have passed the reception desk on the day we left the hotel, and it never occurred to us to ask if there was mail for us. By the time it might have been sent up to our room, we had already gone....If you had not happened to return there tonight...if you hadn't seen this on the letter-rack...we would never have known!"

"And if we had found this out sooner, we'd have been well on our way to Cape Town by now! What a powerful word that little 'if' is!...It comprises all the regrets human beings can ever experience....Perhaps this was all destined to happen to us..."

All at once Dominic seemed to become unaware of Philip's presence, and spoke as though to himself. "Who knows, perhaps this has happened for the best. I have the most extraordinary premonition that I have some sort of mission in this godforsaken place!"

"*What!*" Philip could hardly believe his ears, especially because Dominic's words contrasted so sharply with the expression on his face. "Well, believe me, big brother, I shall not be sticking around long enough to witness that! My one desire is to acquire enough money to get me out of here—and as soon as possible!"

"I hardly think we're going to need evening clothes and black ties for a while, and we certainly can't go trekking around the desert with crocodile skin luggage and Saville Row suits," Dominic reflected, thinking aloud as the idea began to grow on him. "We also don't need our cameras....Probably no place to have films developed and no money to do so, anyway....I don't know much about the sort of clothing we're going to need.—This won't be like hiking through the bushveld, either.—All I have in my mind is movies about Stanley and Livingstone, and archaeologists in pith helmets, but I suggest we start by flogging everything we are not likely to need."

"Good idea," Philip agreed. "And I suggest we start by looking for an army surplus store, to get some idea of what would be the most useful. Perhaps we should keep our riding breeches, but, besides them, we shan't need much more than perhaps a pair or two of khaki pants, and some sort of bush jackets, I imagine—and I'm taking at least three toothbrushes and a goodly supply of toothpaste and soap, as well as underwear. If we run out of razor blades that won't be too serious..."

"A back pack?...A sleeping bag, perhaps?...Oh, and water bottles!" Dominic was also becoming as enthusiastic as his present, shattered self would allow. "One thing I'm taking for sure, is my medical bag. God willing you won't ever get sick, but I'm responsible for you, and I'm a firm believer in being prepared!...No matter how short of money we find ourselves, at any time, I'm determined to hang onto some ready cash, in case we ever find ourselves in a dire emergency! "

CHAPTER THREE

The events of the year that followed are of lesser importance. Dominic and Philip came to know the land—drifting from one kind of work to another; blown hither and thither, by what they deemed the 'Wind of Providence'. The bazaars and the market places held few secrets for them. The smell of camels and the dust of the sand dunes were already in their blood.

Philip's skin darkened to nut brown under the desert sun, and gradually his youthful appearance changed, until the boy was gone, leaving behind a man. Hardly a day passed without his vowing to make arrangements to return to South Africa, on the very next one. Eventually it became a standing joke between the two of them. Dominic, on the other hand, never exhibited any sign of being eager to come to a decision concerning the future. Willing to take each day as it came, whatever it might bring, he enjoyed the sheer aimlessness of living this way.

After all the years of determined dedication to his studies, the responsibility for raising his brother, and the labouring in the various hospitals where he had gained experience, it was incredibly pleasant to drift with the stream....A perfectly natural reaction, he explained to Philip....However, although he did not speak of it again, he could never shake off the feeling that somewhere a different way of life awaited him. It was as though, wherever he went and whatever he did, he was constantly waiting for that 'call'.—Always on the alert for that 'sign'! Looking back at those weeks in Cairo, he could hardly believe that he, Doctor Dominic Verwey, had actually resorted to taking money without permission. He now felt desperately repentant, and prayed about that a great deal.

There were two things he assiduously did during that period....At every opportunity, whenever they rested for any length of time, and if there was sufficient light to do so, he read from the pocket Bible he carried in his backpack, hoping that he might find peace and guidance there....And whenever he found himself in a place where it was possible to do so, he refreshed his medical supplies.

When spring came, he was given the opportunity to wonder whether he had found that calling. Spring, to his mind, was Egypt's worst season. The time for sandstorms. Epidemics seemed to be raging wherever he and Philip went, and immediately realizing that the situation was due more to the unhygienic, unhealthy habits of people than to the season of the year, Dominic had cause to be grateful for the water-purifying kits he carried. He had dealt with such epidemics in the past, and was ever conscious of his responsibility for the health and wellbeing of the brother over whom he had watched for so long.

They were temporarily spending time in some of the numerous small, palm-encircled villages in the Nile delta, where farmers built their houses on artificial mounds of black soil, out of reach of the floodwaters, as they had done since the days of the Pharaohs. Fever and dysentery were endemic, and often, as he walked through the messy streets surrounded by scores of children, heart-rending in their tatters, their sore eyes hardly discernible behind the ubiquitous, inevitable flies, his heart turned over with compassion, and he would wonder: "Is it here?...Or here?"

But a week later he would find himself in another place...
always expectant...always unsure...!

So it went, until one evening, towards sunset, they came
upon Raschid...

In the higher regions of Egypt there is a place where
minerals, especially building stone, are plentiful. Chalk,
sandstone and granite are delved from the cliffs that border on
the valleys. There can also be found the well, 'The Gift of the
Nile'...so called because without the Nile those areas would be
totally desert.

In the late afternoon, that well would usually be the
centre of much feverish activity....There would be the noise of
clinking buckets, the lashing of whips, and above every other
sound would be heard the voices of the camel drivers. But,
on this autumn afternoon, an eerie, deathly quiet reigned over
the place. Dominic and Philip glanced at one another uneasily.
Was there something ominous in this silence?

Very cautiously they approached, and then Philip suddenly
pointed with his forefinger as he whispered: "Look over there,
Dom...over there under that palm...there's a man lying there!"
He went a few steps further...."I...I think he's dead!"

They immediately quickened their steps. It did at first
look as though the man were dead, but at a short distance
from him it became noticeable that he was still breathing.
Dominic touched him with his boot, and when that evoked
no response, he bent down and turned him over so that he lay
on his back, with his face turned towards them. With a cry of
horror, Dominic, the physician, recoiled.

"Don't touch him, Phil. In heaven's name stand back!...
Look at his eyes! Get that bottle of rectified spirits out of my
bag and pour some of it over my hands!...Hurry! And then,

after I've given him a shot, if you can bring me the lid of one of those aluminium army panikins, I'll drop the syringe into it. After that we're going to have to find a way to sterilize everything we use. Perhaps you can think of a way to boil some water quickly, even in the panikin, over a fire"—he kept talking as he swabbed the sick man's arm—"because we can't use up our entire supply of spirits too quickly..."

Philip, although perplexed, obeyed automatically before, with a shudder, he was able to comprehend Dominic's revulsion. The stranger's face, in which the yellowed, grotesquely swollen eyelids were prominent, was smeared with dried blood, especially around his grossly infected eyes.

Thus their first encounter with the man who would change the course of their lives. Later they would come to appreciate how significant this meeting proved to be.

Raschid was another victim of the dreaded, what could be translated as 'The Yellow Eye'. One of the most contagious diseases known, it was also—if the people only knew it—one of the easiest to cure, provided the right treatment was instituted in time. The patient usually reacted to the first injection, and recovery generally followed after the fourth.

The disease indisputably had a ghastly effect, and Dominic, having seen the dreadful symptoms before, during his training, was able to recognize the signs instantly. In years to come, he would, however, continue to remain modest on the score of how he and Philip saved the Indian's life. He would immediately be embarrassed when anyone asked him to relate how they had dragged Raschid to a place where he could lie hidden, and where they tended him for days, until their patient's eyes became normal again and a healthy colour returned to his face. But he would readily tell of how difficult that care had proved to be in the beginning, because, apart from the disease

24

Raschid had contracted, he also suffered cruelly as a result of prolonged, most brutal ill-treatment.

"May Allah reward you richly, *Effendi*!" the man whispered in surprisingly good English when he could open his eyes once more. "You have saved my life!"

"What is your name?" Dominic asked, brushing aside all acknowledgements of gratitude. "And where do you come from?...You are not Egyptian, are you? You speak English very well."

"No, *Effendi*. I was raised in the province of Bengal. I came to this country four years ago, after seeking a home in many other places....My name is Raschid.—And you and the young gentleman are not from here, either...?"

"We are from South Africa....This is my brother," Dominic added pointing at Philip. "I am Dominic, and his name is Philip."

"Samaritans?"

"What?" Dominic frowned, and then grinned as he caught the allusion. "*Africa*," he repeated. "*South* Africa!"

"How can that be, *Effendi*? In my home country we have seen written on many establishments, that dogs and South Africans are prohibited from entering. I am no lover of the Mahatma, because I am a Muslim, but I have always thought he must have had good reason. And yet, even while I was unable to see, I could hear and understand, and I heard you caution your brother to be careful with whatever you were using to cleanse yourselves, because you were running short. You gave me medication which you might have needed for yourselves, and you touched me...when that might have meant death for you!"

"I am a physician, and that is my job."

"Then Allah was especially good to send you, *Effendi*. But

there must be more to it than that! That is why I referred to the Samaritan. You have a name which is difficult for me to remember. I shall call you '*Sahhena el-Hakim*—my friend, the doctor'. And whenever I think of you, I shall forever remember you as my 'Samaritan of the Sahara!' "

Dominic, at a loss for words, could only think of asking: "How would you know how to apply such an expression if you are not a Christian? It comes from a story told by the founder of our faith."

"From an English lady, Mrs. Harriet Hunt, *Effendi*. When I was very young I was a *mahout*. That is..."

"We know what that is," said Philip, interrupting to speak for the first time. "We have seen movies with 'Sabu, the Elephant Boy' and have read many of Kipling's stories. I have always thought that, because it is a Hindi word, only Hindus were elephant drivers..."

"There is much we do not know about other countries," Raschid said, stopping to drink gratefully from the mug Dominic held for him. . "This lady, Mrs. Hunt, told me many things. She was very funny. She did not like her own name, she said, because she hated hunting—especially of our marvellous tigers. She stood in the way, often, to wave a big, black umbrella at her countrymen who came to my province especially for that purpose. She told me about your prophet, Jesus, and about the Samaritan, and she told me that the Mahatma said that, if every Christian could be the way your Jesus once told them to be, from a mountain top, he would be one, too."

Philip glanced questioningly at his brother.

"The 'Beatitudes' ". Dominic explained. "But I don't think that is actually what he, the Mahatma, said. I, too, have read that book, *The Christ of the Mount*. What the writer, E. Stanley Jones, actually wrote, if my memory serves me correctly, was that Ghandi said we should practise our religion without adulterating it or toning it down, and that Ghandi was referring to the 'Sermon on the Mount' when he said so....He said this in response to a question by the author as to what could be done to 'naturalize' Christianity in India so that it would cease to be a 'foreign thing'.

"Now, Raschid," he said, changing the subject, "tell us how you came to be in such a sorry state, otherwise..." And then he heard, for the first time, the name of the Bey, Abdel Sharia, and the well nigh unbelievable account of the man's cruelty...of his slaves and his harem, where, according to Raschid, some of the most beautiful women in the world were held captive. To Dominic the tale was like something straight from the 'Arabian Nights'!

"I don't understand!" he cried, shaking his fair head in bewilderment. "How can such things be allowed...in this day and age?—Is there no one who can put a stop to this?"

"No one!...Those who wish to do so, *Effendi*, cannot...and those who are able, do not know of it!"

"Now you speak in riddles," Philip broke in impatiently. "Explain yourself, man!"

"It is thus..." the Indian explained in his distinctive, singsong Bengalese voice. "The Bey is great and powerful, and the arms of his soldiers are strong. On the day you are apprehended by them, the living death begins! You toil in the gravel pits, or you break your back laying the rails on which the trains must run to transport the minerals that fill the coffers of Abdel Sharia. There is always a whip close by, for encouragement if you should tire too quickly. It is hopeless to think that you can ever escape, because if you are even suspected of planning to do so, the gun speaks only once...!" Raschid's dark eyes clouded and he flinched. "I have had a narrow escape!...Mercifully!"

"In that case, how did you manage to extricate yourself from that situation? Why weren't you followed? Were your captors not afraid that you would tell someone?" Dominic's questions came one after another.

The Indian smiled faintly. He had been through a difficult time and had not yet fully regained his strength. Somewhat short of breath, he answered slowly: "The one thing that should have robbed me of my life, *Effendi*, is what, with your gracious intervention, has saved it!...The 'Yellow Eye'!...No one would come near me, and those who might have taken me back, were so sure that I would die, that I was left alone. It was better for all concerned that I should not expire within the encampment, where I would be a threat to all!"

"I can understand that," Dominic said. "And that explains, too, why the oasis was deserted. But now you must rest, my friend, because you have already overtired yourself!"

"Just one more question, Dom," Philip pleaded. "There is one thing I *must* know!"

"What is it, young sir?" Raschid asked indulgently. "You are free to ask."

"I want to know," Philip responded, "why, if you were so sure that you would probably die, you still tried to escape? Even while your eyesight must have been deteriorating rapidly?"

As he lay there without speaking for some time, Raschid was clearly trying to analyse the situation in which he found himself, and he seemed to weigh the pros and cons very carefully. Then, having faced the fact that, alone, he could never hope to reach his desired destination, he must have felt himself compelled to take the two white strangers into his confidence.

"*Effendi*," he began—and it was pointedly Dominic whom he addressed—"I have said, very recently, that there is no one who can help—but there is...one! He who must needs always be the refuge of the oppressed. I had hoped that, if I could reach even one of his people before I perished, there would be hope someday for the other wretches whom I left behind in what you, of your religion, might perhaps describe as the 'hell' of Abdel Sharia!"

"Who is he?…This man of whom you speak?" asked Dominic. And when the other man still hesitated…"You can trust us. We are virtually fugitives, like you…"

"I have no other choice, *Effendi*," Raschid acknowledged. "I *must* find help…that is why I am compelled to tell you. We call him…El-Bus Mohandess…but of his whereabouts I dare not tell you. For your own sake, as well as his. If I were stronger, I could, however, have taken you to him. My greatest desire is to reach him and to tell him of what I have seen….Unfortunately, no one has ever been able to unveil the identity of Abdel Sharia, but I am now at least enabled to show someone where his camp is situated."

Dominic stared fixedly at the distant dunes, riveted by the Easterner's tale. He was aware of a compulsion that he was unable to repel. Something stronger than himself drove him, to ask: "What must I do to help you? How can I take you to your leader?"

The other two looked at him with amazement….Philip questioningly, and the Indian with rising hope in his eyes.

"*Effendi*!" Raschid was overcome. "I shall lick your hands!…I shall be your watchdog!…No one shall touch one hair of your head when I, Raschid, am present!" He was growing progressively more excited. "First we shall have to acquire a camel, for the road is long and I am not able to walk far without becoming a burden to you. You will also have need of some beast of burden…such as another camel…!"

"*A camel*?" Philip, who had grown up on a South African farm, was aghast. "Why not a horse?"

"Because, Sir, horses are not plentiful.—Only the sheiks have them. What is more, that would be most unfriendly. A sheik would die before he would sell his horse, but to lose it in such a manner would break his heart!"

"What do you mean by 'in such a manner'?" Dominic was visibly perplexed. "How would we, in any case, get hold of a camel?"

"How else?" Raschid replied calmly. "We shall have to steal it, of course!"

Dominic was immediately put off. "No...no!" he protested, shaking his head. "I'm done with stealing! I have no more cheques!...And that reminds me...I have no more prescription forms either, so, even if I ever find myself near a pharmacy again, I cannot buy any more medication. Despite the fact that it was virtually true, I hated having to pretend that my doctor had given me additional prescriptions in case I ran out...and stealing *anything, ever again,* is definitely *OUT...!*"

"*Effendi,*" Raschid said solemnly, "you will have to choose....Peace of mind, your own, for one man—or peace and a better life for thousands! It is like the Christian *Memsahib* Hunt would have said, if someone asks you to go one mile with him...go two! But you have already given all you had for me...! As soon as I am able to walk, *I* will steal the camel!"

Dominic sighed, shrugged his shoulders and took off his watch. Then he extended his palm to Philip. "Give me yours too, little brother..."

"*What?*" Philip exclaimed, in what was fast becoming his habitual manner ever since he had become embroiled in Dominic's plans, obeying, nevertheless. "You must be joking, Dom!...Do you know what these watches cost now? Since the war?"

"I do," Dominic affirmed. "And while I honestly doubt

whether they will buy more than just the one beast, I can only hope that some poor, unsuspecting camel driver will appreciate that fact and get the right price for them!...Here Raschid...!"

"The *memsahib* would have been proud of you, *Sahbena*, my friend," Raschid grinned. "She would say you have given your cloak as well as your shirt!"

CHAPTER FOUR

The better Dominic grew to know Raschid, the more the man astonished him. The Indian spoke at least five languages fluently, could discuss—with admirable conviction—most writers and poets whom Dominic could name, and his general knowledge was surprising.

The brothers had only to mention some part of the world for Raschid to respond with: "I've been there, *Effendi.*" Even about South Africa it seemed that there was not much they could tell him, except that the response differed in a few aspects. "I've been there also, *Effendi,* but only in Natal. I never conversed to any extent with any but Indian people. Some of my family went there to work on the tea plantations and remained to plant sugar. They, and many others, have prospered, and some of them are very wealthy.—Not entirely a good thing, for the Zulus, resenting them as intruders, attacked Indians while I was there, and the government had to bring in detachments of police from many areas to quell the disturbances. I thought it expedient to take a ship from Durban to Mombassa, and finally ended up here!"

"What made you then choose to remain here, in this country, where you have suffered such vicissitudes?" Dominic inquired with interest. He studied the man's classic features, and looked at the straight, jet-black hair. "If your face had not been so distorted when I first set eyes on you, I would have known at once that you were not an Egyptian."

"No, *Sahhena*, I was born in Delhi, and was later taken to Bengal, where I spent my early years, as I have told you."

"That was where you met Mrs. Hunt?"

"Yes, indeed. That is where I met the *memsahib*..."

"You puzzle me, Raschid. You have categorically stated that you were not a follower of Mr. Ghandi, yet you use many Hindi expressions. You refer to her as a *'memsahib'*—the Hindu address of respect for a white woman, and you tell us that you were a *mahout,* which is another Hindi word. You talk of the 'Mahatma', which, if I recall, is the term for an adept in esoteric Buddhism or theosophy....Sanskrit, I think."

"You are correct, *Effendi*. The ancient language of the Hindus, as preserved in their literature, and in which many words in other languages have their root."

"Now there you go again! You call me *'effendi'*, rather than *'sahib'*, as you would do in India. As far as I know, you address me by a Turkish title of respect, reserved for officials and learned men..."

"Correct again, *Effendi*! I do so because you are indeed a learned man. "You are a physician."

"He's more than that!" Philip intervened ferociously, with re-kindled anger. "He's a specialist—or should be! Heaven only knows what he is doing here!...All because of some stupid, empty-headed girl who has wrecked both our lives!"

"Please, Philip!" Dominic protested generously. "You can't call her stupid or empty-headed just because she was swept off her feet by someone else!"

To change the subject, Dominic turned to Raschid once more. "Tell me something more, Raschid. You are forever making these provocative allusions to writings with which your *memsahib,* of whom you speak with such obvious esteem, must have made you familiar. What are you aiming at? Are you testing me?"

Unabashed, Raschid smiled slyly. "You are indeed an astute man, *Effendi*. A man of great perception! Aided by your reactions—and your deeds—I have perceived you to be a Christian, and, I am always on the alert for such a person—if I could ever find one—as the memsahib promised would make me want to be one, too! I am ever seeking...always listening... and I perceive your prophet, Jesus, to have been wise in stating that faith should be like that of a child. However, when you have been in too many places, and have seen so much that is wrong, especially when it is done in the name of Christianity, it is not easy to believe!"

"Tell me what made you want to leave a place where you had a friend you clearly valued so much?"

"My *memsahib*, Mrs. Hunt, herself. In the end, it was because of her I had to leave, *Sahbena*....She was greatly sorrowful when she was dying, because she knew I would have to go away, but what I did that day I would not hesitate to do again. When that hunter, in pursuit of the most magnificent beast I have ever seen, climbed down off his horse and struck her down with her own umbrella where she stood in his path, I ran right in front of his horse to pick up the umbrella, and I hit that man so hard with it, *Effendi*, that he did not recover!"

"And, after all your travels, you ended up here..."

"I did, *Sahbena*. There was so much going on, for some time after the war, with troops still coming and going, leaving Europe to fly or sail home from Egypt, that I felt safe because of that very chaos. At first it was my plan to remain only temporarily...how shall I say...just 'look around' for a while'? But then..."—Raschid's voice changed perceptibly—"then I met El-Bus Mohandess, and from that day I asked no more of life than to serve him!"

"He sounds like a remarkable character," Dominic observed.

"He is, *Effendi*!" Raschid cried passionately. "Oh, he is, indeed! I know that he and his people have searched for me, without rest, from the day the Bey had me apprehended. He has dedicated his life to the under-privileged and the oppressed of his country.—The sick, the poor and the outcasts. Someday he will overcome people such as the Bey, and set all the captives free."

"Mmm," Dominic mused. "I am now more eager than ever to meet this man...but what if he refuses us entry into his 'sanctuary'?"

"Oh, he will not!" Raschid declared confidently. "He has long prayed for a doctor....He, himself, can only offer the sick shelter...not heal them!"

***

Five times every day, with surprising regularity, Raschid would fling himself onto his knees, with his face turned towards Mecca; which, on one occasion, provoked Philip to pose a question while Dominic was assisting the Indian to climb back onto the camel. "Raschid, you have travelled the world, you are an enlightened man, and yet you remain a Mohammedan?"

"A Muslim, Sir," Raschid correct him gently.

"What's the difference?" the young man demanded irritably. He had little patience with what he regarded as trivial semantics.

"It is only those who are outside of our faith who speak of 'Mohammedans' and 'Mohammedanism', Philip, sir. With us it is 'Muslim' and 'Islam'." It was already becoming evident that Raschid, the personification of courtesy, was finding it difficult to restrain himself in Philip's presence. In time, as his admiration for Dominic mounted, he would become so possessive that Philip would constantly complain that, in the presence of his 'watchdog', one was permitted little beyond passing the time of day with his brother.

"Muslim," Raschid continued, "means 'Believer'...Islam, 'Submission to the will of God' ".

"Humph!" said Philip.

(ii)

The journey did not take them more than a day and a half. They could, in fact, have reached their destination sooner but, shortly before noon on the second afternoon, Raschid informed them that they would have to remain at the oasis—which they could see in the distance—for a few hours longer than they usually tarried, when the sun was at its highest.

"But why rest for so long?" Philip demanded. "I want to get you to wherever you need to go, as soon as possible, so that I can start making plans to go home!"

Dominic hid a smile. The old story!

"The Bedouin often spend the whole day in the saddle, Sir, and the leader is then obliged to be absent from the stockade. Even arriving in my company, no stranger will ever gain entrance without his permission, and here we have both shade and water—without which I do not wish to keep you waiting....We shall depart from here at a timely hour which will bring us to our destination shortly after his return."

"Raschid!" Dominic chided him. That is not true—and you know it! Neither my brother nor I are so dense as to accept such a lame excuse!"

Raschid had the grace to lower his head as a gesture of contrition. "May Allah punish me if I ever respond thus to you again, *Effendi*," he said penitently. "You I cannot deceive!" Thereupon he proceeded to explain that he would have to blindfold them as soon as they left the oasis, and, since they could not be made to stumble across the sand with their eyes closed, it was his plan to have both of them climb onto the camel, and he would lead them. He merely wished to rest as long as possible, in order to summon the necessary energy. Later it would also be cooler.

"I'm not allowing myself to be taken, unsuspecting, and to heaven knows where, by a..." Philip began furiously.

"*Philip!*" Dominic glared at him.—This was a new Dominic who reacted so harshly.—"We have made a promise, and as far as I am concerned, promises are not to be broken!" And Philip was not offended by the untoward vehemence with which his brother said this. He could not help wondering how much of it could be attributed to that last communication from a fickle and very shallow girl...

(iii)

Never before had Dominic Verwey experienced any degree of discomfort which could remotely be compared to what he had to endure on that camel. He tried, at first, to sit in front of Philip, and then behind him, but it was hopeless! "I can only compare this to what it must be like to have to spend time on a jagged rock in a concrete mixer—clutching a very awkwardly shaped rucksack!" he groaned at one stage. "This is totally unendurable!...What is it you said, Raschid? About only sheiks having horses?"

"It is so, *Effendi*," Raschid replied, grinning broadly.

"In that case, if I believed in reincarnation—which I don't!—and had to be a Bedouin in that other life, I would earnestly hope for the good fortune to be a sheik!"

Although he was not as heavy as Dominic, Philip also complained that the journey was endless. Blindfolded, he found it excruciatingly boring, but, just before the sun set, Raschid finally announced with excitement: "We are nearly there!"

"We must be relatively high up," Dominic remarked. "The air is noticeably cooler."

"We are in the mountains now, *Effendi*, but the stockade lies in a valley, where it is sheltered from sand and wind. The entrance is very difficult to find. Presently you will become aware that we are descending once more, although our destination is still at a fair altitude."

Mercifully, not five minutes later, the silence was suddenly broken by a rough male voice peremptorily calling out something which the brothers could not understand, but took to be a challenge. Raschid's presumably satisfactory response was immediately followed by a near deafening hubbub. Running footsteps echoed and re-echoed, several people tried to talk at the same time, and the Indian was hardly granted an opportunity to reply to the numerous questions with which he was bombarded.

"The reunion!" Philip observed sarcastically. "Hey, Raschid!" he called out. "It is time you took away this wretched thing from my eyes!"

Raschid came scurrying back. "Ten thousand pardons, Sir," he cried. "Forgive my lack of courtesy!" It was, however, Dominic's blindfold that he removed first.

"Well, come on!" The Indian, very authoritative all of a sudden, issued a command to someone in the crowd around him. "I am instructing him to go and ask the leader if I might be permitted to bring my companions further," he explained for the South Africans' benefit.

"What!" Philip muttered. "Aren't we there *yet?*"

Dominic glanced around him. They appeared to be in a corridor, evidently chiselled out of solid rock, and so narrow that it would be impossible for two horses to pass through, side by side. This explained the echoing footsteps.

In front of them, blocking their path, stood about a dozen bearded Arabs, each armed with a *nabbut*, or thick staff. Upon a signal from someone further down the sloping passageway, the man closest to the brothers raised his *nabbut*.

"You may approach in peace, Raschid. He awaits you and your companions!"

Dominic and Philip, who had dismounted by this time, now walked behind the camel, grateful to be stretching their stiff legs at last. The Arabs in the corridor pressed themselves close to the wall, in order to make room for the new arrivals to pass.

They proceeded in silence until, all at once, they emerged from the tunnel to find themselves looking down upon the valley. Like hundreds of brown toadstools, Bedouin tents—made of animal hide, as is the way of the desert dweller—dotted the landscape. Babies cried, goats bleated, and feathers flew, as screeching fowls scattered in all directions before them. Finally they arrived at the only dwelling which was not a tent.

Raschid went forward alone to speak to someone who awaited him on the top step of a short flight of stairs. After a brief, unmistakeably joyful, verbal exchange, the man, promptly deciding to accompany him, descended to where the newcomers stood, and then—overcome by intense curiosity—Dominic looked up into the wonderful face of El-Bus Mohandess!

"Please make your companions known," the great man instructed in English, favouring the strangers with a friendly smile. His cultured voice, with a slight trace of a French accent in it, revealed a warmth, a magnetic quality, such as Dominic had never heard before.

As Raschid turned to Dominic with almost paternal pride, he, Dominic Verwey heard himself introduced, for the first time, by the name he would bear for many years thereafter.

"This is *Sahbena el-Hakim*," said Raschid. "My friend, the doctor!"

CHAPTER FIVE

For a few days after their arrival, Raschid was not very well. The long journey had clearly overtaxed his already low reserves of energy. Dominic was repentant, and even Philip could find it in his heart to express remorse for having complained so volubly about the discomfort of the camel ride, while the frail Indian had walked on stoically and with almost unbelievable endurance, in his determination to bring a physician to the people desperate for help. They were not the only ones shocked at his appearance, and, after Dominic had obtained permission to administer a sleeping draught, El-Bus Mohandess had immediately given instructions for a bed to be made ready in one of the tents, for the Indian.

Later that night Dominic was astonished when the leader said, "I already knew who you were, *Sahbena*, long before you were introduced to me. I was also aware of how you saved the life of my faithful friend, Raschid. God was indeed good to send you to me....You are needed so acutely at this moment.... Perhaps you might even be persuaded to remain here for some length of time before moving on?"

"May I think about that?" Dominic drew his brows together as though he were already doing that. "I, myself, am in no hurry, but my brother has been restless for some time. I feel responsible for him—he is quite a bit younger than I am—and it is high time that he returned to university and decided what he wants to do with his future."

"Indeed," said the other man. "If he should wait too long he might never find his right place in life....And you, *El-Hakim*, have you found yours?...I do not think so. There is much uncertainty in your eyes. They betray you!"

An extraordinary man! Nothing unsure about El-Bus Mohandess! Every movement deliberate; every word essential and to the point. After passing on to him Raschid's assurance that the camel would be returned to its rightful owner, Dominic happened to add: "But how can he ever know from whom we took it?" And the confidence expressed in that prompt answer was reassuring...."Oh, we shall unquestionably find out!"

Dominic was further surprised to discover that Raschid's hero was not a Muslim.

"My mother was a French girl from Algiers," he told Dominic. "I was taught the tenets of her faith and church, from a very young age, and before her death she had the joy of knowing that my father had embraced them, too."

He regarded Dominic contemplatively. "I wonder, often, whether I should not be doing more to convert these precious people of mine, but they are like children in some respects. When they are first brought here, it takes them a while to realize that they are safe. Later comes the trust...the confidence.—When should the proselytising begin?"

"That is difficult for me to say," Dominic responded. "I have been here for too short a time to risk expressing a firm opinion, yet I seem to think you are already doing enough, for the present. You might preach your head off and only succeed in alienating them, but I believe that you glorify Christ simply by walking the path you do, and the way in which you do so. I would think that, simply by demonstrating the two commandments which our Lord considered to be the greatest of all, you are doing enough for the time being!…You live the Gospel, *Effendi*!"

"My baptismal name is Etienne," El-Bus Mohandess volunteered unexpectedly. "I have not heard it on anyone's lips for more years than I can remember, but it would please me to hear it on yours. You are learned man….Clearly a man of integrity….I am enriched by your company, and I honour you as an equal!"

They were wandering through the camp. The leader made a sweeping gesture with his hand as he drew Dominic's attention to the multitude of tents. "Look at them!…Is this not a terrible responsibility?…You say that I am doing enough, but I know, in my heart, that I have not yet even begun! Where is the hospital that I so earnestly desire?…The Bey, Abdel Sharia, evades me still. No…my greatest task still lies ahead!"

"How can you ever hope to capture the Bey, or to outwit him?" Dominic asked.

"That would be relatively easy once I have succeeding in unveiling his identity. And once I take *him* captive, his cohorts will surrender willingly. I am convinced of that!" Only very much later would Dominic be able to understand what lay behind so categorical a declaration.

All of a sudden the other man stopped in his tracks to look Dominic straight in the eye. "Do you know what my greatest shortcoming is, *El-Hakim*?…You cannot guess? Well, I shall tell you….I am, how would you say, too soft?…A man has to be ruthless and relish a fight, in order to overcome a monster like Abdel Sharia…whereas I…"

He left the sentence hanging in mid-air, and a day would come when Dominic would wish that the leader had gone on to qualify that 'whereas'. The word 'soft' seemed to *El-Hakim*, to be vastly unsuited to a man whose entire being exuded power and strength; of body, mind, soul and spirit.

His very name, 'Etienne' seemed equally incongruous, when something like Alexander, or another of equal historic significance—Constantine, perhaps?—might, in Dominic's view, have been far more apt.

(ii)

Soon after waking on his very first day in the stockade, Dominic began a routine of visiting the sick, going from one dwelling to the next. He had not been at that for long, before reflecting on how much easier it would have been to have had the sick all under one roof; but perhaps due to the fact that he was once more doing what he liked best, the compassion and innate good humour, submerged under bitterness for so long, began to rise to the surface once more. Smiling philosophically, he kept reminding himself of the experience he was gaining, and the advantage of meeting people on their own ground—literally!

Weak though he still was, Raschid was more than willing to serve as the interpreter, and some of his descriptions of various aches and pains sent Dominic into paroxysms of mirth. The wretched condition of many of his patients was, however, enough at times to make it difficult to refrain from gasping. No wonder the leader longed so desperately for a hospital. What he, Dominic, would not have given for the orderliness, the equipment, the routine, and, above all, the pharmacies where he had worked before. How he had taken for granted the many facilities which had been available to him in the past!

He was shocked by the obvious need for a physician, as he saw how desperate the situation was. One man's plight was so particularly pitiful that it tugged at his healer's heart; for, after his long sojourn in the desert, Dominic had very little in the way of palliatives left in his bag. Greatly concerned, he went in search of the leader.

"What is it that you need, my friend?" he wanted to know. Dominic named it. "Write it down for me and before the sun sets you shall have it," the man promised solemnly. "I shall see to it myself!"

"But how...?" Dominic began.

El-Bus Mohandess silenced him with an eloquent movement of his hand. "I have said that you shall have it.—Is not that sufficient?"

That afternoon he brought it to Dominic, personally!

Even Philip, the contrary one, who professed that, on principal, he always made a point of objecting before he acquiesced, admitted to Dominic that he, too, was aware of the leader's powerful magnetism.

"He could never enter a room without everyone in it immediately becoming aware of his presence," he observed on one occasion. And on another: "You know, Dom, there is nothing negative about this man. I imagine that people who know him well must either adore him, or hate him...there can be little ambivalence!"

"That's true," Dominic agreed. "But surely only his enemies could hate him."

"I'm not so sure." Philip frowned thoughtfully. "One could easily, perhaps even unknowingly, resent the effect he has on one. It's actually not a completely comfortable thought that ones own individuality might be overshadowed by the stronger personality of another. As soon as one surrenders and can accept the fact that one is becoming enslaved, the battle's over—but until then...!"

"I know what you mean." And Dominic, who had on one occasion been close to feeling a bit like that, himself, conceded that he could not have expressed himself half as well. On further reflection, he knew he would by no means be unwilling to enter the service of the leader, but for Philip, who was so eager to escape and return home, the situation certainly had to be a difficult one.

The sun was setting as he emerged from the tent where he had administered the morphine to his dying patient, and he stopped for a moment to appreciate the last of the fast-fading, ruddy glow about the rugged peaks surrounding the camp. Then he turned to look back down the hill to where a sickle moon could already be seen rising. He felt a catch in his throat as he saw his brother, a lonely figure silhouetted against the deep blue of the North African night; sitting pensively, chin-in-hand, on a rock. His conscience suddenly smote him as he realized with painfully vivid clarity, that all Philip had long craved was to have him, Dominic, to himself. It hurt him to be reminded of the look on the wistful young face when, after waiting patiently, and for so long, he had been told that Lydia was to accompany them on the homeward journey. Details of many events which had occurred during the time which had elapsed since the shattering discovery of her infidelity, flashed though his mind, as he recalled Philip's practical, sane approach to their selection of suitable clothing and supplies for the journey, the resourcefulness he had exhibited during their vagrant wanderings in the desert, and his obvious pride in providing for the comfort and well-being of his then, still bewildered older sibling. Immediately Dominic's exhilaration in being involved once more in his chosen work, evaporated, and he strode towards Philip.

"I'm sorry, *boetie* (little brother)," he said contritely, sitting down on the rock beside him and putting his arm around the hunched shoulders. " I've been damnably selfish! Because I have allowed myself to think that life had nothing left for me, I have coerced you into wasting a part of the best of yours. Frankly, in taking advantage of your companionship, I have been parasitic to a certain extent. I have taken you for granted....I'm going to speak to El-Bus Mohandess, and request that he take the necessary steps to get us away from here at the very earliest opportunity. However, if you will bear with me for just a day or two longer, there is something I would like to do for him before we leave."

"And what is that, Dom?"

"He longs desperately to establish some sort of hospital, no matter how basic, and will keep striving to achieve that. I believe that his dream will be realized in time—he's passionate enough to make that happen—and I would like to try and lay out a plan of action for him to adopt in the meantime. The man has a tremendous responsibility on his shoulders and there is a critical need for *something* to be done!"

"But where can you begin? To me it seems to be far too daunting a project, for *anyone*!"

"Well," Dominic said thoughtfully, "I have learned one lesson already....When I initially set off, I found myself inwardly complaining with every step I took. It was so time-consuming to have to go from tent to tent to search out people who might need me, but now I have reason to be grateful that the sick are not all herded together under one roof. Having found two with obvious hepatitis, and encountered a number of others with a wide range of infections, both chronic and acute, I now see it as a blessing that the people are at least separated by virtue of the distance between their dwellings.

Even so, the leader is fortunate that he has never had a major epidemic on his hands!"

"Were there any who resisted your ministrations? You are, after all, a sort of infidel to them, aren't you?"

"After what they have been through before being brought here, Phil, there is little that phases them, as long as they recognize a possibility for the improvement of any difficult or painful situation. I actually came across a man in a yarmulke in one of tents, where he and his Arab companions seemed, uncharacteristically, to be in perfect harmony with one another. His name is Ezra. He speaks excellent English, and I found him to be cultured, intelligent, and more than willing to help Raschid out with any obstacles in translation, that might otherwise have occurred. It is a credit to El-Bus Mohandess that his charges have such faith in the fact that he would not subject them to any person or situation that would be detrimental to them, that they tolerate anything he sanctions.

"If problems do occur, it could be with the women, who are not accustomed to having strange males—let alone white men—even briefly glimpse them without their yashmaks, or whatever they call them! I did encounter some in various stages of pregnancy, but, you may be sure, they'll think twice before they let me help them out in an emergency. However, there are obviously not as many women as men in the stockade....It's a wonder there are any at all, but..."

"How come they are, as you say, here at all?" Philip wanted to know, interrupting him. "These are all refugees from Abdel Sharia, aren't they? And surely his women are kept very securely under guard, in the harems?"

"The ones that are here are not former prisoners. They are evidently the wives of former captives, brought here, from their homes, to rejoin their husbands. Raschid tells me that not everyone to whom the opportunity is presented, necessarily takes advantage of the offer—and El-Bus Mohandess draws the line at having women and children kidnapped and brought here under duress. Not only would that mean stooping to the same low tactics as the Bey, but having sulking, discontented females in the camp would only lead to discord. He does, however, insist that those who want to come at the request of their spouses, are brought here, blindfolded."

"That makes sense," Philip said. "But getting back to what you plan to do...what do you envisage as a priority? What will have to be done in the meantime?"

Dominic, who had risen to his feet, sat down again beside him on the rock, drew a deep breath, and the manner in which he exhaled was eloquent. "Phew! Everything's a priority! To begin with, the tents are not numbered, and more than once I went back to check on someone and found myself in the wrong place....I'm too spoilt, Philip! Too used to the efficient secretaries who kept records up to date, filing systems easy to access, and the whole operation running smoothly. Raschid seems to know his way about, but I shall not have time to familiarize myself with the layout of the place—nor can I possibly carry the details of every case entirely in my head. How any physician whom Mohandess ever succeeds in bringing here on a permanent basis, will regard what might appear to some to be a very trivial problem, I can't say, but I would put that difficulty quite high on my chart....Top of that list? Probably a more adequate water supply—and some lessons in hygiene. Teach them, for instance, about the difference between amoebic dysentery and common or garden diarrhoea....And parasites!... Most of the people have been accustomed to bathing in the rivers. To urinate in the water is a common practice. They don't realize that, in doing so, they not only infect the water, but risk inviting the Bilharzia parasite right into their own urinary tracts. I'd bet my bottom dollar that more than a quarter of the patients I examined today are infected.

"Then there are all the other, possible bacteria. I would certainly establish an isolation tent. Of course I haven't had time to make a thorough assessment, but I've seen enough to know that, in many cases, there are those whose health has also been severely compromised by what they have had to endure in the labour camps.

"How El-Bus Mohandess comes by the resources to do what he does, I cannot imagine; however, the man seems to have little difficulty in obtaining medical supplies. So, before I leave, I could very easily draw up a list of the most necessary drugs etc.—but how, and by whom they are administered will be the insurmountable problem. I admire Etienne from the bottom of my heart, but the very thought of all that he has taken upon himself makes me groan!"

He stopped suddenly and patted Philip on the shoulder. "Sorry, bro! I have been rambling on, haven't I? You must be sick of listening to the Jeremiad!...What have you been doing with yourself today?"

"I invited you to vent yourself, didn't I?" Philip said wryly. "I wanted to hear what you had to say....What did I do with myself?...I wandered around and grinned at people to indicate that I was friendly....But I also did a lot of thinking.

"Why can't I help you, Dom? For as long as we are stuck here, until Mohandess sees fit to take us back to wherever we need to go, I have to pass the time somehow...Why can't I follow you around with a pen and paper and make notes for you as you dictate. That should speed up your assessment and get us out of here more quickly! I know they have writing materials, because I have seen you write down the names of medications you needed him to get for you!

"Another thing I could do, if you think that would be helpful...I would need to involve Raschid because he speaks their language...If I could establish some sort of routine, perhaps I could get the ambulatory ones to come up to the house—and if we could maybe erect some sort of shelter for shade, where they can wait their turn, that should save a great deal of time. You would then only need to go down to those who are confined to their tents!"

It had grown too dark for Philip to see his brother's face light up, but he could hear the enthusiasm in his response. "I have always thought of you as the resourceful one, *boetie*, and this is an excellent suggestion. I'd be thrilled to have you help me! Thank you for your offer! By the way, we're not eating on our own tonight. We have an invitation to dine with the leader, and when I tell him of your offer I know he will be most appreciative.—Who knows? In whatever direction you choose to go when you get back home, you may, some day, be able to use some of what you learn here, in your thesis for *your* doctorate!...You know I don't believe in coincidence!"

"Well it most certainly won't be a medical degree, that I can tell you!" Philip grunted fiercely, trying to mask his gratification. "Let's first wait and see how your watchdog reacts to my presence in your retinue!"

They were resident in the home of El-Bus. His personal guests. Frequently he and Dominic would play chess or engage in long, stimulating conversations, and, with each encounter, Dominic became more acutely aware of his host's powerful personality. At first he found it strange and difficult to analyse how he could find such joy and peace in the presence of someone so completely different from himself. Then, by degrees, he came at last to understand much of what had baffled him before.—The marked change in Raschid's voice when he spoke of his rescuer...the boundless trust in the eyes of every man, woman and child in the stockade.—And so it was that he also came, in time, to be able to analyse his own feelings. Finally what he felt became fully understandable. The comprehension of the nameless emotion of which he had immediately become conscious upon reaching the camp of El-Bus Mohandess, was like a blinding light....The feeling that, after a long and arduous journey, he had finally come home!

He recognized that in a flash of wonderment one night, while standing in the moonlight, looking down upon the tents...

"It is *here!*" he cried aloud to the heavens. *"It is here!"*

He had recently fallen into the habit of climbing the ridge behind the leader's house, where he had found his favourite spot for studying his daily passage of Scripture. It was a cool and peaceful place, sheltered by a gigantic rock from the prevailing winds which, while not to be remotely compared with those that whipped up the sandstorms of the desert, could be a hindrance when they set flimsy pages flapping. It was his custom to make his way there in the late afternoon, before sunset, and while there was still sufficient light for him to be able to read small print.

As the year wore on, the days grew progressively shorter, and the light faded sooner, it became necessary to make his way up the mountain earlier and earlier, and so it happened one day, that he found Ezra in his special place, reading his Hebrew *Tanakh*. In years to come, Dominic would say that the times they spent together after that encounter proved to be among the most rewarding of his life.

"Doesn't this help one to understand why Moses felt close

to God in places like this?" was the man's opening gambit, as he moved up to make room for Dominic on the level ledge where he sat. "I come here most days, at this hour....Everyone should be privileged to ascend to a mountain top sometimes, don't you agree?"

Dominic agreed wholeheartedly, but was unprepared for what followed. He was completely taken aback by the provocative question Ezra fired at him: "You are obviously a Christian. Do you mind sharing your quiet time with a Jew?"

"Certainly not!" Dominic shot back emphatically. "After all, the founder of my own faith was a Jew....Not so?"

After the time they spent that day, sharing many things and discussing many weighty and intriguing matters of doctrine, the young physician began to look forward to the possibility of running into Ezra again. Soon they made a point of timing their respective ascents up the cliff, with the special intention of meeting. He learned that the Jew, formerly a wealthy merchant from Palestine, had been in the habit of making frequent trips to Cairo and Alexandria in the course of his business, and it was during one such visit that he had been abducted and taken prisoner by Abdel Sharia's men, for the purpose of extorting ransom.

"My family paid again and again for some time, that I know, but still I was not released," Ezra told Dominic. "One loses all count of time when one is in a situation such as that in which I found myself in Abdel Sharia's prison," he continued, "but as long as I could still cling to hope, it was somehow bearable. When I finally realized that help was not forthcoming, I had to abandon all hope, and it was when that happened, that what had formerly been just 'bearable', became intolerable!"

"But couldn't the British authorities in Cairo have helped?"

"Evidently my brother did appeal to them, but right then, at the time of my capture—as I have since learned from a fellow captive who was brought to the prison a year or so after I was—they had their hands full, simply trying to stem the tide of increasing terrorist violence in Jerusalem and elsewhere."

"That must have been about the time of the Stern Gang and the bombing of the King David Hotel in Jerusalem," Dominic reflected.

"It was. I know that now," Ezra concurred.—The *Irgun* and the Stern Gang....Jewish resistance to the British mandate had already begun before the war, when extremists set up this organization called *The Irgun*, which is short for *Irgun Tseva Leumi*, which can be roughly translated as "National Resistance Movement". Their aim was to campaign for the establishment of the state of Israel. They supported the British during the war but, about four years ago, a splinter group led by a man called Abraham Stern decided to continue the fight against the British. This group, now best known as the 'Stern Gang', have been responsible for many terrorist atrocities and murders since then.

"In addition to the problems already besetting Britain— as described to me—I can well understand that, shortly before the state of Israel was finally established, especially in the face of the cooling American attitude towards them at that stage, there was little to be gained in trying to elicit help from the British authorities anywhere in the Middle East.

"As I have said, when you are held captive and each miserable new day is just followed by another, equally miserable, you become oblivious of the passage of time. When you wake up, you are aware of little more than incredulity at still being alive...but I do seem to think that it must have been at least four years ago that the Stern Gang began their campaign. At the same time, the Americans were then strongly pro-Jewish and very anti-British, in regard to the possible establishment of a state of Israel, and the United States media kept up a barrage of protest against the British attitude.

"I was not really surprised, *El-Hakim*, to learn that, at one point, Winston Churchill became so irritated with the continual American carping about Israel, that he suggested that, if the Americans were so critical of the way Britain was handling Palestine, it might be a better solution for all concerned, if they were to take over the job, themselves.—So now, *Effendi*, can you understand how it was that the British authorities in Cairo would pay little heed to the plight or abduction of an insignificant Jewish merchant?"

Dominic was, however, still far from satisfied.

"But why did they not then try appealing to them via the Egyptian government, in that case? What is, or was, the king's attitude towards both the leadership of Israel, and that of Britain?"

"King Farouk?" Ezra's hollow laugh was significant. "He has not been in good odour with the British since the ill-advised war against the Jews. And his throne is very far from secure. It would surprise me if he were able to hold onto it for very much longer. Quite beside the fact that he is known to be a kleptomaniac—did you know that?—his subjects are very critical of him. My knowledge of the outside world as it is now, is limited, and I only found out, just before I was rescued, that it is the general belief that it will probably not be many years before the king is deposed and sent into exile. I heard this from a man who had been brought there just weeks before I was fortunate enough to be rescued—while outdoors working in a gravel pit—some distance away from the prison. I shall never cease to thank *Hashem*, the Almighty, for a man like El-

Bus Mohandess. Without his intervention, I would be dead by now—and it would have been a blessed release!"

"He, El-Bus Mohandess, is an amazing person," Dominic observed. "I wonder constantly, among other things, where and how he finds the money to provide food and shelter for all of us.—How does he finance all this"

Ezra turned abruptly to face him. "You mean you don't know?"

CHAPTER SIX

The days sped by. December brought the first of the cold weather and, with it, numerous difficulties. The Bedouin who had been out of the camp one day, came back that night with the disquieting information that two of their companions had not returned with them, and after three days without news of them, the visible concern in the dark countenance of El-Bus Mohandess deepened.

"I fear, *Sahbena,* that they, too, are now among the captives of the Bey," he confided to Dominic. "He will press them to reveal the whereabouts of our stockade, and because none of them will be persuaded to do so, their torture will be exceedingly severe.—As it was with Raschid.—I shall have to go to their aid!"

"But what can you do, Etienne *effendi?*" Dominic inquired. "What are you and your men against so many?"

El-Bus Mohandess refused to be discouraged. "Now, thanks to Raschid, we know, at least, where the place is. What we shall do, I can only decide once we get there!"

He would not hear of it that either Dominic or Philip should accompany him. "The sick are in need of you, *El-Hakim.* You cannot be both physician and fighter, and the responsibility for your brother is not one I wish to take upon myself. He is not of us!…I would rather you remained here.—If you would do that for me, watch over my people in my absence. Raschid will help you!"

Shortly after that his horse was saddled and, with his face partly hidden by the hood of his white *burnous* (the woollen cloak of the desert Arab), he galloped off, the hoofs ringing on the stones until the sound became muffled in the tunnel; and, to Dominic, the valley seemed lonelier and colder than before. Philip was in a bad mood and Raschid busied himself with his numerous duties.

The following afternoon Dominic was busy dressing the arm of one of the children when the sound of shouting reached him from the direction of the tunnel entrance. Immediately a commotion ensued, and the guards came running to summon *El-Hakim*. Seconds later, the leader's horse came thundering into the stockade, bearing a motionless figure, slumped across its back. The bright stain on the now torn, once spotless white *burnous*, was evidence of the blood gushing from the gaping wound in the side of El-Bus Mohandess.

"What happened?" Dominic called out concernedly, while still some distance away, and no one needed an interpreter to understand what he meant. He arrived, breathless, as Raschid, Philip, and a dozen or more Bedouin appeared simultaneously, in front of the leader's house.

They lowered their leader very carefully from his mount and carried him inside, where he was laid down gently on his fur-covered divan. Dominic fearfully reached for his wrist.

"He lives," *El-Hakim* told the anxious people around him, "but his pulse is very weak....I shall do what I can...!"

It was not long before the rest of the men came storming into the camp, heart-sore and dead tired. Their attack had ended in failure. They had seen their leader's horse shy and then take off with him, after one of the Bey's soldiers had fired that fatal shot, and now they were almost to afraid to ask...! They stood silently and respectfully at the foot of the steps, anxious to learn *El-Hakim's* verdict. And when Dominic did emerge, the appearance of the doctor caused an immediate stir among the group. They waited in dread upon his pronouncement.

"He has temporarily regained consciousness," Raschid interpreted verbatim, "but I fear it will not be long....He wishes to speak to the headmen....*Only* the headmen!" he emphasized.

Slowly and sorrowfully they followed each other into the chamber, and stood reverently around the divan upon which their friend and protector lay.

El-Bus Mohandess smiled faintly. "Men," he whispered, "do not abandon the struggle!" He breathed with difficulty. "The victory will be yours someday....Be loyal to one another, and obedience itself to your new leader....Conserve all envy, malice, hatred or ruthlessness, until you are faced with the enemy!"

"But who can we find to fill your place, *Effendi?*" came the despairing cry from a burly Arab who struggled to keep his emotion under control. "Who?...*Who?*"

The leader did not hesitate. Without stopping to think, he responded decisively, albeit weakly: "There is only one... *Sahbena el-Hakim!*"

"*Sahbena el-Hakim?*"

"*Sahbena el-Hakim!*" they echoed in chorus. "The leader has spoken with wisdom....May Allah bless him!...*Sahbena el-Hakim!*"

But Dominic instantly came a step closer. "I, *Effendi?* No, no! That is impossible! I am incapable...unworthy...ill-equipped...I..." Meeting the disappointed gaze of El-Bus Mohandess he faltered, and could not go on.

"Will you forsake us, *Sahbena?* Can you not sense that the responsibility is yours?...Have I deluded myself?" Etienne panted. "From the very first moment I looked into your face I felt the bond between us!...I was convinced that you—like me, years ago—had been sent here by Providence....Can you tell me in all truth that you feel nothing?"

Long before the dying man had finished speaking, tears were streaming down Dominic Verwey's face. He flung himself to his knees beside the leader's bed. "I feel it, *Effendi!*" he cried. "I felt it long ago! The very urge to come here, in the first place, was irresistible!"

El-Bus Mohandess allowed one hand to rest on the bowed, blond head beside him. He raised the other. "Greet me, my friends, and go in peace! I wish now to be alone with *El-Hakim* and Raschid. There are many things to discuss...and there is...so...little time!"

He closed his eyes for a moment, and when he opened them again, the three of them were alone.

"I knew, my friend, that you had not come here of your own volition. *You were sent!*"

"Is this then my long-sought destination?...Is it here that I have found my calling?" Dominic had been asking of himself for some time. Now he knew that that question had already been answered, in his heart, weeks before. He could no longer fight this.

"I shall do whatever you say, *Effendi*," he promised solemnly. "And it will be with pride that I shall do so! Just tell me what you want me to do!"

"There is no need for that...nothing I can tell you....You will know when the time comes. I ask only one promise of you. Do not be as soft as I have been. The struggle ahead of you is too bitter...too vicious for that." He pointed to an ancient rapier which hung on the wall opposite, and which Dominic had frequently admired. "It was my father's. Keep it there after I am gone. Keep it as a symbol of the bond between us. Whenever you feel yourself weakening, hold this as a reminder of what I have said to you today." His voice grew weaker. "Finish, *El-Hakim*, what I have begun!"

CHAPTER SEVEN

Thus, six weeks before his twenty-eighth birthday, Dominic Verwey, my friend the doctor, became Hamid Pasha, 'refuge of the refugee and provider of sanctuary for the oppressed'. Healer of the sick and defender of his people's *Istiklal*—their independence.

As might be expected, Philip was utterly aghast when first advised of this. That his brother should have devoted so many years to study, in so many parts of the globe, only to end up as a leader of a ragtag band—a gang of ignorant, uncouth, heathen outlaws—was just too much for him. But, before too long, much against his will, he began to view the situation from a vastly different angle. It gradually began to take on quite an exciting aspect, and Dominic was surprised one day to hear his younger sibling announce that he had decided to stay—for a while! He was no longer quite so eager to return home, Philip declared. After all, he had not yet decided what he wanted to do with his life, and, as he put it, he was still young enough to relish an adventure.

"I rather like having my clothes laundered for me once more," he grinned, "and having my meals served to me. Except for the occasional sheep's eye"—this with a crooked smile—"I have even grown to like couscous and lamb curry!...I wonder how they got the sheep here, in the first place?"

The title bestowed on Dominic, was Raschid's choice. "You must have two names, *Effendi*, he insisted. "A time will come when you have to represent us at the gatherings of the sheiks and the *cadis* in the desert."

"What will be my so-called rank, Raschid? My status?" Dominic was quick to respond, audibly concerned. "Do I?... Will I qualify...?"

For the first time, the brothers saw Raschid double up with laughter. It took him a few moments to compose himself before he could speak. He wiped away the tears with the back of a brown hand. "*Ha, ha, ha...!*"—Still quite convulsed with mirth, he managed to say: "Do not fear, *Effendi*. You have my assurance that you shall not be required to ride a camel! '*Pasha*' is a Turkish title of honour," he spluttered. It means 'Governor' or 'Commander'! Moreover, nearly all the able-bodied men in this camp have their own horses. I can assure you that you are most certainly entitled to a fine mount, and I, Raschid, your humble servant, will choose him for you, myself!"

The Indian promptly, and quite automatically appointed himself the controller of his master's affairs. Dominic was his hero, his ideal, and, furthermore, he, Raschid clearly considered that he deserved special acknowledgement for the fact that it was he who had brought the new leader to that place. Was not that a particular honour? The sorrow they all felt at the loss of El-Bus Mohandess, had now to be tempered with gratitude that so eminently suitable a successor had been given them.

The doctor would need to be well schooled to carry the dual responsibilities he had accepted. Again it was Raschid who would see to that, and any training he could not personally provide for his idol, would be entrusted only to masters of every desired art. Only the best men in the stockade would have a share in equipping and preparing *El-Hakim* for every, possible eventuality.

One by one they were brought before him. There was Ali,

the crack shot. From him Dominic would learn to shoot straight from the hip, on a galloping horse in the Arabian manner; never missing the target, and without having to take aim.... Rameses, the tough, wizened little Turk, was a wizard with the sabre. Then there were the twins, Haroun and Mamoun, both dwarfs, whose turbans nearly swept the floor as they bowed before their new leader; especially grateful because it was to one of them that Dominic had once given a painkiller for toothache. They, together with Raschid, would be the bodyguards of the worthy successor to El-bus Mohandess. Shrewd and amazingly agile, they could also be despatched, and trusted, to carry out the most difficult assignments.

Dominic, whose fine carriage, stature and colouring lent him extraordinary presence—assets of which he was quite oblivious—received the people with great dignity, deeply moved by their solemn pledges of loyalty; knowing in his heart that each and every one of them could be relied upon, without reservation...

***

The days and weeks that followed were intense and exhausting, and he particularly valued the times he could spend up on the ridge with Ezra, who never sent him off without what is possibly one of the most beautiful blessings in the Old Testament. *"The Lord bless thee and keep thee; the Lord make His face to shine upon thee, and be gracious unto thee; the Lord lift up His countenance upon thee and give thee peace!"*

One afternoon Dominic was moved to ask: "Ezra, how did you manage to retain your sanity? What made you even try to stay alive? There must surely have been times when you thought of taking your own life...!"

"I never gave up hope. I resorted to the only way in which to ward off such thoughts, *Effendi.* Three times every day, no matter what I was doing I would recite the *Amida;* also known as the *Tefilla* or *Shemoneh Esre,* the eighteen blessings. This should be a standing prayer, but I had to trust that the Almighty would understand that it was not always possible for one who was bent over, wielding a pickaxe, with a rifle or a whip at his back. I would frequently find myself in tears as I said the *Matir Asurim—Barukh atah she'matir asurim.* 'Blessed is the One who frees those who are held captive'.

"In antiquity, of course, being thrown into a dungeon or prison was tantamount to death, and this daily invocation is second only to giving thanks for the sure and certain hope that life is redeemed from the grave and the soul thereby reunited with the Almighty!"

It was Ezra who prayed for *El-Hakim* at the start of every day, who taught him to pray over his patients, and how to keep calm in the midst of turmoil. And Dominic would have been unable to put into words the delight he derived from the unexpected appearance of Philip one afternoon, or the joy that was his whenever his brother came to join them.

But Dominic also cherished opportunities to have his friend to himself, and to draw upon his wisdom. For, within a few, short weeks, he would often arrive at their appointed meeting place with a heavy heart—as he began to question his own hitherto unimaginable behaviour. He would frequently hold his fair head in his hands and groan with disbelief at the paradox he embodied. Such times invariably followed others of extreme exhilaration, after which he inevitably returned to the camp, filled with self-loathing and doubt. "I hate myself, Ezra! I hate the person I have become! How dare I ever let Philip know the truth behind these nocturnal activities?..."

"What a rotten example I set!" he cried out on another occasion, out of the agony in his heart and mind. "For my people...and my brother! How can *you* tolerate my presence?" he would demand of the man who had perforce become his father confessor. And the sage Jew would always have the right answer. One day it was: "Dominic, *effendi*, even if I had not learned to love you as a son, I would still remind myself of the words in *'The Wisdom of Yeshua Ben Sira'*, known by you Christians as Ecclesiasticus....'*Show the physician due honour, for the Lord has created him.*' To me you will always remain what the Bedouin call you.—*'Sahbena el-Hakim....*My friend the doctor.'*

"As for the rest?—What can I say? Am I not one of those who benefit from what you do? How dare I be hypocritical or self-righteous about this?...I, Ezra, who quoted to you from the Amida *'Blessed is the One who frees those who are held captive'?*

" While I acknowledge that the reference is to the Almighty, I have only to study the *Tanakh* to find numerous stories of people who, for the sake of others, were called upon to do all manner of things which, by today's standards would be considered utterly despicable."

He did not tell *El-Hakim* of the times when his brother came alone. In Dominic's absence, it would often now be Philip who sought to pour out his heart, as his concern mounted for *El-Hakim* and what he had taken upon himself. Nor did Ezra tell the doctor immediately, how it had surprised him to have to put to Philip the same question he had once had to ask him, Dominic.—*"You mean you don't know?"*

This time was different because he had been moved to add: "Why don't you ask your brother?"

For Dominic, sleep was never a problem—he was out for

the count the moment his head touched his pillow—and the splendid rapier of El-Bus Mohandess was there as a symbol of encouragement when the going was rough.

Before sunrise every morning he was in the saddle, thankful for the many years on his father's farm where both he and Phil had spent a large part of their lives on horseback. Wherever he went he was accompanied by Ali and the faithful Raschid. After every shot that was fired, Raschid would nearly fall out of his saddle to learn Ali's verdict. To hit a moving target at two hundred yards was difficult enough, but from the back of a galloping Arab stallion…! It was because Ali was a man of few words, that Dominic derived such pride from being informed that he was the best pupil the expert marksman had ever had.

In the beginning, Rameses, the sabre fighter, would carefully cover his master's arms and legs with thick protective pads of densely woven wool, before each lesson, and there was a guard for his face. But the day came when these precautions were no longer necessary. Dominic was taught how to virtually undress a man with sword, without sustaining a single scratch himself.

Then there were the sick, as well. He often smiled to himself as he recalled the words of El-Bus Mohandess, "You cannot be both fighter and physician!" And, when he did so, he could not help wondering if the leader hadn't perhaps silently added the word…"yet!"

No matter how full, or how hectic his day had been, he could not neglect his patients. Every evening, before dusk and sometimes also early in the morning, they would line up before his house, as directed by Philip. His young brother came to be of inestimable help, once he had voluntarily learned how to use a syringe, to apply a bandage, and splint a limb, becoming so skilful that Dominic told him that he was as good as any nurse or army medic he had known in the past.

"When I have my own practice again...that is, *if* I ever I have my own practice again, I'll give you a job any day!"

"Dominic Verwey!" Phillip retorted. "How many more times must I tell you...!"

"Okay, okay," said Dominic. "I know that you're determined not to study medicine, but whatever you do decide to do, you could always take me up on that offer during university vacs! There are few students who don't need to earn money, any way they can!"

No sooner had they eaten supper every evening than *El-Hakim* would cast longing glances in the direction of his divan, but Raschid was relentless. "No, *Effendi*. The pronunciation is still not good enough.—Kasr doubara...d.o.u.b.a.r.a.—That is better. One more time, please!" Dominic's throat tightened as he struggled with this strange tongue. Because he knew Afrikaans, *ch* sounds as in *och,* presented no problem, but he complained that, in order to say some of the Arabic words, one had almost to gargle. "No wonder that, to the British in Palestine, 'Haza' had sounded like 'Gaza', by the time they had gagged on the 'h'!"

Or perhaps the lesson would be about the tribal customs of the Bedouin.

"'Bedouin' is an Arabic word, *Effendi*. It means 'dweller in the desert'. They are nomads, and that is why they live in tents."

"As if he did not already know that!" Philip put in scathingly.

"The religion they profess is a crude form of Mohammedanism," Raschid continued, ignoring him. "They are governed by sheiks and *cadis*. 'Cadi' is a Turkish word, and the *cadis* are like your judges or magistrates." His voice droned on, tirelessly.

Like all *El-Hakim's* mentors, Raschid was elated with the progress of his student.

(ii)

Finally the day has arrived. Who can say who is the proudest—Raschid, Philip, or Dominic, himself? Today *El-Hakim* has become a true man, well versed in the ways of the desert....From this day forward, *Sahhena el Hakim*, our friend the doctor, becomes known, also, as 'Hamid Pasha', the leader of his people!

His white cloak, the *burnous*, is draped ceremoniously about his shoulders.

Dominic *el-Hakim* is the friend of the friendless and the rejected, healer of the sick, protector of our *Istiklal*—our freedom—and the refuge of the refugee!

Solemnly his white stallion is led forward, Hamid Pasha vaults lithely onto his horse, takes up his position on the silver-emblazoned saddle...a rousing cheer goes up. The lost children of El-Bus Mohandess have found a new father!

Over the heads of the headmen, Dominic meets Philip's gaze. With complete mutual understanding, they smile at one another...

PART TWO

CHAPTER ONE

There is a saying that Cairo is Egypt, and Egypt is Cairo. That is absolutely true. There one finds the Arab from the desert, the farmer from the Nile valley, the Jew, the Greek, the beggar and the prince...millions of people in one city.

The southern suburb is Maadi, where, in post-war Egypt, writers, poets and other intellectuals chose to live. West are the pyramids and a sphinx. East is the Citadel where, centuries ago, Saladin housed a part of his army. Later the British army took it over to be used as a casern or barracks. North is Alabasia, where the soldiers lived, and still further north is situated Heliopolis, where wealthy Egyptian officials had their palaces. There, too, was the mansion of Sir Humphrey and Lady Talbot.

Of all the inhabitants of exclusive Heliopolis, Sir Humphrey was probably the most concerned about the manner in which the robber-captain, Hamid Pasha, continued to evade the law.

In his position, Sir Humphrey frequently had occasion to entertain ambassadors, senior officials of various states, and others of the 'rich and famous' class. This at a time when it was said that no one was safe for long with cash in the pocket, or jewels around the neck.

Whenever Sir Humphrey was called upon to arrange a function, he was so weighed down with anxiety that, for nights before the time, he never slept. He could talk about nothing else! Would the guests be safe? If only Hamid Pasha could be

kept in ignorance of the forthcoming reception, or whatever!...
Eventually Hamid Pasha became such an obsession with him
that he would dream up, and confer upon him, all manner of
attributes not remotely possible for any one man to possess. In
his own mind, the pasha was capable of anything dastardly,
and was almost superhuman.

"He's been having his own way for close on five years
now," he fumed at the breakfast table one morning. Spread
out before him was the morning paper with a comprehensive
account of yet another escapade. "The blighter gets away with
far too much! If a law is not to his liking, he simply changes
it!" He read further, purple in the face and irately keeping up
a running commentary, until eventually, with an exclamation
of impotent rage, he hurled the paper from him and stamped
on it.

"Please, dear, what will the servants think!" Lady Talbot
murmured absentmindedly, her thoughts elsewhere. "Will the
king be coming to the ball tonight, do you think?"

"I sincerely hope not!" Sir Humphrey's florid face turned
a deeper shade of purple. "That's all we need to make the
evening complete!—A renegade robber and a kleptomaniac
king! Heaven preserve us! It is no secret that Farouk is light-
fingered, even when on state visits. Didn't he help himself to
the Shah's ceremonial sword while he was in Persia, and make
off in England with a valuable watch, very dear to Churchill's
heart?...Heaven forbid...!" He choked at the very thought of
it, and had to gulp down a mouthful of limejuice. "As if it isn't
enough to be plagued with concern about the bloody pasha!"

"Humphrey...the servants..." Lady Talbot began, but he
ignored her.

"The damned reprobate is really getting to be too much!
If the so-and-so wants something, he just calmly walks in and

takes it…just like that!" He snapped his fingers to emphasize his meaning. "Just like that! As easy as it sounds!—What is the matter with the police? They must be in cahoots with him! How else can they allow this to go on any longer?"

"Perhaps it's just that they *can't* catch him, dear," his wife suggested mildly.

"Humph!" her husband grunted. "Of course they can't! Don't be so silly, Ida! They're too damned useless to do that!"

"I heartily concur, Sir," *his aide-de-camp*, Valentine Morgan, joined in from the other end of the table, taking his eyes off a stunning girl seated opposite him, only long enough to stab his grapefruit with the ferocity he would gladly have expended on the notorious pasha. Staring at the recently arrived guest, he was not sure whether it was a good thing or not that, as rumour had it, the reprobate apparently despised women. Ruth, the Talbots' daughter, had listened to her father's tirade with amusement. Personally she found the capers of the elusive daredevil fascinating and highly entertaining. "I wonder what he does with all the stuff that he steals," she sighed dreamily.

Their guest, Thérèse, smiled sympathetically. Ruth was at the romantic stage when such things were exciting. She could remember all too well how silly she was at that age; in the good old days when…but she dared not think of them. Courageously the young princess fought to repel the thoughts that could so easily come crowding in on her, but it was strange how memory perpetually intruded.…Would a time ever come, she wondered, when life would be so joyous and so meaningful again that it would be possible to think back upon those days without bitterness or longing?

Once more, in her imagination, she was back in the garden of the castle. She saw the flowers and the fountains, and heard again the cooing of doves in the old cypress tree nearby.

Her father would come walking across the bridge, his noble silver head bowed in deep, earnest conversation with one of the advisers to his court. Later, she knew, her mother, charming in a cool, floral muslin gown, would come to call her because the dancing master waited in the salon...

Unfortunately, experience had proved that it was impossible to suppress memories, and it was never only the happier ones that were recalled. Thérèse had been along that path before, and she knew that all too well. She shuddered as she saw the flames once again; she shrank from the image of her mother's mangled body. Involuntarily she held her hands to her ears to muffle the noise of the exploding bombs.

"Thérèse!" Ruth regarded her questioningly. "Come back! Whatever can you be thinking about so seriously? I've twice tried speaking to you?"

(ii)

Since coming to stay with the Talbots, Thérèse had become very familiar with the name of Hamid Pasha, as with all his comings and goings. Ruth had told her that he only robbed the very rich. He had never, as far as she knew, murdered anyone, but senior officials and other important people sometimes disappeared, and 'everyone'—according to Ruth—suspected that he had either abducted or done away with them. One thing, though, it was said that he never preyed on the elderly, or targeted young women.

"Oh dear," Ruth murmured plaintively, "I suppose that excludes me! I don't have any diamonds, and would I perhaps be considered too young? How people can know what he looks like, if no one ever gets to have a good look at him, I don't know, but I've heard it said that he is still quite young, himself, is *very* handsome, and *very* well built! Oh, Thérèse, I *wish* I could see him! He is welcome to pick on *me,* whenever he likes!"

"I trust that that is unlikely, my child," Sir Humphrey said sternly. "And I continue to hope that he finds this place too difficult to get into." He turned to Morgan. "You will arrange for extra guards, Valentine?"

"I certainly shall, Sir!" The ADC rose from the table with ill-concealed reluctance....Lady Talbot...Princess...Miss Ruth—if you will please excuse me?"

Although Thérèse could appreciate how a sheltered, seventeen-year-old like Ruth might find the pasha's adventures riveting, she, herself, could only think of them with annoyance and disgust. A criminal like that belonged behind bars— illiterate, unwashed, uncivilized Arab that he doubtless was. More attention than that she did not devote to the man, until...but that's another story!

She was dressing for the ball when there was a knock at the door and the Baroness Gerda von Mölendorff entered, resplendent in a full-length evening gown, emeralds at her throat, and a tiara befitting what, either foolishly—or optimistically—she still considered to be her official status. "I want to talk to you," she said. "May I sit on your bed?"

"Of course!" Thérèse smiled. "You sound mysterious. Have you come to gossip?"

"No, of course not!...All frivolity aside, Ferdinand and I are most concerned about you. It is at his request that I have come. There are so many people in this house at the moment that I have not found a single opportunity to talk to you privately all day, so I took my bath and dressed early, in order to speak to you before you go down to the reception hall."

"That is very kind of both you and Ferdinand," Thérèse

responded, "but I am still completely nonplussed....You have not yet told me why you are so concerned!"

"My girlie"—the baroness took her hand affectionately—"what do you plan to do when your visit with the Talbots comes to an end? Will you leave Egypt? Where do you plan to go, and on what do you hope to exist?...Will you arrange yet another visit...with other people?"

Greatly discomfited by the unexpected confrontation, Thérèse considered that possibility for a moment. "No, Gerda," she then replied calmly. "I think I'm ready now to pick up the shattered pieces of my life, and I plan to make use of the nursing experience I acquired during the war. I hope to find suitable employment somewhere, and thus become independent of my friends—upon whom I have imposed for long enough!"

The older woman looked at her sternly. "Don't you ever dare to talk like that again in my presence, young lady!... Imposed?...I ask you! When we have repeatedly implored you to make your home with us! You make me cross when you adopt this humble, quite ridiculously obsequious attitude!" Suddenly realizing that she was getting nowhere, she changed her approach, and her smile was warm once more. "Thérèse, my child, how can a princess of the Royal House of Soravia be reduced to earning her own living! That would be nothing short of shameful!...A disgrace!"

Had the baroness only known it, the ice onto which she had just ventured was extremely thin. The princess drew her slender shoulders back proudly, and sparks of anger flashed from the brown eyes, to make them appear almost violet. It was not the first time Gerda von Mölendorff had been struck by the girl's beauty, but at that moment, she was breathtaking. However irate Thérèse might be, the baroness decided, she was quite the most beautiful girl she had ever seen.

As far as appearance went, Thérèse was everything a princess should be. From the top of her head, so defiantly held high, to the tips of her small, dainty feet she was—even devoid of coronet and all fine jewellery—the epitome of grace and dignity. Although her simple white organdie dress, worn with a blue velvet sash, and trimmed at the neck and around the fluted sleeves with a border of matching velvet ribbon, was a very far cry from any of the magnificent evening gowns she might have worn in days gone by, she was nothing short of exquisite.

Intently and affectionately appraising, anew, the aureole of shining dark curls, and the creamy perfection of the girl's skin, the baroness felt a pang of sadness at the thought of all that her young charge had lost, but the object of this appraisal was oblivious of the fact that she was under scrutiny. Cheeks flushed, she was far too upset.

"Gerda," she retaliated, striving to keep her temper under control, "there is no disgrace in honest work!...And...and...it's high time you all accepted the fact that there is no longer a Royal House of Soravia!—Is there still a Soravia? Does it still exist?" she demanded fiercely.

"My dear child!" The baroness was overcome with contrition. "Please don't talk like that! It breaks my heart that you are still so bitter! You know how I meant that. We are only so eager for you to accept Otto's proposal of marriage. That was what I was hinting at, but I can be so clumsy at times!"

Immediately, Thérèse was also contrite. Her anger faded swiftly. Sobbing, she jumped up and went over quickly to throw her arms around the baroness. "Please forgive me, too, Gerda! I'm not bitter—only heartbroken....If you only knew how deeply it grieves me to be reminded of my home!...That is why I have become so quick-tempered! I suppose it's a sort of defence mechanism!"

Gerda gently stroked the glossy hair until the tears abated. "Never mind, never mind," she crooned softly, as if Thérèse were an infant. "Everything will come right some day, you'll see…"

Finally the princess raised her head, and smiled tremulously as she dried her eyes. On one soft cheek tears still glistened like dewdrops. She sat down beside the baroness on the bed.

"Gerda," she said earnestly, "you understand better that anyone else what it is like to be homeless, but mercifully it is only a question of time before your period of exile will be over. Of course you must wait upon word from the officials, but you and Ferdinand will return to your country, and your nephew, to his. You have confidence that your home, although damaged, waits for you.…My future, on the other hand, stretches out hopelessly before me…lonely and bleak…"

"But Otto…" the baroness began.

"I cannot marry Otto just as a hedge against loneliness, Gerda. Please believe me, it has nothing to do with his wanting to return to Germany.…The past is the past and I harbour no hatred. As far as I am concerned, the war has been over for long enough, for it to make any difference now, and I can think of nothing more pleasant than to be your niece by marriage, but it would never work. I am fond of him, but shall never learn to love him.…That's why I must seek another way out!"

She was silent for a moment before resuming thoughtfully: "During the war, despite the vicissitudes, I was far happier than I am now. I know that it was because I had less time to dwell on hurtful memories. I was useful, and I was busy.…I *must* work again!"

"But where do you plan to go, child? You are surely not bent on settling here, are you?"

"No. I may possibly go to South Africa. Some of the girls

I learnt to know at the hospital, have found good jobs there, as nurses, and there might well be an opening for me too, somewhere."

Gerda rose to her feet and tried to smoothe the wrinkles around her hips. "I shall not argue with you any longer, dear child. I can understand far more than I did before. But now..."—she propelled Thérèse toward the cheval mirror— "you must hurry or we shall miss both the banquet and the dancing!"

(ii)

By eleven o'clock the ball was in full swing. From where Thérèse stood watching with Otto von Mölendorff, the scene before her was like one from a picture book. The gold braid on the officers' colourful uniforms, the shimmer of satin and the rustle of taffeta—so it was in the days of her childhood....The sparkle of diamonds and the lustre of priceless pearls; with, here and there, a glimpse of priceless, but highly unnecessary furs. Now and then she caught a whiff of costly perfume.

Otto touched her arm lightly. "I spy a tray of what appears to be a fresh supply of champagne. May I fetch you a glass?"

"That would be very nice, thank you, Otto," she replied, smiling at him, and he walked over to where several other men were already clustered around the footman.

He had hardly left her side, when she heard the whistle. Loud and shrill it came, a second time, and suddenly the ballroom was teeming with what the princess took to be Arabs. Women screamed...men cursed...and above the clamour she heard the jingle of spurs.

"HAMID PASHA!" the name scorched through the room like a flame.

"Please remain where you are, ladies," the robber-captain commanded calmly but authoritatively, in remarkably good English, but with an accent that she was unable to define. Thérèse could detect amusement in the mocking voice, and imagined that his lips curled with disdain.—"And no one will be harmed!"

At first she could not determine the direction from which the voice had come until, glancing over her shoulder, she saw— with a shudder of apprehension—the tall, powerful figure in the white *burnous*, not very far from where she stood. His back was to her and the hood of his cloak temporarily hid his face from view.

Her hand immediately flew to cover the finely crafted locket on a heavy gold chain, the only article of adornment she was wearing. All that remained to her of her mother's jewellery, she was not going to allow any common thief to deprive her of it. Behind her was a short flight of stairs which, she knew, led to one of the many parapets not far above street level; rather like small, outside galleries, surrounded by wrought iron balustrades, and probably intended as fire-escapes.

In a flash she was down the steps, through the door, and out on this balcony, where she leant against a wall, panting for a moment, before moving to where, out of the direct rays of a street lamp, it was comparatively dark. Keeping very still, she could hear that, whereas there had momentarily been dead silence in the ballroom, pandemonium had since ensued. Somewhat weak in the knees, and almost afraid to breathe, she remained crouched in that corner of the gallery until, all at once, she became aware of the white-cloaked apparition towering over her. Out of the corner of his eye, the pasha had obviously detected a movement on the stairs, and had followed her. She saw the glint of a sword as he transferred it from his right hand to his left, before grasping her by the wrist, bent on drawing her into the light.

"My dear little lady," he laughed derisively, with an eye on the small hand still clutching desperately at the locket, "can your bauble possibly be of such value that you would disobey my instruction?"

"I...I..." she stammered hoarsely. From her crouched position, the man seemed even taller than she had thought, and his hold on her wrist, as he bent over to pull her to her feet, was a grip of iron. "It was my mother's," she managed to say. " It has her picture in it...and...and..." To her exasperation, tears stung her eyes.

He threw his head back and laughed out loud. She found it incredible that anyone should remain so casual in the face of the *fracas* he had just engendered. "Don't fret!" he said, with a noticeable change of voice. "I really don't relish making such enchanting young ladies miserable!" He raised her chin with a forefinger. "Keep your trinket....I am more than willing to accept a substitute!" And before she knew what was happening, he had pulled her into his arms, and pressed a burning kiss on her lips. He let go of her so suddenly that she staggered, and then, with a leap that, for want of a better word, she could only think of later as graceful, he was over the railings of the balcony. From down in the street, he waved to her and blew her a kiss. "Till we meet again, sweetheart! Perhaps I'll return to steal from you again some day—if you're lucky!"

He ran a short distance to where a man waited, already mounted on one of two horses, and then, with an agile, effortless spring, he was astride the saddle of the second, a magnificent white stallion. As he galloped past, with his companion beside him, he waved to her again and she caught a fleeting glimpse of the face under the hood.

For a few moments Thérèse wondered whether she had dreamt the whole incident, until she became conscious of the wild beating of her heart. She touched her mouth tremulously, as though expecting to find it bruised.

"The nerve!" she panted furiously. "The sheer, effrontery!"

***

Shaken though she was, she could barely refrain from laughing when she saw the expression on Otto's face. He was as white as a sheet as he and Gerda came running down the steps, with Baron von Mölendorff, his wife, and Sir Humphrey Talbot hot on their heels. Did he think that the pasha had dragged her off to his lair?

The baroness was hardly less agitated. "Thérèse!" she cried with relief, as she caught up with the others. "You are safe, thank God! I am nearly dead with fright!"

But Otto was quite incoherent. "*Fräulein*!...Princess!...My dearest Thérèse, when I saw him on the stairs, so soon after you...the most dreadful thoughts came to me!"

"But of course you could not bring yourself to come after me, yourself!" she retorted coldly.

"I could not...!" he tried helplessly to defend himself.

Sir Humphrey looked as though he were about to suffer a seizure. His heavy face was flushed an even deeper hue than usual, and he mopped his brow with a shaking hand.

"My dear princess, it was too *dreadful*! Two of the miscreant's lackeys took up a position at the foot of the steps, with swords crossed, challenging anyone who might dare to try and follow their misbegotten leader! *O-o-o-h!*" he groaned.

"What will my guests think? All robbed blind without anyone attempting to lay a finger on the bandits to stop them! None of them was armed with anything more than a scimitar, so, had our men only been wearing side arms we could have had him! I think I shall have to institute that requirement very promptly....*Oh*...! *This is dreadful! Dreadful!*"

His ranting was cut short by the arrival of his ADC. If anything, Valentine Morgan appeared to be even more agitated than the rest of them. "Princess!" the *aide-de-camp* burst out. "You are safe! I can hardly believe my eyes! I thought he might have made off with you! The man has a reputation for abduction and I feared...!"

Thérèse, who was by this time beginning to feel that if she were to give in to her wild desire to laugh, she would never be able to stop, tried to speak as normally as she could. She despised the kind of women who permitted themselves the luxury of hysteria, at the drop of a hat.

"Though I am highly flattered, Captain Morgan," she responded as evenly as she was able, "that would have been rather a waste of his time, would it not?" Involuntarily a note of cynicism crept into her voice. "He probably knew that, with very few exceptions, the remaining members of the European nobility are virtually penniless at this time.—Who could possibly have come up with the ransom?"

She turned to the younger Von Mölendorff. "Otto, why don't you go in search of a footman—if they're not all hiding under a table or something—and see if you can rustle up that glass of champagne of which we were deprived earlier?"

"An excellent idea!" said Gerda. "I can certainly do with a drink—Make mine a stiff brandy, please Otto!"

"But please, first tell me, Thérèse," Otto pleaded, having not yet completely recovered from the shock. "Did he not encounter you out there on the balcony?"

She hesitated for a moment, wondering what restrained her from talking openly about the incident. "He did pass by me," she prevaricated shamelessly, "and then he jumped over the railings. I hid in the shadows, which made it difficult for him to see me!"

Just then Ruth, still breathless with excitement, came running to join them. "Wasn't that all just too wildly thrilling?" she cried. "To have him right here, in our very own ballroom?...Oh, Thérèse, you lucky dog, I am *sooo* jealous! It must have been quite spine tingling to be alone with him like that!...He was facing me before he ran out after you, and now I know it is true that he is so tall. I also saw for myself that he certainly can't be an Arab, because he has the bluest eyes I have ever seen!"

"Blue eyes be damned!" her father fumed. "The brigand should have been shot! He could have killed us all!"

"That, Sir, I would venture to say, might have been rather difficult, even for a man with Hamid Pasha's reputation," Baron von Mölendorff put in with an amused smile. "Considering that there must have been more than three-hundred of us in the room!"

"It is also true," Ruth continued, ignoring the interruption, "that he never lays hands on anyone, personally. I also saw that, for myself!"

"That makes him no less guilty, Miss Ruth," the ADC put in. "He is still an accessory after the fact, and what about all his other crimes?"

"We shouldn't believe half of what we hear," she retaliated defensively. "I certainly don't!...But I still can't help wondering what he does with all the money?" She tilted her head thoughtfully. "Probably has an enormous house...with an enormous swimming pool..."—she was warming to the idea—

"and, for all we know he might live right here in Heliopolis, almost next door to us!"

"Heaven forbid!" Sir Humphrey threw up his hands in horror!—"Thank God!…Here come Otto and the footman with our drinks!"

***

Meanwhile Hamid Pasha and his cohorts were exuberantly charging through the night, shouting triumphant remarks back and forth to one another, and Dominic began to laugh uproariously, loud enough for Philip to be able hear him above the exultant word-exchange and the rhythmic clatter of the horses' hooves on the paved street. He spurred his horse forward so that he could ride alongside his brother.

"I'll bet they still don't know what hit them!" he shouted against the wind, referring to Sir Humphrey and his guests.

"No! Totally unprepared!" Dominic yelled back cheerfully, but all of a sudden his exhilaration evaporated. The inevitable reaction against which he had determinedly steeled himself, set in, but this time it was worse. If he had not been on the back of a galloping horse, he would have held his hands to his face and cowered with remorse. The only redeeming part of all that had transpired that night—and for which he was grateful—was that he had somehow been able to restrain Philip from coming inside with them. He should not have brought him at all!

He had never intended Philip to have any part of 'Hamid Pasha's' life, and he deeply regretted ever having told his brother the whole truth. At first only the fact that Philip had been prompted by Ezra to question him, and to brook no evasion, had made him open up to any degree, at all. After that, one thing had led to another, and finally Philip had wormed it all out of him.

It had been a big decision, in the first place, to establish a precedent by allowing his younger sibling to accompany small groups of the men who rode out in daylight hours to fetch supplies. The only consolation was that while he, Dominic, would have stuck out like a sore thumb, Philip, with his dark hair and beard, was far less conspicuous. In his brown *burnous* and, with his Arabic becoming more and more fluent, he could be any other young Bedouin, coming to the marketplace with friends, on a totally innocuous errand. Although Philip had promised that he would never approach any of the vendors, directly, his companions studiously obeyed the instruction that they should vary their routine by not frequenting the same village too often, and never in quick succession.

While it pleased *El-Hakim* to know that his brother felt less trapped once he was not permanently restricted to the confines of the stockade, it was a joy and a delight to observe his growing interest in the sick. Of late Philip had begun to exhibit a surprising willingness to assist wherever he was needed, and the manner in which this newfound enthusiasm had been precipitated, had been nothing short of miraculous.

It was difficult to think of Ali, the crack shot, in terms of domesticity and gentle family life, but he had felt free to unburden his heart to *El Hakim*, whenever they had come cantering back at a leisurely pace, after a strenuous time of what Philip referred to as 'shooting practice'. After having been captured by Abdel Sharia's men, and incarcerated in one of his dungeons, Ali—who could never understand what commercial value he could possibly have held, for the nefarious Bey—had drawn comfort solely from the fact that, as his wife was pregnant, he would not perish without leaving behind something of himself. In some respects, like Raschid, he had been rescued some distance from the prison, but, in his case it had been while working on an extension of one of Sharia's railways lines and not toiling in the dreaded gravel pits. From the day he had been brought to the stockade, the marksman had lived only for the day when El-Bus Mohandess could fulfil a promise to bring his, Ali's, wife, and the child he had never seen, to the stockade. It had thus nearly broken his heart when she arrived without the son whom, he was to discover, had been stillborn.

Having seen some of the consequences of the crude botching of the 'midwife', among other women in the camp, Dominic had not been surprised. Blessedly, by the time Ali's wife, now approaching forty, expected her second child, much of the women's attitude concerning the ministrations of a physician—and a male at that—had changed dramatically. Was not *El-Hakim* unlike all other men? Was he not the leader and the almost supernatural being with the golden hair, to whom even small children ran when they were in trouble?

This change of view proved to be fortuitous, indeed, when it became obvious to the doctor that the infant would not be born alive without his performing a caesarean section. It was also fortunate that, because of his relationship to *El-Hakim* and his regular presence during consulting hours, 'Philip-brother' had also come to be accepted as a perfectly normal part of medical assistance. Later, when the baby boy was presented to his well-nigh speechless father, it was to Philip that the honour was given to do so. And then had come a night, two weeks later, when the same 'Philip-brother', who could no longer be regarded merely as the '*little*' brother, was able wait up and greet Hamid Pasha and his returning outriders with surprising news, as they came thundering into the stockade at one o'clock in the morning....In the absence of the doctor, he, Philip, had been obliged to perform a delivery. All on his own! It would, however, be quite a few weeks before he found himself able to proclaim, categorically, that he had decided what he wanted to do with his life.

Neither of the brothers could have foreseen what a wonderful family physician Philip would someday prove to be; nor how many children he would help to bring into the world. Nevertheless, Dominic was pensive on this particular night, as, with his brother alongside of him, they covered the miles that still lay between the Talbot mansion and the mountain refuge. They had spoken earlier about their respective futures, as a result of Philip's insistence on accompanying Dominic on this raid.

"I'm quite old enough to decide for myself what I am prepared to risk, Dom," Philip had insisted. "And being cooped up with so many sick people all week has given me a perpetual headache. I rather fancy having the wind in my face....I can take good care of myself....All those who had high fevers seem to be improving, and Raschid has been up and about for a few days, so he is well enough now to be left safely. Fortunately he is no longer the frail man we brought back with us from the oasis....*Please* take me with you next time!—You owe me!" he added, grinning.

"There is little chance of my ever being able to leave Egypt and go home, now, *boetie*," Dominic had tried to convince him. "There is a price on my head, and I'm told that I am now even suspected of abducting some visiting head-of-state from the king's palace. The obstacles in my way are insurmountable, and, in any case, I am wholly committed to my charges here. But it's different for you. You are, in effect, not guilty of any crime other than outstaying your welcome, and money is no longer a problem, is it?"—This with a rueful smile.—"Since our home country is part of the Commonwealth, and we have, to our very recent credit, people like Jan Smuts and Sailor Malan, for example, still revered for their part in the North African campaign and the Battle of Britain, you could even walk into Talbot's office with some cooked up tale of having escaped from me, yourself, and he'd help you like a shot.

"You're only twenty-seven now, Phil, and many guys older than you, who came back to South Africa from the war determined to further their education, must be well on their way by now....Go home now! Go home and go to med school. In the meantime, while you are still here, stay clear of anything that might connect you with Hamid Pasha, I implore you!"

"I'll go home when you can, or not at all!" Philip had remained adamant. "And I'm going on that raid with you tonight, even if just to hold your horse!"

Now, returning to the stockade, they rode further, in silence and without any interference, first going south through the city, itself, and then veering off slightly to the west, sticking to the back streets, until they reached the western exit, where they were temporality held up by a stream of traffic, coming and going from all directions.

"Last time we came out through the north end," Dominic explained. "We have to keep covering our..." He was about to say 'tracks', but broke off instead, almost open mouthed, to fix his eyes incredulously on something not far from him.

Philip, who had heard Dominic's sharp intake of breath, allowed his own gaze to follow the direction of his brother's fixed stare, and thus also managed to get a good look at a luxury limousine gliding slowly past them.

"But it's...! Dom, isn't that Lydia in that car?" he called out excitedly. "Did you see her?"

"Mamoun! Haroun!" Dominic shouted to the twins, a dangerous glint in his eye. "Follow that car!" he commanded. "Right to its destination, do you hear me? I want to know whose house it is, and the names of all who live there. Take twenty men with you, and do not return until you have deprived the lady of all the valuables she has with her!"

"But, *Effendi...*" Rameses, catching up with him, was about to protest.

"Rameses!" Dominic thundered. "When I say something, I mean it! If we have to establish one precedent, then let it be this one!" Although his eyes still flashed angrily, he had to admit that the Turk was right; and immediately the familiar, good-natured smile appeared once more. "Do not fret, old friend," he called out. "That one is not a lady—she's a vixen!"

CHAPTER TWO

I wonder if Lydia always toffs herself up like that when she goes out?" was Philip's cynical observation next morning, when he saw the collection of jewellery that the dwarf, Haroun, had spread out on the table in front of Dominic. "She must hang everything she possesses, about her person, and that's certainly not in very good taste!"

Dominic laughed derisively. "Perhaps, after this encounter, she'll develop a better sense of style! Anyway as charming as these objects might have looked on her, they'll be far more appreciated here. I think that this lot, together with the rest of what we collected last night, will be quite enough for us to be able to acquire some much-needed new equipment, and complete at least one of the building projects.

"As soon as Raschid is truly fit enough to make the journey to Cairo, I'll send him, with as many men as he deems necessary, to make inquiries about purchasing what we need most urgently, and as soon as I have next week's meeting behind me, I hope to get stuck in and finish the isolation ward." He looked up from what he was doing. "I am convinced that we would have little or no infection in this camp if Sharia had the decency to provide some sort of medical care, in his."

For as long as he could remember, Philip had hero-worshipped his brother. Although, as he grew up, there had been times when he had exasperated him, he had been able to rationalize Dominic's gullibility on the grounds that, as he had spent so much of his life studying or doing research, he had a right to be so ridiculously unworldly. Now he found himself in awe of him.

"Did you know about this...this kind of thing when you signed on, Dom? Did you realize that you would have to go to these lengths to carry on where Etienne left off?"

Dominic shook his head. "No, *boet*, I assure you I did not! I once tried to question Ezra in an oblique way, but his only response was another question."

Philip was dumbfounded. "Well then, when you found out, why did you not back out? You had every right to..."

Dominic looked him very solemnly in the eye, and said simply: "Because I promised, Philip. I made a promise...and to me, going back on a promise is like the worst, possible form of lying. What a dreadful place the world would be, if one could never be sure of, or rely on anyone's word!—And now I stay because I love these people. They are like my children. I don't want to compare myself, for one minute, with the poor wretches in the stories we used to read at school, who had to go out into the damp and fog to steal, in order to feed the hungry mouths at home, but there is something almost Dickensian about the situation here, you must admit. What would become of my people?...Who would feed them?—But now you know why I have tried so hard to keep you in ignorance."

For a few minutes Philip was silent as he pondered what his brother had said. Then, still very much perplexed, he asked very simply: "What about the Bible, Dom? What about the Ten Commandments?...What about Christ?"

"What about Christ, Phil? I can only trust in what he said about 'Whosoever giveth a cup of water to one of these little ones, in My name.'...I admit that it might sound sacrilegious, but I do...I really do try to do this in His name...and I can only pray to God that I will someday be forgiven for the manner in which I do so!"

He rose to his feet as though the subject were closed.

"Now I must get back to work.—There's a ward waiting to be completed!"

"It's high time, Dom," Philip agreed, following him outside. "Even for this time of the year the number of cases is unusually high, and the symptoms vary so much. Can't we move some of the patients to there, in the meantime? For instance, that English banker, Christopher Brent, whom you brought back last Wednesday, has so far presented none of the signs of this weird fever. He should not be in with the others.

"He is still in a great deal of pain and, as you said yourself, in that rundown condition, he's a prime candidate for infection....Fortunately the weather is still quite mild, so that the north side doesn't matter so much yet. I can get some of the men to help me hammer a few planks over those windows on the south, that really need them, but don't have panes as yet. Raschid maintains that he is quite well enough already, to help us."

"Very well. I'll leave that to you. Start as soon as you have eaten....But tonight, if he really is up to it, I shall need Raschid, myself. I have a date!" Dominic smiled wickedly. "Tonight I intend to pay a visit to the wife of the Sheik Mohammed Ahmed!"

"*What*!" Philip was astounded, "*Lydia?*"

"Who else?" Dominic savoured the amazement on Philip's face. "I'll let you know how it went....Mamoun," he addressed one of the twins, "tell my brother what you found out last night."

Mamoun bowed low before Philip, as was his custom, before reciting the required information in his strange, squeaky monotone. "His name is Mohammed Ahmed, *Effendi*," he began, bestowing on Philip a more respectful form of address, "but, in Egypt, he chooses to be known as Mohammed Alfit. He is a member of the *Barlaman* (parliament), the representative of this *mudiria* (province), and the possessor of great wealth. The lady Lydia is his only wife...for the present! Business frequently compels the sheik to absent himself from his home, and..."— he winked slyly at Philip—"he is *not there now*!"

"Do you see why I have to grab the opportunity while I may?" Dominic asked, giving Philip a similar, but more challenging wink.

"But you can't do that! You just *can't*! You are simply looking for trouble....It's too risky! And she is, moreover, another man's wife! You have always been such a stickler about things like that..."

"That, my dear respected brother, was Dominic Verwey. Hamid Pasha follows a different set of rules. Have you not heard that the notorious pasha allows nothing to get in his way?"

Philip shook his head. What a paradox Dom presented. Hamid Pasha and his unpredictability presented a far greater problem than the patient, sensitive Dominic Verwey, for all his artlessness and total lack of guile had ever been! He found it very difficult to reconcile this attitude with the way Dominic had spoken but a few moments before, and as soon as Dominic, Raschid, and the rest of the entourage had ridden off in the late afternoon, he went in search of Ezra to pour out his concern.

"If you think that you are the only one who is troubled, my dear, devoted young brother of our leader and protector, you are mistaken," said Ezra. "Never think, for one moment, that *El-Hakim* does not agonize constantly about the very things that trouble you. Give him the benefit of the doubt.

Don't begrudge him the opportunity of going tonight, to try
and rid his heart of all residual resentment. That should be of
least concern to you. Pray for him as Raschid and I do. We are
of different faiths, but we are united in this.

"Your brother has fulfilled almost every one of the dreams
of El-Bus Mohandess. However, as I was privileged to be present
in the room, just prior the death of our departed leader, I can
tell you that, as it was for him, so *El-Hakim's* greatest task still
lies ahead! The Bey, Abdel Sharia, evades him still, and he can
never hope to expose him until he succeeds in unveiling his
identity. As El-Bus Mohandess so wisely said, once the Bey is
taken captive, his cohorts will surrender willingly."

"I don't understand..." Philip began.

"You will," Ezra assured him. "When the time comes. Just
pray for your brother that it happens soon. In the meantime,
none of us—and least of all *El-Hakim*—will be safe to leave
this place until that happens!"

(ii)

Screened from view by a huge Oleander, Dominic removed
his *burnous* and handed it to a strangely morose Raschid. The
Indian had not spoken a word to him since they had left the
stockade, erroneously believing that he would thus leave *El-
Hakim* in no doubt as to the reason for his disapproval. He had
called out cheerfully enough to others in their group, as they
were all wont to do whenever they were on their way to some
assignation, adrenalin flowing, free of the confines of the camp
and enjoying the wind in their faces. However, his conspicuous
lack of communication on this occasion, actually led Dominic
to find a different cause, thus putting an incorrect slant on
Raschid's attitude towards this particular venture.

It was quite clear that Philip had shared his views with Raschid, and that they were in complete agreement on some score..... What he did not know was that, as they saw it, this woman for whom Dominic might be risking his life, had broken his heart once and had perhaps left it so fragile that he might be facing a greater risk.—That of having it fractured beyond all possibility of repair.

Precisely what that score was, however—beyond the fact that Lydia was married—Dominic could not determine. Had he known what they feared, he could soon have put their minds at rest. In fact, now that the twins had brought him so unerringly to the right place, he was no longer quite sure why he had come. There was no quickening of his pulse, and no thrill attached to the prospect of seeing his former love again.

Had it ever been love, he wondered? He had been so pathetically ill-versed in the ways of women. Unlike some of his colleagues, he had never been tempted to flirt or enter into a relationship with any of the nurses, or even with girls he had met during his student days, and he certainly would have balked at an affair with any of his patients.

Thinking back over the months of their engagement, he almost blushed at the memory of the diffident, almost apologetic kisses he had pressed on Lydia's cheek from time to time. He had hardly ventured to hold her hand, and somehow he could not blame her if she had been swept off her feet by the mysterious and more passionate Mohammed Ahmed.

He could not recall ever having been shaken by any of the more daring kisses he had occasionally risked, seldom venturing more than a peck on the mouth. During his courtship of Lydia there had never been that magic moment when the earth had seemed to shake or stand still, or whatever it was supposed to do. Moreover, as he now recalled, there were moments cruising the Mediterranean in the stifling heat, when Lydia's heavy perfume had almost sickened him. And as this thought came to him, he was suddenly shaken by the memory of the sweetness of the kiss he had stolen on Sir Humphrey's balcony the night before. He cringed at the recollection of the girl's vulnerability and the brutality with which he had inflicted that kiss upon her quivering lips.

Dwelling on the encounter, he despised himself for making her cry, and, recalling the tears that he had seen her eyes, despite the dimness of the light, he was made to realize that she had been defensive rather than afraid for herself. She had been fearful lest he take from her something very precious, and it touched him to remember that it had been a beloved souvenir and not an item of costly jewellery that she had held onto so fiercely. Because of the manner in which he had gripped her wrist before drawing her to her feet, he had been able to feel that her pulse was racing, and he could not help admiring the courage which had driven her to escape to the balcony. He was shocked to discover how deeply he regretted the fact that she should have been aware only of his reputation, and not of the circumstances that had thrust it upon him.

He was guided by the twins as far as the gap in the dense cypress hedge, which they had fortuitously discovered the previous night, and that shielded the sheik's house from the wind. There he cautioned them to come no further with him. Squeezing through the gap, he found himself beside a blue-tiled swimming pool, and stopped for a moment to enjoy the reflection of the moon in its shimmering surface. A fine, velvety lawn lay stretched out at his feet and, surveying it in the moonlight, he wondered how Mohammed Ahmed's lackeys could maintain it in this climate. Momentarily comparing the confines of the enclosed garden with the openness of his mountain top retreat, he wondered how he would ever again adapt to living at a low altitude.——And then, unexpectedly, he spotted her...

"Lydia!" he called softly, and again, a little louder... "LYDIA!"

Startled, she swung around, and the expression on her face when she recognized him was almost comical.

"Dominic? What on earth are you doing here?...Where have you come from?"

He came strolling casually towards her in his very ordinary, white, tropical suit, as though his presence there was the most normal thing on earth...."As though I've just been to the corner store and back," he thought dryly, smiling crookedly to himself.

"Hullo, Lydia," he greeted her calmly. "I'm spending a few days in Cairo on my way to the continent, and I suddenly got this inspiration. 'Dominic,' I said to myself, 'you really can't go away without going to see how Lydia is doing!' "

"But how did you find me?" There was a perplexed, worried little frown between her eyebrows. "Ahmed is not..."

"No. I am already aware," he interjected, deliberately misconstruing what she was about to say, "that he is not commonly referred to as Mohammed Ahmed, but someone where I am staying, knows him, and he explained to me how to get here. Taxis are still just as readily available as they have ever been..."

"Oh, I see."

But it was perfectly obvious that she did not see, and was still uneasy. However, he seemed so innocent, and she, of all people, knew very well how artless he could be. An arch, inviting smile appeared on the doll face. "Aren't you going to greet me more appropriately after all these years, Dom? I assure you that I am still eminently kissable!"

He came closer and asked mockingly, "And what about the jealous Ahmed? What would he have say about that?"

"Forget him!" she murmured, sensing a recklessness in Dominic that had not been there before, and she found it fascinating. Her arms crept slowly around his neck and she held her face up, puckering her mouth for the kiss.

But Dominic, who had never found himself in such a situation before, was beginning to find this game enjoyable. He felt an irresistible urge to tantalize her. His lips were very close to hers, before he pushed her away. "Lydia!" he rebuked her, pretending disapproval. "Shame on you! To speak in those terms about your own husband!" He sounded shocked. And then he drew her towards him again, and dropped a fleeting kiss on her forehead.

"Hullo, Lydia," he chuckled, and let her go. "Why don't we sit on this bench for a while and have a nice chat."

Bewildered and temporarily at a loss for words, she was angry enough to have slapped him, but she thought better of it. Instead, she managed to restrain herself, and sit down beside him.

"What's the problem, sweetie?" he asked, sounding amused. "Why the pout? Aren't you pleased to see your old friend?" The sardonic grin on his face was infuriating.

She studied him as intently as the moonlight permitted. He seemed the same, and yet different. Five years could change anybody, but what was it that was so different about him? Apart from the fact that he had allowed his hair to grow so long that it was more like a golden mane, this new Dominic was a hundred times more attractive than the old one had ever been, and it was propitious that he should have made his appearance at a time when life was at it's most trying.

"Why are you being like this, Dom?" she asked him, with genuine concern. "There was time when you would not have been so cold. You would not have treated me like this!"

"Good heavens, woman!" he cried furiously. He sprang up, and looking down at her, there was fire in his eyes. "Did you expect me to kneel at your feet!" At that he angrily pulled her to her feet and held her to him so tightly that she feared her would crush every bone in her body. His lips, when he did kiss her, were cold and hard, and hurt her mouth. "This is what I think of you, you shameless little coquette!" And he kissed her again with such brutality that she wrenched herself free of his hold, and stumbled back to where she has been sitting on the wrought iron garden seat. Despite the warmth in the night air, she began to shake as though she were freezing. She raised tearful blue eyes to his.

"I deserved that, Dom. You have good reason to despise me, but I would never have believed that it would hurt so deeply to lose your love! I was always so sure of it!"

"What did you expect?" he demanded more kindly. "That I would go through my entire life nursing a broken heart?" He grinned, reverting to disdain. "You, my incorrigible little Jezebel, really do over-estimate your charms, don't you?"

Lydia had now begun to sniffle from sheer frustration. At the same time she was flummoxed to such a degree that she could not decide what to do next. Could this really be Dominic? The shy, long-suffering fiancé whom she had so often ridiculed as soon he was out of earshot? Her not inconsiderable feminine wiles were clearly useless in the face of such open contempt.

Before she had been able to decide upon the next step, however, Dominic became aware that they were no longer alone, and a chill moved down his spine as he realized how silently the fellow had approached. There was something threatening and catlike in his movements. How long, Dominic wondered, could he have been skulking in the bushes? The man loudly cleared his throat. "Excellency!" He addressed Lydia, stepping out of the shadows. As the moonlight fell full on the newcomer's face, Dominic had difficulty suppressing the cry of horror that instinctively rose up in him. Never in his life had he seen anyone quite so repulsive and, while, human-like, he instinctively recoiled, as a physician he could not help wondering why nothing had been done to repair such gross damage to that face.

"What is it, Farao?" Lydia inquired. "I have a guest and I do not appreciate being disturbed." She spoke haughtily, but Dominic detected a degree of nervousness in her manner.

"A thousand pardons, Excellency," he responded with such exaggerated obsequiousness that it bordered on impertinence. "It is urgent that I speak with you!"

To Dominic's surprise she obeyed instantly, and followed the man across the lawn. By the time she had walked as far as the opposite end of the pool, it must have occurred to her that she was being discourteous, because she turned around and called out: "Please excuse me for one moment, Dom. I am only going to give orders that refreshments be served to us out here..."

With that she disappeared into the house and, left alone, Dominic sat down again on the hard seat to ponder the situation. He could have kicked himself for being such a fool. In coming to this place he had risked considerable danger—for both himself and his comrades—and what for? What had he hoped to gain? What exactly had he anticipated? He remained deep in thought for quite some time, and then, all at once, many things became clear to him.

He could now admit to himself that, during the early

stages of disillusionment, after Lydia's callous treatment of him, he had, albeit subconsciously, wished her to be so miserable that she would forever think back longingly, with regret and remorse, of the happiness she had experienced with him, Dominic Verwey. In time, as his experience of life and the world had widened, he had been able to acknowledge that there was no such happiness to be recalled. She had never loved him. Why then would she have suffered any regret?

With that realization behind him, a revised desire had begun replace the former. Lydia should be so unhappy that, when she met him again some day, she would appreciate what she had missed. He would return, rich, acclaimed in his field, and brimming over with self-confidence, and she would fling herself at his feet and beg for forgiveness. Many a time, in his imagination, he had heard her…."Dom," she would declare, "I made the biggest mistake of my life! Please take me back, I beseech you!"

Here he sat then, this night, back in her company—or what there was of it!—far from wealthy, and yet she had unmistakably shown that he was not unwelcome. What was it that she had said? *"I would never have believed that it would hurt me so deeply to lose your love…"*

Where was the jubilation? The exultation? The satisfaction? "Face it, Dominic," he acknowledged to himself, "you are so bored that you can't wait to get away!"

It would have been easy to reason that, since he had come so far, he might as well take advantage of the situation and make the visit worthwhile, but Lydia no longer held the slightest attraction for him. As soon as she returned, he resolved, he would make some excuse and go back to rejoin Raschid and the others. They were probably growing anxious by this time, and he thought affectionately of how much more he could have been enjoying their company, rough and ready as some of them were. As a result, he was thoroughly put out when, instead of the returning Lydia, he saw a servant coming towards him, bearing refreshments on a silver tray.

"I shall place this on the small table beside you, *Effendi*," the young Turk said politely. "You are invited to pour yourself something to drink while you wait." With that he bowed and left the guest to himself.

With the ghastly face of Lydia's repugnant dark friend still fresh in his memory, Dominic did not trust the contents of any of the carafes or bottles on the tray; and, in any case, he very seldom drank alcohol. With a fleeting glance at the bushes around him, he filled a glass with whatever was nearest to him, immediately emptied it and then, relieved to see a tap nearby, he went over and rinsed the glass thoroughly before filling it again, this time with water. Trusting that it was potable, he was still sipping the tepid water with a convincing pretence of enjoyment, when Lydia returned.

"Oh," she observed with somewhat overdone animation. "I am so glad to see that you have made yourself at home." She took a biscuit and nibbled at it. "No thank you, Dom," as he pointed to the tray. "Please don't trouble...I am not at all thirsty!"

Dominic was struggling desperately not to squirm. How was he ever going to escape? He wanted to laugh as he recognized the old, garrulous Lydia in the way she suddenly leaned forward conversationally...in what Philip had more than once sarcastically referred to as "LYDIA'S TELL ME ALL ABOUT IT—LET'S HAVE A CHAT MODE!"

"Well, this is all very nice," she began. "Tell me about Philip. How is he, what is he doing with himself these days? And what have you been up to since we last met?...You probably have a large practice by now?"

"Indeed I do," he replied. "Bigger than you think!"

The moon had temporarily gone behind a cloud, and some distance away he heard a door close very quietly. Protected now by the gloom, Lydia leant forward. With her mouth very close to his ear, she hissed: "Be very careful of what you say. Alfit has spies everywhere!" Several seconds later the garden was flooded with light as someone flicked a switch somewhere, and he was able to note that she was markedly tense. It happened that, just then, the unsightly man he had previously seen, galloped past on horseback, close by them, and only when the sound of hooves had faded away in the distance did she appear to relax once more.

This was when Dominic's interest in the sheik Mohammed Alfit's sinister ménage was kindled. Before long it would transpire that his visit had been worthwhile, after all, in more ways than one!

"What on earth is going on here, Lydia?" he asked with a deceptively innocent smile. "Do you still go to see so many movies? As I can recall you have always been inclined towards melodrama…"

"No work of fiction can be compared even remotely with the state of my life as it is at present, Dom." She said this so seriously that he was convinced that she spoke the truth. "I am seldom if ever permitted visitors, and then only with Alfit's permission. The loneliness and monotony of it will someday drive me insane!"

"Don't you ever go out?" He was thinking of the previous night, when he and Philip had caught that glimpse of her on the outskirts of the city.

"I don't know whether they are all the same, but a Moslem such as my husband, does certainly not readily display his wife in public. When I sometimes escape from here for an hour or two, it is always without his knowledge. Luckily I have a few friends among the servants. The chauffeur occasionally smuggles me out of here, but only for a drive. I possibly have more clothes and jewellery than any woman alive, but who ever sees them?...They are to be for Alfit's eyes only."

Dominic, involuntarily touched by the bitterness on her voice, took her hand and said sympathetically, "Poor Lydia! You haven't struck as good a bargain as you envisioned, have you?"

At this slight gesture of encouragement, she veritably sparkled with charm once more. "Dom, I *must* see you again! Is there a place where I can contact you?"

He hesitated. He would prefer not to have to see her again, ever, and he had already wasted too much time. He could have been helping Philip with the windows.

"Well you see, it's like this..." he responded evasively. "I am not always easy to reach...and...I do not have a fixed address at the moment. I come and go as the mood hits me!"

"But can't you at least come just one more time, before you leave Cairo? Surely you won't go away without coming to say goodbye!" She had never been a woman easily put off. Her mouth began to tremble pathetically, and, in a tiny voice, she said, "Dom, you don't know how badly I need a friend!...Please say you'll come just once more, for the sake of what there once was between us!"

How, he could not help wondering, did she think this might be achieved, even if he wanted to?—Which he did not!

Now decidedly uncomfortable, he stood up and looked down at her. "Lydia," he said emphatically, "I have to be brutally honest, I'm afraid. I came here tonight for a reason that now seems ridiculous to me. I had hoped to return briefly to an old, almost forgotten dream world. Now I see that that is impossible to recapture—and, please understand me, it will *always* be impossible! That dream is dead! And now I wonder if it ever was real. It would serve no purpose for either of us to pretend that a flame could possibly be coaxed from cold ashes. I don't believe there ever was a flame, and there *is* no fire to be rekindled.—Believe me, there never was! Now I really must go!"

At that she jumped up and, facing him, she grasped his lapels frantically. "How can you be so cruel? Even if the fire has gone out, can you refuse me help when I need it so desperately? I am, after all, a stranger in this land, and there is no one but you!"

"Say goodbye to me now," he said firmly. "And let me go, Lydia!" He was all too familiar with the histrionics of the past. "You managed very well until I happened to show up again. As you coped before, so you will again." He freed himself from the grasping hands and moved towards the gap in the hedge. "My transport is waiting, and I really need to hurry now. Do you want me see you to your door before I go...?"

"Dom! Dom! Why can't you believe me? There are terrible things going on here...things I don't understand, and I am so afraid! I do need help, truly I do, and I beg of you to hear me out before Farao or Alfit return."

All the while she was speaking, she had been hanging onto his arm, and she half-ran to keep up with his longer stride.

At the opening in the hedge, because she would not let go, he was forced to stand aside in order to let her pass, for the gap was too narrow for two of them to squeeze through together. She took advantage of this by running ahead to take up a position in front of him on the path, impeding his progress.

"I ask for nothing but that you should hear me out, Dom. Just let me tell you what I know, and then you can judge for yourself."

He gave a sigh of resignation. "Very well, then. Tell—but make it snappy. I honestly must hurry now!"

"Oh, I shall," she promised, talking so fast that she was quite short of breath. "Thank you! What troubles me is that many times, when people come here, Farao calls me, to get me out of the way, just as he did tonight. Refreshments are then sent to them—wherever they happen to be waiting—and, just in case I might decide to return too soon, I am always forbidden to partake of any liquid whatsoever. As a result, I have seriously begun to wonder if the drinks could be spiked. Naturally, since you now appear to be okay, I am feeling somewhat ashamed of my suspicions but..."

"Is that not perhaps because of something to do with Alfit's religion?" Dominic suggested, being careful to hide the sudden interest she had evoked.

"I don't know. In the beginning I did accept the fact that Moslems do not drink alcohol, and therefore their spouses should not do so either. And, as I have said, I feel a bit ashamed of my suspicions because your being unaffected makes them seem so ridiculous—but there is something else that bothers me. Every single one of the people who do indulge, invariably end up obliged to spend the night in our house. And..."—she lowered her voice—"when they leave next day, they do not do so without Farao and five or six of the servants to accompany them!"

"Hmm," he said thoughtfully, "I wonder where they go from here. Do you have any idea? And do you ever see them again?"

"No." She shook her head. "I have never again seen any of them, but I did unsuccessfully attempt once or twice to find out where they had gone. When I could not, I began to wonder if...No! That was too silly of me!...I am convinced now that I was mistaken."

"How so?"

Lydia looked down at her feet. "I am almost embarrassed… ashamed to tell you, Dom. It was hateful of me to have had so little confidence in my own husband! In the beginning it was easy to let my imagination run away with me…"

"Cut the excuses! I do not have time for them!" he interrupted her impatiently. "I have known you too long. Get to the point, Lydia!—Out with it! Of what did you suspect him?"

"Well…I…" Even Lydia, who loved to be dramatic, found herself stammering as she uttered the words.—"Have you ever heard of Hamid Pasha?"

Dominic stiffened. "Sort of," he responded, struck by the crass irony of the situation. "Why?"

"Well" she began again, "I know it makes me sound stupid to admit this, but I have at times feared that Alfit might perhaps be Hamid Pasha!"

"*No!*" Dominic opened his eyes wide. "Lydia! Your own husband! To be so lacking in trust! Imagine that!…*Hamid Pasha*, of all people!…However did you come to that conclusion?"

"Alfit often attends functions where the elite gather. As the representative of this province he is invited as matter of course.…And then, in addition, he happens to be very popular. Unfortunately, it's usually at such receptions that the pasha makes his appearance. Only last night the bandit raided the residence of a high-ranking British official, Sir Humphrey Talbot. Can you wonder that I get these way-out ideas?"

"*If I had only known!*" Dominic was thinking. "If had stayed in the ballroom long enough, I might have broken the rule, and made a beeline for the worthy member of the *Barlaman,* myself!" Aloud he said, "And now you no longer suspect him? What has brought about this change of heart?"

"Last night I took the opportunity to get out for a bit while Alfit was absent, and on my return, before I was able to get back into the house, I was personally robbed by some of the pasha's ruffians. When my husband came home, I learned that he had suffered a similar experience!"

"Ah!" The exclamation escaped him with such overt gratification that, seeing Lydia glance at him quizzically, he immediately assumed an attitude suggestive of polite boredom. "So he also fell victim, did he? I can understand now how guilty you must feel, Lydia, but it must be a great relief to find out that your suspicions were unfounded, after all..." He nonchalantly began to button his jacket. "But now I really *must* go!"

Even as he moved to pass her, a possibility that had sprung to mind some minutes before, now became more credible, and he knew that he could be in imminent danger. In all probability that hideous person had gone to fetch Mohammed Alfit to examine the latest bird caught in their trap, and, having foiled them once already, he dared not be around for the second attempt

It transpired, however, that Lydia was still not done. "You have not given me a chance to tell you why I am so frightened, Dom. Hamid Pasha's men followed me here last night. They could very easily attack this house....I am absolutely terrified, but I dare not tell Alfit, because then he would find out that I went out last night....Now do you see? I only told you about the weird things that go on here, so that you would understand how cross Alfit would be because I unwittingly led them here. I suppose they came because one of them happened to spot my jewels through the windows of the car. I am so worried that I never slept a wink last night!"

"Do not worry any more, Lydia," he consoled her. "I feel

sure that the pasha will be quite content with whatever he has already taken from you. Why should he suspect that there would be any more valuables left in your home? Very likely thinks that he has already deprived you of every jewel you ever possessed!"

"But this place is an absolute treasure-trove of antiques and other priceless articles, Dom. It would actually be worth his while to come..."

"You don't say!" He bit his bottom lip thoughtfully. "Who would ever have suspected that!" Impulsively he took a scrap of paper from his jacket pocket, and scribbled on it the address of Rameses' aunt in Cairo. "Look, little girl, I think you are making more of this than you need. Your conscience is pricking you, and now you are allowing your imagination to work overtime....If you really need me before I leave, you may send me a message to this address. I visit a patient there, whose case I find extremely interesting, and I like to learn as much as I can....But how would you be able to let me know without Alfit's knowledge?

"As I said, the chauffeur..." she began.

"I see. That goes without saying," was the dry rejoinder. "I understand perfectly!"

Before she could say another word, he took her firmly by the hand. He determinedly drew her along with him as far as the hedge, and then he began to run.

Raschid was so morose as they set off on the journey back to the stockade, that Dominic burst out laughing. "What has bitten you, oh joyful spirit of the East?" he teased him.

"In the Koran we also read about Adam and Eve, *Effendi*!... *Pff*!" He spat contemptuously. "Even the proud Hamid Pasha can be tempted and ensnared in a trap by a serpent!"

Dominic roared with laughter. He found Raschid's jealous disapproval, priceless, and a wonderful antidote for tension, and he was about to retaliate when the laughter died on his lips. Before his mind's eye, like an elusive, perfect cameo, rose the memory of a lovely face with rosy lips and eyes like violets, under an aureole of shining black curls. He took a deep breath, as though inhaling the soft fragrance of a dainty girl in the half-light on a balcony, and he recalled a tiny hand clasping a treasure more priceless than all Lydia's jewels put together...

"That's funny!" He murmured to himself. "Philip was right!...Lydia really is an insipid, faded blonde!"

(iii)

Set free from the resentment he had subconsciously harboured since that fateful night in Cairo, *El-Hakim's* heart felt lighter than it had for more than five years. Relieved of all residual anger towards Lydia, who now seemed only pathetic to him, he was already planning his next project. The children in the camp were growing up too rapidly to be left only to parental instruction of the Koran, and nothing else, and, because he had faith that they would someday be returned safely to the outside world, it was high time they were taught the three R's. They should by now have been learning at least the rudiments of history and the geography of the outside world, and he resolved to send the twins and some others of their choice, to the city the very next day, in order to purchase a globe of the world, slates, and whatever else they could bring back with them at short notice. He dreamt of constructing a proper schoolhouse some day, but in the meantime, as soon as he was back home, he would give Ezra the go-ahead to start teaching them—in the open air if necessary. He could begin while he, Dominic, was away attending the crucial meeting which he had called in the desert.

There were other things he could not wait to tell his mentor, and much he also needed to share with Philip. How he longed to confess to them both that he finally understood how the anger bottled up inside of him had found an outlet in Hamid Pasha. He felt as though to be, as it were, three persons in one, had given him licence for actions he would never have sanctioned in anyone else, and had also motivated some of his most outrageous behaviour.

He felt positively euphoric as the air cooled, and the fresh mountain breeze was in his nostrils once more, but, at the entrance to the tunnel, a shock awaited him.

Rameses, the swordsman, and Ali, the marksman, awaited him with sombre faces.

"Greetings, Hamid Pasha," one of them greeted him. And, "A hundred-thousand *salaams*," said the other. Both looked so distressed that Dominic jumped down from his horse to inquire of them anxiously: "What is it, friends? Has there been trouble in my absence?"

The one glanced at the other, neither anxious to speak first. Then, Ali, the older of the two, said sorrowfully, "It is the young man...the Philip-brother! We found him lying on the floor where he had been working. We picked him up and carried him to his divan. He is sick with the fever, *Effendi*, and, we surmise, to a serious degree!"

CHAPTER THREE

The princess Thérèse had accompanied Baron and Baroness von Mölendorff as far as Alexandria where, without any regret whatsoever, she had taken leave of Otto, who still looked a bit jaded as a result of the stress he had suffered the previous night. She had waved her handkerchief at him dutifully—entirely for Gerda's sake—until the steamship disappeared over the horizon, and had then taken a *demitasse* of strong, sweet Turkish coffee with the senior Von Mölendorffs in one of the cafés, before returning with them to Cairo, shortly before the evening meal. Now back in her bedroom at the Talbots', she listened listlessly to Ruth's ceaseless, schoolgirlish babble.

The young girl was in her glory; ecstatic that Hamid Pasha should have come so close to her. She had felt like swooning, she avowed, but at the same time she repeatedly bemoaned the fact that she had not been able to get a better look at his face. Unlike Otto, she declared the events of the previous night to have been positively the most exciting of her 'entire existence'!

Finally Thérèse decided that she had had enough. Her eyes hurt from having the sun in her face all the way back to Cairo, and she could neither afford to listen to any more chatter, nor waste time staring through the window. There was far too much to be done.

"Ruth," she requested gently, "won't you be a dear and ask the maid to come and help me with my packing? There are at least ten other people who will require her services tomorrow, and I want to take advantage of the opportunity while I still may....In the meantime I think I shall go and enjoy my bath."

"Let her draw the bath for you, Thérèse," Ruth protested. "Why should you do it yourself?"

The princess laughed. "My dear child, in a wartime hospital there is often an insufficiency of water, let alone servants! I have grown accustomed to taking care of myself. Besides"— she hesitated in the doorway to the bathroom—"I have to get used to doing without a great deal more than a personal maid! One of these days I shall be a working girl, hopefully earning a living, like thousands of others...!"

Ruth sighed. It made her *so* unhappy to hear her dear Thérèse speak like that. Deep in thought, she temporarily forgot about the enthralling robber-captain, and went to find the chambermaid.

Relieved to be alone at last, Thérèse turned both taps on fully, and let them run until the enormous marble bath was close to overflowing. Then she lay back, twiddling her toes and happily soaking in the warm, perfumed water; content just to dream. It was wonderful to be able to relax like this at last, and she valued the opportunity to be left to herself for long enough to sort out at least some of the many confused—and confusing—thoughts that had plagued her all day.

Tomorrow her visit with the Talbots would come to an end, and she would then go to a hotel until she received a further communication from South Africa, concerning her most recent job-application. She was confident that she would not be lonely while she waited, because, until Gerda and Ferdinand went home, they would visit her as often as they were able, and then she could always depend on Ruth and her parents. Sir

Humphrey and his kind-hearted spouse were most concerned about her, and it was nice that they had made it so clear that she was not leaving their home without protest on their part. But it was time to stand on her own feet. Time she was wholly independent.

Everyone had been so loving and so kind—even Otto!... Why did his adoration bore her so? She had to pull herself up sharply to refrain from giggling at the recollection of his bulging eyes, and cheeks ashen with fright, when he had come rushing out onto the balcony.

But now she was also reminded of the barbarian, Hamid Pasha, and the blood rose to her face so that she was sure her very ears burned with futile anger. Her jaw tightened as she thought, for the hundredth time, of all the crushing things she could have said to him....What had she done, instead? Gaped at him like a naïve, inexperienced adolescent. She permitted herself several almost censorable expressions of exasperation as she jumped out of the tub, grabbed a towel, and vigorously dried herself as though she were bent on rubbing her skin right off.—As though, in doing this, she was venting her rage at him.

Back in her bedroom she found that Lucille had already completed her packing for her. Her luggage had been placed tidily in one corner of the room, and only the clothes she would need next morning still hung in the cupboard. Her nightie had been placed invitingly on her pillow.

She stretched herself out on the bed and yawned sleepily. The clock on the night table told her that it was only half-past nine, but she did not feel like going downstairs in search of company. For a moment she hesitated, eyeing the fresh bed linen, and then pressed the bell again for the maid. "Please tell Sir Humphrey and Lady Talbot that I am very tired after the long trip, Lucille, and I am going to bed early."

MARIE WARDER

Within a few minutes she was ready. She picked up a few of the glossy magazines she had bought at the steamship terminal that morning, placed them within easy reach on the table next to her bed, and, with a glorious sense of anticipation, crept in between the cool, white sheets. The pleated satin shade on the bedside lamp threw a rosy glow over everything in the luxurious bedroom, highlighting the gilt embellishments on the gracious Louis XVl suite, and she looked around her with no small measure of sadness, before opening a magazine to begin reading.

Before very long, however, she found that the sheets were not as cool as she had hoped. The room was becoming uncomfortably close. As there was a wind blowing, Lucille had very likely closed the window, as well as the French doors that led to a balcony similar to the one on which she had sought refuge the night before; but deciding that she preferred the wind to the heat, Thérèse climbed out of bed and opened the casement nearest her.

Back in her bed, she resumed reading where she had left off, and was quickly absorbed in the tragic love story of a popular opera singer from Milan. Outside in the passage footsteps sounded, and she heard Gerda's voice as she bade her hostess a good night. There was silence once more.

What first caught her attention, Thérèse does not know, to this day. She was only aware of an overpowering urge that drove her to look towards her window, to where the heavy drapes had been pushed aside. A stab of horror made her gasp as she looked up into the most awful face she had ever seen. Through the open window the man was staring fixedly at her. The purple scar running down one side of his swarthy face had screwed his cheek up into a ghastly grimace, exposing his yellowed teeth. She noticed the dirty, broken fingernails where

120

his thick, stubby fingers clung to the windowsill, and she who had seen many gruesome sights during the war, felt as though her heart would stop from sheer terror. There was something so menacing in the man's appearance that she was temporarily robbed of speech. For a period of time that seemed endless to her, she stared at him in silence, overcome with revulsion, and then suddenly she closed her eyes, and screamed...and screamed...and screamed...

By the time she risked another look, he was gone, as silently as he had come...and when Ferdinand and Gerda came running from the room next-door, exclaiming how fortunate it was that she had not locked her door, she could almost have convinced herself that she had indeed, as they insisted, dozed off for a moment and had a nightmare. All she could think of then was that, if he was one of Hamid Pasha's henchmen sent to kidnap her, she could only be grateful that he had not been the one who had found her alone on the north balcony, the night before.

After Ferdinand had closed the windows and Gerda had tucked her back in bed as if she were a child, she turned off the light, and lay thinking about the pasha for a while before falling asleep. Her would-be intruder had not only looked repulsive, he had smelled so bad that, even from six feet away she had almost been nauseated by the odour of stale sweat and tobacco; whereas—for a man whom she had unfailingly thought of as 'unwashed'—Hamid Pasha had smelled surprisingly pleasant. And she knew, because, at one stage, her nose had been pressed up against his chest. His hands, too, had not been rough, despite the firm grip, and she thought again of the strange manner in which he had grasped her wrist, almost instinctively it had seemed....Not as though restraining a captive, but as one would automatically do when reaching for a pulse.

CHAPTER FOUR

All night long Dominic kept vigil at Philip's bedside. When the first rays of the sun bathed the valley in gold, Raschid found him still there. In the tent that Philip called home, his brother sat like a graven image. In a face, grey with fatigue, the blue eyes were bloodshot, and Raschid saw deep lines about the mouth of his beloved leader.

"*Effendi*," the Indian whispered sympathetically, "I have brought you coffee to ward off the fatigue." He placed the cup on the stool next to Dominic and confessed, "I have added a drop of that cognac we took from Lord Epsom's villa for you to administer to the sick Englishman."

"Thank you, my friend," *El-Hakim* said dispiritedly. "I shall drink it later…"

"No, *Effendi*," Raschid chided, shaking his head. "You will drink it *now*!" With that he lifted the cup and held it so close to Dominic's mouth that he was forced to swallow the strong, syrupy liquid. The cognac burned his throat as it went down, and presently it began to spread a warm glow though his veins.

With a glimmer of his old smile, Dominic looked at Raschid. "There was very little coffee in that coffee, you rascal!"

The Indian grinned. "That is indeed true, *Effendi*, but both Ezra and I—who, as you know, are not familiar with the effects of this additive—agreed that coffee was perhaps a little too weak for our purpose." He took the empty cup from Dominic and walked respectfully backwards. He would never turn his back in the presence of the leader. "Do you have any instructions for me before I go?"

With his eyes once more fixed on Philip's flushed face, Dominic thought for a moment. "I would rather not leave my brother alone now. Please do the rounds, if you will, and let me know how our other people are doing. If there is one who needs me urgently, please call me! Ezra will help you, but keep him away from here, and from wherever we have patients with the fever. He is extremely susceptible to infection..."

"I go, *Effendi*," the other man promised, and, quite unnecessarily, went out from the tent on tiptoe.

"Remember to wear clean coveralls, Raschid!—Leave the ones you are wearing, here, and cleanse yourself thoroughly, before you go near anyone who is not sick with the fever," Dominic called over his shoulder. "We don't want this to spread any further!"

Raschid would obey, he knew, but it had taken a great deal to convince anyone else to wear a mask or gown, and, for the first time—perhaps because he was exhausted—Dominic despaired of ever instilling in every one of his charges, much more than the basic rules of hygiene that he had always taken as read.

Philip sighed and muttered something unintelligible, and Dominic immediately turned his attention back to him, bending solicitously over him. So far he had not lost one patient to this latest scourge, but he was groping in the dark. How desperately he longed for a facility equipped to test blood and establish precisely what he was up against. As all seven of the 'recently rescued', with the exception of the Englishman, had been similarly afflicted, there was no doubt in his mind that six of the men in his make-shift isolation area had come from the same place, and had brought the bacterium into the stockade with them.

He put his hand against his brother's burning cheek, and stroked his hair. As he did so, he felt a tug at his heart, and a lump in his throat. What had happened to that little boy for whom he had cared so devotedly? It was painful to dwell on how drastically, during the past five years, their rôles had been reversed. Philip had become his brothers' keeper—plural. In the true sense of the word. With the passage of time, not only of his brother, but also of everyone other person in this camp.

He had only to think of Raschid's reaction to the news that Philip had been taken ill. "That cannot be, *Effendi!*" he had wailed, in great distress. "I will implore Allah to have mercy! He seldom left my side while I was the sick one, except to help others!" And Dominic was overwhelmed by the recollection of what Philip had said, only a day before: "After being cooped up with sick people all week, I rather fancy having the wind in my face!"...Now it was Raschid who had expressed, in so many words, his awareness of the hidden depths in a young man with whom he had long been at odds; a young man whom he had gradually grown to value and appreciate...as much as every other man, woman and child in the stockade had learned to do.

Deeply moved by this reflection, Dominic again measured Philip's heart rate, took his temperature, and sponged his hands and face. No change. There was nothing he could do until sufficient time had elapsed before the next injection, and he sat down disconsolately once more.

It was an ugly thing, this fever. One of the few with which he was unfamiliar. How some of the wretches who were deprived of medical care, ever survived it, he would never understand, because, even with what he had at his disposal, it could be touch and go. He found it strange how the Bedouin, without any medical knowledge whatsoever, could diagnose symptoms of various diseases so quickly. They were seldom wrong about the signs of any fever once they had come into contact with it, but this time he was not so sure. They had this peculiar habit of naming a disease according to the effect the malady had upon the hue of the afflicted one's complexion—and yet, when he came to think of it, it was not really that strange. There was the 'Yellow Eye' which made the eyelids swell and fester, as in Raschid's case, until the eyes did indeed take on a jaundiced colour; there was the 'Red Fever', and there was the appalling 'Black Shadow'.—The very thought of this last plague, made him cringe.

Were they possibly referring to the 'Back Death'? Surely not! How ironic that he, the so-called specialist, had failed to hear alarm bells go off when Philip had talked about a "perpetual headache!" He had also added that his joints were stiff, and it usually took from one to seven days for patients to become symptomatic. Would Philip's handsome, beloved young face come to display that ominous 'black shadow'?— God forbid! It could not be *Bubonic...*!

There was plenty of evidence that the same plague which had killed millions in Europe during the fourteenth century, had originated in ancient Egypt, but it was carried by lice and fleas; and, besides, there was no swelling of any of Philip's lymph nodes....Pneumonic plague? *That* could be passed on from person-to-person—but no! No one was coughing or showing any other sign of it. Septicemic? From blood infection or neglect of any of the former?...Also not spread person to person. In all these, the common denominator was the *Yersinia* bacterium, but unfortunately he had no way of establishing its presence.

He made a mental note. Priority number one...*microscope*! He wouldn't mind putting some item of Lydia's jewellery towards that...! If he'd had one now, he'd at least have been able to check a gram stain.—If the light from the generator was bright enough for that....

Even though he had ruled out the 'Black Death', the mere possibility had triggered self-reproach on many counts. It was his fault that Philip lay sick this day, in this place. He, Dominic, should have made a better job of being *his* brother's keeper. From the time Philip was ten, and he, fifteen, he had tried to be father and mother, as well as older brother to the boy. Had he really made a good job of that? He doubted it. A remote 'outlaw-colony' was hardly the best place for a man of Philip's age to be.—Philip, who, for as long as he could remember, had far too frequently found himself obliged to commence a sentence with, "But Dom, you *can't*!" That had been his catchphrase. He loved to boast that it was his responsibility to restrain his brilliant brother's wild impulses. And yet, Dominic reproached himself, it was through him that Philip, himself, had ironically been enticed to become a part of the wildest and most reckless venture of all!

"As soon as Philip is well again—and I pray to God that he will be"—Dominic vowed—"he is going home!"

(ii)

By two o'clock that afternoon there was a slight improvement, but still Dominic refused to sleep. Philip remained in a delirium. During the past fourteen hours he, Dominic, had only twice left his brother for any length of time, first going to scrub up and put on the gown he wore over his clothes, for the protection of other patients whom he personally needed to see. Each time, after he had done this, he had returned promptly to take up his position at Philip's bedside once more.

In vain, Raschid and others—who, having recovered, were now known to be immune—came to the tent, imploring him to rest, and promising to call him, in an emergency. The Indian kept coming, bringing fruit and whatever else he could think of, in a vain attempt to make the doctor take refreshment, but Dominic had reached the stage where he refused even coffee. Supposing that perhaps the brew he had produced that morning, had not been satisfactory, Raschid resorted to summoning Rameses' wife, who, she assured him, had once been stricken by the 'Black Shadow', herself, and who could serve coffee to the leader in a *finjan*—the small cup he preferred—poured straight from the *brikini,* in the Bedouin manner, just as he liked it.

Greatly honoured, and delighted to show off the few treasures she had managed to carry with her on the camel, when El-Bus Mohandess had brought her to join her husband, Farida proceeded to go through the whole sequence, the way she, as a good housewife, would have served Dominic in her own home. The age-old ritual required her to taste the first cup, the *El-Heif,* herself, in order to demonstrate that it was safe to drink. Then she poured the second cup, or *El-Keif,* which was supposed to be tasted by *El-Hakim,* before he actually drank the *El-Deif,* or guest's cup, but Dominic, who was never known to be anything other than gracious, wearily shook his head and waved her away. And that was when Raschid finally lost patience.

"*Effendi,*" he said firmly, "they are saying outside that, in his concern for his brother, Hamid Pasha is forgetting his many other children. The father is forsaking those other children!"

Dominic looked up questioningly. "What on earth do you mean, Raschid?"

The man hid the sympathy welling up in him. "Hamid Pasha has a great responsibility on his shoulders. He made a promise to El-Bus Mohandess. His people have to rely on his strength—yet he values them so little that he pays no heed to their pleas to rest and conserve his strength!"

"But Raschid, surely they must understand how things are? Am I not permitted to do all that is in my power, for my brother?" Dominic asked, taken aback.

"You have already done so, *Effendi*," Raschid replied more gently. "And you can do that again, later. But what does it profit the Philip-brother to have you sitting here, waiting? You, *Sahhena*, have sufficient experience of this thing to know that it is time alone that will tell....Go now and rest, we implore you. Ali and I will keep watch. We shall not leave him for one moment!"

"You sly old fox!" Dominic exclaimed. Nevertheless, he rose from the chair and stretched his stiff body. "Very well. I shall go and lie down, but I make no promises that I shall sleep." He went as far as the door. "There must be two of you, at all times, in case one of you has to come and call me—but, for the protection of Meriam and the child, I do not want Ali!...Summon Rameses, instead..."

Apparently Raschid was not done. He faced Dominic determinedly. "*Effendi*, what about the gathering?...Within three days we have to depart, in order to be there in time, and we cannot cancel it at such short notice. Many will have travelled from far already!"

"Oh!" Distractedly running his fingers through his hair, Dominic frowned. "The meeting! I had completely forgotten about it!"

"You have *forgotten, Effendi?*" Raschid pretended to be almost speechless. "Is it not you who called it? This gathering that can be so vital to all of us?—Including *El-Hakim* and his brother!"

Dominic stiffened. A defiant expression crept across his face and his blue eyes darkened. Why should he feel guilty?... Raschid was becoming far too presumptuous. "Is Philip's life then of so little importance to you? Send messengers to say that I apologize, but cannot possibly attend this meeting." However he had no sooner uttered the words than he knew he had spoken rashly.

It transpired that Raschid knew his leader better than that leader suspected. The Indian knew, too, that it was not the normal *El-Hakim* who spoke, but he was far too astute to betray this. Assuming an attitude rather like that of the humble *mahout* of his youth, and lowering his head, he adopted an expression of both innocent remorse and feigned anxiety. "May Allah punish your unworthy servant if ever again he should dare to presuppose his leader's instructions..."

"What have you done, man? Explain yourself!" was Dominic's impatient reaction.

"I only thought to spare you further concern, *Effendi*," Raschid explained apologetically. "It was unforgivable of me. I have already communicated to the messengers that they should convey Hamid Pasha's gratitude to all who have indicated that they are willing to attend. It is said that the opportunity to meet with him there is keenly anticipated....Alas! May Allah be merciful to the low dog who bears the name of Raschid!" He peered sideways at Dominic to see what effect this information was having on him. "The messengers, none of whom has been near any infected person, now wait only upon the word to depart!"

But the leader of this 'low dog' was not stupid. He was perfectly aware of the sly look, and a smile of grudging admiration lit up his face. Five years had taught him a great deal. He had not known Raschid that long, for nothing! Shaking his head, he moved towards the Indian and patted him on the shoulder. "You win...as usual! Not long ago I called you a fox....That term was inadequate!"

He studied the other man intently for moment, and then his tone changed yet again. "Tell me, my friend, how can I possibly go? I am responsible for my brother. Every time I remember how concerned he was yesterday about others, I feel twice as guilty as before. He wanted to prepare a place for the sick ones while I..."

"If it were only to establish that there are items of value in the home of Mohammed Alfit, *Effendi*, your excursion would still have been worthwhile," Raschid reminded him. But the doctor continued to look so downcast that he deemed it important to consider the problem in greater depth, before opening his mouth again. His introspection was rewarded. All of a sudden a thought occurred to him and he asked: "In those big hospitals where you worked, *Sahbena,* did the physicians always remain thus, throughout the night, without rest, to watch over their patients....No, I did not think so!—What was the alternative, then?"

"We had nurses, of course!" Dominic's irritation was evident, because he could not see where this line of reasoning was taking them.

"Aha!" cried Raschid. "Then that is what is required here!—How soon can Philip-brother, safely be left in the care of a nurse?"

Dominic showed little enthusiasm.

"His fever would have to break, and although I have seen

no evidence in anyone so far, there would have to be convincing evidence that this sickness is not as deadly as the 'Black Shadow'. In any case, that is a ridiculous question, Raschid, and I shall not dignify it with a response, other than to ask how, in your opinion, we would ever get hold of a nurse?"

"How, honourable Hamid Pasha?" Raschid echoed patiently. "When we need money, we steal it!—When we need a nurse, we have to steal a nurse. Of course!" He made a sweeping gesture with his hand...."Just like that!...No other alternative is open to us"

Dominic had to smile. It suddenly seemed like yesterday that Raschid had said, in response to the question regarding the acquisition of a camel: "How else? We shall have to steal it, of course!" But he also remembered that El-Bus Mohandess had returned the camel to its rightful owner, because it was part of their strange code of honour to take nothing that was not absolutely necessary, to return whatever it happened to be, as soon as it was no longer required, and never to take anything from those who were not in a position to replace it.

"And, when we no longer need her, Raschid," he asked dryly, "do we give her back?"

(iii)

Some hours later, Philip having begun to show signs of improvement, Mamoun and Haroun were summoned, and came speedily to ascertain what the leader required of them. On their short, sturdy bowlegs, they came waddling in like identical ducks. They *salaamed* with great solemnity before Dominic, and waited patiently for him to speak.

"The young brother is still seriously ill," he told them in Arabic, "but, mercifully, I am sure now that he is not afflicted with the 'Black Shadow'. The treatment is having the right effect, but he cannot be left without someone who is capable of giving him his injections and following the procedure I have instituted—which, by the Grace of God, already seems to have worked for Raschid and several of the others. On the other hand, I do not want to neglect my other responsibilities, or risk affronting the sheiks and the *cadis* who have agreed to meet with me in the desert, by remaining here with my brother.

"I have discussed the situation with Raschid, and it is his suggestion that we find a nurse who can watch over Philip-brother, until I return. It is your duty to find her and bring her here!"

Not intimidated in the slightest, the two nodded their turbaned heads.

"You will need to make inquiries in several places, because it will not profit us if the lady is above carrying out my instructions. No one can describe the facilities here as being of the best, so, although she must have experience, she must be accustomed to working under less than perfect conditions. Do you understand?"

Again the nod, slow and deliberate. He found it incredible that two people could look so much alike, and so automatically move in unison. Dominic felt the corners of his mouth twitch, but managed to restrain himself.

"Yes. It won't help to come back here with someone who is nervous, helpless, or too critical of the conditions under which she will be required to work," Raschid put in. "And make sure you bring us someone who won't immediately be missed.—We don't want to upset the entire police force!" He added mockingly: "There are enough of them with headaches already!"

Even Dominic found these demands more than a trifle

challenging, but the twins did not bat an eyelid. Mamoun, the spokesperson for the two, took a step forward. "With permission of the leader, we will take Little Brother with us. He will possibly be of help to us."

'Little Brother', so named because he was about five years younger than the twins, was the last person on earth deserving of such a moniker, considering that he was a good five inches taller than Dominic. It was doubtful whether anyone in the camp knew his real name, but it explained why Philip—whom Dominic often addressed as *boetie,* or 'little brother'—was distinguished by the name, 'Philip-brother'...the brother of *El-Hakim.*

The dwarfs and the gangling 'Little Brother' were cause for much good-natured amusement among the Bedouin in the camp, for no one had ever been able to ascertain whether or not they were indeed brothers. From a physician's point of view, Dominic doubted it, but, like everyone else, he had the greatest respect for the capabilities of the twins. And if they thought that it would be helpful to have Little Brother with them, that was sufficient for him. He gave his permission, and the two waddled off happily to advise Little Brother of what was required of him.

Dominic went back to his seat at Philip's bedside, and Raschid went off to brew the inevitable coffee.

(iv)

Just before sundown the next afternoon, Mamoun came galloping into the stockade. For one with his build, he sprang from his horse, in front of Philip's tent, with amazing agility, and surrendered the sweating mare into the care of a fellow Turk, who was waiting there. The doctor's brother, he was informed, had now been moved to the hospital building. *El-Hakim* had been summoned and would be out right away. Moments later, the dwarf was able to present himself to the leader.

Both Dominic, and Raschid—who came running behind him, to see what all the excitement was about—were surprised to see Mamoun back so soon, but upon hearing his report, surprise very quickly gave way to admiration. They were left in awe.

"We have found her, *Effendi*," the dwarf announced, breathlessly. Despite his rather peculiar dialect, he spoke in terms which were easy to understand; telling them, in effect: "The others are bringing her. We have learnt that she spent some part of the war with the Soravian Red Cross in the Philippines, where she gained considerable experience in a makeshift hospital, situated in a convent. She is familiar with various maladies—perhaps even the one which has come upon us." He shook his head sadly. "Alas, unfortunate Philip-brother! May Allah look kindly upon him!"

CHAPTER FIVE

The princess Thérèse was thus not destined to remain in her hotel room for very long. No matter how philosophical she had tried to be when contemplating her move from the Talbot mansion, she had not found the reality of being entirely on her own, as pleasant as she had thought it would be. As it happened, however, she was not given an opportunity to begin unpacking, before, for the second time in less than forty-eight hours, she was again subjected to a very strange experience.

Within an hour after her arrival at the hotel, there was a barely audible tap at her door, and she secretly hoped that it was not Valentine Morgan finding some excuse for coming back. By the manner in which he had vied for the honour of accompanying her from the Talbots, and then, upon his departure, holding her hand so long that she thought he would never let go, he had betrayed an unwanted affection which made her uncomfortable. Nevertheless, she went to the door with an expression of pleasant anticipation. Perhaps a message from Gerda, or a welcoming bouquet from someone....Instead, the most extraordinary thing happened....Before she could open her mouth, the people waiting in the passage, pushed unceremoniously past her, and one of them locked the door behind him.

Before her astonished eyes was the most odd sight. The two comical little brown-skinned men who stood before her, were identical, and neither could have been more than four feet tall. In contrast, the skinny apparition with the long, sad face, behind them, appeared as tall as Jack's beanstalk. At least seven foot, she thought.

At first she was dumbfounded, to the extent that she did not speak. She says, however, that, for some reason, she did not feel the least bit afraid. Actually, her only thought was that she had seldom before encountered such colossal audacity.

That was her first thought, but after the twins had bowed so courteously before her, and the tall man had almost dusted her shoes with his turban, she began to think that perhaps she had judged them unfairly. It was indeed an unmitigated impertinence for them to have thrust their way into her room, but in their demeanour they were respect and courtesy itself.

It was not for nothing that El-Bus Mohandess, long ago, and now *El-Hakim*, had chosen the twins to carry out the most difficult—and, as in this case—most sensitive and delicate assignments. Mamoun, with his underdeveloped body and clown face, was remarkably intelligent, and his insight was nothing short of amazing. Haroun, on the other hand, while not as quick thinking as his brother, was capable of grasping precisely what Mamoun expected of him, sometimes even before the command was given.

Mamoun sensed instinctively that the princess Thérèse was not the kind of woman to be easily intimidated; nor would she, like the silly, hysterical female he had had to follow two nights before, react to any direct attempt to scare her. The clear, sparkling eyes met his fearlessly, and there was something impressively courageous in the way in which she carried herself, head held high. Only a slight flaring of her nostrils and a quickening of her breath betrayed that she was not completely at ease. The dwarf decided to be frank with this princess, and he bowed again, politely.

"Excellency, if you will be so kind, please pardon the impertinence of your unworthy servants. It is only due to the need for caution, and the fear that we might be discovered here, which has occasioned such effrontery on our part. I beg your permission to explain."

Not quite sure whether or not this was really happening, she nodded wordlessly.

"I am Mamoun, the servant and watchdog of *Sahbena el-Hakim*, father of the desert. He sends us...I, Mamoun, he... Haroun, and the Little Brother with a request to you."

"And what is that?" Thérèse asked, still thoroughly bewildered. "How can I help him, and how does he know about me?"

"He does not!" Mamoun informed her honestly. "It is we who have found you! This year the curse of a fever, not unlike the 'Black Shadow', rests heavily upon the unfortunate children of *El-Hakim*. He toils day and night to help us, but now that he has an urgent need to go away, the plague has stricken the brother of *El-Hakim*, himself."

"I am sorry to hear that," Thérèse replied uncertainly. "But how can I help you?"

Mamoun looked up and faced her squarely—with tension evident in every fibre of his small body—while the other two held their breath. "Highness, it is a long story. The leader has instructed us to find a nurse who might be familiar with similar situations, and the precautions to be taken for the protection of herself and others, while attending such a patient. Someone with the ability to watch over his brother, in his absence. . Without her we may not return....'Find one,' we are commanded, 'who will not too soon be missed, in case she has to be brought here against her will.' That is why we seek one who is not of this country.

"We visit the Bureau of Information, we go to the hotels and read their registers; and we rifle through files. We have friends who search the desks of tourist agencies. Finally we learn about you, Excellency. We are shown a newspaper in which it is stated that the princess Thérèse, who is the guest of Sir Humphrey Talbot, has cared for the sick under difficult conditions, and our hearts sing. We learn from Sir Humphrey's servants that the princess is now in a hotel room, alone, and then we know, with gratitude, that we have found her!"

All at once Thérèse was reminded of her repulsive visitor of the night before. Was this why he was spying on her? She shuddered. "And if I refuse to come?"

Mamoun did not hesitate. "Then, honourable lady, we are obliged to take you by force." He shook his head sympathetically. "The commands of *El-Hakim* are always to be obeyed. You have no choice!"

Thérèse bit her lip thoughtfully. "How do I know that I can trust you? Perhaps you intend to murder me along the way!—What is there to prevent me from immediately summoning the police?"

"I advise you rather to come, Madame," Mamoun said gently. "We three have instructions to protect you with our own lives. Why would we not bring you safely to our leader? I who bear the name, Mamoun, will swear on the head of the prophet, himself, that you may return as soon as the young *effendi* has recovered."

Meanwhile, Haroun and Little Brother had been searching for a pen and paper, which, having found, they handed to Mamoun.

"Kindly write a letter here to the manager and inform him that you have unexpectedly been called away, but that you will return shortly," Mamoun instructed her politely, "and bring with you whatever clothing you might require....It grows late....Haroun," he said to his brother. "It is now your responsibility to bring the princess to our leader. I go ahead to advise him of our success..."

"You will regret this!" Thérèse called out to him. "Who is this so-called leader who despises the law?"

In her imagination she could already see this 'father of the desert'—a filthy, doddering old man, with a host of filthy wives, and dozens of equally filthy offspring!

(ii)

Led by Little Brother, the journey, on horseback and in the dark, seemed endless to Thérèse for, despite the fact that there was no moon, Haroun and Little Brother insisted that she be blindfolded. This secretive behaviour made her wonder anew whether she would ever be returned alive. Why had she not rather married Otto...or at least remained with the Talbots? "Someone who will not immediately be missed," the man had said....*Now I am that someone! Who will ever come and look for me?...Why did I ever write that wretched letter?...I am just a miserable coward!*

All the way there, she damned the man, *El-Hakim*, in her heart. How dare he do things like this? How could he get away with it, and how would she survive amongst barbarians? Her greatest fear, however, was that this *El-Hakim* would turn out to be the revolting, terrifying man she had seen at her window.

When finally, stiff and close to tears, she was helped down from the saddle and had the blindfold removed, she found herself in front of a low, whitewashed building with light streaming from its windows, and an unmistakeable hospital smell in the air. This made her feel slightly better, because she felt at home in such an environment, and it was a considerable improvement over the slave market she had envisioned. She looked around her and noticed that a high wall surrounded the place. To her left, within the enclosure, was a large Bedouin tent, several smaller, animal-hide dwellings of the same type, and here and there a campfire flickered sociably.

At this stage, the other dwarf, Mamoun, suddenly made his appearance, accompanied by an Indian with a distinctly refined appearance. When both bowed low before her, welcoming her, her courage was fully restored. No reluctant captive was received in this manner.…She had almost expected to be dragged in by the hair!

"The leader awaits you within, Princess," the Indian informed her. "It is his request that you be brought to him without delay! But first, before we go through those doors at the end, we must find you a mask and a gown, which he says, you may need later…"

With her heart in her mouth and her throat so dry that she had to keep swallowing nervously, Thérèse followed him. What would this old man, this 'Father of the desert' look like, she wondered apprehensively. What if he proved to be some slobbering, lascivious old letch? Was he a cruel man…a Turk?…Or perhaps an Arab?

Finally the Indian held one of the heavy doors open for her, went ahead to a room leading from the corridor on the other side of it, and gestured to her to enter. "*Sahbena el-Hakim*," he said. "My friend, the doctor!"

She looked up hesitantly and stared in amazement. The man in the white coat, with a stethoscope around his neck… this *El-Hakim*…was a white man, powerfully built, with a mane of thick, sun bleached blond hair, and eyes as blue as the heavens—but like hard, blue steel!

He was sitting casually on the corner of his desk, swinging one leg rhythmically back and forth, as he flipped through a sheaf of papers. He studied her intently for a moment, one eyebrow raised contemplatively, as though he were assessing her worth. Then he must have decided that he could possibly be a little more polite, because he rose to his feet and set the papers down on the desk. "Good evening, Princess!" he said in a tone that came across as pure arrogance. This remark was followed by his asking, with such undisguised boredom in his voice that it was made abundantly clear that he did not care, one way or another, what her response would be: "Have you had a good journey?"

Therese's blood boiled. Where she came from, one was not subjected to such cavalier treatment....The ill-mannered barbarian! He had not even invited her to be seated!

"Allow me to remind you, Sir, that abduction is a punishable offence! A crime punishable by death?—Or perhaps you did not know that!"

El-Hakim grinned mockingly. "That is not what I consider to be a really friendly reply to the question I put to you, my dear princess, but I shall try to do better. I know that very well—in fact, I am quite well aware of the law—but here it is so often necessary to transgress it, that it becomes boring to try and calculate the extent of the punishment due to us!"

Raschid, who had left them alone, chose to return just then, with a tray on which he had arranged an assortment of fruit, as well as pita with falafel, a bowl of yoghurt to spoon over it, and two cups of coffee. "Her highness must be hungry, *Effendi*," he said apologetically. "Haroun and the Little Brother tell me that none of them has eaten since leaving the princess's hotel, and you have been without food all day."

El-Hakim took the tray from the Indian, set it down on the desk, and, in thanking him, favoured the man with a smile of such extraordinary charm, that it lit up his entire face. His appearance changed completely. In his tanned face, perfect white teeth sparkled, and laughter lines crinkled the corners of his eyes, making them seem to be an even deeper blue than before. Thérèse' suddenly realized that he was not as old as she had expected him to be.—Probably not more than thirty-three or four, at most. There was something quite charmingly youthful about him when his expression softened.

"Raschid is a better host than his leader," he observed wryly. "Years of isolation in the desert eventually tend to make a man so loutish that he gradually unlearns, and eventually loses all social graces." The smile was then focused on her. "Please pardon my disgraceful lack of courtesy, Princess Thérèse. I have just realized how tired you must be…"

Highly delighted to see his leader no longer looking quite so intimidating, Raschid rubbed his hands together and ventured a suggestion. "With your permission, *Effendi*, I shall show the lady to the bathroom before she eats….Highness, if you will please follow me!"

(iii)

While she ate, *El-Hakim* explained to Thérèse what was expected of her. She was tired, but now that she was seated and closer to him, facing him across the desk, she was able to see how tired he was, too, and found herself involuntarily pitying him. She also noticed that he, himself, ate nothing.

"Raschid is the guilty one," he confided, after the latter had removed the tray. "It is vital that I attend this…this medical conference, but I cannot possibly leave my brother alone in his present condition. There is a definite and encouraging improvement tonight, and I believe he can be safely left now in the care of someone else. However, that someone must be more knowledgeable than any of the people I have here. Normally my brother acts as my assistant, but now, while everyone who helps me in the hospital is more than willing, they are, in this instance, so ill equipped that I have to be constantly available to advise on even the least complication....Which is why Raschid suggested that I have a nurse brought here."

It was on the tip of Therese's tongue to ask what he would do if she refused to undertake the care of his brother. He had had her brought a considerable distance across the desert, but he could not force her to do anything!

As though he read her thoughts, the hint of a mocking smile on his face reminded her of someone she had seen before, and she drew her lovely brows together in a frown of concentration. Where had she seen that provocative grin before? From the moment she had entered his office, there had been something familiar in the appearance of this mysterious desert physician.

"In case you are wanting to ask me how I can force you to carry out my instructions, Princess, I shall reassure you at once, on that score. It is always our ultimate threat that we shall kill anyone who will not cooperate, but, in your case, the situation is different. I am a doctor and would thus never refuse to treat anyone—be he, or she, my greatest enemy. You are a nurse... and I shall never permit myself to believe that a good nurse does not uphold that same tradition. That sense of duty." His tone became less formal. "Are you a good nurse, Thérèse?"

What else could she do but gaze at him silently? He had such a peculiar effect on her that she found herself completely incoherent in his presence. "I despise him!" she tried to convince herself. "He is so smug and so cynical!"

Unexpectedly he rose and took her arm. "Come, Thérèse," he said kindly, "it's time you went to bed. Tomorrow I shall introduce you to my brother, but now I see shadows under those beautiful eyes!"

She allowed him to lead her to the door, but kept stealing surreptitious glances at him. *Where* had she seen him before? Perhaps during the war, it occurred to her. Some time, if ever she should encounter him in an indulgent mood, she would ask him. Now he walked ahead of her down the corridor, in the direction of the door where she had earlier dismounted from her horse, and, completely against her will, she found herself—as exhausted as she was—admiring from behind him, the breadth of his shoulders in his white coat, his easy, graceful stride, the shape of his head, and the thick, almost silver hair that came down to his collar.

He took her outside, to the big tent she had noticed earlier, and lifted the flap so that she might enter. "Since the house which belonged to my predecessor was converted to become the nucleus of the hospital, this has become my own abode", he explained, with quite boyish diffidence. "I hope you will be comfortable. There is only one spare room in the hospital and I shall sleep there tonight, to be close to my brother. Tomorrow you can move in there, or, if you prefer, Rameses will see to it that a tent of your own is made ready for you. Unfortunately I cannot make my brother, Philip's, tent available to you until it has been thoroughly disinfected, but that can also be sorted out later.

"Meriam, the wife of Ali, will see to you tonight. She is gentle and will take good care of you. I shall instruct her to have as much hot water as you wish, brought in, and my tub will be filled for you....Have no fear, you will be quite safe—and any valuables you may have brought, will be equally safe. It is a matter of honour here, to protect our people, and everything they possess!...Good night, Princess Thérèse..." And then he was gone—but not for long!

A moment later, she heard her name called. "Thérèse, may I come in for a second? Are you decent, or can you pass something out to me?...There's a camel saddle, which I use as a table, beside my divan....There's a small, black book on it that I want to read to my brother before I go to sleep, whether he is conscious or not!...Found it...?

"Thank you!" he acknowledged as she passed it to him through the flap, noticing, as she did so, that it was his Bible!... What an enigma this 'Father of the desert' was proving to be!

***

As she relaxed in the tub that had been carried in for her by a smiling Meriam, and another woman whose name she had not caught, she gazed around her at the *kaross* (fur-rug) on the doctor's divan, and the costly Persian rugs that lined both the floor and some sections of the insides of the tent. There were other wall hangings, too. Handmade tapestries lent an impression of luxury here, high up on this mountain of the Sahara. Reflecting on how an isolated, monk-like physician could have chosen to furnish his 'abode' in this quite incongruously opulent manner, she was not to know that all that surrounded the doctor, had once belonged to another man; another who had dedicated himself in the same, selfless way. Etienne had brought them there....The only relics saved from his former, palatial dwelling....Sacrificed in favour of a life dedicated to the care of the 'children' for whom *El-Hakim* was now responsible. What was most compelling of all, however, from the moment it drew her attention, was a rapier that hung across from *El-Hakim*'s bed. The exquisitely crafted hilt was embellished with precious stones that flashed many different hues in the lamplight, depending on which way she moved her head...

Wrapped in a large towel—a luxury she had not expected—she was still absorbed in the fascinating examination of her surroundings, when the middle-aged Bedouin woman returned, after first coughing tactfully from outside, and Thérèse decided that she really liked Meriam with the kindly brown face. She, Meriam, smiled continuously, as though to convey that, although she could not speak the princess's language, she welcomed her and wanted to assure her that she was available to serve her.

Suddenly Thérèse had a most unexpected thought. She was glad she had come. Every part of what had transpired since the dwarfs had tapped at her door—most especially her meeting with *El-Hakim*—was surreal enough, in retrospect, to have been part of a dream, but here, in this animal-hide tent, she felt at home, to a far greater extent than had ever been the case in the Talbots' sumptuous mansion....As though she belonged here. Inexplicably, among these strangers, she felt safe, and less lonely than when she had been surrounded by her friends. For the first time since she had been forced to flee her homeland, the ache in her heart was stilled.

***

Sitting at Philip's bedside, Dominic's thoughts were in a turmoil. The girl Haroun had brought to him was, without a doubt, the one he had kissed on the balcony of Sir Humphrey's house. Now he could recognize the dream image that had been haunting him ever since then, and his one fear was that she would, in turn, recognize him. How would he ever be able to have her sent back to Cairo if she knew that the desert-physician, *El-Hakim,* and Hamid Pasha, the brigand with a price on his head, were one and the same?

What bothered him, too, was that foolish remark about 'beautiful eyes'! They were, of course. He had never seen eyes quite like that before, and tonight he had been able to prove to himself that they really were like violets. But that still did not excuse comments that might be misconstrued as flirtatious. It was fortunate that, because she was there as a nurse, it should be easier to maintain their association on a purely a professional basis. The bit about her possessions being safe, had been intended to set her mind at ease, for, apart from her voice and those eyes, he would have known her at once by the locket around her neck. But he would never have dreamt that she was a princess, and he speculated on her circumstances, and her lack of other jewellery. There had to be an interesting story there. What could have motivated a royal lady to volunteer for work in a Red Cross hospital, and that not in her own country?

Although he was dead on his feet, almost to a point of staggering when he walked, he was far too disturbed to go to bed. He sat with Philip for another hour, wrestling mentally with far too many problems. The line of treatment he had adopted, was working for Philip. The medication he had been administering to him was clearly effective—but there had to be some way of protecting the nurse and the rest of his people. Raschid brought him the medical book he had requested, and sat with him, patiently keeping him company while he consulted it. Then the two of them went into the small, still inadequate lab he, Dominic, had managed to build up, over the years, and there they spent another hour or two.

"Raschid," Dominic said thoughtfully to his friend, "I think El-Bus Mohandess is satisfied with what we have done, so far. Out of his house, the hospital has arisen, and the people have food and clothing. We have brought many here to find shelter. When we triumph over Abdel Sharia, our task will have been accomplished."

"The day will come, *Sahhena*," Raschid replied with conviction. "Much depends on the meeting."

"That is true," Dominic agreed. "But Rameses and the ones who stay behind, will have to ensure that the girl does not wander beyond the hospital enclave. Especially now that our goal is in sight. The gate will have to be kept securely locked at all times, for as long as she is here, and a watch must be posted there for the benefit of anyone in need of medical treatment, who might seek admittance.

"I am already fearful of her recognizing me, and if she should venture outside of the walls, she might very well arrive at a dangerous and very inconvenient conclusion. In order to honour my pledge to El-Bus Mohandess, I have long had to remind myself of a promise I made to myself....Before I would allow anyone to disrupt my plans—I would be forced to have that individual removed!"

CHAPTER SIX

When Philip returned to full consciousness, and opened his eyes for the first time after the crisis had passed, his first impression was that he must have died. Lying on his back, he saw, looking at him over the top of a facemask, a pair of eyes that could only have belonged to an angel.

For a few moments he did not speak. He examined the whitewashed walls of the small room in which he lay, saw the one wooden chair, the rickety table laden with all manner of hospital paraphernalia on it, and only then could he believe that he was still on the good old earth.

The door opened and Dominic came in, a joyous smile on his face because he had heard that Philip was awake. He smiled broadly at Thérèse, too, pleased to see that she was obeying orders, and walked over to take Philip's pulse.

"Good morning, old fellow," he grinned, overcome with gratitude and brimming over with good humour as he saw the temperature Thérèse had noted earlier. "You have really given us a scare! Let me introduce you to your very charming nurse, Thérèse—the Crown Princess Thérèse of Soravia, to be exact. See that you treat her accordingly."

Philip smiled back, with comical astonishment, but his throat and lips were so dry that, when he tried to speak, his reply was hardly more than a hoarse whisper.

"A princess?" he croaked. "I don't know which I find

more unbelievable.—A girl who is probably gorgeous behind that mask, or the fact that she is a princess!…Dominic, your hospital is making progress, pal!"

To cover her embarrassment, Thérèse, about to take the young man's temperature again, fiddled with the thermometer, which she shook and placed under his tongue before he could say any more. "I can assure you that I find the fact that I am here, just as unbelievable as you do!" she responded dryly, with a glance in Dominic's direction. "I assure you that this has come about quite unexpectedly, and without much enthusiasm on my part!"

Dominic seemed to think this amusing. He laughed as he explained to Philip: "Mamoun, Haroun and Little Brother have personally brought the princess to take care of you in my absence, Phil. I am almost ready to leave."

With the thermometer in his mouth, Philip could only mumble something unintelligible, but the twinkle in his eyes and the expression on his pallid face, expressed eloquently that he also found the situation entertaining.

While she stood beside him, Thérèse's eyes wandered briefly from the watch on her wrist to the face of the doctor, a tiny frown wrinkling her brow, while all manner of thoughts went through her mind.…So his name was Dominic.…*El-Hakim's* brother had to be quite a few years younger than he was, and although Philip was covered with blankets, it was clear that he did not have the same powerful build as his older sibling.…. *El-Hakim* was wearing riding breeches this morning, and the open neck of his khaki shirt revealed a tanned chest that, to her small self, seemed massive.

He had rolled up his sleeves, and she could not help noticing the way the muscles in his arms rippled as he prepared the hypodermic syringe, holding it up in order to have a good look at it, and making sure that every bubble had been expelled. She found this intriguing. A man would need vigorous exercise to look like that. When, where, and how did he find the opportunity? Tearing her gaze away from *El-Hakim*, she removed the thermometer from Philip's mouth, and very efficiently entered his temperature on the chart, while his brother swabbed his arm for the injection.

Philip, now able to speak, inspected his arm. "Good heavens, Dom! I look like a strawberry or a fruitcake, or something! How many times a day have you been doing this to me, man—and for how much longer?"

Dominic chuckled. "After this, only three times a day, I promise you, but Thérèse has permission to give you a stab every time you misbehave!" He ruffled Philip's hair. "'Bye, *boetie*! I will try to look in on you again, briefly, before I leave, but, in case I can't, I'll just say, 'See you soon, and bless you.... Pray for me!' "

He then turned to Thérèse. "May I speak to you alone, for a moment, please! I have to leave shortly and there are others I must see before I go."

Outside in the passage, she found that the *El-Hakim* who awaited her was very different from the approachable, indulgent Dominic so briefly revealed in his brother's presence. He addressed her impersonally, and spoke so crisply that she had cause to wonder if this could be the same man. Philip, and perhaps Raschid, were undoubtedly favoured, because it seemed that the face of friendship and gentleness was there for them only to see.

"You have made it quite clear that you are here against your will, Princess, and I cannot say that I blame you—but unfortunately I now have need of you. I cannot go into details, but the meeting I go to attend is of immeasurable importance.

It would hardly be an overstatement to say that hundreds—perhaps even thousands of lives are at stake....Much depends on the outcome. Right at his moment Raschid is probably having my horse saddled, but you still have time to reconsider....Are you prepared to help me, or should we take you back, right now?"

Despite his attitude, she was involuntarily affected by the sincerity in his voice. His earnestness impressed and touched her; nevertheless she still felt far from content....How could she tell him that she had already made a decision the night before, and really did want to help him? How could she confide to him the frustration of which she had so constantly been aware while obliged to follow the useless, meaningless lifestyle of the past few years; of the loneliness and sorrow that could only be alleviated by work? Could she, while he was in his present frame of mind, explain to him eloquently enough, how much joy and fulfilment she would derive from being useful to someone, *anybody* at all? More than anything else she wanted to be needed, considered indispensable—have someone *dependent* upon her!

No! With that steely gaze fixed upon her, it was impossible to speak frankly. The icy blue eyes gave the impression that they could look right into her very soul, but she knew that *El-Hakim* was incapable of seeing into her heart....A temperamental, spoilt little fool was probably his opinion of her. A deposed princess, but still ridiculously proud and selfish. Well then, that was how she would behave.

She removed her mask, looked into his eyes for a moment without speaking, and then said simply: "I am prepared to help you, *El-Hakim!*"

(ii)

Having already looked in on the other quarantined patients, they scrubbed up, and Dominic led her on a quick tour of the rest of the building, pointing out where everything she might need, was kept. "Now that we're out of the isolation area, you will be able to meet Ezra," he told her. I don't allow him down there because his immune system has been severely compromised, but he'll be available, elsewhere, in case you have a problem. He's quite accustomed to standing in for Phil in a small way when called, but eventually I want to use him as a teacher in the schoolroom I am hoping to establish...

Then he took her to see the patients in the rest of the hospital. Although she was unable to converse with anyone other than a man who spoke French, and an Englishman who seemed rather bewildered, she smiled disarmingly and exclaimed approvingly at what she saw, marvelling at the existence of a small, well-equipped cottage hospital and clinic, miles from what she would have termed 'civilization'. *El-Hakim* was justifiably proud of what had been accomplished by converting the house he had been given, to serve this purpose.

"All this must have cost a great deal of money, Doctor," she remarked. "Are you supported by the government in any way?"

"Not exactly," was his reply. "Mostly through contributions. Usually people are loath to give, but we usually succeed in persuading them!"

As far as they went, people met him with beaming faces, ambulatory patients hastening forward to greet him. Although she could not understand what they were saying, she was beginning to realize that this singular man was more than their physician to them. *"Father of the desert"* Mamoun had called him. She had no option but to admit to herself that it was beginning to look as if he deserved that reputation...

"Some day I hope to have a really well-equipped lab, and the isolation ward has still to be completed," he was saying as they walked towards his laboratory. "You may have noticed that the room in which we have had to accommodate Philip, has no window panes as yet, and we had to scrape together some furniture for it before we took him there. This fever thing, brought into our midst by some recent arrivals, hit us when we were least prepared, and my brother was actually trying to do some last minute upgrading when he, himself, was taken ill. I reproach myself bitterly for allowing him to spend so much time with the afflicted ones, but there was no one else.—Perhaps I have bitten off more than I can chew."

"It seems formidable to me. Is this your full-time occupation? Running the hospital, I mean."

"No, it isn't," he answered quite curtly, becoming taciturn once more. "But we shan't go into that right now!...I only took you on the tour of the hospital and clinic, in case of an emergency, but I hope that you will not have to be called. My request to you, was that you watch over Philip. That is all— and for that you will have my undying gratitude."

"But I would *like* to do more!" she cried, almost pleading. "I miss my work! Your brother is not going to need me every hour of the day, and I shall need to fill in the time, somehow!"

"In that case, I'd appreciate it if you would also help out in the clinic. There is no one else who is really capable of doing that while I'm away—and, if you ever feel so inclined, perhaps you could just pop in sometimes and have a further word with Christopher Brent. We brought him here unconscious, and we have only come to know his name, nationality, and profession, by some papers we discovered in his wallet....He, himself, remembers nothing. Not even the circumstances of the attack....He only knows that he is a banker, because we have told him so.

"He needs to talk more...to be stimulated. Philip, Ezra and Raschid have tried to spend time with him as often as they were able, because he does not understand Arabic....Oh," the doctor chuckled, "and we allow him the odd snifter of cognac occasionally...because he seems to like it, and it cheers him up!"

They then went into the lab, where he caught her by surprise by asking her to roll up her sleeve.

"Whatever for?"

"Don't ask. Just trust me! I'm trying to do everything I know how, in order to provide you with as much protection from this illness, as I possibly can. I can't have you getting sick as well!"

She stretched out her left arm and pushed up her sleeve with her right hand. "We wouldn't want that, would we?" she commented expressionlessly, not at all proud of the sudden, overwhelming bitterness that rose up in her. It was not as if she still expected to be treated like a princess, but it hurt somehow that he should be concerned only about the people in his hospital. Most certainly not about *her*!

El-Hakim made no comment. He saturated a tuft of cotton wool with spirits and took hold of her arm to disinfect it. Unexpectedly, and to her consternation, something akin to an electric shock went through her entire body at the touch of his long, cool fingers, and she was obliged to lower her head lest her eyes betray this foreign emotion.

She felt ashamed to think that her equilibrium could be so easily unhinged by an obscure desert physician, who, judging by the secrecy pervading the whole place, might not even be completely honest. Temporarily she had cast aside the reluctant admiration she had felt for him but a few minutes before, but when, in looking down, she saw his hands, she was utterly riveted by them. She had never before seen such beautiful hands on a man! These were the hands of a musician, an artist or a surgeon. Certainly not those of a criminal!

"What's the matter, Princess?" he asked, making fun of her. "Afraid of needles?"

"Of course not!" She shook her head angrily. "In the nursing services, injections were an everyday occurrence!" And then, tossing her dark curls defiantly, she stalked out and he followed, chuckling to himself.

He found two well-worn, but spotless white coats, which probably belonged to his brother, for her to wear. She could have drowned in them, but decided that there was no way they could be the property of the doctor, himself, because they were not large enough. As she tried one on, he quite automatically stretched out his hands to help her roll up the sleeves, and she could only hope that he was oblivious of the minor storm he created in doing so. She had already begun to dread that mocking smile.

***

Finally all his last minute jobs were done. All pressing responsibilities dealt with, and others less urgent, shelved—for the time being! He went back into the hospital and talked with his brother, alone, for as long as time permitted.

Thérèse, preparing to move over to the hospital, was busy in his tent and trying, amid much mirth and comical gesturing, to direct Meriam to where her things should be taken, when

El-Hakim made his appearance. Their hilarity was so infectious that a fleeting smile lit up his eyes. In fluent Arabic he explained to Meriam what the princess desired of her, and with a nod, the woman began to gather up the visitor's belongings. Thérèse, could hardly believe her eyes when he helped the woman take some of the luggage outside, and then carried it for her to where Ali relieved him of it. Clearly a respectful, familial system was followed here, she concluded—with the 'Father of the desert' as its head—and her thoughts went back contemptuously to Otto and his insufferable hauteur.

Presently, Dominic came back and stood right in front of her. In the tent he seemed particularly tall, his blond head almost touching the roof, and something about that pricked her memory. Somewhere, recently she had seen another man like that....*Where* could it have been?

"Thérèse," he said, "in view of the manner in which you were brought here, this might sound a bit hollow, but I am indebted to you. Some day I hope to be in a position to repay you....Meanwhile, please make yourself at home. Mamoun and Haroun—and also Meriam—have been placed at your disposal. They will attend to you personally." He took her hand in his for moment, spun around on his heel, and strode from the tent.

All at once it was painfully lonely in the tent, and she had the feeling that time stood still. Before her hung the magnificent rapier with the sparkling hilt. Outside she could hear the voice of *El-Hakim* summoning his men. Suddenly she felt compelled to jump up and run outside.

"Dominic! Dominic!" she called after him, breathless with the urgency of what she wanted to say to him. "Wait a moment, please!"

"Dominic," she panted as she approached him, and then

restrained herself, blushing and immediately reverting to his desert name.—"*El-Hakim...Doctor...!*"

"What is it?" He did not seem exactly overjoyed to see her. One foot already in the stirrup, he sounded impatient. Around his shoulders hung a white *burnous*, the woollen cloak of the desert Bedouin, and a hood covered the brightness of his hair. Now realizing that she had embarrassed both the doctor and herself, by her impulsive action, her courage wavered before his penetrating stare.

"What is it, Thérèse?" he asked again.

She took a step forward and looked at him apologetically. "*El-Hakim,* I have made you a promise. May I now ask one favour of you?"

Although he was in no less of a hurry, he nodded affirmatively. "As long as you don't expect the impossible..."

Speaking hurriedly, so that she need not hold him up any longer than was necessary, she said: "I am not afraid to be left behind, but I just need your solemn assurance that that awful man will not spy on me again! He thoroughly unnerved me the other night and I tremble at the mere prospect of ever seeing him again!"

Unexpectedly an expression of unfeigned perplexity crossed the tanned face of the physician. "What man, Thérèse? I don't know what you are talking about! Did the twins frighten you?"

In her heart Thérèse knew that he spoke the truth. But now an even more terrifying thought struck her. If her abhorrent 'peeping tom' had not come at the behest of *El-Hakim*, who had sent him? And what had he come to do?

"He came on the night before the twins visited me.... Before I moved to the hotel where the twins found me, I was a guest at the home of Sir Humphrey Talbot, whose name may be familiar to you. I was already in bed when I saw this simply dreadful face peering at me through my open window! As my bedroom was on the second floor, he could not just have happened to be passing by, *El-Hakim.*

"He had purposely, and for some reason known only to him, climbed up there to see where I slept. Naturally, when the twins turned up at my hotel on the following day, I concluded that the man had been sent ahead by you, to check out my whereabouts!"

El-Hakim had meanwhile withdrawn his foot from the stirrup and stood listening attentively to her. He frowned thoughtfully. "I cannot think who that might have been, Princess," he said sincerely. "We only decided quite late in the day to try and find a nurse for Philip, and by the time Mamoun and Haroun arrived in Cairo, you must already have checked into your hotel. I shall give the matter some thought while I'm away, but don't concern yourself in the meantime. Allow me to assure you, once again, that you are very well protected here. Any one of the men whom I am leaving behind in this place, would give his own life to protect you!"

He stroked her cheek lightly, as though she were a child in need of comforting, then sprang lightly into the saddle, and, without looking back, spurred his horse forward. On the other side of the wall, more horsemen awaited him, and Thérèse caught a brief glimpse of them before the dust obscured them from view.

She remained standing where she was, deep in thought. When the air cleared, she noticed that the gate that led to the outside world had been securely locked. And she found it significant that it should be so.

In the distance she heard hooves strike rock once more, and then a chorus of voices calling out in unison from some place higher up the mountain, possibly sending *El-Hakim* on his way with a blessing.

CHAPTER SEVEN

The golden sand stretches out interminably before you, reflecting the light—and the heat—into your eyes and face. Above you the bright blue, cloudless sky. Upon everything and everyone, the sun blazes down mercilessly. Everything is dead quiet. Only the dull thud of hooves and the rhythmic movement of the horse beneath you can penetrate your consciousness, because your mind is dulled by the heat. Eventually the sweat around your eyes, and the glare from the desert sand, make it very difficult to see clearly.

Here and there a vulture, and sometimes an eagle, swoops down, only to return swiftly to seek the safety of the sky.

To Dominic, after the sleepless nights at Philip's bedside, and two days in the saddle, the monotony of his surroundings and the movement of his white stallion, Snow—whose name was the only cool thing left in the world—was hypnotic. It was some time since he had last been able to sleep long enough to feel completely rested, and he was unbearably drowsy. He could only concentrate on trivialities, which did not require any effort. The problem of the princess Thérèse, her nocturnal visitor, and how to take her back to where she belonged, would have to be left in abeyance for the time being. Soon they would reach one of the small settlements that bordered on the pre-determined meeting place. Cairo, Medinet and El-Fayoum lay far behind them; the Suef Oasis just over the next sand dune.

As they began to encounter other people along the way,

his tired brain caused him to ponder a singular attribute of the average Egyptian...a sort of sixth sense that lent them the uncanny capability of somehow, instinctively, knowing one another's names. Egyptian names could be very long and very difficult, but that never seemed to deter anyone. You could stop in the middle of the desert and instruct your servant to ask the way. "In which direction is Zagazig, Ahmed Meguid Shams el Din?" he would yell at someone feeding his camel more than a hundred yards away. The man would most probably not know where Zagazig was, despite the fact that it was, metaphorically speaking, just around the corner, and that he lived there himself, but you could lay your head on a block that his name would really be Ahmed Meguid Shams el Din! The man in question would then prove that he, in turn, knew your servant to be Rameses, or Ali, or Osman Abdel Wahab!

(ii)

Dominic and his band were the last to arrive. All around the oasis, in the shade of every palm tree, numerous Bedouin already lay resting on their blankets, deep in conversation with others whom they might not have seen for many a day. Camel drivers were busy, bringing food and water to their animals, and *haratin* were occupied with the putting up of tents. But that was how it should be. Hamid Pasha was a man of some consequence in the desert, and it was at his request that they were gathered there. How would it have looked if he had arrived early and had had to wait for others?

All rose to their feet as he jumped down from his horse. Each made a gesture of welcome with his hand. Slowly, proudly and with befitting dignity, the pasha walked ahead of his men to lay his sabre and gun down ceremoniously at the entrance to the camp, along with others already placed there. One-by-one his companions followed suit.

First they would eat, and then would come the business proceedings. Raschid and his leader were taken to the tent of Fuzad the *Cadi,* where they were heartily welcomed by the venerable old man. The rest of Hamid Pasha's entourage would see to their own food.

Dominic took up his position on the mat, sitting cross-legged opposite Fuzad, while Raschid stood respectfully behind him in order to serve him. Never would the food be handed directly to Hamid Pasha. His servant would be expected to accept it on his behalf and then set it before him.

"You are more than welcome, Hamid Pasha," Fuzad addressed him. "The unworthy hospitality of Fuzad the *Cadi* is at your disposal..."

Dominic greeted him with matching courtesy, and indicated, in the customary manner, that he accepted the meat Raschid held out to him.

He and the old *Cadi* chatted companionably. Fuzad was a man of wide experience with many interesting tales to tell. But after a while Dominic looked at him very earnestly. "Fuzad," he said directly, "you all know that there is a price on my head. Many of the sheiks have been through hard times of late. Why don't they take the chance, now, to capture me? Besides, how is it that they would travel so many, many miles at the request of a 'robber' pasha?"

The old man smiled kindly. "We do not know where your stockade is, Hamid Pasha, but we know full well what you do there. The eldest son of my brother is known to be among your men—'Rameses, the sabre fighter' is the name by which he is known. Up against Abdel Sharia on our own, we are lost. Who knows? Hamid Pasha may very well, at any time, have to shelter some of the Arabs who are in this very camp tonight....When injustice triumphs, as it does at the present time, it is not impossible for any one of us, whether we break the law or not, to be incarcerated in one of the Bey's prisons. It is not necessary to have a price on one's head—like, Hamid Pasha—in order to be taken captive....We all know this, and we all recognize that he would be our one hope...and refuge!"

There was a long silence. Dominic weighed the *cadi's* words very carefully. Finally he said: "Thank you Fuzad....If ever that should happen, God forbid, there would always be room in my camp for you! As long as I am alive and the need exists, I shall, with God's help, endeavour to justify your confidence in me....There would always be enough food at my table for you, too!"

"And I shall pray for the protection of Allah for you, my son!"

(iii)

The sheiks and the *cadis* sat or sprawled in a wide circle on the warm sand to listen to what Hamid Pasha had to say. The sun had begun to set and all around them fires were already being lit. A last red ray caught Hamid Pasha's face and illuminated his white *burnous*. He was unmistakable as he stood there....Everyone present, said Fuzad, introducing Dominic, knew that Hamid Pasha had come there to elicit their help in the struggle against Abdel Sharia. They were pleased to listen attentively, without interruption. Later they would be given the opportunity to question the pasha.

There was dead silence as Dominic began to speak. He had a feeling that they were kindly disposed and, with the support of Fuzad he *had* to succeed. Beside him, Raschid was very tense.

He addressed them candidly in the desert dialect, briefly describing Raschid's dreadful suffering in Abdel Sharia's prison camp. He also listed other inhuman and dastardly practices ascribed to the Bey. "You, yourselves, know, friends, that prominent officials frequently disappear, and the blame is always placed squarely on my head.…Tonight I want to assure you that that is not only unwarranted, it is absurd!

"Who are these people who are being 'removed'...? I shall tell you! Only those who are honest; only those who have the courage of their own convictions; only those who dare to oppose tyranny and injustice.…. Who is this Abdel Sharia? Has anyone outside of his own circle ever seen him?.... Never! And he cannot be outwitted because as soon as someone in the *Barlaman* dares to institute an inquiry, that 'someone' suspiciously disappears without a trace!

"There must be some of his henchman in the *Barlaman* itself. We all know—some of you already have experienced this—that innocent, quite ordinary Bedouin, too, are unjustly being sentenced every day for crimes they have not committed. The moment they emerge from the prisons, Abdel Sharia sucks another felony out of his thumb to send them back.

"Why he does this, you also know. He needs labourers in his mines, his gravel pits and on his railway. I firmly believe that the missing officials are to be found among the Bey's wretched captives.…No amount paid in ransom ever secures their release, and it does not help to try and escape. You are either shot or—if you are lucky—sent back by the false 'court'!"

Hamid Pasha was silent for a moment, in order to catch his breath. The slightest rustle of a dry autumn leaf would have been audible in that silence. A few hundred pairs of eyes were focused on his inspired countenance. When he spoke again, it was hardly above whisper. "My men are ready to fight to the death, if necessary, but there are too few of us....Will you help us, friends? Can we count on you?"

It was clear that the pasha had made a great impression on his listeners. Some hands were already raised to pledge allegiance. Fuzad had Dominic admiringly by the arm.—Then the unexpected occurred. A tall, spare man, sitting alone on the fringe of the crowd, suddenly rose to his feet.

"Honourable Hamid Pasha," the man said regretfully, "we have listened with much interest and great admiration to you tonight..... We sincerely desire to help...but we *dare* not! Someday, when the identity of Abdel Sharia is revealed, we can talk once more, but now we do so in vain. If we resist him, we bring down the fury of the Caliph upon our heads. Everyone here knows that it is said that Abdel Sharia is a holy man, and, although we cannot understand his motives, we are not allowed to offer resistance. Who are we to oppose the will of a chosen one?"

He sat down again and immediately tongues were loosed. Everyone speaking at once created a noise under the palm trees, that was like the roar of the ocean.

Long ago Raschid had told Dominic that the Bedouin embraced a crude form of Mohammedanism. Nevertheless it came as a great shock to find that these men of the desert could be so ignorant that they would even believe that a monster like Abdel Sharia was holy!.... With a superstitious, Islamic fanatic, one could do nothing, Raschid had told him once, and Dominic remembered enough of Raschid's nightly lessons to know that the Caliph, who was the successor to the prophet, himself, and considered to be supreme in both civil and religious affairs, was more important to the Mohammedan than the Pope to a Catholic!

***

Dominic motioned to Raschid and the rest of his men, that they were not staying. There was no need to pitch the tents. He wished only to get back to the stockade. He would never have believed that he could miss it so acutely!

CHAPTER EIGHT

His one desire was to get as much as possible of the distance that separated him from the stockade, behind him, but fatigue soon got the better of him. Before they had covered much more than six miles, he was made to realize that, in leaving the oasis so precipitously, he had been selfish. In his initial disappointment and anger, he had not been in a fit state to consider others. He had not been thinking clearly, but he soon noticed that Raschid, who had only recently risen from a sickbed, had slumped forward on his saddle, and yet, while many of the others exhibited similar signs of weariness, not one of them complained. With a sigh of resignation he gave the order to halt at the first suitable place and set up camp.

There were a hundred-and-one matters he was anxious to discuss with Raschid, but, in comparison with a saddle, the hollows they made in the sand under their blankets, were better than any featherbed, and the warmth radiating from the flickering fire quickly sent them off to sleep.

Early next morning they were once more on their way. During the worst heat of the day, they temporarily took advantage of shade provided by a few isolated palms, resting just long enough to give each man his ration of food and water, and to feed, water and wipe down their steaming mounts.

It was consequently only after the evening meal on the second night, that Dominic was granted an opportunity to seek relief from the confusion raging in his thoughts. He waited for Raschid to finish eating and then beckoned to him.

"I need some time alone to think, Raschid, but I really must talk with you! I am going to that rock behind the sand dune", he said, pointing to it with a forefinger, "where I will wait for you. But please allow me some time, just to be alone…" And, nodding, the Indian went obediently, to wait.

Because the Bey's spies were everywhere, Hamid Pasha never dared set to up camp at any of the commonly frequented resting places in the desert. As a precaution he had chosen, for their campsite, a hollow between two curved dunes, from where his sentries could watch, unseen, to be sure that no one was following them, and the conveniently shaped, semicircular walls of sand would provide shelter on all sides.

His long legs carried him easily up and over the slope, to where, with a deep sigh, he flung himself down and leant against the rock for a short while, drawing comfort from it because it signalled that he was nearing his beloved mountain. Then, not wanting to be so conspicuous, he stretched out on his back, and lay there in the sand, deep in thought. Far above him, in a sky far bluer that anything he had seen since he had left South Africa, myriads of stars began to twinkle in the twilight, and a crescent moon was rising behind the dunes in the distance.

It was an ideal evening for dreaming and introspection. As soon as the sun set over the desert, the air cooled rapidly, but now the sand still retained enough heat to make the ground a pleasant place for self-searching. His present existence was so surreal that he was grateful for this rare opportunity to try and find the real Dominic Verwey….To search for the child who had once played 'Five Stones' with the Basotho children on his parents' farm….What had happened to the boy whose greatest pride had been derived from being simultaneously selected for both the school's cricket and rugby teams? How had that farm boy grown up to be an outlaw, when all he had ever wanted was to be a doctor?

He wondered how Philip was doing, and whether Thérèse was coping with the responsibilities he had dumped on her slender shoulders. Despite the disdain he felt for women, he was confident that she was quite up to the task; however, now that he was able to shed, even temporarily, the persona he had embraced, and be just himself for a while, he was surprised at himself for expecting anything at all of her. Considering the circumstances under which she had come to be in his camp, she must be finding her situation untenable. And for his own behaviour, he could find no better word than 'reprehensible'!

At times he found it hard to believe that she could actually be a crown princess. There was indeed that inherent refinement in her appearance and bearing, and something eminently regal about her demeanour, despite the fact that she was so small, and yet she did not put on airs. Without being haughty, she gave an impression of quiet dignity, and that, together with something childlike—or rather, a certain shyness—made her an interesting study. Instinctively he knew that she was a good nurse...capable but sympathetic and gentle. She also happened to be tremendously attractive, but naturally, to a confirmed cynic and woman-hater like himself that was of minor importance....It was of course only the mystery of her life that fascinated him.—How did a crown princess come to be a nurse?

Philip was his greatest concern. There was an expression in the lad's eyes when he looked at Thérèse that was disquieting, and he did not trust it. What might happen when she removed the mask and he could take a look at that exquisite face, was anyone's guess. Philip could not be allowed to get ideas about a foreign princess who was, in any case, beyond his reach. To make matters worse, when a man had not seen a white woman for so long he could very easily be thrown off balance—and that accent was certainly charming. In an absolutely impersonal way, he, himself, liked hearing her voice.

From Thérèse his thoughts turned to her nocturnal visitor, and he resolved to question her further, before he sent her home...but the arrival of Raschid, just then, made it impossible to repel other more pressing concerns, any longer.

"Raschid," he began broaching the subject with great reluctance, unwilling to hear the truth, "you, yourself, are Muslim. Do you believe what that man said? Do you also want to give up the fight? I cannot say I blame you if you do."

Raschid only smiled, shaking his head. "No, *Effendi*. Not all, but most of these desert people with whom we have to deal, are ignorant and know nothing of the outside world. I think I can say of myself that, because I have been fortunate to visit many other parts of the world, I have a wider view...a broadness of mind that you cannot expect of them.—And besides..."

He looked into Dominic's eyes, and paused meaningfully.

"Besides what, Raschid? What were you going to say?" Dominic asked gently.

"What I was going to say, *Sahbena*, was that besides having travelled abroad, I no longer believe all I did long ago, because, starting with my *memsahib*, Mrs. Hunt, and later El-Bus Mohandess—four of the most excellent people it has ever been my good fortune to know—have all been Christians...! The third is Philip-brother—and you know the other...

"My life has changed much, Dominic *Effendi*, because of you. So much so, that I can be grateful for the 'Yellow Eye' affliction. Because of you I also have a friend who is a Jew.

A Jew with whom, together with several others, I shared the same tent for some years—but with whom I never spoke, until I saw you do that....Without Ezra, my life would be the poorer. I do not consider it to be by chance that you saw fit to move us into a smaller tent, only large enough to accommodate two..."

There was a significant pause, and by the way the Indian continued to look at Dominic, there was no mistaking what he intended to convey....And something happened to Dominic at that moment. Something that had not happened to him since he had become a man.—Tears stung his eyes...!

It took a few moments for Dominic to compose himself, and when he did speak, it was to say a very husky: "Thank you, my friend!" He then took a deep breath, shrugged, and said, "We were talking about Abdel Sharia, and what happened at the gathering. You were putting the blame for much of the reaction, on people who are ignorant...but what about the rest? You can't say the same for all of them..."

The Indian no longer seemed quite so comfortable. "I don't know, *Effendi*. I do not know! There are indeed others who would not desert you in any other battle, but who might consider this one to be against their religion..... And then there are also others who would consider it a glorious and holy martyrdom to die for the Bey..."

Dominic knew this to be true, and he was suddenly overcome by a feeling of the most overpowering despair. He felt utterly powerless, and he felt trapped. He mulled over what Raschid had just said, and then requested earnestly: "Please explain it all to me in greater detail. Perhaps I shall then know better what to do."

"Good, *Effendi*, I shall endeavour to do so," replied the Indian. "It is like this....But I shall begin with some of what was explained to me many years ago, by my *memsahib,* because I know well that you are a student of your Bible.

"When I was young—and that is when, in my experience, memory is most deeply stored—she read to me a part of your New Testament which she said, as I recall, was frequently referred to as *'Revelations'* or the *'Revelation of John'*. This she said was incorrect on two counts, because it was one, great 'Apocalypse' or, in English, 'Revelation' of your prophet Jesus *to* a man called John. She talked about herself as being an esca...esca...?" He appealed to Dominic.

"Eschatologist?" he suggested. "A person who believes in the coming of a Messiah whom, to Christians like me, would be our Lord Jesus Christ?"

"That is correct, *Sahhena*. Thank you. I discussed this once with Ezra, and he told me that you had said to him that there was only one difference between him and yourself. His Messiah had not yet come, you said, but yours had already done so....In other words you considered yourself to be a 'completed Jew', and when yours comes again, He will still be that same Messiah....His coming will be for the *second* time!"

Dominic grinned. "I did tell him that! Fancy his repeating that to you!"

"Now you will understand better what could possibly be the situation you face in pitting yourself against Abdel Sharia. You have one Messiah, and when He comes again, He will still be the one who, to you, is the 'one and only"—but here it is different. Here a different one rises up, every so often, claiming to be the anticipated one...

"All pious followers of Islam believe that one day another great prophet called the *Mahdi* will appear and, every so often a leader rises up who declares himself to be that *Mahdi*. Abdel Sharia is another of these.—Thus far, however, it has always transpired, in the end, that the claims of these men were false, but there are many people, among them the Bedouin, who are more gullible than one would suppose. The fact that Abdel Sharia has never shown himself openly, veils his personality with a mysterious, even magical quality which captures the imagination..."

"I see, yes!...El–bus Mohandess has indeed set me an enormous and difficult task, and I also see now why I have so frequently had to hear the expression 'when his identity is unveiled'!—But those others, Raschid? The false leaders of whom you have spoken....How were they outwitted? Tell me about them."

Raschid thought for a moment. "There was one, right here in the Sudan, in the last century. The instigator of a great uprising. He called upon the men of the desert to support him, and it was during the British campaign to subdue the rebellion, and during the siege of Khartoum, that General Gordon was killed in 1885. You, *Sahbena* must have heard tell of 'Gordon of Khartoum'?"

"I most certainly have," Dominic exclaimed. "We learned about him in school—but he was never real to me until this moment!...That's amazing, Raschid! What makes you so sure that Abdel Sharia is not 'your' *Mahdi?*"

"Because, *Effendi*, your *Mahdi* was said to be loving. My memsahib believed that, although he was the son of her God, He loved her enough to die for her. I would want mine to be the same. This man, Abdel Sharia, cares nothing for others. Everything he does, *Effendi,* is for his own gain. He is cruel, he is dishonest and he is merciless. I am suspicious even of the fact that he chooses to include the word 'Sharia' in his name, in order to impact the minds of those who might not believe.

"I can tell you much about which definitions of the word 'Sharia' are accurate and which are not, but I believe that, whoever this man is, he trades on what we are all taught—

namely, that it is the law system of Muslims, that it is based upon the Koran, and that that makes it the will of God. Is that not sufficient to instil awe in the minds of all who would go against him?"

"It would certainly, if one were receptive. But, to get back to the one who used his supposed god-like status to stir up the people who killed Gordon..."

"That so-called prophet was killed the same year," Raschid replied, "and the rebellion..." All at once he broke off and stared fixedly in front of him.

Dominic looked around to see what had caught his attention. "What is it, Raschid?"

For a moment Raschid held his breath. Then he threw himself down flat and whispered urgently, "We are not alone, *Effendi*!—Look over there!" He pointed with a forefinger.

Clearly silhouetted against the glow that still lingered above the horizon, Dominic saw a small caravan of horses and camels, leaving a light cloud of dust in its wake.

Dominic hastily slid backwards down the bank, and Raschid followed his example. Screened by the sand, they looked at one another.

"They can't see us," Dominic said with conviction. "Unless they are looking down at us from the very closest dunes—but no, they are not high enough....One thing is certain...we *have* to know who those people are. We can too easily be followed when we leave here."

Raschid nodded. "Anyone at the gathering, now knowing that you are Hamid Pasha, could have followed us."

Dominic had to consider the predicament from every angle before voicing any comment, but then he said: "Please go and fetch Ali and Sezit, Raschid. I shall wait here and keep my eye on the horsemen so that I can establish whether they intend setting up camp there, or going further."

Lying on his stomach, Raschid slid a little further down the bank, and ran back to their own camp, to do Dominic's bidding…

(ii)

By the time the other three joined him, Dominic had come to several conclusions, which he shared with them.

It was unnecessary to be able to see the strangers, themselves, he informed them. Even hidden from sight amid the dunes, the rising dust had clearly indicated their progress until, about a quarter of a mile from where he and his men now lay watching, there was no longer any dust to be seen.. He was thus able to assess more or less where the caravan had halted. Presently they would know whether their newly arrived neighbours were friendly, and innocently camping there, or not, because, while the twilight lingered, smoke would clearly betray their presence. Anyone wishing to be hidden, would never risk lighting a fire before it was completely dark.

"Just now, when Raschid first noticed them," said Hamid Pasha, "my first reaction was to regret that we, ourselves, had made a fire, but I am now inclined to think that that could yet be to our advantage. Whoever the people over there might be, they might be led to assume that we are unaware of their presence, and quite unconcernedly preparing for the night, as ordinary travellers would."

"That is true, *Effendi*," Raschid concurred. "We can only wait."

In silence they gazed across the desert. Dominic was of the opinion that they would not be attacked. Even if the men, now too close for comfort, did turn out to be Sharia's spies, as he suspected, it was probably their intention to stay out of sight for as long as possible, in order to follow Hamid Pasha all the way to his hiding place.

After thirty minutes, Dominic shook his head. "They are setting up camp without a fire, as I suspected," he observed. "We must go closer and investigate. What I would give, right at this minute, to have the twins here!"

He looked at the watch which had once belonged to El-Bus Mohandess, and then studied the position of the moon. "That moon will spread little light over the sand," he remarked, "but unfortunately, where the sun has set, the horizon does not darken until late, at this time of the year. Against that backdrop, we have consistently been travelling northwest since we left Suef, and that is why our mysterious pursuers have approached from the east. If Raschid had not providentially been sitting higher up on the dune, we would never have suspected that we had company."

"That is indeed fortunate," Raschid agreed, "but now it becomes necessary to approach from the west. As soon as we make the least movement on the dunes, we become an easy target!"

"I would rather go around like *this*," Dominic said, pointing to the east, "in a wide semi-circle, so that I can surprise them from the opposite direction. Even had the afterglow of the sun not been to our disadvantage, it would have been unwise to approach from the direction of our camp. Very likely they have posted their sentries on this side, in preparation for precisely that eventuality."

"You are quite right, *Effendi*!" Raschid could never find fault with Hamid Pasha's reasoning. "What would you have us do?"

Dominic removed his cloak, handed it to Raschid, studied the moon again, and then said, "I want you and Sezit to return to our companions. Take the watch and if, after one hour, Ali and I have not returned, you must attack the camp of those strangers. But, in the meantime, while you are waiting, you must erect my tent."

He held up his hand to preclude any protest. "Yes, I know, it is unnecessary, when we plan to remain for only one night, but we must give the impression that we are here for an indeterminate length of time. First light a few more fires, then all except six of you, must roll out your blankets and lie down. There must be little activity in our camp. If it seems that we are asleep, that will further aid my plan. However, the six men you select, must sit in my tent and stay awake, in case the rest do fall asleep. As I have said, if Ali and I have not returned after one hour, those who are keeping watch in my tent must wake the others and come in search of us....Is that all clear?"

"Perfectly, *Sahbena*," Raschid assured him. "May Allah preserve you!"

"I shall be praying to God incessantly for His protection— for all of us, Raschid," he responded solemnly, patting the latter on the arm...."But there's one more thing!"—Dominic, who had already started walking, turned around.—"Those of you in the tent, must laugh raucously and talk loudly, as if you have all had too much wine!"

"It shall be as you say, *Effendi*!" the Indian promised...

(iii)

Hamid Pasha and Ali circled around the dunes, avoiding the higher places so that they would not been seen. Maintaining strict silence, they proceeded, sometimes walking upright and often sliding on their stomachs through the sand. Before long, it became easier to pinpoint the situation of the camp for which they were headed, because the sounds always associated with such places were unmistakable. The low drone of many voices, the clinking of tin spoons on tin plates, and the neighing of horses, carried to them on the evening breeze, became louder as they neared the place.

Finally they had only to climb over a last wall of sand to look down on the camp. The strangers had also chosen a hollow, and, as they moved closer, Dominic and Ali kept pushing the sand out before them so that, when they reached the highest point, only their heads would stick out. Both would be lying in a hollow and not provide a noticeable silhouette on the dune.

There they lay looking down. It was just as Dominic had predicted. Not a single fire burned. Everyone carried on with whatever he was supposed to be doing, by the half-light of the crescent moon. That would stand him, Dominic, in good stead, making it a great deal easier to get closer. In his khaki breeches and shirt, he was hardly visible on the sand, and he was glad that he had left his cloak behind. Like two snakes he and Ali glided down, head first, and then crawled further on their hands and knees.

It was fortunate that they first reached the 'horse camp', where two strapping young Arabs, each carrying a bucket, were moving around among the animals. A mare near Ali lifted her head and whinnied loudly, but, before the man closest to them could investigate, Dominic went up noiselessly behind him, and chopped him smartly on the neck with the side of his hand....Physicians do not easily kill, and, to them, the anatomy of humans is an open book. Dominic knew exactly how and where to deliver the blow—without fatal consequences—and the young man immediately folded neatly before him.

The other Arab was bent over, with his head under a horse, when Ali gave him a mighty push from behind. The man fell forward, with his mouth in the sand, and before he could properly catch his breath, Hamid Pasha's skilful Turk, had silenced him for an hour or two.

Grinning broadly, and highly pleased with themselves, they looked at each other with satisfaction. Dominic took the water bucket which the first Arab had been obliged to relinquish, and crouched down, as the other man had been doing, as low as he could under the horse. Ali sat on his haunches beside him and, looking between the legs of the animal, they could examine the camp and the strangers in it, reasonably well.

"Ali," Hamid Pasha whispered. "Take note, the horses have not been off-saddled. Probably in anticipation of a sudden departure."

"As soon as we make the first move, *Effendi*," the Turk agreed.

Dominic noted, too, that there were none of the ornamental silver trappings, beloved of the desert horseman, on either saddles or bridles. Anything that jingled unnecessarily had also been removed. No doubt to avoid undue noise, or flashes of reflected light.

Nowhere was a tent to be seen. Obviously all would sleep on the ground, in the open air, so that they could be in the saddle as speedily as possible. To the west sat two watchmen, each with a rifle on his knee.

"What did I tell you?" Dominic exulted, under his breath. "They anticipate that any possible spies will come from that direction!"

As he was speaking, a man walked over to where the guards sat, talked to them for a moment, and came back to stand not more than twenty feet from where Dominic and Ali, were hiding. The Turk gasped.

"*Effendi!*" he hissed. "It is he—the man from the gathering!

The tall, thin sheik! I *thought* that he had been primed by Abdel Sharia! "

Dominic was gratified to find that Ali was another who had not been fooled, and was about to tell him so, when the sheik began to speak, and they pricked up their ears.

"Osman! Menit!" the sheik called out. "Come here!" Two of his henchmen came hurrying at his command. His voice was so penetrating that Dominic could hear every word as audibly as if he stood right beside him.

"I wish you to go now to the camp of Hamid Pasha," he said clearly. "You, Menit must return at once to report, while you, Osman, must remain there until you bring me word that the pasha prepares to depart!"

The two spies *salaamed*, and set off, and Dominic waited only long enough to listen to what the sheik might add for the benefit of another man, who had joined him.

"We have been unpleasantly surprised by the outlaw's knowledge of our master's affairs," his words drifted through the air. "Our updated orders are that we are no longer only to follow. As soon as we have established the whereabouts of his stockade, we are to proceed with the destruction of Hamid Pasha and everyone he harbours there."

With that, the sheik and his companion walked away, chatting without disclosing any further information, and Dominic saw no point in lingering a moment longer. He realized that he would learn nothing more to his advantage.

"Come, Ali," he whispered urgently. "We need to follow those men, but we can only return by a round-about way." His knife flashed as, with lightning speed, he cut a length from the rope with which the animal nearest to him was tethered, before the two of them crept away, following the same route by which they had come, and dragging the unconscious men over the first sandbank with them. Because they dared not risk their recovering too soon and raising the alarm, they took the added precaution of tying them up and ramming a scrap of cloth torn from Ali's shirt, into each man's mouth, before proceeding further.

***

Moving stealthily and with the utmost caution, they managed to catch up with Sharia's spies, from behind, but kept their distance, awaiting a suitable opportunity and moving forward, flat on the sand wherever possible, as the men ahead of them were doing. Down below them in Hamid Pasha's own camp, there was no sign of movement, it seemed. Around the flickering fires, his men lay asleep, and all was quiet.— Everywhere else but in his tent, where loud, boisterous and uproarious merriment reigned.

There lamps burnt brightly, throwing clear shadows onto the walls, and even from where Dominic and Ali lay, it was not difficult to guess what the people inside were up to. Every so often a rough voice would loudly shout out something supposedly hilarious, provoking much raucous, drunken laughter. It was enough to make the leader grow pale at the sound of what seemed like the vilest cursing going on in his tent. Hamid Pasha smiled a fleeting smile....Raschid's idea of how his leader would entertain guests, was priceless!

"Ha!" the man called Osman, spat with contempt. "After suffering a defeat, the pig drowns his sorrows in this way!"

The other one, Menit, laughed mockingly. "See how sweetly his followers sleep. So innocently that no one keeps watch!"

The two spies lay down for a minute or two longer, in silence, and then, having reassured himself, Menit recklessly stood up. "I must return as I was instructed. Stay here so that you can watch everything that goes on."

Osman nodded. "Tell them back there, that there is no need for concern. The whole lot outside, are snoring, and the ones in the tent will doubtless soon be, too. Hamid Pasha will certainly not want to be on his way too early....Send someone in about two hours, to relieve me!"

Menit responded affirmatively and disappeared over the bank. Along with Ali, Dominic watched his progress as he went from one dune to the next, until he was out of earshot, and then gave the signal. With one bound, Ali was upon the remaining spy. Too late the man called Osman realized that he had walked into a trap. He rolled about in the sand, struggling with Ali, but the latter was both too quick, and too strong for him. Very soon, Osman, like two of his friends further back, slept peacefully among the dunes.—And as Hamid Pasha and Ali rushed into the camp, Raschid consulted the watch of El-Bus Mohandess. The leader had returned with six minutes to spare!

Dominic came running, calling out to the men in the tent to wake the others with all haste, and to strike camp as quickly as possible. "Put out the fires! Saddle the horses! Hurry! Hurry!" he urged them. He had only two hours before the relief spies would come to take over, and by that time he wanted to be well on his way.

Just before it grows light, a gentle wind always moves across the desert, and their tracks had to be obliterated by it. By the time the sun rose, they had to be in the mountains, because there, on the hard ground between the rocks, no hoof left a mark.

CHAPTER NINE

During the first four days of *El-Hakim*'s absence Thérèse was happier than she had ever hoped to be again. During the day she was too busy to sit down, and at night she slept like a top, unless she was called to a patient.—Even then, when she was able to return to her cot, she had only to put her head down to fall sound asleep once more. Sometimes Rameses and the twins had to beg her to stay in one place long enough to eat a proper meal, and, as she began to know one patient from the other, she derived a great deal of joy from their welcoming smiles. It was wonderful to be of use once more, and to feel necessary to people.

After supper each evening she would usually visit with Philip for a while, before going on her evening rounds. By the time she went back later, to take to him the goats' milk drink she had prepared, and as his brother had prescribed, she was more than ready for sleep. The coir mattress on her narrow, iron bed, was hard, but there was a comfortable hollow in the centre of it, and every night, long before she had finished undressing and taking her bath, she was already anticipating the glorious moment when she could slide in under the blankets.

For three nights she was asleep before her head touched the pillow. That awful habit of tossing and turning was a thing of the past. She did not concern herself with the future. She could think of her parents, her destroyed home and pillaged country, without cringing with the pain of it. For three blessed nights, she did not lie awake grinding her teeth in an agony of futile rage because the word 'neutral' had meant so little. There were no air raids, and no bombs to haunt her dreams.

But on the fourth night, sleep once more eluded her.

Even during the war, however they steeled themselves against it, the nurses had sometimes acquired a favourite among their patients, and now, probably because *El-Hakim's* attachment to his brother had touched her so deeply—or perhaps because Philip was so pathetically weak and run down after his illness—she put herself out to be extra nice to him. The doctor had not yet definitively put a name to whatever it was that had afflicted eight of his people, among them Raschid and Philip, although he had sounded pretty sure that he was on the right track, but, just by looking at Philip's chart, she concluded that he was lucky to be alive. She had had experience of diseases that resulted in such high fevers, and she knew that the victims were often left depressed.

Philip was no exception, and whenever she went into his room, and found him with a long face, she made allowances for him. It was so easy to cheer him up by simply smiling at him, that, every time she passed his door, she would poke her head around it to exchange a joke with him.

On the third day, she allowed him to sit up, and was pleasantly surprised when he requested Rameses to help him shave. He was sick of that beard, he said....It was always a good sign when a patient started to take an interest in his or her appearance.

On the following day, with no untoward consequences, he sat in a chair by the window, for an hour. Thérèse was adamant, however, that he should not walk anywhere until *El-Hakim* had personally given his permission, but this did not explain why, when she went in after the evening meal, he was staring disconsolately at the ceiling.

"The picture of cheerfulness!" she observed good-humouredly. "Are you bored?"

Immediately a smile lit up his gloomy face. "Come and sit here with me for a while," he pleaded. "I am so tired of bed that I could die!"

"Shall I go and borrow a pack of cards or a set of dice from Mamoun?" she asked sympathetically. "You are strong enough now to play a game."

But he shook his head impatiently. "I don't want to play cards, Thérèse. I want to look at *you*! What good is the *Queen* of Hearts to me, when what I want to see is the *'Princess* of Hearts'?"

"A lovely compliment," she replied flippantly, favouring him with an exaggerated, sweeping, bow. "You are a true poet, Mr. Philip!"

"And you are making fun of me," he complained. "Why won't you take me seriously, Thérèse?"

She read such disappointment in his eyes that she suddenly realized that he was in dead earnest. This greatly concerned her, and she sat down at the foot of his bed, looking searchingly at him, and raising one dark eyebrow questioningly.

"What is wrong with you tonight, Philip? Are you feeling overtired from being up too long? You cannot expect to regain your strength immediately. Tomorrow, or the next day, your brother will return, and then you can start walking about..."

Unexpectedly he was not satisfied with this.—On the contrary! "That is precisely what bothers me. I very badly want Dominic to come home....Even in my sleep I cannot help feeling anxious, and I shall be ever so grateful to see him safely back here; but, on the other hand, the thought that you must leave here, is like a knife through my heart!"

Thérèse was startled, but managed not to show it. "Just because I'm not so callous when it come to injections?" she asked, forcing a laugh, and determined that he would receive no encouragement in *that* direction. Then she had a thought and the smile vanished. "Why do you feel so uneasy, Philip? Is your brother in any danger?"

Dominic had already put the fear of death into him, and he somehow succeeded in not lowering his guard. "In the desert everyone is in danger," he responded evasively.

Thankful that the awkward moment had passed, she remarked, "Oh, yes—Hamid Pasha!—Does he bother you here, too? "

" Not exactly.—But Thérèse..."

"It is unlikely that such a criminal will be able to evade the gallows for much longer!" she was quick to interrupt him. "Don't you think so? I know what I would do if *I* ever got hold of him!" Concerned that he might be leading up to some sort of declaration of affection, she talked so fast that she said the first words that came into her head. "I regard it as the duty of all lovers of justice to join forces, and not to rest until that felon is behind bars! "

To her amazement, Philip burst out laughing, and being so weak, mirth, and the effort exacted of him, made tears roll down his cheeks. "My dearest Thérèse," he gasped, "you should not be so transparent!" Suddenly, out of the blue, he stopped, and asked: "How old are you?"

"Twenty-six." She was totally bewildered. "Why?"

"I'm just curious," he replied, smiling. "Twenty-six, and you are still as naïve as a schoolgirl! You are terrified that I am about to become amorous, but, at the same time, you don't want to hurt my feelings....You sweet thing!...As though I couldn't see right away how hard you have been trying to avoid the subject at all costs!" He squeezed her hand gently. "Never mind, honey. I shall behave myself. As of now, *you* shall have the privilege of choosing every subject of conversation....Think carefully.—What would you like to talk about? "

At first she was so embarrassed that she could not reply, while Philip looked as if he were about to explode again at any minute. Finally her sense of humour took over, and she, too, began to laugh. She soon took advantage of the opportunity, however.

"Let...me see..." she said slowly, pretending to think very hard, and then: "Tell me how you and your brother came to be here, in the first place. I can't help wondering..."

Still being very cautious not to let slip anything incriminating, he related briefly how, after Dominic had completed his studies in Edinburgh, the two of them had come to Egypt on holiday, and he told of meeting a philanthropic man whose dreams had influenced Dominic to a great extent. When the man was suddenly killed, Dominic in particular— and, through him, he, himself—had remained to devote himself to the realization of the ideal towards which that man had striven for so long. "*El-Hakim* will never return to South Africa until that has been achieved," he continued, and his eyes shone with admiration for his brother.

All the time he was speaking, Thérèse sat with lips parted and eyes dreamy, caught up in the fascinating tale. She sighed when it came to an end, and the dark brown of her eyes seemed quite violet in that light. "Isn't that just the most wonderful thing to have done?...But your brother is a singular man!"

"How so?" Philip instantly demanded, suddenly jealous.

"I don't know..." She frowned thoughtfully. "It is difficult to explain because he is so complex. Often so inscrutable, he can be disarmingly friendly at times.—In your company he is even nice to me—and the patients adore him—but as soon as he has to become personal, it is as if he immediately withdraws into a shell of cynicism. His mood can change so quickly that I never know what to expect!"

"Oh, that!" Philip was relieved. "That's just because you are a female. He can't stand women…or, no, that's putting it a bit crudely. Let us rather say he despises them. He says one should never rely on them. Apparently they are 'artificial and fickle'. He has sometimes expressed the opinion that their 'heads are empty!'" He laughed at the recollection. "That brother of mine! But, never mind, Thérèse, as long as you—as you have put it—remain 'impersonal', and faithfully carry out orders, he is not that fearsome!"

"Yes, but what was the cause of this attitude? Was he always like this? It all smacks of a failed romance, if you ask me!"

"It was," Philip affirmed, and he told her about Lydia. "She could never really have loved him. In my opinion she only wanted him, to prove that she could get him. As soon as she was sure of him, the novelty began to wear off. But I am positive that they were most unsuited. Dominic would have become so tired of her within the first year, that he might have gone to the dogs from sheer boredom and disillusionment. As for me, I can only be grateful that it happened like that, because I found her hard to tolerate. A little of Lydia went a long way!"

"But it is unbelievable that a woman could do something like that!" What she really meant was that she failed to understand how any woman would let a man like *El-Hakim* slip through her fingers. "And that for an Arab about whom she knew nothing!" Thérèse was visibly shocked.

"For heaven's sake, don't ever let on that I have told you all this, Thérèse," he pleaded. "Dominic would be furious!"

"I shall be gone from here before the end of the week," she reminded him, "and what I know will never make any difference..."

She told him of how, coincidentally, she happened to be planning to go to South Africa, and about the hospital post for which she had applied, but realizing all at once, how late it was, she jumped to her feet.

"This will never do, Philip-brother. It's high time you were asleep, and I can hardly keep my eyes open!"

Philip was about to protest because there were many things he would still have liked to talk about, but she shook her head with mock sternness. "No, no! I'm not going to listen. The doctor gave orders that you should get plenty of rest. If you would like another glass of milk, I'll send it with Rameses." And with that she walked determinedly towards the door. "Night, Philip. Sleep well!"

(ii)

But she, herself, was unable to sleep. Too many thoughts were whirling through her brain

As she lay rehashing what Philip had told her, her own admiration for the desert physician mounted. To her mind, the fact that he was a specialist, made the sacrifice all the greater. She could not understand how she could have been so insulting on that first night, when, already dead tired from the responsibilities he carried, he was consumed with concern for his brother. One man could not possibly be expected to cope with all this alone.

In vain she tried to convince herself that her indignation had been warranted, that he had had no right to have her abducted, and that he, himself, was to blame for the arrogance that had so angered her. He had so infuriated her that she had wanted nothing more than to insult and humiliate him. Admittedly though, it was precisely that consummate self-confidence that made him so attractive.

She relived every moment that she had spent in his company. In her head she could hear that rich, vibrant voice, which could change so readily from amiable to contemptuous, and she could clearly recall every word he had ever said to her. Clear in her memory was a picture of blue eyes and golden hair, broad shoulders and, and—most vivid of all, those beautiful hands....

"For heaven's sake," she chided herself as she lay in the dark. "To fantasize like this about a man you've only seen half-a-dozen times, and must forget in a few days' time is ridiculous!" But still she could not fall asleep. *"El-Hakim,"* she said aloud in the darkness. *"Sahbena el Hakim*—my friend the doctor....I like it. It suits him!"

His personality was so compelling, she reflected, that his presence was almost tangible. The moment he left a room, it became like a deflated balloon; yet that magnetism still hovered in the air. Even in his tent she had been aware of it.

Suddenly she longed to be back there, to sleep again, among his personal possessions. Impulsively, but recalling that there was no electricity in the tent, she lit the lantern, grabbed her white coat, and ran outside barefoot, carrying the lantern with her.

Emerging from the hospital, she encountered Rameses—who was sitting on a step at the entrance—and almost startled him out of his wits. He immediately concluded that there must be some sort of trouble, but she only laughed roguishly. She felt daring, and was gripped with the wildest excitement.

"It is too hot inside, Rameses," she explained in her limited Arabic. "*Maleesh*!—It is nothing!" She pointed to Dominic's tent, miming, with her hand against her ear and tilting her head. "I go to sleep *there*...in the *Effendi*...in *El-Hakim's* tent."

Rameses must have understood, because he smiled and nodded his head. He took the lantern from her and carried it, leading the way, until they reached the tent, where he handed the light back to her, *salaaming* respectfully as he did so.

Once inside, she lit the bedside lamp, doused the lantern, and threw her coat over the camel saddle beside the divan, taking note of the fact that the little black book was not there. Then she climbed in under *El-Hakim's kaross*. She looked around her at the tapestries, smiled almost affectionately at the old rapier, blew out the lamp, and turned over with a sigh of contentment, to sleep.

(iii)

When, dusty and dead tired, Hamid Pasha returned to the stockade, the new day was dawning, and here and there a cock crowed. While still some distance away from where he would dismount at the gate of the hospital enclosure, he took leave of his men, first thanking them, and then giving instructions for them to be as quiet as possible as they went back to their tents. The sick were not to be disturbed. He and Raschid then proceeded alone, while the rest returned to their dwellings beyond the enclosure.

Both men and horses were almost stumbling with fatigue, and, for that reason, as soon as they had fetched two lanterns from the hospital, and had seen to the animals, Dominic told Raschid to go off to bed. The Indian was far too exhausted to attend to his leader's needs and it was not expected of him.

Dominic went straight to his tent. Oh, just to be able to sleep! At that moment nothing could be as enticing as a soft bed!

At the entrance to the tent, he stood still for a moment. He shook the sand from his hair, and beat the dust from his riding breeches with the flat of his hand. Never before had he felt so filthy. There was sand in his eyes, and grit between his teeth, and his throat was dry with it. He bent over, intending to light the lamp, but suddenly a muffled exclamation of astonishment escaped him. Someone was already in his bed, and a cloud of dark curls was spread across his pillow.

Perhaps because the turn of events at the meeting had left him so dejected, or perhaps because he, himself, felt so dirty, Thérèse, at that moment, seemed to him the cleanest and loveliest thing he had ever seen in his life. After the dust of the desert and the roughness of the men with whom he had been associating, she was like a fresh, spring breeze in South Africa. As she lay there with her eyelashes shadowing her face, she looked incredibly vulnerable...so innocent, and so small...and, with the rosy blush of sleep on her cheeks, so sweet. One tiny hand hung over the side of the divan.

He went closer, and looking down at her, his heart turned over. A feeling of tenderness, such as he had never experienced before, rose up in him, overwhelming him to the extent that, for a moment, he could hardly see. It overpowered him, and he knelt down beside her. He gently lifted the little hand that was resting on the floor, and tucked it under the blankets. Careful not to wake her, he pulled the *kaross* up to cover her shoulders, and then impulsively pressed a soft kiss on her forehead, before picking up the lantern and tiptoeing out to find an empty bed somewhere else.

CHAPTER TEN

That very afternoon he had Thérèse taken back to Cairo.

This time, besides the twins and Little Brother, whose responsibility it was to take her right to the hotel, she was also accompanied to the outskirts of the city by Raschid, Sezit, Rameses, Ali and half a dozen others, which she found strange. Considering that Haroun and Little Brother, by themselves, had brought her the whole way to the hospital, why did *El-Hakim* now suddenly find it necessary to send such a large contingent to accompany her on the way back?

While she found this very odd, what she could understand, even less, was the reason for his wanting to be rid of her so quickly. Although there were no further cases of the mysterious fever, the care of the remaining patients still demanded much time and energy, and he was visibly almost dead on his feet. However, they had no sooner risen from the noon repast, than he informed her that she was free to return.

"I am not expected at the hotel until tomorrow," she reminded him. "When Mamoun dictated that letter, he obviously anticipated that you would be away longer than you actually were. Perhaps I can continue to be of use to you for a short while longer, *El-Hakim*. I have already decided to bury the hatchet and I am quite willing to stand in for you tonight."

But *El-Hakim* firmly, albeit politely, refused the offer, and once back in her room at the hotel, she felt bitterly hurt, and constantly found herself mulling over the turn of events. It was true that he had promised that he would allow her to return as soon as possible, but that was before they had come to know each other better. Could he not see that she was no longer either as unwilling or uncooperative as—for good reason—she had seemed upon her arrival? Besides, the speculated incubation period for the fever had not yet expired.

No! There had to be another reason, and she was despondently forced to face up to what that reason was. He disliked women.—To him they were nothing but a burden and an aggravation—and he could not get her out of his way fast enough.

There was however, one, small incident which provided a degree of consolation. Just before he had tied the blindfold over her eyes, he had looked at her closely for a moment and then, taking both her hands firmly in his, he had said: "Thank you, Princess Thérèse, for all that you have done for us. You did your work here with amazing competence, and, from all that I have heard from my patients, I know that you did more than your duty....Far more than I had asked of you...and I sincerely appreciate that!"

He could at least have come a little way with her, she thought. Philip was probably the only one who might perhaps miss her.

***

She wandered listlessly through her suite, and half-heartedly smelled the roses that the hotel manager had sent up to her, as soon as he had learned that she was back. *Here* Mamoun had stood while explaining his assignment to her.

There the pen and pad still lay where she had left them. If it had not been for a slight tenderness in her upper arm, where Dominic had given her that injection, she could easily have believed that the events of the past week had been only a dream.

Eventually, lonely and tired of her own company, she picked up the telephone and put a call through to Gerda. Everyone at the Talbots' seemed gratifyingly pleased to learn that she was back, but, of course, Gerda was not happy that she had not let anyone know that she planned to go away. Thérèse responded with a garbled story about an old school friend from Soravia who had been taken ill while visiting in Alexandria, and because the baroness had no reason to doubt her, she believed her unconditionally. She, Gerda, went on to tell that she had received a cable from Otto, to say that he had arrived at his destination safely. She also invited Thérèse to go to the theatre with her crowd, after dinner that evening.

But *there* it was no different....Thérèse simply could not become immersed in the tragedy unfolding before their eyes. And back in her suite she rolled around restlessly in her bed until the early hours.

(ii)

It was actually a relief when Gerda suggested the tour. Two days after the princess's return, the Von Mölendorffs telephoned to give her the great news. They were finally returning home the following week. The baron had expressed the desire to revisit as much of the area as possible, during the time they had left in Egypt, and once again Thérèse was invited to accompany them.

They spent four days looking at the pyramids, museums,

the sphinx and other places of interest—all of which she saw in a blur. In the great mosque of Mohamed Ali she listened half-heartedly to the guide's explanation of the fact that no statues were permitted, and how the Muezzin called the faithful to prayer because bells were also prohibited.

The Gezira Club offered facilities for every sport and pastime, but no remedy for a lead weight in the heart.

In the Nile valley she learned disinterestedly that the name, 'Egypt', meant 'Black Land', but was hardly excited by the explanation that the name actually referred only to the black earth of the Nile. The famous blue Egyptian lotus, the *Nymphaea caerula*, was just another water lily.

But there, in the valley, she made two other discoveries.... Two discoveries that, to her, were more important than life itself. First she discovered that she could not live without Dominic Verwey, and secondly?...Well, their hotel was brimming over with tourists—all particularly wealthy. An irresistible target for Hamid Pasha!

On the same night on which the Baron and Baroness Von Mölendorff, and the Princess Thérèse of Soravia arrived at the place, the pasha launched a raid and got away with more than five hundred pounds sterling, in jewellery and cash. On the small patio where Thérèse sat, sipping a cold drink, she witnessed the entire affair, speechless with shock. Although they waited with the horses, some distance away, she would have recognized the dwarfs and Raschid anywhere; and it so happened that, when the robber-captain galloped past her, a strong gust of wind just happened to blow back the hood of his *burnous.* It was with great difficulty that she restrained herself from crying out. That blond head was unmistakeable. And Arabs do not have golden hair!

CHAPTER ELEVEN

She came back to the hotel in a wretched state of mind. After having to take leave of Gerda and Ferdinand von Mölendorff, she felt deserted and utterly desolate.

Against her better judgment she had fallen in love with a man about whom she knew nothing. A mysterious, enigmatic desert-physician who had, in any case, not given her the slightest encouragement—and now she had to discover that he was a thief, and, quite probably, a murderer to boot. She should have recognized him the moment she walked into his office, but her subconscious mind had refused that. How, at the hospital gate, she had not connected that magnificent white stallion and the white *burnous* with Hamid Pasha, she would never be able to fathom, but now she understood why he had seemed impatient, and so visibly disconcerted when she had run after him.

Why did women always have to be so perverse? There was Otto; upright, decent, honest, and the nephew of her best friend, but she could not choose *him*!...Oh, no! She had to go and throw away her love on the outlaw, Hamid Pasha! What made it so very much worse, was that the discovery that *El-Hakim* and 'Hamid Pasha' were one and the same, could do nothing to dull the longing in her heart!

On the way back to the hotel she was further disturbed when, everywhere on the streets, she saw newspaper vendors in white trousers and red fezzes, carrying placards on which she read headlines printed in scarlet The words danced before her eyes like flames…

MUSTAPHA MISSING
HAMID PASHA SUSPECTED OF ABDUCTION

In one English newspaper the headlines read: "Important official missing, believed kidnapped. Reward for capture of Hamid Pasha doubled."

She should have known that the hotel *dragoman* would wax eloquent on the subject of the pasha. It is said that when a *dragoman* attaches himself to a group of tourists, nothing less than a shotgun can shake him off, and, like all other members of his profession, this one's excellent command of several languages stood him in good stead, as he latched onto tourists well before they set foot on the threshold of the establishment. He tried hard to live up to the reputation of 'knowing everything about everybody'. Their line of business, where they came from, and their financial situation.…The first, by skilful probing, and the last, of course, by the size of the tip.

The one at Thérèse's hotel might well have been knowledgeable, but when he started airing his views on the subject of the pasha, she immediately wrote him off angrily as a 'know-all'. How perverse of her, she thought, when she had to acknowledge that the man could be right.

"That Hamid Pasha has really overstepped the mark this time, Excellency," he informed her garrulously, helping her out of the taxi, and observing that she had glanced at the placard held up by a boy on the sidewalk. "Mustapha is indeed an important man. A member of the *Maglis ash Shuyukh*—the senate, no less!"

"How can you be so sure that Hamid Pasha is involved?" she asked hesitantly, cold right down to her toes.

"Oh, he's the one, without a doubt," the dragoman assured her. "Apparently Mustapha informed the police last night that he would shortly be able to furnish them with proof of the kidnapper's identity. He promised to bring the truth concerning all these crimes that have lately been committed, before the senate next week!"

"So you have automatically concluded that he was referring to Hamid Pasha?"

"Highness, I don't just think so.—Everyone *knows* it!"

***

On the small table in her hallway she found a letter bearing a South African postmark. Upon reading it, she was informed of her acceptance at a clinic in East London. Quite beside herself, she tossed the envelope back onto the table, for the *dragoman* had done nothing to improve the situation by adding, as an afterthought: "Right at this moment we have a representative of the Bank of England here, searching for a missing colleague, and they reckon the pasha's got him, too!"—She had not considered it necessary to ask him if he could tell her the missing man's name...!

Far too upset to mingle with other people, she ordered room service, but later, when the waiter came to take the tray away, it was to find her dinner untouched.

She went to bed early—but not to sleep. How she missed the clear, cooler air to which she was fast becoming accustomed when *El-Hakim* had seen fit to banish her to the city once more!

Despite the suffocating heat, she was obliged to keep the windows shut on account of the deafening noise. It was the ninth month of the Mohammedan year, and the start of Ramadan, and she could easily have believed that the entire population of Cairo was milling around in the street directly below her. Ramadan being the period of fasting during which all pious Muslims ate and drank nothing between sunrise and sunset, she thought it was probably relief from hunger that drove the people to stay awake all night and carry on like this. At intervals, old-fashioned fifteen-pounders were fired off to call the faithful to prayer. Only with the ascent of the new moon, would Ramadan come to an end.

Her thoughts wandered to Raschid and others of Dominic's people, speculating on how they would be observing the fast, and it was then that the most awful thought occurred to her.... Could not that so-called 'medical conference' he had gone to attend, perhaps have been another raid on yet another poor, innocent individual? Had she toiled away in the hospital only to enable Hamid Pasha to go out and commit another crime? Tears stung her eyes as she saw the bitter irony in her offer to stay longer. Of course she had to be taken out of the way—to make room for the unsuspecting Mustapha!

The only comfort she could find in this ghastly mess lay in the memory of how well the banker was treated. It must have been the doctor in Hamid Pasha who had suggested, *"Perhaps you could just pop in sometimes and have a further word with Christopher Brent. He needs to talk more...to be stimulated..."* And she could hear Dominic's kindly, indulgent chuckle as he said: *"We allow him the odd snifter of cognac occasionally...because he seems to like it, and it cheers him up!"*—But then, to counteract that, there was also the disquieting memory of: *"We brought him here unconscious....He only knows that he is a banker, because we have told him so...!"*

How had Brent been rendered unconscious, in the first

place? Reduced to not even knowing who he was? Would they treat Mustapha less kindly?...Torture him, perhaps?...Could a doctor bring himself to do things like that?

How she wished that, during the times she and Ezra had worked together in the clinic, and she had had the opportunity to question him, she had probed more deeply into the subject of the two brothers, whose last name she had learned from him.

What a nice man Ezra was! And so knowledgeable, on so many subjects. While he was as devout a Jew as her father had been a Christian, there was something about him that reminded her acutely of her revered parent. She had also been quick to notice that, whenever he spoke of Dominic, there was the same warmth in his voice that she had detected in Philip's. At the same time, he had made it abundantly clear that, while he loved and respected both Verweys, his admiration for *El-Hakim* knew no bounds.

In the doctor's absence, he seemed to feel responsible for the younger brother, and more than once expressed his frustration at not being permitted to venture into the isolation area, though masked and gowned. He wanted to see for himself that all was well with Philip, he insisted, and also complained good naturedly about the fact that his good friend and 'tent mate' Raschid, had no sooner been let out of quarantine than he was off somewhere with *El-Hakim*!

It was interesting how, on one occasion, when she happened to comment on the opulence of *El-Hakim's* tent, Ezra had been very quick to point out that that was certainly not due to any extravagance on the doctor's part.

"That boy has nothing but the clothes on his back!" he had chuckled indulgently. "And he would not have spent a single piaster on them, himself, if there had been anything else here, big enough to fit him!"

"Surely he must receive quite generous remuneration for all that he does!" she had exclaimed. "His qualifications alone—and added to that, the isolation of this hospital—would warrant it."

This time Ezra, turning to look at her with undisguised surprise, had to laugh out loud. "No one here receives *monetary* remuneration, Princess!...Least of all our friend, the doctor. I believe that what he derives from his work is far more precious to him than money. The man is completely dedicated..."

"But then, who feeds and clothes everyone?" She was growing more confused by the minute.

"*He* does!—But I think we had better leave it at that," Ezra said, firmly but tactfully, giving her to suspect that she had been asking too many intrusive questions.

Somewhat crestfallen, and needing to change the subject, she said conversationally: "Among all the Persian and Arabian wall-hangings in his tent, there is one that puzzles me. The one with the elephants...I would perhaps have expected camels..."

"I know the one you mean," Ezra responded. "It's Raschid's favourite, very likely because he was a *mahout* in India once, but remember that Hannibal is said to have crossed the Alps with African elephants, so it is not quite as incongruous as one would think. Everything in *El-Hakim's* tent was entrusted to him by his predecessor who, in turn, must have brought with him a few family treasures, inherited from his family..."

"Like that wonderful rapier?" she interposed enthusiastically. "Was it used in some significant battle perhaps? Could the man's father have been a soldier?"

"In that case," Ezra told her, with a benevolent, quite paternal smile, "he most certainly would not have used *that* one! Rapiers were designed for duelling and not as weapons of war, as sabres were. *El-Hakim's* predecessor was a humble and extremely modest man—not a physician, but as dedicated, in his way, as our friend the doctor is—and would never have boasted of wealthy or aristocratic ancestry. But, to me, that rapier suggests an owner who could have been of the nobility, or at least a man holding a high position in society.

"Rapiers with jewelled hilts were typically not used in any form of combat, but as a dress accessory among the very wealthy. Just as a woman of status would wear costly jewellery, so a man of high standing would carry an expensive rapier at his side. Being made of soft, precious metal, perhaps gold—or at least silver—such hilts would not stand up to the rigors of combat; nor would their owners risk damaging them by actually using them.

"A usable weapon would have a hilt made of steel which would probably not be much adorned, other than perhaps a jewel set in the pommel".—He warmed to the subject.— "Somewhere, where it would not likely be dislodged and lost during combat. Furthermore, usable blades and hilts of that period were made of steel, either cast or forged by hand, and even the best-made weapons could crack or break....A cracked or broken hilt could likely be repaired but a damaged blade would need to be replaced or re-forged."

This was a fascinating subject, but she had to risk another question while the going was good. "Would *El-Hakim* ever use it in, say, a duel?"

"Maybe he'd take it to a ball or feast, or some other such gala affair," Ezra chuckled, "if he ever had the time or the opportunity, but definitely not into battle."

"Yes, but what I really meant to ask was, is he skilled with a sword?"

"My dear young lady," was the emphatic response, "he is

amazingly skilled! And not only with the rapier!…I would never want to come against him brandishing a sabre, a scimitar…or a rifle, either!"

Those words had been etched into her brain!

She with all her boasting! *"I regard it as the duty of all lovers of justice to join forces, and not to rest until that felon is behind bars!"*

No wonder Philip had laughed! Why should she not call Sir Humphrey, right away, and tell him what she knew? In fact, she had a good mind to do so

She tossed and turned, desperately punching her pillow, threshing about and wriggling her toes until the sheets lay in a disorderly heap on the floor.

It was her duty to inform the police, but wouldn't it be better to take the easy way out, cable South Africa, and leave right away?…Would her conscience haunt her forever, if she were to leave Egypt without doing her civic duty?

Once before she had protected Hamid Pasha. Her cheeks burned at the recollection of that burning kiss on the balcony. Had he remembered it when he saw her again? How he must have been laughing up his sleeve at her! Even just for that, he deserved that she should tell!—But oh, as Ruth had said: "He has the bluest eyes I have ever seen!"

Involuntarily her thoughts shot off at a tangent here.

One night, during one of their chats, Philip had told her how Dominic had come by his uncommon name. His father, also a specialist in tropical medicine, had been in Central Africa when he died; stricken with one of the very diseases he was researching. Alone in the jungle, his widow had had to give birth to her first child. Providentially she was found by a group of Dominican nuns who saved both her life and that of her son.

Out of gratitude she had named her boy after the founder of their order. Philip was the child of her second marriage, which explained why the brothers differed so much from one another in appearance.

Thérèse had quite an extensive knowledge of the Roman saints. Convents had traditionally been the schools of choice for children of the Soravian nobility, and although, like the Verwey brothers, she was not a Catholic, herself, she was well acquainted with the story of Saint Dominic.—The man with the beautiful face, about whom, from the time of his birth, there had been numerous prophecies concerning what a great, heroic man of God he would be...The saint who had founded an order of which the monks had become the foremost scholars of philosophy and theology in the whole of Europe.

Saint Dominic, it was said, had loathed any idea of fighting, and had believed, with all his heart, that Truth would triumph...without bloodshed or violence! Well, thought Thérèse bitterly, he had certainly acquired a fine namesake for himself! She could not help wondering what his mother would have thought of *her* Dominic!

***

It is indeed wondrous how the small things in life often turn out to be the most vital. Dominic Verwey would never have dreamt how a coincidence would save him.—But was it coincidence? Actually, although Thérèse did not believe that there was any such thing, she would, for some time, be unable to find a more suitable word to apply to what happened next. At this critical juncture, in a desperately unhappy state, and so bewildered that she could hardly think straight, she had already moved towards the telephone—but then...just as she was about to phone Sir Humphrey...what should save Dominic Verwey?—His *hands*!

Still reminiscing about all that the nuns at the convent had taught about the saint, among other things that, in addition to the perfection of his face, he had such remarkably beautiful hands, she grew quite weak in the knees as she permitted her thoughts to dwell on the singular, heart-stopping beauty of *El-Hakim's*. That he who had dedicated himself to the healing of the sick, and brought new lives into the world—the 'Father of the desert' and of everyone to whom his skill was freely available—should perhaps hang like a common murderer! The vision of that proud, golden head bent in shame, left her in the most extreme agony of spirit. She shrank from the mental image of those powerful wrists in shackles.

With an audible groan of pain, she sank down onto her bed.

"Oh, Dominic, Dominic!" she moaned. "Why did you have to do this?"

In great agitation, she could not sit still. She rose to her feet and went to stand by the window. Far below her, people appeared to crawl around like ants. Neon lights flashed all over the city, rendering the stars dull by contrast. It was not like this in the desert. There it was peaceful and the stars twinkled as brightly as the stones in the hilt of the rapier that hung in *El-Hakim's* tent.

And then she knew that she was lost! Let him do what he would, she loved him and nothing could ever change that! She would go to a land that would, forever, painfully remind her of him—but his secret would be safe!

What if he really had abducted that man?—Hadn't she seen for herself that his men robbed people?—But did he not perhaps have a reason for doing so?...What was love without trust? She supposedly loved him so madly, but how quick she had been to condemn him!

What was it he had said about the hospital's being funded 'mostly by contributions'? *"Usually people are loathe to give,"* he had said, *"but we usually succeed in persuading them!"* That was of course what he had meant. 'Persuaded'—with a gun or a sabre!

The sincerity in his voice when he had stated that hundreds of lives depended upon his attending that gathering, had not been feigned. Even if the 'meeting' had been of a less conventional nature than was normally the case, she now believed with all her heart, that he had not gone there for his own gain.

A thousand times happier than she had been when she had previously climbed into bed she was asleep as soon as her head touched the pillow.

(ii)

Morning presented its own problems.—First of all, there was that letter from South Africa. She had made up her mind the night before, that she would go, but in the secret places of her heart a different plan had begun to unfold. At some stage between sleep and waking, a vague aspiration had begin to sprout, and, as the day wore on, that desire grew into a wild, irrepressible urge. Not since the day when she had taken that last, heartbreaking look at the ruins of her family's palace, and had impulsively asked to be taken straight to the nearest Red Cross dépôt to volunteer for duty—anywhere she could be of service—had she felt like this. But the compulsion she had felt that day, now paled in comparison. Then she had been trying to escape from horror, she knew that now. This time she was running after happiness.

Philip had told her that Dominic had dedicated himself to an ideal; one that he would not relinquish until his goal had been reached. Surely, somewhere on earth, a mission that would make her life worthwhile awaited her, too....But why did it necessarily have to be in South Africa?

Dominic Verwey did not have the slightest interest in her, but it would bring her the greatest joy and fulfilment to know that she was contributing to the realization of his dream. Besides, how could she go so far away, never to see him again?

Her eyes sparkled and her face shone with excitement. She hurried over to the telephone, and this time she did call the Talbots.

Ruth took her call, and Thérèse rapidly expressed her request. She was leaving again, immediately, and would be away for an indefinite time, she told the girl, and she had called to ask if she might have her mail forwarded to the mansion as she did not yet know what her permanent address would be. She also asked, and received permission from Lady Talbot, to send some of her things over, for storage until she returned. Where she was going, her large trunks would be unnecessary.

Then she requested the clerk at the front desk to ask the *dragoman* to come up to her room, and to have her bill ready as soon as possible, as she expected to depart at any moment.

CHAPTER TWELVE

When Mamoun, Haroun and Little Brother set off from the stockade early that morning, they had no premonition of what the day would bring. It was their habit to leave before dawn on Thursdays, in order to reach Cairo and complete their business in the marketplaces before the worst heat of the day. After that they would eat, have a snooze somewhere in the shade, and then point their camels in a homeward direction.

When she had been in the hospital enclosure on the previous Thursday, Thérèse had been able to infer, from something Mamoun said, that he and the other two were off to the city for supplies. She found the dwarf's French/Arabic pronunciation of English a trifle difficult to understand at times, but there had been nothing obscure in his kind offer to bring back for her anything she might require.

Unless there was a sudden, urgent need for something, he had explained, they only did this once a week, and because of that they had to take more than one camel. Now, this again being a Thursday, she would have to bank on that one day a week always being the same....Her entire future depended on that seven-to-one chance. The cable bearing the news that she was unable to take up the position, was on its way to South Africa, and she had already said her goodbyes to the Talbots.

Clad in her riding habit and accompanied by the *dragoman,* she roamed the marketplace, wandering through one bazaar after another, fascinated by the colourful, striped canvas booths, and the variety of tempting merchandise. She looked with delight at the enchanting little pointed slippers that hung over every doorway, between bunches of luscious, exotic fruit. She fingered finely crafted ornaments of ivory, silver, and gold wire mesh, turned over scarab rings, brooches and necklaces, and examined jewellery boxes skilfully crafted in olive and aromatic sandalwood. Despite the novelty of all she saw, she was never, for one second, left unaware of the excitement in her wildly beating heart.

The *dragoman* stayed close to her side as she squeezed her way between Indians with teeth, lips and tongues stained red from the inevitable betel nut, or 'pugua'—the 'palm nuts' from the areca—that they constantly chewed. Fumes of incense assailed her nostrils, while fragrances emanating from every perfume boutique, mingled with the aroma of the strong, Turkish coffee traditionally served to clients within.

And then, suddenly, she saw them and froze in her tracks!

She fumbled frantically in the pockets of her breeches for a few piasters and dropped them into the *dragoman's* palm. "Please bring the horse I hired this morning, to me, here, as quickly as possible, and I will pay you then. After that you may return to the hotel.—And please *hurry!*"

Because, in this crowd, it was easy to lose sight of them, she fixed her eyes on the twins and Little Brother, taking careful note of where they went to rest in a patch of shade cast by the booths. During Ramadan they would not linger to eat.

As soon as the dragoman brought the horse, she paid him, and then led her hired mount to within thirty yards of where the three were sitting. There, with her head and shoulders covered by the coarse, brown *burnous* she had earlier purchased especially for this purpose, she sat down, too, to wait. Her heart was beating even more tumultuously than before, and the hand with which she clutched at the bridle shook ridiculously, in spite of her efforts to control it.

After what seemed like an eternity, the twins rose to their feet, and Mamoun gestured to Haroun and Little Brother to bring the animals. Thérèse rechecked the straps of the saddlebag into which she had stuffed only the direst necessities, and then, with an unspoken prayer on her lips, she led her horse closer.

(ii)

They had hardly gone two miles beyond the city limits when Mamoun, the observant one, realized that all was not well. Back home in Soravia Thérèse had been considered an above average horsewoman, but she lacked a great deal in the art of tracking and pursuit. In addition, she was ignorant of that unwritten rule of the desert, that one never crept up on anyone from behind. Far safer to approach boldly and openly— unless you were particularly well practised.

After a while Mamoun turned around in his saddle and pointed to the dust cloud behind them.

"I am now inclined to suspect that person of following us. Every time we have urged our horses into a gallop, he has also accelerated his pace—but, whoever he is, he follows with such ineptness that he can hardly be a formidable enemy."

"That might be," Haroun remarked in his squeaky voice, "but that does not mean that we may allow him to approach unimpeded. You know very well, esteemed brother, how even Hamid Pasha, the wise one, and the others were followed. Someone is assuredly trying to find our hiding place."

Mamoun had to agree, but planned no confrontation while

they were in the open desert. He deemed it wiser to give the spy a chance to engender his own downfall.

Eventually they reached the slopes of the mountain chain in which the stockade was situated, and dragging the camels behind them, immediately headed for the mouth of the narrow pass so familiar to them. Once there, they dismounted quickly, and while Little Brother, led the animals to where he could hide with them behind a massive outcrop of rock, the twins nimbly climbed up two relatively leafy trees which grew on either side of the path, secreting themselves where they had the best view of their surroundings.

Meanwhile Thérèse had valiantly kept going, spurred on by sheer adrenalin. She became concerned, however, when she lost sight of the three ahead of her. In the open desert it had been easy to keep them in sight, but she had not foreseen the problem that the mountains now presented. Her first thought was that she had turned the wrong way at some stage. In front of her were only rocks and a few, scrubby trees. Not the slightest puff of dust betrayed the direction the others had taken.

The sun blazed down upon her mercilessly, her back felt as if it would break, and she was so thirsty that she was close to hallucinating, but she did not for a single moment regret that she had come.—Nothing mattered as long as, at the end of the journey, she found Dominic. Meanwhile her only fear was that she might be lost.

At the entrance to the pass, she reined in her horse, uncertain of how to proceed and looking anxiously around her. She listened intently, but everything was deathly quiet. Suddenly a staff swished through the air, and then everything around her went black.

***

Mamoun let go of his *nabbut* before scrambling down the tree, as the pursuer, slumped in the saddle, slowly began to topple over to one side. Then the mountains echoed with the strangest sound ever heard there before. It was not unlike the pitiable trumpeting of a wounded elephant in agony.

Little Brother, seeing the hood fall back to expose the person's head and face, had immediately recognized Thérèse. It needed only one or two strides of his uncommonly long legs to reach her side, and his great height enabled him to reach over and catch her before she fell. Lifting her carefully from the saddle, and taking her into his equally long, spindly arms, he sank down upon the ground, cradling her like a baby. "*Ahwee, ahwee!*" he keened inarticulately, rocking her gently while tears streamed down his gaunt face. "*Ahwee!* We have killed the princess!...We have destroyed the dear little thing!"

Mamoun rushed over to look, waddling as fast as he could. "May Allah be merciful!" he cried fearfully. "You are right, Little Brother. It is indeed the princess, and we have killed her!"

(iii)

Dominic was strolling through the stockade with Philip, followed by a string of healthy, sturdy little ones—many of whom they had, from time to time, treated for various ailments, scrapes and bruises, and some they had brought into the world. His people could see that *El-Hakim* was happy, now that his brother was well enough to enjoy a walk in the sunshine at last. Rejoicing with him, as far as he went, the Bedouin welcomed them both with friendly smiles that lit up their faces.

Women sat on their haunches outside of their tents,

occupied with their individual chores. Many were engaged in grinding their own semolina, which they would later steam with meat and vegetables to make *couscous* for their families to eat during the hours in which they were permitted to break their fast. Others, perhaps waiting for the camels to return with supplies that Mamoun and the other two were bringing back from the city, were occupied with various activities such as the weaving of cloth. Meanwhile, making the most of a quiet day, the men lay around wherever there was shade, trying to outdo each other with tales of their heroic youth, but rose to their feet as their leader appeared.

It was sublimely still and peaceful in the valley. Not a cloud marred the clear blue of the sky, and not a blade of grass stirred. But suddenly the peace was disturbed by a commotion up at the hospital gate. At the same time, Dominic noticed Little Brother hastening towards him, and there was blood on his garments.

"*Sahbena*!" he panted, approaching as fast as his spidery legs could carry him. "Come quickly!"

As Philip was still too weak to run, and seemed to enjoy just being in the open air once more, Dominic left him to follow at his leisure, assuring him that he did not need help. Mystified, he himself hurriedly accompanied the trembling and obviously shaken Little Brother.

A sizeable crowd had already gathered around Thérèse where she lay on her cloak in the sand at the foot of the hospital steps, but as soon as they saw him coming, people made room for Dominic to pass. He stared with disbelief at the unconscious girl on the ground, and then with a smothered cry, he sprang forward and knelt beside her.

"Oh, my Lord! How did this happen?"

"It was my fault, *Effendi*," Mamoun whimpered anxiously.

"I struck her on the head with my *nabbut*!...The poor, dear little thing!" he echoed Little Brother. "What has Mamoun done?"

Dominic hardly heard him. He effortlessly picked up the limp little body in his powerful arms, and carried her into the hospital where, with great care, and hating to make her lie on the hard surface, he laid her down on the table in the clinic. With quick, practised fingers, he took her pulse, and then expertly examining her head, found, among the silky blue-black curls, the wound from which she had been bleeding. He looked around fleetingly and saw Mamoun cowering in the doorway.

"If you have cracked her skull, Mamoun," he vowed, totally unlike himself, "I'll darned well crack yours, too!"

The unhappy dwarf nodded. "That is what I deserve, *Effendi*," he replied resignedly.

Dominic, normally so self-assured, needed a moment to compose himself. He furiously kicked the door shut with his foot. But then, not wanting to remove any of Thérèse's clothing unnecessarily, in order to check for further injury, he thought better of it, and opened the door again, to find Mamoun still standing in the passage, together with Haroun and Little Brother, who had joined him in the meantime.

"She is not bleeding so profusely any more, you will be pleased to know, and you can tell me later how this happened," he told them, a little more calmly. "But what I need to know now is, how did she fall? Could any bones be broken?"

"No, *Sahbena*," Mamoun assured him. "She was on her horse, and Little Brother caught her before she fell. He carried her from the pass to here."

"Good...Thank you. Now please fetch Meriam immediately, and ask Philip-brother to send me one of his clean shirts for her to wear. Like this "—he indicated, by placing his hand sideways against his upper arm, that it should be short-sleeved—"or did she bring any clothing with her?"

"There is a saddle bag, *Effendi*..." Haroun volunteered.

"Well bring that, too. Please be quick!"

He cut away as little as possible of the lovely hair, dressed the wound, filled a basin with warm water and then, as though she were a child, gently wiped away the blood and desert dust from the exquisite face and incredibly small hands and feet. He would have to wait until she regained consciousness to see how good her reflexes were. In the meantime, when Meriam arrived she helped him remove Thérèse's bloodstained blouse and replace it with the shirt she, Meriam, had brought. Then Dominic carried the precious burden down the corridor, and, as he set her down on the bed in which she had slept less than two weeks before, he could only offer a prayer of thanksgiving...

What a blessing it was that Mamoun's insecure position in the tree, coupled with the shortness of his arms and the length and weight of the *nabbut*, had deprived him of sufficient leverage to inflict what could have been a fatal blow!

CHAPTER THIRTEEN

Thérèse found herself floating in a haze of pain. Her pulse hammered at her temples and the sound of it grew louder…and louder…until she felt that her head would burst if she did not open her eyes. In addition to the pounding in her ears, a different sound coaxed her to return to her senses. A sound to which, with her whole heart and soul, she wanted to respond.

"Thérèse!"

That was surely the most wonderful voice in the world, and it sounded so concerned.

"Thérèse…open your eyes," the voice pleaded from a very long way off. If it would only come closer, it might possibly be Dominic's.

The pounding became a roar, so overpowering now, that she could hold out no longer. The voice also seemed nearer to her, and it was too enticing to withstand. Her eyes flew open and she sighed. It was only a dream!

Dominic was sitting beside her bed with the most anxious look on his face, but frustratingly, before she could determine what he was doing there, the dream-image faded. However, he *did* have a very nice face, her wandering thoughts led her to conclude.

"Thérèse!" He called again and, opening her eyes, she saw that he was smiling, and that his teeth were perfect, and very white in that suntanned face. "You *must* try to keep awake!" He shook her arm gently.

It was *not* a dream! He was really here. There was no mistake! Her hand was being held very tightly in one of his, oh, so comforting ones. An answering smile of contentment spread across her face and she closed her eyes again. He was so big and so strong, and she was safely here with him at last...

Presently the hammering in her temples began again. She slowly raised her heavy eyelids and groaned. "I have such a headache!"

"Never mind," he comforted her. "Now that you are conscious, and as soon as I have had a good look at you, I shall give you something for the pain. Just lie still while I check your pupils and your eye movements.—Do you feel at all nauseous?...No?...Good!...Now squeeze my fingers..."

He pulled down the sheets. "Let me see you lift your legs slowly, one at a time, and see how slowly you can put them down again....So far, so good!"

After he had covered her again, he opened the door and the window, hoping to create a draught because the room was like an oven, and then he brought the promised capsules, which he held out to her, and a glass of water which he set down on the table beside her.

She was lying flat on her back, and Dominic slid his arm under her shoulders to raise her slightly before she drank the water he proffered. Even this slight movement made her wince with pain. She moaned involuntarily.

"It is better that you lie flat," he told her sympathetically as he lowered her again, very gently. "Now you must not be concerned about anything at all. It is *our* turn to take care of *you*."

It was unbelievable that it was to her that he could speak so lovingly. He was clearly unaware of the fact that he still had his arm under her shoulders, and he softly stroked the hair sticking out from under the bandage, from her forehead. In spite of the wooziness, she could detect a look in his eyes that had never been there before. They were no longer that cold, steely blue, but like the warm, friendly ocean in summer.

For a wild moment she wondered if her were about to kiss her, but his arm tightened suddenly, as he was distracted and had to turn his head. It was at that moment that Philip, as white as a sheet, came storming through the door. He took one look at the bandage and stumbled forward.

"Thérèse, dear Princess Of Hearts, what have they done to you?"

As dizzy as Thérèse was, she was immediately aware of the change in Dominic. His expression hardened, as his face took on that unapproachable look once more. He slowly withdrew his arm and stood up, stretching himself to his full height, as though challenging anyone to suspect that *El-Hakim* of the desert would ever be guilty of weakness.

"There is nothing about which you need to concern yourself unduly, Phil," he said stiffly. "I have done only a baseline evaluation, but the lady fortunately seems to have an uncomplicated concussion, if my diagnosis it correct..."

In his agitation, Philip had bumped against the bed and Thérèse was unable to hide the pain this caused, prompting Dominic, who had been watching her, to command: "The princess has to try and sleep now, Philip. I have given her capsules for her headache."

"CAPSULES! For what must be excruciating pain!" Philip cried furiously. "You could at least have given her a shot of morphine!"

"Don't be ridiculous, Philip," was Dominic's sharp response. "You have assisted me often enough to know by now that morphine can disguise a serious head injury! This is not the first time I have mourned the fact that we do not have X-Ray equipment, but, as we don't, I'm giving her nothing else until I can satisfy myself that there is nothing more serious wrong with her. I doubt if she has suffered any serious degree of bruising or haemorrhage, but as soon as I have had sufficient time to establish what there might be, she will be given a shot of Pethedine—if necessary—and nothing else! Ten years ago," he went on defensively, and quite unnecessarily belabouring the point, "I would not have believed that I would have penicillin to treat infection—instead of having to rely solely on sulfa drugs—so, maybe some day, someone will come up with an alternative painkiller for this purpose....But that's all I have to work with right now!"

For only the second time in their lives, the brothers confronted one another with hostility. Years before it had been because Philip had dared to suggest that Lydia was fickle and untrustworthy. This time it was worse, because, while both were equally angry, neither would have admitted the cause of that anger, even to themselves. The atmosphere in the room had become charged with tension, and antagonism hung between them like a naked sword.

All at once Dominic felt guilty and, stabbed by the expression on his patient's sweet face, his demeanour changed instantly. "Thérèse is definitely not in the mood for an altercation at the moment," he said crisply. "Besides, I have work to do. If you can pull yourself together sufficiently, brother, I feel sure that you won't need too much persuasion to sit here with her.... Please let me know if she needs anything..."

And with that he marched out of the room.

(ii)

She did later fall asleep for a while for, apart from taking the medication, she had been up before dawn, and the journey across the desert had been long and tiring. Her last thought before she dozed, was that Philip was himself still too weak to be sitting there for so long.

Her first thought, when she awoke, was to wonder when and how she had come to be wearing a man's shirt, and then she noticed that Philip had gone and Dominic was once more at her bedside. It was pitch dark outside. A lamp on the table in the corner had been lit to provide the light by which *El-Hakim* sat reading his little book.

"What is the time?" she asked drowsily. "Have I been asleep for long?"

He looked up and his smile, though still friendly, was more guarded, which did not escape her. "It's about eleven-thirty. I sent Philip off to bed."

"But you should not be up so late, either, *El-Hakim...*"

"I'm not a bit tired," he assured her. "I have become accustomed to ungodly hours.—How are you feeling now?"

"Still a trifle dizzy and a bit confused," she smiled faintly. "But the headache is better."

"I'm very pleased to hear that." He stood up. "Lie very quietly. I'll be back in a minute."

He went out, to return some minutes later with the famous 'egg-flip', made of goats' milk, fruit and egg, which he had prescribed for Philip, and he helped her to sit up and drink it. She was disappointed to realize that, although he still treated her kindly, there was no tenderness. Instead there was a decided restraint in his manner. That precious moment was gone, never to return.

"There is a little sugar and a trace of vanilla in this, to take away the taste of the goats' milk.—Raschid's speciality, because he is a Muslim....He tells me, however, that the inventor of this beverage, the father of my predecessor, had recommended the addition of a drop of brandy, on appropriate occasions, as a 'pick-me-up' for battle fatigue."

"That's what you told me to give to Philip," she reminded him. "I learnt to drink goats' milk while I was nursing during the war," she reassured him. "We all did, and there was never a single case of Malta fever among the lot of us."

"It was the same with us, depending on where we were," he replied, helping her to lie down again.

This was the first time they had ever engaged in anything akin to conversation. "So you were in the army too," she remarked thoughtfully. "Do you know, Doctor, when I arrived here on that very first night, I was absolutely certain that I had seen you somewhere before."

"And now? Have you decided where that was?" He set the glass down carefully, not betraying any sign of the concern she had just provoked.

"Yes, I have. After hours of pondering that very question, I had come to the conclusion that it must perhaps have been in a Red Cross hospital but—" she began, but broke off when Mamoun knocked softly on the door.

"What is it?" Dominic asked, with untoward impatience of which only he knew the cause.

"I come to find out how the princess is, and to express my great sorrow for what I did," the dwarf replied, sounding so unhappy that Dominic could not bring himself to prolong his suffering.

"She is much improved, Mamoun, thank you," he said, far more indulgently. "I believe that the princess is out of danger and will most certainly live."

"Allah be praised!" Mamoun murmured earnestly. "I go to bring the good news to Haroun and Little Brother." He went out as fast as his short, bowlegs permitted, and they heard his footsteps disappear in the distance.

"What's going on here?" Thérèse was quite bewildered. "What actually happened to me, and did anyone really think that I might die?"

And then she heard from Dominic of Mamoun's plan to outwit the unknown rider, how he had struck her with his *nabbut,* and how she had been brought to the hospital.

"Naturally he would not have recognized me because of the cloak and hood I was wearing," she exclaimed concernedly. "I deserved it! Please promise me that you will tell him that I do not blame him at all for what happened!...Poor Mamoun! He looked so guilty!"

"I shall certainly tell him," *El-Hakim* promised. "But tell me, Thérèse, why did you do it?"

She considered carefully what to say, before venturing to reply. She had to put it to him in such a way that he would not suspect the truth. Hoping that she was clear-headed enough to get away with this successfully, she worded her response as if she had misunderstood the question.

"Because I knew that they would not agree to bring me, if I had asked. That is also why I wore the cloak, to disguise myself..."

El-Hakim studied her closely, his intense blue eyes fixed on her face and obviously noting her every change of expression. "It is a good sign that your memory, up to the time that you were struck, appears to be unimpaired—but you are evading the question, Princess Thérèse, and you know it!"

"That is true," she admitted, with no small measure of embarrassment. "But it is a very long story!"

"I have all the time in the world," he assured her, and then suddenly felt remorseful. "I have kept you talking to satisfy myself that you are not confused, but to stay longer would be selfish of me, when you must rest." He leaned over, held his cool fingers to her pulse, and then put his hand on her forehead. "How is the head now?"

Thankful for any encouragement to postpone the explanation, but giving him a truthful answer, nonetheless, she admitted: "Not as good as when I first woke up."

Dominic frowned and she knew what he was thinking. She was, after all, a fairly experienced nurse. It was not impossible that, within the next twenty-four hours, complications might yet arise. He had not reprimanded Phil unnecessarily.

Raschid made his appearance just then, bringing coffee for his leader, and simultaneously coming to inquire after the princess.

"Good evening, Highness," he greeted her with a flourishing *salaam,* after handing Dominic his cup. "Ali and many others are outside, and all are eager for news of the princess."

"I find myself considerably improved, thank you, Raschid," was Thérèse's dignified response. "Please advise them of my appreciation for their interest and concern."

"I shall inform them, Highness....None shall omit to give thanks that your life has been spared." Then he added a very strange thing. "My *personal* gratitude," he informed them solemnly, "shall be expressed to the God of Ezra, *El-Hakim,* and Philip-brother. I know they have petitioned Him, and He has answered!"

He turned to Dominic. "May the princess have coffee now?"

Dominic looked questioningly at Thérèse, but she shook her head. "No thank you, Raschid....*Ouch*! That hurt! I dare not move my head!"

"That will come right, Highness," Raschid said confidently, bowed to her, and left.

"Why are they all awake so late?" she asked Dominic when they were alone again. "It must be past midnight by now..."

"It's Ramadan. They are usually very noisy, but I guess that, out of deference to you, they are keeping themselves awake some other way. They pray until very late at night, and then they are on the go again, well before dawn, in order to have a quick meal before the sun rises."

"Oh, yes! I remember now. That was of course why there was such feverish activity in Cairo. I judged the people unfairly.—Perhaps because I was too agitated, anyway, to go to sleep until very late."

That thought immediately rekindled the memory of the previous night, and the misery Dominic had caused her.... Would she ever be able to tell him about it?

He was quick to observe the shadow that crossed her face, and taking it that she was in physical pain, he rose from his chair. "Now you may safely have another painkiller."

He brought her another capsule and glass of water. "Before you are too groggy, Meriam will come and see to you. She will unpack your saddlebag for you, and please don't hesitate to ask if there is anything you need.

"Don't try to get up, even to go to the bathroom. She knows exactly what to do for you, and will be here for most of the night, until Ezra comes. He has volunteered to take over from her." He touched her shoulder lightly. "Good night, Thérèse. Sweet dreams!"

Meriam came in shortly after that, to ready Thérèse for the night, and before she turned down the lamp, she was pleased to see that the princess was already asleep.

(iii)

Now it was Dominic's turn to be tortured by uncertainty. He had been let down by a woman so unconscionably in the past, that, for his own protection, he had erected for himself a hitherto impenetrable barricade of distrust. As a result it was impossible for him to find any good, acceptable reason for Thérèse's coming.

Both Mamoun and the other two were convinced that she had visited the bazaars that morning, with the express purpose of finding and following them. She had acquired a horse, and had, by her own admission, purchased a *burnous*, with the firm intention of disguising herself.—But why?

In the early stages of shock and anxiety, he had almost made a fool of himself. But alone in his tent, after leaving her with Meriam, he paced back and forth, trying to convince himself that it was only sympathy for her helplessness, and concern about her condition, that had knocked him off balance to such an extent.

Philip behaved as though he might be in love with the girl, and yet he had probably never even had a good look at her. And she? Dominic knew that he ought to resent her because she could so easily become the cause of unpleasantness between himself and his brother. But then again, he could only hope, perversely, that it was rather because she was attracted to Philip that she had gone to such lengths to find her way back to the camp...

No matter how much a princess—a person of royal birth—loved a man, there was no way she would come running after him....And that, after knowing him for such a short period of time. A member of an exclusive, wealthy, social set, and undeniably of uncommon beauty, she was probably besieged by young blades who were far more eligible....How could a girl of her rank hope to find lasting happiness with a commoner like his brother...or he, with her? She, accustomed to the luxury of life in a palace...a princess...while Philip, however good-looking and likeable he might be, was an unknown young man not yet equipped to earn his own living!

Because she was clearly in great pain and still suffering a measure of shock, herself, he had not wanted to force an explanation from her, but hadn't she been a trifle too reticent... or perhaps, evasive? Her headache had not been so violent that she had been unable to talk about other matters.

Around and around went such thoughts. The situation was as much beyond comprehension, as it was beyond resolution. Acting on impulse, he went over to the old rapier of El-Bus Mohandess, took it down from where it hung, and sat down on his divan, holding it in his hands. It had been given to him as a gift...a sort of talisman against weakness. If only it could have emanated some sort of power! For here he sat, already vulnerable, trying to convince himself that Thérèse had come there for Philip's sake; because he, Dominic, was simply too cowardly to face up to the fact that she might be a spy.

Quite panic-stricken at the mere thought, he jumped up frantically and returned the rapier to its usual place. Then the indecisive pacing began again.

Of course, as he had already tried to tell himself, there was no way Philip could have been the reason. Plain and simply, such reckless behaviour was out of character for a crown princess. In addition, it suddenly occurred to him, there was her close friendship with the family of his archenemy, Sir Humphrey Talbot. If she had made any mention at all, to Talbot, of a mysterious physician who had forcibly abducted her and taken her to some remote hospital in the mountains, the man would want to bring the malefactor to justice, even if he made no connection with Hamid Pasha….But then…?—Would this dreadful uncertainty never end?—Why had Thérèse come alone?

Eventually he had to admit that he was confounded. Utterly bewildered, and at a loss to find the solution, he could only wait and see. The greatest danger, to her as well as to him, was that she was now able to point out where, in that range of mountains, the stockade lay.

Fortunately it would be a good few days before she would want to go horse riding again!

CHAPTER FOURTEEN

In the days that followed, Dominic kept a watchful eye on Thérèse, and was constantly tortured by his own thoughts. For some inexplicable reason, he lacked the courage to go and question her outright—probably because he feared what her response might be. He was so uncharacteristically short-tempered that even Raschid noticed it.

Meanwhile Thérèse healed quickly. After only one day in bed she was allowed to get up, and although she felt dizzy as she took the first, hesitant steps, she persevered until she gradually regained her strength. Just to be where she longed to be, where she could see Dominic, was all the encouragement she needed.

She immediately offered him whatever help he might require, and although he initially refused the offer, when finally, stammering with nervousness, she managed to explain that it was for precisely that reason that she had come, he took her up on it. His acceptance was expressed so grudgingly however, that it hurt her. She had not expected *El-Hakim* to welcome her with open arms, but his kindness during her indisposition had kindled the hope that he might perhaps be friendlier than during her previous visit.

Before long she was obliged to conclude that the doctor's kindness was reserved entirely for the sick. Healthy, she was once more relegated to the ranks of the despised and the 'empty headed'. She had to acknowledge that if ever she had really deserved the latter designation, it was when she had behaved like a romantic fool. It was natural to ascribe to her delirious condition at the time, the fact that she could ever have imagined that he had been about to kiss her.—But then, as the saying went, the wish was often father to the thought!

There was some consolation, however. She was warmly welcomed by the patients, and also by Ezra and others with whom she worked closely. Meriam was her devoted slave and Mamoun her faithful shadow. His humble adoration could have been almost comical, if it had not been so touching. Surprisingly, however, the patient who seemed the most pleased to see her back, was Christopher Brent.

The improvement in the condition of the banker was amazing. He was walking about freely, chatting to whomever spoke English, and even helping to carry trays. But Dominic still insisted that he should rest a great deal, and because Brent had to be back in bed early in the evenings, which made the nights very long for him, she would sometimes take her own cup of tea to his ward, while he was enjoying his, just to keep him company. Either Dominic or Philip must have told him who she was, because, as his memory began to return, they found that they even had a few acquaintances in common.

He had a vague, recurring impression of being at the home of someone important—perhaps that of a government official—from where, he believed, he was taken away, and that, against his will. Most intriguing of all, was his description, though equally vague, of the man who had been assigned to remove him from that house....The person who must have dealt him the blow that had resulted in his being unable to recall very much after that. Somehow the words Brent used to describe the man in question, convinced her that it could only have been the same person whose face had so unnerved her!

What a relief it had been to find that he did not appear to be associated with *El-Hakim*, after all.

Of all the people confined to the hospital, the Englishman was perhaps the most resigned. There was no point in his wanting to leave while he remembered so little of his former life, and to know that he was safe was enough for him, for the time being. He was grateful for the kindness and excellent care he was receiving. In fact, it was Dominic who was in the greatest quandary about Brent, because he would have liked to have been able to put the man's family—if he had one—out of their misery, and also bring an end to any ransom payments Abdel Sharia might possibly be exacting, but his hands were tied. He did not know how to do this, without putting everyone else in the stockade at risk.

At that stage in the drama unfolding in the camp, nothing seemed to be quite like it had been before the fever, and Hamid Pasha's failure at the oasis gathering. Ezra and Raschid were concerned about Dominic. In all the time he had been in the stockade, he had never had a break from responsibility and tension. Both noticed that, whenever he could escape from that responsibility for even a brief period, he would disappear up the mountain with his little book, and they had surprised him, more than once, on his knees—in his tent and also in his favourite retreat. Ezra just happened to encounter him there one day, but he no longer went there specifically to meet him, as before. This was because, for some reason, *El-Hakim* plainly shunned company.

Philip felt wretched, too. He hated to see the tightening of his brother's face, and the tautness of his jaw, in particular. It disturbed him to have to witness Dominic's innate good humour, once more become submerged by something not unlike the bitterness that had clouded his handsome face for so long after they had come to Egypt.

Meanwhile, Thérèse's only real problem seemed to be with the brothers Verwey, themselves.

Philip no longer kept his devotion secret. Very obviously wanting to keep the promise made when he was her patient, that he would not 'become amorous', he said little, but made it clear in numerous ways that he was in love with her. The result was that she was consumed with the problem of how to make it clear to him that she would never feel the same about him.

In that respect, Dominic became even more of a problem. Sometimes she had the uncomfortable feeling that he blamed her for her effect on his brother. He would constantly drop scornful hints about the imprudence of any possible relationship between them, and his favourite subject of conversation appeared to be 'stupid women who allowed their hearts to triumph over common sense'...

Before long, having seen another side to the man, and no longer buoyed up by that glorious prospect of contributing to the realization of *El-Hakim's* dream—whatever that was!—she felt that she could stand Dominic's provocative behaviour no longer. There were times when he would quite blatantly try to drive her into Philip's arms....Philip should go and keep the princess company because she was lonely and looking dejected.... Or, would she go and see what Philip was doing...?

She had to admit to herself that she would take the old mocking smile any day, in preference to this brutal manipulation. But worst of all was the cold mask of indifference he could assume on some occasions. The times when he became as intractable as granite.

One afternoon, at the end of her tether, she sought him out in his pharmacy where he was making up prescriptions, for once without Philip or Ezra to help him. She waited patiently, in silence, for him to finish, and then she blurted out: "*El-Hakim*, I have to talk to you!"

He took his time about turning his head, and then, frowning, regarded her expressionlessly.

"Well, here I am....Talk!"

That really took the wind out of her sails, and she was embarrassed by the flush she felt spreading up her neck and into her face. "I want to go back to Cairo, *at once*!" she somehow managed to blurt out, clenching her small fists nervously.

"Why are you telling me this?" he asked in that bored tone of voice that so exasperated her. "Philip is the one who might be interested, not I!"

"Because you are the one with the key to the gate, of course!" she cried. What did one do with such a man? "You know well enough that I can't leave here without either your permission, or your assistance, and goodness knows what you have done with my horse!"

"Hmm..." He pretended to weigh the subject very seriously. "Well, it grieves me to have to disappoint you, Princess, but after due consideration, I find it inconvenient to let you go!"

"But why?" Thérèse lost all control of herself. It was torture to remain in his company any longer under such circumstances. "Just because you want to see me crawl!" she yelled at him. "You are so full of your own importance that you want to control the lives of everyone around you!"

Now he had been thoroughly roused from any semblance of indifference. He sprang up and took her by the shoulders, so hard that it felt as though his fingers bruised her.

"I can't let you go, you little fool," he muttered, "because I dare not risk it!"

"Are you afraid that I might show someone the way?" she mocked him. "Of whom are you afraid—*Hamid Pasha*?"

Immediately she had said that, she knew that she had

overstepped the mark. Dominic blanched so markedly that his eyes were like blue flames in his face. He was the one with clenched fists now, and it was clear that he restrained himself with difficulty. She found it hard to breathe while he regarded her so furiously.

The very next minute, his very obvious tension suddenly appeared to dissipate, and there was an unexpected, noticeable, and quite dramatic change in his attitude. As though, beaten, he was prepared to subject himself to the inevitable. He sat down heavily and, with shoulders bent, he leant forward with his hands on his knees, staring fixedly in front of him. He no longer looked just exhausted. His face was grooved with devastating concern, and Thérèse could not bear it that he should look like that.

"Dominic, I am so sorry!" she cried regretfully and grabbed him by the arm. "I did not mean anything by that.—Dominic, I beg of you…!"

But he shook her hands off roughly. "Don't you *ever* mention that name in my presence again, Thérèse!" he said threateningly, and his voice cut like a whip.

She, too, now subsided onto the nearest chair, and covered her face with her hands, as he stalked out, slamming the door behind him. Alone among the scales, the vials, and the miscellany of other equipment in the pharmacy, she allowed the tears she had been holding back for so long, to flow unrestrainedly.

How long she sat there, she did not know, and she did not care. She says now, that it was through Raschid that the first vestige of comfort came to her. It was already dark in the pharmacy when, all at once, the room was flooded with light. The Indian, coming to fetch something, turned around from the switch beside the door, and was greatly alarmed to find the princess sitting on a low three-legged stool, looking harrowed. Taking in, at a glance, her disconsolate attitude and red-rimmed eyes, he went over to her with concern written in every line of his face.

"Highness!" he exclaimed. "Are you ill?"

She raised her tearstained face and, breathing with small hiccoughs—as children sometimes do after prolonged weeping—she said the first thing that came into her head.

"Raschid, how did you know that *El-Hakim* prayed for me?"

"Because I heard him, Excellency," was the simple reply.

(ii)

After that scene with Thérèse, *El-Hakim* went straight to his tent. He flung himself down despairingly on his divan, only to jump up restlessly again. More troubled that he had ever been in his life, he went over to stand under the old rapier. When he had said so confidently to Raschid that he would have to remove anyone who interfered with his plans, he had meant every word of it. Of course he had not been speaking of *killing* anyone, but *remove?* Most certainly! He would have thought of something, he was sure....But now?

As he hesitated, consumed with doubt and driven by overwhelming distress, he prayed aloud: "Help me, Lord!... What must I do?"

He was startled, by the sound of his own voice in the silence of the tent, but as he turned around to go out again, he could have sworn that he heard another...

"Give her a chance, my son!"

CHAPTER FIFTEEN

Although Thérèse did not know it, her entire future hung in the balance for the next two weeks. Dominic put her to the test in every conceivable—and inconceivable—manner. He dreamt up the most far-fetched scenarios, and tempted her in the most ridiculous manner, to betray his trust.

The most outrageous plan of all was to have the gate of the hospital enclosure left wide open. That was to be the 'trial by fire'! The idea came to him after he had overheard her talking to Christopher Brent about Mustapha, and the enormous reward being offered in Cairo for news of the missing senator. Dominic went out directly, and had Ali and Rameses summoned. Something told him that Raschid's ever-growing admiration for the princess would make him too reluctant a participant to be included in the scheme.

"Rameses," he said, not entirely happy about this, himself, "I want you to give orders for the gate that leads to the stockade to be unlocked after sunset tonight, and you must make yourself personally responsible to ensure that it remains wide open at all times. The guards must remain in the shadows, unseen, and no one is to be seen walking about there, either, until I change the order....No one, that is, except the princess."

"But, *Effendi*, will she not then see too much?" Rameses protested, in some confusion.

"She already knows the worst there is to know," Dominic told him dismally. "But do as I say....And you, Ali..."

"Yes, *Effendi?*"

"You have a more difficult task. It was difficult for him to express, in Arabic, precisely what he was trying to say, but the gist of it was: "You must go and talk to the princess on some pretext or another. Tell her that, for some reason, the gate has to be kept open, and that you are concerned about that. Hint broadly at all manner of dark secrets hidden beyond it. In the course of your conversation, you are to let slip that *El-Hakim* is terrified about her having discovered his personal secret. Somehow, just casually, get her to promise that she will not attempt to go beyond the enclosure, because that could make the lives of all of us very uncomfortable."

The next time Thérèse came into the courtyard, after hearing all that Ali had to say, Dominic and Rameses watched her tensely, from behind the tamarisks that grew in a dense clump near the entrance. She walked as far as the open gate and back—twice—only to turn around each time, without venturing further....Each time Dominic held his breath. "Thérèse, Thérèse," his heart cried out with every beat, "if you only knew how desperately I am depending on you!" A third time she went, stood there for a short while, clearly undecided, and then, tossing her glossy black curls, she walked away resolutely—without as much as risking a peek beyond the gate...

Bemused beyond description, he rose to follow her. Perhaps a trustworthy woman actually did exist!...Then it *was* because of Philip that she had come!

In sharp contrast with the relief that this knowledge should have brought, he was aware only of a sharp ache in the region of his heart...!

***

On her way back to the tent which she had been occupying since her recovery, Thérèse passed by Philip's, and found him standing outside, looking at the stars. "Come inside and visit for a while," he invited her, lifting the flap. "I have been waiting all day for a chance to talk to you."

She went in, but not to stay. "I have only come to take a quick look at your house," she smiled. "Then I am going to bed. What did you want to talk to me about?"

Philip regarded her unhappily.

"Thérèse, you have no idea how utterly wretched I am. I know that I made you a promise to avoid this subject, but won't you please listen—even just this once?"

Through the opening in the tent, Philip's words were carried clearly on the night air, and Dominic who could hear him, froze in his tracks.

"I love you, Thérèse," came the passionate young voice. "I know that this is a colossal cheek, but I, insignificant lout that I am, have had the temerity to fall madly in love with the crown princess of Soravia!"

"My dear Philip," Thérèse replied, her charming accent made more evident than usual by her anxiety not to hurt him. "You must not think like that! That is not a cheek! How could it be? I am unable to express how honoured I am that you should consider me worthy and, were I able to return your love, nothing else would matter!"

Outside, Dominic suddenly realized that he was listening to words not meant for his ears. Hastily, and feeling almost panic-stricken, he ducked into his own tent, and closed the flap securely behind him.

Philip took Thérèse's hands in both of his; his lean, earnest face very serious. "Is it that you don't find me at all attractive, dear Princess of Hearts, or perhaps because there is someone else?"

If only not to hurt his pride, she decided to be honest. "There *is* someone, Philip, but I'm afraid that my situation, in that regard, is no different from yours."

Then Philip nearly took her breath away. "Thérèse, are you perhaps referring to my brother?"

She stared at him wordlessly, her cheeks burning. "However did you come by such a ridiculous idea?"

He shook his head knowingly. "I don't know that it is so ridiculous at all, little girl. He's about the only man to whom I would be prepared to lose you." He said this with a crooked grin that tore at her heart. "You can trust me! I shall not give you away!"

Thérèse sat down on his divan. Her eyes brimmed over, and there was a colossal lump in her throat. "How did you know?" she asked huskily, unconsciously affirming the fact by that question. "How *could* you know, Phil?"

"I think I expected this the very first time I saw you."

"But I did not yet know it, myself..." she protested.

"That may well be. Who knows when or where love begins? Can anyone say, 'It was here...or there...or then?'...The night you sat with me...when I told you about Dominic...*I* was sure!"

"But *how?*" Thérèse was dumbfounded. That Philip could display such perception!

"Do you remember how you reacted...how quick you were to ask, 'Is your brother in any danger?'—Lovey, you were an open book!"

She sat in silence for a few moments, weighing his words. Then she laughed shakily. "Heavens! You are scaring me! In future I shall have to think twice before I utter another idle word in your presence!" Out of the blue, as she said that, another declaration, made on the same night, came back to her. She winced at the recollection, and decided that perhaps she had better sit down after all.

"Philip," she requested gently. "Please come and sit here, next to me. There is something I now have to tell *you*!" Waiting for him to comply, she took a deep breath and then blurted out: "Last week I found out who Hamid Pasha is!"

If he had not already been seated, it would have been necessary for him to take the weight off his legs. "This is indeed a night for revelations," he chuckled nervously. "And for shocks!"

"You don't have to worry," she said softly. "If you believe that I love him, you ought to know that I would never betray him!"

"How is it that whenever you endeavour to try and ward off possible declarations of love on my part, you always seem to switch to the subject of Hamid Pasha? Do you remember last time?"

"I do," she replied. "All too well. That is what I was leading up to. I recall the idiotic speech I made, *apropos* that very subject, and how I went on about the duty of all law-abiding citizens. And yet, when I found out that it was in my power to put Hamid Pasha behind those bars about which I spoke so smugly"—she smiled wryly—"I attached so much importance to my civic duty that I actually ran away!"

"So that's why you followed the twins and Little Brother back here?"

She nodded.

"But hasn't that knowledge changed how you feel about Dom?" He was incredulous

"Not one bit! I have come to believe that Dominic could

never bring himself to do the things he does, no matter how bad they might seem, without good reason!"

"I wish he could hear you!" was Philip's heartfelt rejoinder. "But, if he did, he would probably only respond as he has inevitably done in the past, in the days when Ezra and I were still welcome to meet with him up on the mountain. No matter how we would try to reassure him, he would still groan and protest with something like: '*But I am a thief!....It does not matter how you try and whitewash it, the fact remains...I have become a thief, plain and simple!*'...Oh, Princess, you cannot imagine what that does to me, to see him suffer like that!...It is as though he has to wear 'Hamid Pasha' like a suit of armour sometimes, to steel himself.—He has to be a different person!"

She took his hand gently in her small, comforting one. "Philip-brother, never fail to remind him that one of the last things Jesus did on the cross, was to forgive a thief!"

He could hardly believe his ears. "Thérèse!" he exclaimed in wonderment, "you are a girl in a million!...Even if I can't have you, myself," he grinned ruefully, "you could be a real asset as a sister-in-law!"

He had made this comment bravely, but the pain of it was visible in his eyes, and his lips were stiff. However, at the same time, he had been quick to notice the sadness with which his own words had been received, and he put his arm comfortingly about her shoulders. "I know that Dom will want to murder me for this, but I think it's time to tell you the whole story. You deserve it!"

And then he filled in all the details he had been obliged to omit before, leaving nothing out this time. He told of Raschid and the 'Yellow Eye', of the Bey, Abdel Sharia, and El-Bus Mohandess. Telling about how Rameses, Ali and others had been selected as Dominic's mentors, he described in detail the rigorous and gruelling training *El-Hakim* had gone through to fit him for the enormous task of protecting his people. Finally, he went into the details of his brother's disappointing defeat at the gathering in the desert, explaining why she had been brought to look after him, Philip, and stressing how critical it had been for Hamid Pasha to be at the oasis. Thérèse listened so intently that, for fear of missing something, she was almost afraid to breathe.

"This whole story is so fantastic," she remarked when he had finished, "that I can hardly believe it!" All the time she had been talking, she had kept fingering her locket, as she frequently did, but the fact that she did so was of no significance to him...."Were you with him on the night he came to Sir. Humphrey's mansion?"

He nodded. "I was—but only outside, holding Dom's horse. He did not want to involve me in any way, but I insisted, so for the sake of peace, he let me go that far with him."

"Then it was you I saw! You were the one who passed by the balcony with him, when he waved to me!—But you say there are more people, *here?*—Where?"

"Lower down in the valley. A whole stockade of them... Almost an entire village, which you have not been able to see because you have been confined to the hospital enclosure."

"I wondered where the new patients kept coming from!" she exclaimed, holding her hands to her lovely mouth, which was open wide with surprise. "I also saw Dominic bring someone on his horse once, and another time he and Rameses arrived at the hospital, carrying someone on a sort of crude litter....I can appreciate now why Dominic needs to keep the stockade a secret, but how did all the people come to be here in the first place, Philip?"

"All fugitives! Some have lived here for years. The new

arrivals have probably been rescued lately.—Since Raschid has shown Dominic where to go, that happens more and more frequently.— Among the lot of them, there can't be more than a handful who have actually committed any sort of misdemeanour, but, as I have tried to explain, it is not necessary for them actually to have committed the crimes of which they were accused, to have been found guilty.

"Abdel Sharia has people arrested left, right and centre, cooks up imaginary charges against them, and sentences them to life imprisonment in his prisons . Raschid was one, only he was never sentenced. He was caught and dragged off by the Bey's men when he and El-Bus Mohandess were actually on a failed rescue mission—such as the one from which, blessedly, Dominic had successfully returned when he brought that man back on his horse! Ezra, on the other hand was kidnapped for ransom....Some are fortunate to escape the dungeons, but when they do, they have no refuge except Hamid Pasha—my brother!"

By now she was completely bereft of speech, and could only nod in awed comprehension. It was shattering to discover that things like this could happen in what was supposed to be a civilized world. Everything was suddenly crystal clear. Mustapha was not here....He was the prisoner of Abdel Sharia, and Dominic was unjustly being blamed for his disappearance.

"And Brent?...The Englishman?" she asked, finding her voice at last. "Do you know that he is under the impression that he was somehow abducted, too."

Philip nodded. "He was in the process of being dragged off, probably also for ransom, when Dom, Raschid and Rameses appeared on the scene. Dominic fired a few shots into the air, to startle his captors, and they let him go—literally! One of them bashed him, Brent, over the head so that he would fall from the horse on which he was being transported. Probably meant to kill him, to be on the safe side so that he could not talk. He'd be in worse danger now, if my brother decided to have him taken back to Cairo, and if Sharia were to find out that he was alive!"

By this time, the Princess Thérèse was thoroughly stunned. Philip had given her much food for thought. As if *El-Hakim,* the 'Father of the desert' were not already sufficiently dedicated, Hamid Pasha had willingly taken upon himself an even more awful responsibility. No wonder *El-Hakim* had looked so devastated when she had taunted him with the mention of Hamid Pasha. She pondered this conundrum in silence for while, and then a dreadful thought struck her. "Oh, Philip," she cried, "I swear Dominic thinks that I am a spy!"

CHAPTER SIXTEEN

The following day was, unseasonably, the hottest of the whole summer thus far, and, as later transpired, the heat—albeit indirectly—had a profound effect on the lives of everyone in the stockade.

Dominic was sitting listlessly in the armchair in his tent, grateful to be in the mountains and not down in the desert, and trying to decide whether it had been any hotter during the *Khamsin* than it was that day, when Raschid came in, carrying a cold drink on a tray.

The Indian moved sluggishly in his long, white toga, and his forehead was beaded with perspiration. As he reached for the glass, Dominic felt guilty. It must have been sheer torture for Raschid to have had to prepare the juice in this heat when he, himself, was not permitted even a drop of water to quench his own thirst.

"It's a good job that the *Khamsin* doesn't blow during Ramadan, isn't it Raschid?" *El-Hakim* asked, referring to the hot wind, the name of which was derived from the word for 'fifty', because it blew for fifty days of every year.

"If the Creator of the universe so decrees it, who are we to complain, *Effendi?*" Raschid replied resignedly.

Dominic shook his head. This Indian friend of his was a singular person. Would he ever be able to understand him? He studied him with new interest.

"Sit down here for a while, Raschid," he requested. "I

would just like to talk to you." He smiled. "I promise that I shall not touch a single drop of this juice in your presence!"

Raschid obediently sat down, cross-legged, on the mat, and wiped his face with his long, wide sleeve.

"You Muslims are a weird bunch," Dominic observed thoughtfully. "In some ways you are far more devout than we Christians.—Do you really believe in the power of your prophet?"

"Muslims do not surround their prophet with the same, godly power that you ascribe to your Christ, *Sahhena*," he explained patiently. "The battle cry of the Muslim is always, 'There is no God besides Allah, and Mohammed is his prophet!' "

"The only one?"

"No, *Effendi*! Mohammed is the most important, but there are hundreds. Abraham, Noah and Jesus are among them." He looked up into Dominic's face. "This belief had been instilled in me since I was a child and I had never had the opportunity to know anyone who believed differently, until I met my *Memsahib* Hunt. Since then, I have learned much from Ezra, who has reminded me that Isaac and Ishmael were brothers, after all, and I have lately been leaning more towards his *El-Shaddai*, the Almighty God. But I do not believe that I am any more devout than you are, *Sahhena*!"

"How can you say that, Raschid?" Dominic was astonished.

"*El-Hakim*, as I see it, your whole life is a fast. You have had to relinquish much for which you had prepared yourself! You have had to abstain from contact with your own kind. Your life is not your own." Raschid's voice faltered, and when Dominic looked into his eyes, he noticed that they were shining with tears.

"Some months ago," Raschid went on, when he had pulled himself together, "I asked Philip-brother to bring back from the city, for me, a book such as the one you read. For Mamoun to do it would have been to risk his own life....In this book I have seen that your God is 'Love'—a word I had not yet really begun to understand until you took pity on me!...Do you remember that you laughed, *Effendi*, when I called you by the name of 'Samaritan'? I am thinking of my *memsahib*, too, now that I have been able to read that story for myself...

"Your book also tells us that we should love our neighbour as we do ourselves.—And when I recalled the night you pledged to give up your own hopes for the future, in order to take upon you the responsibility for the children of El-Bus Mohandess, I was finally able to understand *that*!

"*Sahbena*, I know what you do when you disappear with your small book!...As you pray, you search in it for words that will bring you hope of forgiveness—for what you are driven to do, to provide for the big family you have been given—and salvation for those of us that you deem lost....Today I confess to you that I do not fast because it is Ramadan....I fast for my own forgiveness, as much as I pray for you!"

There was silence for some time, as both men, too overcome for further words, struggled to regain their composure. *El-Hakim* could only take the brown hands in his, and nod his thanks, swallowing hard as he did so.

When he was finally able to speak, and more for something to say, Dominic asked, "You have mentioned some of the Muslim prophets...but there is one more, isn't there, Raschid? The one that is still expected....I am referring, of course, to our discussion about the false prophet of whom you spoke on the sand dune. Do you remember?...We were talking about Abdel Sharia, and then, among other things, you told me about someone who tried a similar ruse during the last century. You did not finish the story, and I can't remember that you ever told me his name..."

Raschid thought about that for a moment. "Ah, yes, *Effendi.* I remember.—Mohammed Ahmed. That was his name....I was interrupted that night by..." He broke off, perplexed by the expression on Dominic's face. *El-Hakim* had sprung to his feet with such violence that he had knocked the chair over backwards. His eyes had widened and he seemed to have a very dry throat, for he swallowed with difficulty.

"What did you say?" he cried hoarsely. "*What* was his name?"

"Mohammed Ahmed," Raschid repeated with increasing bewilderment. And once again he was not destined to complete that story, for Dominic jerked him to his feet, as the astonishment on his, Dominic's, face gave way to incredulous excitement.

"Raschid!" he cried jubilantly. "The coincidence is too great! Don't look so overwhelmed man! That's who he is.— The Sheik Mohammed Ahmed!...Lydia's husband! I'm talking about *Abdel Sharia!*...Praise God!"

(ii)

Philip, Ezra, Ali, Rameses, Sezit, the twins and Little Brother, were summoned in haste. Dominic gestured to them to be seated, and as he faced them he was so overcome, that he could hardly speak. It was difficult to believe that the moment had finally arrived.

"My friends," he began, oblivious of the heat in his overcrowded tent—and it was mainly to his brother that he spoke—"the most incredible thing has happened! Some might attribute this to coincidence, but I know better!" He waited a moment before continuing. His news was far too momentous to be imparted in any but the most dramatic manner possible. "This will be a long story, but I hope that you will bear with me, because what I have to tell you is too important to be skimmed through...

"When, a little more than two weeks ago, I paid a visit to the wife of the Sheik Mohammed Ahmed—a man better known to you as the member of the *Barlaman,* Mohammed Alfit—she described to me many strange things that happen in their house from time to time. But, as those of you who accompanied me there will know, I returned here to find Philip-brother sick with the fever, and was then too distracted by my concern for him, to think again about what she had told me....Very soon after that, some of us left here to attend the gathering at the Suef oasis, where we hoped to persuade the sheiks and the *cadis* to join us in launching an attack on the camp of Abdel Sharia.—You all know what transpired there, and I am ashamed that, for the first time, I gave up all hope that any of us would ever again be able to return to anything like a normal way of life.

"On the way home from the oasis, Raschid started to tell me about a man who, more than seventy years ago, became as powerful and as wealthy as Abdel Sharia. He achieved this by claiming to be the long-awaited *Mahdi,* but unfortunately Raschid was not granted the opportunity to tell me that man's name. This was because we discovered that we were being followed, and due to the haste in which we departed from that place, and in the midst of disturbing events that have taken place since our return, I have never, until today, thought to ask Raschid to complete his story.

"If, this afternoon, the intense heat had not indirectly

led to a discussion between us, Raschid and I would not have spoken again about the prophet. That was only the first of several wondrous and inexplicable developments. Only now have I heard that the name of that false prophet was *Mohammed Ahmed*! That is the second of the revelations, and it is too great to be taken for granted...for that is a name of great significance to all of us, although to none of the rest of you will it immediately be as meaningful as it is to my brother and to me. We *know* such a man, and..."

Philip was the first to grasp where this was leading, and Dominic was not given the opportunity to say more, before his brother leapt up, exclaiming exuberantly, "I can see that, Dom! I know what you're getting at—and it is precisely the sort of masquerade that would capture the imagination of a monster like him!"

"Exactly!" Dominic smiled approvingly at Philip. However, with the exception of Raschid, everyone else in the tent, including Ezra, quite understandably appeared to be baffled. Dominic was not surprised. He would have been the first to admit that, apart from the complexity of the tale, when he became over enthusiastic about something, he was inclined to speak so fast that his Arabic became less than satisfactory. He decided to try speaking more slowly, and to make what he so urgently wanted to convey, more comprehensible.

"Let me put it this way," he explained for everyone's benefit. "It is said that history repeats itself, over and over again. Let us suppose then that, at the present time, there is a man called Mohammed Ahmed, who learned at school about that other, bearing the same name as his, who lived years ago, and who had become exceedingly wealthy, world famous, and even powerful enough to incite others to lead a battle against the British. All because of a daring plan. He had led his followers to believe that he was the *Mahdi*.

"Supposing our present day Mohammed Ahmed, the scholar, grew up to be a genius—although an evil one—and let us further suppose that, out of the similarity in their names, there grew a plan with a multitude of possibilities. One that would make him equally rich and powerful.

"He starts off by getting himself elected to the *Barlaman*, possibly with the support of other equally unprincipled people, but now calls himself Mohammed Alfit, so that no one will connect him in any way with that other name; for, by this time, he is already in the process of creating a mythical, non-existent character, namely the Bey, Abdel Sharia, to carry the responsibility for his crimes.—What police force, no matter how good, is able to arrest a man who does not exist?...In addition to the mystery, the elusive attributes of Sharia would make the myth that he is a holy man, wholly acceptable....Now do you understand?"

As one man they nodded, too astonished to comment. Raschid made a sort of hissing noise as he blew out his breath, shaking his head in reluctant admiration. "Your suspicions are far-fetched, *Effendi*, but in my heart I believe them to be correct!"

"But you will need proof, Dom," Philip cautioned his brother. "Not only is it dangerous to act on suspicion, but your proof has to be conclusive enough to be of use against Sharia. Especially as the one who will be providing it, namely Hamid Pasha, is not in the best of standings, himself."

"I shall get that proof!" Dominic assured them. "Just wait and see!"

Lydia had told of people who left her house under mysterious circumstances and now *El-Hakim* could make an accurate guess at whom those people must have been.—The missing officials, all of whom knew Ahmed well enough to visit him. All must have been entertained by him and given some sort of sleeping draught, after which they had been taken away by the hideous Farao and company, to 'Sharia's' stronghold. The unfortunate Mustapha, having unwisely made known his intention to disclose his suspicions to the authorities, whether correct or not, had probably been whisked away similarly, before he could do this.

Although in the banker's case, a substantial ransom had been the objective, Christopher Brent was undoubtedly another who would have suffered the same fate, if he had not been rescued in time. What Dominic could not fathom out, however, was why—unless the eminently recognizable Farao usually handed his charges over to someone else, halfway— he had failed to recognize him among the group whom he, Dominic, had, with such surprising ease, been able to despatch with only a single shot into the air. Perhaps if he had, the mystery might have been solved long before this.

But there was no time to waste on such speculation. *El-Hakim* underlined his plans to his men, and each was given his own, explicit, as well as implicit, instructions....The twins, accompanied by Little Brother and as many other men as they deemed necessary, were to leave immediately for Cairo, where they were to spread out and make inquiries about Mustapha. Mamoun, who had long since proved the effectiveness of his own methods of gaining entrance into the kitchens of Cairo's elite, and worming information out of household servants, was to visit the senator's house, with the object of ascertaining whether Mustapha had been in the company of *Barlaman* member, Mohammed Alfit, at any time during the week prior to his disappearance.

"I'll wager anything you like," Dominic declared confidently, "that you will find that Senator Mustapha was a frequent visitor to the home of his nefarious colleague!"

He had very reluctantly acceded to Lydia's plea for a contact address at which she could reach him, but now any communication from her had suddenly become of vital importance. Rameses and Ali were instructed to go at once to the home of the sabre-fighter's supposed 'aunt', to see if there might be any messages waiting there.

One-by-one, bent solely on carrying out their leader's commands, faithfully and unconditionally, they went their way, leaving only Raschid and Philip in the tent with *El-Hakim.*

***

Dominic took the old rapier down from its hanging place, and holding it, his thoughts were so far away that he looked at the other two without seeing them, and with a strange expression on his face which Philip could not fathom. "It has been a long time, *Effendi*!" *El-Hakim* murmured, half to himself.

Presently, becoming aware again, of the others, he smiled with some embarrassment. "One day, not long after the death of El-Bus Mohandess," he confided to them, "I was sitting here with this in my hands, thinking of the manner in which I acquired it, when all at once it almost seemed to move, as though it had a life of its own....I know you will probably think I am crazy," he went on, "but I made a vow that day that I would never use Etienne's rapier in a duel until I could meet Abdel Sharia, face to face. I have saved it for that—but I have had to wait a very long time for the opportunity!"

"What do you mean, Dom? What do you intend to do?" Philip demanded, after a long pause, and with some anxiety. "That is a dress sword, *boet,* and is, in any case, not intended for use!"

For a few minutes Dominic remained deep in thought. He drew his fingers through his thick golden mane, in the manner Philip knew so well, and bit his lower lip between his strong, white teeth. At last, ignoring Philip's last remark, he said: "To begin with, as I see it, it is imperative that we put Fuzad, the *Cadi*, into the picture. He will need time to call the sheiks and others together, so I cannot afford to wait for further developments before letting him know how things stand.... Then I shall also have to pay Lydia another visit, to 'pump' a little more information out of her, and also to ascertain when I might find her honourable spouse at home, before I finally decide what to do with the devil, himself!"

He frowned indecisively, and absentmindedly groped for a handkerchief, "Phew! It's hot!" he exclaimed, but suddenly meeting Raschid's calm, fixed gaze, he remained, looking at the Indian, handkerchief still in hand, and forgetting to wipe his forehead. He had known Raschid for too long not to guess what was going on in his head. He smiled his thanks.

"I shall be lost here without you, old friend," *El-Hakim* acknowledged, "but it *is* the only way! You will have to be the one who goes to Fuzad, to show him where Sharia's camp is."

"I, too, have waited a long time, *Effendi*," the Indian said simply. "More than five years! From the day you cured me of the 'Yellow Eye', *my* vow has been that I would return to set those other poor wretches free. Only provide me with the details of your plan. I shall do the rest."

Although he did so with some misgivings concerning the safety of his friend, Dominic complied. "Just explain the situation to Fuzad, for now," he instructed Raschid, "and ask him to wait for word from me. Prepare to leave just after sunrise tomorrow, and then, if you have not, within a day after your arrival, received a message to the effect that my suspicions were unfounded, he and the other sheiks are to attack Sharia's camp. We will come to your aid, as soon as our other business has been attended to."

Raschid *salaamed* solemnly. "It shall be as you wish, *Effendi*!"

Before he left, he picked up the tray on which the significant glass remained untouched, intending to carry it out with him, but he set it down again, as Dominic reached out to give him his hand.

"May God go with you tomorrow, Raschid. Choose ten good men to go with you!"

(iii)

At last Dominic and his brother were alone. Both sat down, not saying a word. The silence and inactivity seemed almost to be an anticlimax after the intense, fast moving events of the past hour, and there was, moreover an unfamiliar feeling of restraint between them. Dominic stared into space and Phillip distractedly picked up Dominic's glass and drained it.

"It's hot, hey?" Philip remarked.

"Terribly!" Dominic agreed.

Another long silence.

Philip made another attempt. "Will Raschid make it there safely, do you think?"

"I sincerely hope so!"

"Dom," Philip finally said tentatively, "there seems to be some sort of awkwardness between us, which I can't quite define....Why?"

"What do you mean, 'why'?" Dominic was instantly rattled. "Am I supposed to know the answer?"

"You are so touchy lately, that one hardly dares to speak to you, and you're making Thérèse's life a misery!"

"I did not ask her to come back here, did I?" Dominic snapped back tersely. "She should have prepared herself for a cold reception!"

"Perhaps she did…" Philip ventured gently.

Dominic slapped his leg impatiently, and sprang up, outraged. "For Pete's sake, Philip," he thundered. "What's got into you, man?…You hint at this and that, and you carry on like an idiot. What's come over you? Has the girl robbed you of your senses?…You make me so mad sometimes!"

Philip stood up and regarded Dominic with matching fury. "And you make me sick!" His lip curled sarcastically. "Everyone else is always wrong…but never the almighty *El-Hakim*!…Oh, no!…He is, of course, totally without fault! I think it's high time I got away from here. This place is apparently no longer big enough for the two of us!"

If Philip's tirade had taken Dominic off his stride, he gave no sign of it. Instead, he hid his feelings behind a veil of amused tolerance.

"This seems to be infectious. It's fast becoming a habit here.—*Everyone* suddenly wants to leave. First Thérèse informs me that she wants to go, and now you!"

At this Philip decided to throw all caution to the winds. He grabbed Dominic by the arm. "Did she tell you that, Dom? And will you let her go?"

"Of course not," was the reply. "How can I risk it? The girl is a threat, especially at this crucial time, and she stays where I can keep an eye on her!"

"Dominic!" Philip smiled, frowning incredulously. He angrily shook his head. "How can you even think such things? Don't you ever use your not insignificant intelligence?"

Still standing on his dignity, Dominic said stiffly, "I can't see anything to grin about. This is a very serious matter. At first I wanted to give her the benefit of the doubt. I knew she must have come here either for your sake, or as a spy for Talbot. Last night I actually heard her declare that she did not care for you—so, to which conclusion should I come now?"

"You precious fool!" Philip felt like kicking him. "Were those the only reasons you could come up with?" He dared not break his promise to Thérèse, but he felt that he had to say something or explode!

"How much of our conversation did you overhear last night?"

"Enough!...I did not stay to listen, Philip!" Dominic snapped.

"Well that was a pity! If you had, you might by now have come to your senses!" Philip was growing angry again. "Do you mean to tell me that you are going to condemn her, just like that? Are you blind, man?...Why don't you just go and ask her, outright, what's she's doing here?"

The expression on Dominic's face was slowly undergoing a change. He looked at Philip as if he were seeing him for the first time, and liked what he saw. Gradually, as he considered his brother's words, a light began to go up, and he suddenly smiled so broadly that his relief was reflected in his eyes.

"I think I shall, Phil! That's an excellent idea!" He slapped Philip on the back. "You're a really nice, guy, bro," he said. Then, being a man accustomed to planning ahead, and for some reason, puzzling to his brother, he tucked a small pillow under his arm and strode out of the tent.

"Tell her I absolve her of any promises she made to me!" Philip shouted after him.

***

Alone in the heat of the tent, Philip sat down again on his brother's divan...

CHAPTER SEVENTEEN

With a new spring in his step, Hamid Pasha made straight for the Crown Princess's tent. He did not wait upon an invitation to enter. The flap was open and he could see her inside. Why unnecessarily waste any more time?

She was lying on her divan, staring up at the roof of the tent, but sat up in surprise at his unexpected appearance And, as was inevitably the case in his presence, the atmosphere immediately became so charged with tension that she reacted, quite involuntarily, by nervously clenching her small fists once again.

"I came to find you earlier, to report something to you, but you were having some sort of meeting in your tent and I did not wish to disturb you," she stammered, trying her best to sound professional.

"That will have to keep until later," he responded, and she realized, from the tone of his voice that he had not come to quarrel. There was determination in his attitude, but his face was not unfriendly.—On the contrary! She had never seen him quite so amicable!

To her amazement, he took her by the hand and drew her to her feet.

"Come," he said. "I want to talk to you," and then, allowing her only enough time to slip on a suitable pair of shoes, he led her purposefully towards the doorway.

If Thérèse had wanted to, she could very well also have responded coolly, as he had once done, with, "Well, here I am.—Talk!" But, as he, himself, had once observed, women invariably allow their hearts to rule their heads. If the beloved says, "Come!"...they come!

So, without offering any resistance, she let him take her where he would.—From the very beginning, she had found his self-assurance magnetic—and, for the first time, she went through the gate of the hospital enclosure. She could hardly believe her eyes, for as far as she could see, in the valley and up against the mountain slopes, there were tents, tents, and more tents.

"Take a good look now, Princess," he said, with an unfamiliar, boyish lilt to his voice, that had not been there before. "This is what lies beyond the gate!" But he did not let go of her hand.

He led her between the tents, past shy, smiling, Arab women, and dignified, bearded Bedouin men. He took pride in showing her the healthy children in the stockade. Fowls squawked, flapped their wings and scattered before their feet, as he took her further, until, reaching his well-trodden path, they began to climb a short distance up the mountain.

Eventually they were alone among the rocks and the tamarisks, in the shadow of the peaks. It was pleasantly cool up there, and far below them lay the stockade, spread out in the sunshine. When he had found a good place, he put the pillow down for her to sit on, sat down beside her, and then, for the first time, looked directly at her. Something she saw in his blue eyes made the blood rise to her face, and her heart beat faster.

"Thérèse," he said diffidently, "I have revealed my 'secret' to you. Won't you share yours with me, now?...As a sign of trust, I have shown you my people. Do you trust *me* sufficiently now, to tell me the 'long story' that you avoided telling on the night of your accident?"

Nervously, but resigned to her lot, she replied, "It is a long story, but if you are prepared to listen, I would very much like to tell it to you."

"I am more than prepared to listen!" He made himself comfortable on the rock and settled down to listen. "Please start at the beginning and leave nothing out!"

But she did not know how to begin, and she stared out for a while across the valley, as though seeking inspiration. She could find no suitable words at all, until she happened to fix her gaze on the beautiful hands which, as he sat with his legs crossed, were clasped about one knee. Inconsequentially wondering how a man like Hamid Pasha could find the time to keep his hands in such immaculate condition, especially when the rough circumstances of life in the desert were taken into consideration, she summoned the courage to say, "I can only tell if you don't look at me!"

"Why?"

"Because you look right into people, Doctor Verwey! I might cry and I don't want you to see me!"

He took her hand in his again as he said softly, "I've seen you cry before, Princess. And I have felt like kicking myself ever since. Every time I have thought about that!"

Sitting on her right, it was her right hand that he held in his left, and, turning towards her, he flattened his and spread hers so that it lay on his palm, and he marvelled at the daintiness of it. He would have given a great deal to lift it to his lips, but thought better of it. Instead he put his other hand on top of hers, smiling as he saw how completely his own covered it. Then he said: "Thérèse, I am so sorry that I referred to your precious locket as a 'bauble'." He turned towards her again. "I see you holding onto it, even now, and I want you to know that I have berated myself for that, too—but I am *not* sorry that I stole that kiss!"

He moved closer, "I'll try not to look at you if it makes you nervous, but I want you to know that I am extremely nervous, too! I can face up to a horde of dangerous people in the desert, but I am actually terrified of you. I have no idea of how—when I'm not *El-Hakim* or Hamid Pasha—I should handle a princess...and I'm hopeless with girls.

"I beg of you to tell me the story because I shall be on tenterhooks until you have done so! I am afraid of what it is that you have to tell me, and I need to get that behind me, too, before I, myself know how to proceed from now on.— Meanwhile, do you mind if I put my arm around you, because, perhaps if you lean against me, neither of us will feel quite so nervous any more!"

Not being able to restrain himself, he was already looking directly at her, and was able to see the wistful smile that moved across the exquisite face. She gave a deep sigh.

"My childhood was certainly the happiest with which any child could be blest," she began..... "Soravia was one of those fairytale-like places where the birds seemed to sing more sweetly, and the colours of the flowers were brighter than anywhere else on earth. The people were contented, the harvests good, and there was always enough work for everyone.—Doesn't that sound like a fairytale existence? Well it was, while it lasted!"

"My parents were greatly loved, throughout the land. Their marriage had not been one of those cold alliances so often arranged between crown princes and princesses for the good of the state. I know that when they had been married nineteen years, they were as much in love as when first they met.

"I was their only child, but I was never lonely. Although she was older than I by a few years, Gerda, the daughter of the head chancellor, was my faithful friend and companion, and she constantly kept me company until the day she met, and later married Ferdinand von Mölendorff, a German count.

"Then came the war. Gerda and I could still keep in contact with one another—for a while—because our small country remained neutral!" Her voice wavered. "Unfortunately, her country by marriage was not quite so eager to respect that fact. My country was ravaged and the castle bombed. I saw my father, together with Gerda's, fall as the first air raid began. They were crossing a small bridge at the time, walking towards me, and later I saw their corpses floating in the water! What happened after that is not quite clear—except for another ghastly image....I ran through the burning entrance to the castle, to find my mother...and I saw...I saw...!"

She stopped talking and stared fixedly in front of her as though she were seeing the gruesome scene once more, and Dominic who had been listening attentively to the soft voice of this small person with the most charming accent he had ever heard, was so deeply moved that he lifted her hand to his mouth and kissed it sympathetically, while hardly realizing that he was doing so.

"And then?" he gently encouraged her.

"I was fortunate enough to escape and be taken to Switzerland by friends of my parents..."

"Perhaps you should try to put into words what you could not bring yourself to say, Thérèse," he suggested. "I have a strong sense that you have never gone into the details of that day with anyone before, and I know from experience that saying something out loud can be a catharsis..."

"You are right," she said, nodding. "Gerda knows the gist

of it, because she suffered the loss of her father...but she was not *there*!...*She was not there...*!"

By this time she was sobbing, and he had reason to be thankful for the fact that he had not, after all, used his handkerchief to mop his brow. He tilted her chin, to make her turn her face to his, and then he wiped her tears away, as unselfconsciously as if she were the tiniest of his patients. And she realized anew why his people loved him so much...

"Thank you," she said tremulously when he was done, involuntarily thinking of how completely natural all this was. She could have known him all her life!

"I think you're right, Dominic. I have this recurring nightmare. Sometimes it even overwhelms me in the daytime, and I have been so grateful to have been kept busy while I have been here. I have felt safe—which reminds me of what I meant to tell you earlier. But perhaps I'd better finish my own story first...

"In my most vivid memories of my mother, I always see her in one of the lovely, pastel gowns she loved to wear. She is about to come out, to meet me in the garden...but she did not reach me that day....I ran into the castle, and found her barely recognizable body, just inside the door, and then someone dragged me away before everything burst into flames...!"

"How awful for you!—And then you went to Switzerland?"

"I did. I first enlisted in the Soravian underground, and later joined a Red Cross nursing unit..."

"But you must have been a mere child!...How old were you when you did that?"

"Nearly seventeen. Before my eighteenth birthday I was already in the thick of the fighting. But you know all about that part of it already. The war was bad enough, but, for me, the worst really came after the last shots had been fired. Then I had to wrestle with two of the most powerful enemies in the world—memories, and loneliness!

"I roamed about for a year or two, desperately seeking diversion and forgetfulness, and finally accepted Lady Talbot's invitation to visit them in Cairo. She had been to school in Switzerland with my mother, and because, at the same time, she decided to invite Gerda, together with her husband and brother-in-law, I came. But even among old friends, it was no better.

"So-called 'pleasure' can only dull memories—not erase them. Shortly before I came here to you for the first time, I had applied for a position at a clinic in South Africa, and later I learnt that my application had been successful but then...I..."

Dominic perceived her confusion and was wondering what he could say to help her, when he suddenly remembered the strange remark Philip had shouted after him when he had left his tent.

"I don't know what all this is about," he told her, "but Philip asked me to tell you that he was releasing you from any promises you made to him.—Does that help?"

She was clearly relieved, and smiled reminiscently. "It does. It makes the rest of the story easier to relate. As I was saying, because I had realized that comfort could only be found in hard work, I had been seeking employment—and so I came here! Philip had made me promise that I would not tell you this, but one night, while you were busy with something, he told me quite a few things about your life, past and present. The story made a great impression on me, and then something else happened to convince me, and on the day I meant to post my letter of acceptance to South Africa, I decided, instead, that my mission might just as well be here, as there....I followed

Mamoun and the other two, in order to come and offer you my help!"

"What!" Dominic was stunned. "My dearest Thérèse, I admire you, more than I can say, and I appreciate the fact that you were willing to make such a sacrifice for me....But my dear girl I can't allow you to do that!"

As he said this, he was suddenly overcome with the deepest remorse, coupled with the most tremendous sense of loss. For a brief, enchanted moment, he had allowed himself to enter into a fool's paradise. Like a lovesick boy, he had been carried away on a tide of emotion such as he had never known before...but now, putting the situation into the perspective of harsh reality, he had been brought to his senses by his very own words

"There is no future for you here!...No...What I mean to say is, you are a crown princess, and as your father's only child you are, after all, his successor....You have a responsibility to your own people!"

Thérèse looked at him in surprise. "Which people? My dear Doctor Dominic, I have just been trying to explain to you that there aren't any. Not any longer! I no longer have a country, either. I am homeless and I am 'people-less'...I am like the wandering Jew! All I want now is to find a place somewhere where I can be of use and make my life worthwhile. I must have survived the bombs for *something*! "

While she was speaking, the wildest ideas were beginning to take root in Dominic's mind, and, as they unfolded, he was overwhelmed by one, hitherto unimaginable possibility.— Thérèse was not beyond his reach as he had thought. Circumstances had made them equal!

But, no! There was still one mighty obstacle, and the mere thought of it was worse than a dash of cold water in the face.

"Thérèse," he began, consumed with anxiety. "When did you find out...?"

"You mean, that you are Hamid Pasha?" She leaned away from him in order to survey him thoughtfully. "The night you sat by me in the hospital I started to tell you that I had seen you somewhere before. I thought it might have been in another hospital, somewhere, but I was not able to decide exactly where that could have been. Last week I suddenly remembered!"

"Where was that, Thérèse? What I'm trying to ask is, 'Where did you see me?'" He knew well enough, but he wanted to hear her say it.

Her face reddened and she suddenly seemed to have some trouble with her tongue. "It was on the balcony of Sir Humphrey Talbot's house!" she admitted, at last.

Dominic laughed delightedly when he saw her blush, and he held her hand more tightly "I kissed you, didn't I?" he asked, teasing her. "Were you very angry with me?"

Rosy to the very tips of her ears, she could not reply, and he laughed all the harder....Exultantly.

"What helped you to remember?" He noticed that she hesitated, and he asked again, "Did something prick your memory?"

"I was staying at a resort in the Nile valley last week, with Gerda and her husband," she said quietly, "and you came there. I first recognized the twins, who were waiting for you in the street, and then when I was outside on the veranda, you rode past. The wind blew your hood off and I recognized you at once. That was when I knew!"

"Oh!" At once he was serious once more. "Did you tell anyone of your discovery?"

"No one. At first I wanted to take Sir Humphrey into my confidence, but I couldn't do it! The very next day I decided to come here."

Dominic could only look at her in wonderment. Then the

full significance of what she had said, hit him. "You knew that *before* you left Cairo, and yet you came? You know what I am, but you still wanted to help me?" He found it incomprehensible that such a woman could exist! "Why, Thérèse?" he demanded urgently. "Why?" His heart was in his eyes as he waited in suspense upon her reply. "Please tell me truthfully, Princess!"

"Because I felt that, for whatever you were doing, there had to be a good reason! Last night Philip told me about Abdel Sharia and now I *know* that to be the case!"

This was not exactly the response he was hoping for, but he realized that he could not be too hasty. "What would you say if you knew that I was enabled to uncover the identity of Abdel Sharia today?" he asked.

"Oh, Dominic! Really?" She could not hide her excitement. "I am so happy for you! And now what will you do?"

"What am I going to do?...Well, it's like this..." He pursed his lips and answered her with a casual shrug of his shoulders, while watching her out of the corner of his eye. "I shall have to fight him, of course! It's a dangerous business, but what else can I do?"

His words had the desired result! The violet eyes widened and, with a cry of alarm she clung to his arm. "No, Dominic! No! You must not do that! What if he wounds you or..." She shuddered. "He could *kill* you! You mustn't risk it!"

It was with the utmost satisfaction that Hamid Pasha drew the Princess of Soravia into his arms. He had to put his mouth very close to one shell-like ear, to whisper, "Before I go to my death, may I, at least once, have the pleasure..."

"DOMINIC!" Philip's anxious voiced reached them from the pathway.

Startled, Dominic let go of Thérèse, and his arms dropped to his sides as his brother emerged from the surrounding foliage.

Philip was acutely aware of Thérèse's flaming cheeks and Dominic's resentful face. Stammering apologetically, he said, "I was told down in the stockade that I would find you here," and handed Dominic the note he had brought. It was written on pale lavender notepaper and reeked of some exotic perfume. Unfortunately it did not occur to him to consider how this must sound to Thérèse when he added, "It's from Lydia!"

Dominic jumped to his feet, and asked the other two to excuse him as he hastily ripped open the envelope, and read the contents with undisguised eagerness. He glanced at once at the watch which had once been Etienne's. Everything else was forgotten. All he could think of was that the confrontation with Abdel Sharia was finally at hand.

"Come!" he said to Thérèse and his brother. "We have to go back immediately!"

And neither he nor Philip noticed the expression on Thérèse's small, pale face.

(ii)

Dominic could never have anticipated that a night and day of such indescribable strain lay head for him. Roughly ninety minutes after Rameses and Ali had returned from the city with Lydia's note, the twins and their band stormed into the camp with ominous news. They had been able to establish that Mustapha was indeed well acquainted with Mohammed Ahmed, as Dominic had surmised, and what was more important, he had last been seen in the company of Farao the Ugly. It appeared, however, that someone had found it inconvenient for such inquiries to be made, because Mamoun and company were hardly beyond the city limits, when they were attacked by about twenty unknown horsemen who had obviously followed them from Mustapha's house. They had been fortunate enough to get away—but without Sezit.

That night no one could sleep. Dominic paced back and forth in his tent for most of it, and Philip alternately wandered around outside, or, kept his brother company. Involuntarily their thoughts kept going back to night before Etienne's death. Would Sezit suffer the same fate?

"And I sent him!" Dominic repeatedly reproached himself.

No one thought to enlighten Thérèse who went sadly to her tent, and blew her lamp out much earlier than usual.

***

Just as the new day dawned, urgent shouting drew Dominic and Philip, to the compound. They heard the clatter of hooves and almost fell over one another in their haste to get outside.

There a dreadful sight awaited them.

Philip shuddered and covered his face with his hands, but *El-Hakim* rushed forward. The gate was open and from all over the stockade the Bedouin came running. Sezit's two wives, who normally fought like cats and dogs, were now having to cling to one another for support.

"Mamoun!" *El-Hakim* sharply commanded the dwarf. "Stay in front of the princess's tent. I don't want her to see this!"

Sezit's feet had been fastened to the stirrups of his horse, in such a way that his battered head would drag on the ground, and the miles through desert sand and later rock, had left their mark. In addition, his back and shoulders were scored with deep, raw grooves, such as could have been caused by a rake or a pitchfork. Even Dominic winced at the sight.

With infinite care, they carried him inside, but as soon as they came under the light it was obvious that there was nothing to be done for the poor wretch, apart from the customary washing and shrouding of his body, and beginning the preparations for his burial. Because cremation was forbidden, this would have to be carried out before the sun rose too high in the sky, and the day grew too hot.

"Abdel Sharia shall pay for this," Dominic promised Sezit's wives, but suddenly the significance of all of this struck him with such force that it took his breath away.

Without touching Sezit—because a Muslim was not to be defiled by any Christian, not even *El-Hakim*—he left the others to do whatever was necessary, and ran to find Philip, who had meanwhile returned to his, Dominic's, tent.

"Phil, do you understand what this means?" he asked urgently when he found him, and quickly explained. "They must have used a gaffle or something similar, to try and get information out of him—probably to find out the name of his leader. When he would not talk, they tied him to his horse, and one good slap on the rump would have been sufficient to make the terrified animal bolt...so that it would lead them right to our doorstep, as it were! Now they not only know where Hamid Pasha hides out, but realizing that he will undoubtedly soon be hot on their tracks, they will have to act speedily!"

"What do you think they will do?" Philip, who was in complete agreement, wanted to know.

"Their best strategy would be to attack us first," *El-Hakim* decided, "and as soon as possible, but somehow I doubt that Abdel Sharia would have sufficient men at his disposal in this area....Dare I wait to find out? Our only hope is to forestall them."

Philip nodded. He was about to ask Dominic how he planned to do this, when he heard him gasp.

"Oh, dear God!" *El-Hakim* cried, and his brother knew that he was not just being profane. "We have to get Thérèse out of here!"

The reality of his responsibility suddenly weighed very heavily upon Dominic. If anyone had asked him, at any other time, how he had ever managed to accomplish all that he had, he would probably just have shrugged his shoulders. He would have passed the question off with something facetious, like 'just taking it one day at a time', or 'by putting one foot in front of the other', but on that day it was difficult for him to get his head around the enormity of what was actually at stake. The lives of so many depended upon him, not least among them, that of his very own brother.

"*Boetie*," he said reflectively, appreciating the rare moment of communion alone with Philip "we're a long way from the polo field at Concordia today, aren't we? I don't think we're going to get through this without God's help....Will you pray with me?...For all of us, *boetie*, but I have a special request for myself...

"I'm almost ashamed to confess that, even in this dire situation, I would *hate* to kill anybody!...I've knocked a good few blokes out lately...but *kill*!—I can't be a coward about this and I'm ready to die....I want to honour my promise to Etienne—but Phil, I'm a *doctor*! Now I don't even know how to pray about this, myself....Will you please pray as you are led..."

"Of course!" Philip said at once.

He came over and put his hand on his brother's shoulder, and they had hardly closed their eyes, when they were interrupted by a discreet cough from outside.

"*Effendi*," came Raschid's voice. "May I come in?" And, seeing the brothers together like that, he said apologetically, upon entering, "I intrude, and for that I ask your pardon. I come to say that I am ready to depart. Having now already heard what Mamoun has been able to tell us, I do not believe that you would either wish, or need Fuzad the *Cadi* to wait upon further word from you.....I also come to say that the wives of Sezit, request the honour of *El-Hakim's* presence. They say that he would have wanted his leader to be with them at this time"

"Of course," Dominic replied, as Philip had done only a few minutes before. "That would be an honour, and I shall go, but first I need to tell you about the situation in which we find ourselves here today.—Or perhaps Philip-brother can do that for me?"

Philip nodded. "Go, Dom!" To Raschid he said, "My brother and I were about to offer prayers for Sezit and his family, and for you, Raschid. For your safety and for the safety of us all. With God's help, Sharia's reign of terror is coming to an end, but we all would like to live long enough to see that happen."

As quick-witted as usual, the astute Raschid grasped at once what Philip-brother was trying to tell him. "Go, *Sahbena*!" He said to Dominic. "I go quickly to fetch Ezra."

And so on this day, while Dominic Verwey, also known as *Sahbena El-Hakim* and *Hamid Pasha*, went to assist with the arrangements for the burial of his Muslim friend, a Christian, a Jew, and a Muslim prayed together in his tent, for God's mercy on the soul of Sezit, and the safety of everyone in the stockade of El-Bus Mohandess.

(iii)

Thérèse was woken from a troubled sleep by Meriam, who was apologetically shaking her by the shoulder. "Wake up, Highness," the girl said, speaking as clearly as she could in English, liberally interspersed with Arabic.—And, as if to make sure that she was understood, she illustrated the words with eloquent gestures. "The *Effendi* has requested that you rise quickly and make ready to depart, as soon as you have eaten." She then pointed to the tray at the princess's bedside.

A moment later Philip burst into the tent.

"Thérèse," he inquired urgently, "is there any place in Cairo to which you can go? What I mean is, have you given up your rooms at the hotel?"

"But why?" Thérèse frowned, sitting up, disgruntled and still half asleep. "What's going on here?"

"Dominic wants you to be taken back as soon as possible, and I was just wondering where you would prefer to go?"

"Oh, I see." Now wide-awake, she was beginning to get the picture. She tossed her dark curls proudly, and, with mounting anger, responded haughtily: "Of course I have somewhere to go! Why would you even need to ask? Lady Talbot has made it clear that she is only too eager to have me return to the mansion, at any time....You go and tell Dominic Verwey from me, that it is quite unnecessary for me to avail myself of his hospitality any longer!"

But once Philip had gone, she could not suppress a sob. That effusive friendliness on the part of Hamid Pasha had been no more than a ploy to ensure that she could safely be sent on her way. Now that his precious Lydia had surfaced again, he naturally could not wait to be reconciled with her, and plainly the presence of another woman would cause him nothing but embarrassment.

So much for his pathetic, "I'm hopeless with girls!"—when it was clear that he had females coming out of the woodwork! Most disgusting of all was that he did not seem to care that this Lydia was a married woman!

Having a quick wash, she was grateful for the ewer of warm water and the clean towel, brought to her for that purpose. She then dressed hastily in her riding habit, and while Meriam packed the rest of her belongings in the saddlebag for her, she ran a quick comb though her hair, before sitting down on the divan to drink her coffee, which had been kept warm on the small charcoal burner placed under the pot. Despite her anger and her eagerness to depart, something more than jealousy and profound hurt nagged at her, and though trying to convince herself that she would actually be quite pleased to be back in Cairo, she suddenly recognized that disquieting feeling, as fear.

Simultaneously she realized that she was afraid to return to the Talbots, and, in a panic, she ran outside where she was relieved to see Philip, with his head down, in earnest conversation with someone, not far from her tent. He was obviously waiting for her, because, hearing her call out to him, he looked up and called back, "There you are! That was quick work."

"What has Dominic done with my horse?" was the first thing she could think of to say, and Philip came towards her at once, nodding to the man with whom he had been talking, as though their conversation had been terminated.

"He had it sent back to the person from whom you hired it. It's a kind of weird thing we do here." Then he noticed that she was trembling. "Are you alright, Princess of Hearts?"

"No, Phillip," she admitted. "I am not....Far from it!" And then it all came out in a rush. She found herself telling him about the hideous man who had appeared at her window at the Talbots, adding, "I tried to tell Dominic about this before, the first time I came here, and again yesterday, but he would not give me a chance to do so.

"I don't know if he has had the time to talk at any length with Christopher Brent, since then, but I was able to spend some time with him, and I wanted to report to Dominic, as he is his doctor, that the patient's memory seems to be fast returning. Mr. Brent recalls a tall figure in a white *burnous* coming to his rescue, but what I now find so disquieting is his mention of abduction, and his description of the kidnapper. There is no doubt in my mind, Philip, that Brent was indeed being taken somewhere against his will, that it was Hamid Pasha who rescued him, and that the person by whom he was abducted was the same dreadful person I saw looking at me through my window, the last time I stayed with the Talbots.

"Philip-brother," she confessed, putting her hand on his arm, "I know that you are the one person I can trust….I am ashamed to have to confess that I am terrified! I have weathered bombs and air raids, but perhaps because I was surrounded by so many other people, all in the same boat as I, I was never as scared as I am now….What if that dreadful person had been sent to kidnap *me*? He would not have known that he would be wasting his time. That I have no friends or family from whom he could exact ransom!"

Philip was clearly alarmed. "Please wait in your tent for me, Princess. I'll be back as soon as I can. Dominic is involved with a burial at the moment, but I am going to try and catch his eye. No one will be offended by an interruption. Everyone is constantly on the alert in this camp, and, as you must have discovered by now, it is rare for a whole day to pass without some form of disturbance!"

She did wait as requested, until, listening to the loud wailing in the distance, she was reminded of what Philip had said about Dominic, and she could not help wondering about the funeral and what rôle *El-Hakim* had to play in it At the same time, thinking again about Christopher Brent, she decided to go across to the hospital, to satisfy herself that it was not perhaps one of her patients who died in the night, and to wish the Englishman well before she left. To her surprise, she found Philip and Ezra both in the ward with him, helping him to dress.

"Dominic has decided to send Mr. Brent back at the same time," was Philip's surprising explanation. "You are to wear your *burnous*, and Farida has gone to borrow one for Mr. Brent, who is unused to riding, and is now having to decide whether he prefers to be taken on a camel, or behind me on my horse."

Reading the unspoken question in her eyes, he drew her out into the passage and quickly explained: "Yes, I am to go with you, and deliver both of you personally to Sir Humphrey. I'm lending Mr. Brent some of my own clothes because those he was wearing when he was brought here, are too badly stained.

"No one knows who I am, Princess," he added, when he saw that she seemed concerned. "I am not as conspicuous as Dom is. He has always done his best to ensure that the twins, Little Brother, and I are not seen to be connected with him in any way, which is why we can fetch supplies and so on with impunity. So, I shall be okay, you'll see…as long as I can rely on your discretion! My only hope is that, when you introduce me—and beyond informing Sir Humphrey of the experience both of you have had, with the not very handsome man who has so frightened you—you would tell him only that you have been working as a volunteer in a small desert hospital, where you happened to come across the missing banker. I am supposedly one of the interns, detailed to help you keep an eye on a still weak patient, and to see you both safely back to the mansion.—May I rely on you to go along with that?" He grinned wryly. " My future sort of depends on it, you know!"

"I am very grateful to you, Phil, and I shall never forget your kindness to me. You may rely on me. But what will you do, once you've handed us over to the Talbots? Will you be safe to return here on your own?"

"I'll be fine," he assured her with a smile. "I shan't be returning immediately, and I shan't be on my own. My brother insists that you have either me, or one of the burly Arabs— whom you have so captivated, and whom we're taking along with us—to guard you night and day!"

He had been about to add, "Until *El-Hakim* comes to get you," but remembering the look on his brother's face when he had learned about Thérèse's frightening nocturnal visitor, he thought better of it. His own stomach was in such a knot that he did not want to dwell on the rest of what Dominic, had said...."And promise me, *boetie*, that if I don't make it, you will take care of my sweetheart, for the rest of your life!"

CHAPTER EIGHTEEN

Lydia had written to say that she would be waiting in the lounge of the Hotel el-Wak every evening between five and six, but unfortunately, by the time Dominic had received the note, it had already been too late for him to go. That had contributed to his being unable to rest the night before, and, besides the sorrow of Sezit's funeral, and the ache in his heart at having to send Thérèse away so precipitously that he had not been granted a moment alone with her, he went through the whole day in suspense and uncertainty, waiting for the time to leave for Cairo.

The suspense was killing. At any moment the stockade could be attacked by Abdel Sharia, but *El-Hakim* dared not make any move until he had established from Lydia where Mohammed Ahmed was. He wondered whether posting extra guards in the foothills and at the entrance to the camp, would be an adequate precaution. He was quite sick with anxiety about the safety of Thérèse, Philip and the others, and tense with concern about the women and children under his care. Lydia was the only one who could provide him with information that could help him plan his next move.

Her letter had been composed in precisely the manner one would have expected of her. Every time Dominic re-read it, he could hear the affectation in that voice more and more clearly in his imagination, and he could also picture the tragic, melodramatic hand-gestures, as she decided upon her choice of words. Many were liberally underscored.

"Dom—I __MUST__ see you! This is a matter of __LIFE AND__ __DEATH__ *to me!!! The most TERRIBLE things are happening here, and there is* __NOT A MOMENT TO BE LOST__*!!! Please be merciful and meet me even JUST ONCE! I shall never bother you again!!!*

"Seeing that I cannot be certain of when you will receive this note, I shall be waiting, until the end of this week, between five and six pm, in the lounge of the El-Wak for you.

"__PLEASE COME, I BESEECH YOU!__
LYDIA"

Under the present circumstances, he had needed at least fifty men to accompany him as far as the city, and had deemed it advisable to post a minimum of twenty others to wait for him.—Some in strategic positions around the hotel, and others to hold the horses, about a block down the street. He gave one of the men his rapier and his *burnous* to hold.

With a cry of pleasure Lydia came tripping out to meet him on the steps. She was dressed according to the very latest fashion, known internationally as the 'New Look', but he was totally unable to appreciate that fact. Her makeup was flawless, but the doll face left him completely unmoved.

He could not understand what he had ever seen in this shallow woman, and, with a catch in his throat, he suddenly realized that he was unconsciously comparing her with Thérèse. In contrast with the sweetness and clear, shining, beauty that was hers, Lydia seemed brassy, and he could also not help comparing this girl's weak chin and mouth, with the firmness and character of Thérèse's enchanting face. He had to pull himself up sharply to listen to what Lydia was saying, when all he could think of was Thérèse's lovely mouth, whether Philip had arrived safely with his charges, and the impending confrontation with Abdel Sharia.

"Oh, Dom!" Lydia cried, welcoming him. "You have really come!"

"That is obvious, isn't it?" he replied, brusquely. "Or do your eyes trouble you?" At a time like this he was not in the mood for inane remarks.

"Oh, come now!" she chided, archly fluttering her eyelashes at him. "Don't you go fighting with little old Lydia, now!"

She took his hand possessively, and would have led him inside, but pointing to his riding breeches and boots, and his open-necked shirt, he persuaded her to walk with him instead, in the garden on one side of the building. She read more into this invitation than he had intended, and giggled coyly when he pointed to a bench in the darkest corner, but Dominic was too distracted to notice that.

"Well then," he said, once they were seated. "What are some of the 'terrible' things you wanted to tell me?"

Lydia pouted and regarded him accusingly. "It's already more than four days since I wrote the letter!"

"I know," he acknowledged, "but I only received it yesterday."

"Then I forgive you, of course," she said. She grasped his sleeve. "Dominic, take me with you, wherever you are going when you leave here!"

"What!" The request had come so unexpectedly that, for a moment, he could only stare at her with unfeigned astonishment. "*What?*"

"I made a dreadful mistake, Dom," she said sadly. "And I realize that now. You are the one I truly love!"

He looked at her sternly. "My dear Lydia, is this the reason why you needed to see me so urgently?...Is *this* one of the terrible things? That you picked the wrong man?" He heaved a sigh of sheer exasperation, praying for patience.

"No," she admitted. "But I really do love you!"

"Didn't I make it clear enough at our last meeting that there can never again be anything between us?" he stormed at her. Time was flying by, and he dared not waste a moment of it on such nonsense.

To his consternation, she covered her face with her hands and burst into a storm of tears, weeping as she poured out her story.

"Alfit—that's what I have to call him—made me a promise that I would be the only one, Dom," she sniffed wretchedly, " but he is entitled to have four wives, and he has recently seen someone for whom he is about to break that promise!"

After all he had already been through that day, and considering the dramatic wording of her note, this was a colossal anticlimax. That this should turn out to be the reason for the urgency of her request to meet him, at such a critical moment in his own life, was laughable, but he curbed himself and put his hand on her shoulder.

"Look here, Lydia," he said, not unkindly. "I cannot begin to understand how you must feel, but I can't say that I am surprised. Perhaps you should have expected this." He wondered fleetingly what she would do if he were to tell her about the harems of Abdel Sharia. She was only one of hundreds!

Suddenly he felt sorry for her. This was not a time for him to forget that everyone was equally important to God. Remembering what Raschid had said about him, Dominic, he was ashamed. He could almost hear his friend's voice....*"Today I confess to you that I do not fast because it is Ramadan....I fast for my own forgiveness, as much as I pray for you!"*

And it was then that Dominic realized that he had never really forgiven Lydia. He and Philip prayed for many people, but it had never occurred to them to pray for her.

How strange that it was she who had been responsible, in the first place, for his still being in Egypt. And for the paths along which both he and Philip had been led to walk since the day they had set out to search for her....How utterly beyond all comprehension it was, that the man for whom she had jilted him, was the very one with whom he now had to settle a score, for such a vastly different reason.

"To run away with me, Lydia," he said more gently, "is not an option. Perhaps you are just mistaken, and if you decide later that you still want to leave your husband, I am prepared to help you to get back to England. Tonight I am unfortunately in a bit of a hurry!"

"You're always in too much of a hurry!" she cried wildly. "And I am not mistaken! I distinctly heard him tell Farao about her, with my very own ears!...They have been planning this for more than a week." She looked pleadingly at him. "Please just listen for a moment longer!...

"The night you came to visit me, I told you about the strange goings on in my home—for two reasons. Firstly to spark your interest and elicit you sympathy, and secondly, I reckoned that, if I could make you appreciate how ruthless my husband can be, you would help me to get away from him.

"On the previous night, Alfit had been to a banquet and apparently—from what I was able to make out—that was where he saw her, and he later ordered Farao to bring her to our house. Whether she perhaps does not wish to marry Alfit, or whatever the case may be, I only know that she disappeared, and that Alfit was furious. Early this week, he told me outright of his intention to marry another wife, which was when I wrote to you.—I had to find someone to help me!

"When at first you did not come, I began to fear that you would be too late. I either had to get her out of the way, or leave before she arrived—but, happily, she still was nowhere to be found, and Alfit, himself, has had be absent from home a great deal, on business…!"

"Is he there now?" Dominic hastily interrupted her, determined at least to derive some benefit from the interminable tale of woe to which he was reluctantly being subjected.

"Yes. He and Farao returned early this morning with about twenty other men, whom I have not seen before. Alfit said he did not want to have to leave the house again, but Farao has kept coming and going at intervals. Just before I left to come here, I overheard him telling my husband that he had heard along the grapevine that the wretched creature was back in Cairo, and he has possibly already gone to fetch her…!" By this time, Lydia was becoming hysterical. "Perhaps, right at this moment, Alfit is waiting for her to arrive!…Now I have to face it that the situation is quite hopeless, Dom! You *must* take me away with you!"

"Why don't you just go home and tell him to choose between the two of you?" Dominic suggested, anxious to get this over with. "You are, after all is said and done, his first wife—which gives you a certain standing—and perhaps if you threaten to leave him, he might forget about taking another one!"

"I have tried that," she cried hopelessly, "but it made no difference! What makes everything worse is that he won't let me go, either. I'm trapped! *O-o-o-h!*" She began to sob afresh. "Talk about just desserts! I was awful to you, and this is how I am being punished! Alfit calmly informed me that she is far more important to him than I am, and that, with her as his wife, he can rise to great heights in the *Barlaman.* He is a very ambitious man.

"He believes that the king is soon to be deposed and

exiled, and he sees himself as Egypt's first president. There is no doubt that the lady he has in mind would be a great asset to him in that position, and, in the face of that, *my* place as 'first wife' in our home, would mean less than nothing. This lady is a princess, no less, and has many influential friends, even among the British. As a matter of fact she is, at this moment, a guest in the mansion of Sir Humphrey Talbot!"

"*What!*" Dominic yelled, for the third time that evening. "Oh, my dear God!"

An icy hand had suddenly closed around his heart, his throat contracted and his mouth was dry, as the most dreadful possibilities went through his brain. He had lately overlooked far too many important clues. He had become complacent and careless about far too many things. Why had he not paid more attention to Thérèse, the very first time she had spoken about a man who had so terrified her? Why had he not given her a chance to tell him about Farao while they were on the mountain together? With his mind's eye he could again see the hideous horseman gallop past them, while he, Dominic, and Lydia had been in the garden, and it shocked him to realize that Farao had probably, at that very moment, been on his way to Sir Humphrey's home, where he would presently terrify Thérèse by looking at her through an open window.

If he had known that Lydia's spouse was on Sir Humphrey's guest list, and probably on friendly terms with the Talbots, he would never have sent her back to that house! How grateful he was that Philip had taken him aside at Sezit's funeral, to enlighten him. Now he could only give thanks for the fact that he had not let him go with her alone, and pray that he and the people he had with him, could forestall Farao.

He did not speak for a while, pondering the question of how Farao had found out that Thérèse was with the Talbots once more. The twins had an 'in', as he knew well, but somehow he could not believe that Abdel Sharia had spies in the mansion. He then considered what Lydia had meant by the 'grapevine', and decided that she had simply been using a figure of speech....On the other hand. what about the men who had turned up at with Farao at Lydia's home earlier that day, and whom she said she had never seen before?

All at once he felt cold shivers go down his spine as the significance hit him....Those were undoubtedly the men responsible for the cruel death of Sezit. He felt sure of it. And, supposing that they had lain in wait near his stockade, all night, awaiting further developments, it could only be that they had seen Philip and his small contingent emerge from the tunnel, and had followed them right to the Talbots' front door. If Farao had been with them at the time—which, judging by what Lydia had said, must have been the case—he would have recognized Thérèse instantly.

If there was an atom of comfort in what he surmised, it was that Sharia's men were no longer in the foothills, and that meant that no attack on his people in the stockade, was imminent.—But the ghastly truth was that Thérèse was more valuable to the ambitious Mohammed Ahmed than she knew.

When Philip had told him about Farao's rôle in the kidnapping of Brent, he had repeated what Thérèse had said to him about having no one from whom ransom could have been exacted for her. Evidently, for Mohammed Ahmed's purposes, she possessed far more than flawless beauty, mere monetary value, or wealthy connections....She had a title!

For the first time in Dominic Verwey's life he was scared stiff. He was so terrified that he began to tremble like an old man with the ague. His hands shook, and he could barely control the chattering of his teeth. His heart thumped so hard that he could hardly breathe, making him so short of breath that he was slightly nauseous.

"Lydia," he croaked hoarsely, "when is Farao going to fetch her, did you say?"

"He was still at the house when I left, and I remember now that Alfit told him to wait until the sun had set." She sounded surprised at his question. "What's the matter, Dominic? You don't look well!"

He hastily consulted his watch and looked anxiously at the darkening sky in which the last, sharp rays of the sun were already fading. And then the fear began to give way to a deathly calm. He sprang up and drew Lydia up with him.

"I shall try to intercept Farao," he said hurriedly. "Later tonight I shall go to your house, but, while I am there, it would be safer for you to stay out of the way....If you can manage to do so, leave a window open for me. Now think carefully, girl," he pleaded. "How many men would there be in the house with Alfit now? I am going to try and help you, but I can only do that if you tell me everything I need to know!"

She frowned, trying to concentrate. "Together with the men who arrived today, and those that are normally there, I'd say about twenty-five. Of course I can't say whether or not others have joined them in my absence....Alfit will be there for sure, because that's what he told me."

Dominic had already begun to walk away, but he turned around impulsively and kissed her on the cheek. "Do not worry any more," he promised her solemnly. "While I live, he will not have the princess....She doesn't know it yet, but, you see, with God's help, I plan to marry her myself!"

He began to run then, whistling for his men as he did so. When he reached his horse, he waited only long enough to hang his white *burnous* around his shoulders, and put Etienne's rapier in place, before he was in the saddle, urging his companions forward.

"We're going to the home of Sir Humphrey Talbot," he shouted to Rameses. "Abdel Sharia is attempting to get the princess!"

(ii)

In the beginning Dominic's involvement in the struggle against Abdel Sharia had been because of his pledge to El-Bus Mohandess. In due course he had been further motivated by an urge to avenge Etienne, and the knowledge of what Raschid and Ezra, and others like them, had suffered, had spurred him on. Today, when he had left the stockade a few hours earlier, he had considered the murder of Sezit to be the last straw—but until Lydia had told him about the Bey's designs on Thérèse, the fight had been largely an impersonal one. Now it had become a matter of life and death to him.

On the way to the Talbot mansion, a consuming hatred for Abdel Sharia rose up in him, and the closer he got, the more angry he became. There was a red haze of fury before his eyes, and a throbbing in his temples. With every stride of Snow's powerful legs, the hatred for Sharia mounted, because this time the monster was poaching on the preserves of Hamid Pasha, himself! He could not wait for the reckoning...

A short distance from the mansion, he held up his hand, motioning the cavalcade to halt briefly. "We will attack Mohammed Ahmed's house, as soon as we have accomplished our mission at Sir Humphrey's," he told his companions, and directed two of them to return to the stockade. Their instructions were to muster all the able-bodied men in the camp, and to go at once to the aid of Fuzad and Raschid. On their way back to the stockade, they were to advise the horsemen he had left behind on the outskirts of the city, of his intention to attack. There were, among them, several who had been to the Bey's residence, with him before. They would know the way, were to proceed directly, and could lead the rest to where they had concealed themselves previously. Once there, they were to await his arrival.

Mamoun, Haroun and Little Brother were normally his chosen messengers, but something told him that it would be heartless to send them away this time. Mamoun would give his life for the princess, and neither he nor the other two should be deprived of the opportunity to be a part of her rescue.

And so they raced on through the busy streets of Cairo. It was a hot wind that blew in their faces this night, and *El-Hakim's* heart beat wildly, from both rage, and fear....Fear not for himself, but for Thérèse. The road seemed endless and one question beat like a drum in his brain.—Would he be in time?

For on this day, Dominic had, almost unconsciously, begun to realize what she really meant to him. The emotion he had felt on the mountain with her had been part of a dream, and the words he had used when asking his brother to protect her, and in saying what he did to Lydia, had slipped out. He had not understood whence they had come....But *now* he knew!...He knew what had evaded him....He loved Thérèse desperately, with his heart and soul. He could finally understand why he had tortured himself with such uncertainty. Being in love was very new to him—and, for all he knew, that was perhaps the very kind of perversity that love could provoke!

At the thought of her, his throat tightened. In his imagination he could see the enchanting little face and the soft roundings of her figure. He recalled the sweetness of her voice as she was telling him her story, he remembered the tiny feet he had washed, and love and longing for her overwhelmed him so powerfully that he felt as though his heart would burst

What he had felt for Lydia seemed foolish in retrospect. The clumsy fascination of an inexperienced young man, with the first pretty girl he had come to know after years of study and long deprivation of feminine companionship. There had never been for Lydia, this blinding passion or desire. Never the tenderness, the urge to protect her, or the pride in having the privilege of doing so, that he felt at that moment. Lydia had never had the power to accelerate his pulse in the way the mere proximity of Thérèse could.

On they went. He felt the steady rhythm of Snow's even gait beneath him, and heard the clatter of the hoof-beats on paved road. They were now on the fringe of Heliopolis and, within five blocks of their destination. Dominic knew that he could drive himself crazy by dwelling on the thought of his princess in the arms of Mohammed Ahmed or—no, that was too horrendous to contemplate—perhaps even among the women in one of his harems! Then and there he resolved that, if he lived through this, he would never waste another moment away from her. No obstacle would be too great for him to overcome!

They halted in front of the mansion and, as they did so, a sudden thought stabbed Dominic like a knife. If Farao had climbed up to Thérèse's bedroom once before, he could have done so again. He could very well already be there. There was no alternative for him, Dominic, and his people, but to barge straight in, through the house.

Loudly and urgently Hamid Pasha rapped on the front

door of Sir Humphrey Talbot's mansion with the hilt of his rapier, and the moment the door was opened, he and his men stormed inside, sweeping the petrified footman along with them. The entire mansion echoed with the sound of footsteps and spurs.

"This way!" Dominic called out, and running across the wide hallway, made for the stairs that led to the next floor. At the same time, from inside the dining hall where the tables were already set, a group of uniformed serving maids and other liveried servants emerged, to stare at him, dumb with terror.

One girl began to scream.. *"Hamid Pasha!"* she shrieked.

Doors immediately flew open all over the place. As he ascended the steps, two at a time, with Rameses hot on his heels, Dominic saw, on the landing, a number of wide-eyed people, in varied stages of dressing for dinner.

"Hamid Pasha!" other women now took up the cry, and Dominic swore under his breath. If Farao were anywhere in the house, this would certainly alert him, but one good thing did come of this. Somewhere upstairs, his brother had heard him.

He raised his rapier, and being so tall, himself, he had no difficulty in catching everyone's attention. "No one will come to any harm," he announced authoritatively. "Please stand back.—We are only looking for the Princess Thérèse!"

By now he had just about reached the second floor, and could see some of the doors leading out of the passage. Which of them was Thérèse's?

Just then, Ruth Talbot, who had also heard the uproar, came running excitedly down the passage. This was an opportunity she was determined not to miss!—Her father obviously had the same idea! Before Dominic could set foot on the top step, Sir Humphrey appeared before him and he, Dominic, looked up—directly into the barrels of the two revolvers Talbot was holding, one in each hand

"This is an opportunity for which I have long waited," the man muttered viciously. "If either you or any of your cohorts make the slightest movement, Hamid Pasha, you are as good as dead!"

Dominic froze, and so did his men, some of them who were already on the staircase, too. Not a single one of them would dare to move, because without Hamid Pasha they were lost, and Humphrey Talbot was known to be a crack shot. There was a pregnant silence during which all held their breath.

For a split second, Dominic wondered whether he should risk tackling the man, but time was too precious. If he and his men were to become involved in a fracas, even if they won, Farao could easily slip away with his prey, unseen, under cover of the commotion. He also had to consider the stockade of now unprotected people he had left behind him, and bear in mind the dire consequences of his not being able to prevent Abdel Sharia from getting to them.

"Sir Humphrey," he said despairingly, surprising the man with his educated and refined voice, "it is absolutely imperative that I reach the princess!—Her life is in danger. Even as we stand here, wasting time, there are individuals—perhaps already in her room—who may succeed in abducting her!"

"So!" Talbot sneered contemptuously. "Cornered, the coward would try to talk himself out of this! Stay where you are!" he bellowed as Dominic made a move towards him.

Pearls of perspiration beaded Hamid Pasha's forehead, and he impatiently thrust his hood back, almost causing Ruth Talbot to swoon at what, without his knowledge, she later described as his 'magnificence!' He *had* to think of a plan...

To this day Thérèse does not know how she managed it, because fear generally rendered her speechless—and Dominic shudders when he thinks of what might have happened if she had not chosen that precise moment—but as Dominic and Talbot stared fixedly at one another, the impasse and the silence were broken by an ear-splitting scream.

"DOMINIC!" they heard her terrified voice.

Now, totally disregarding the threat before him, Dominic frantically pushed Sir Humphrey aside. He was oblivious of every threat or danger as he tore down the passage, with his men in hot pursuit. Sir Humphrey's guests hastily made way and then, to the pasha's surprise, there was Ruth Talbot running ahead of him, and eagerly shouting, "This way!...Here is Thérèse's room!"

With a mighty heave, he and his men burst through the door, almost falling over each other as it gave way. Dominic managed to retain his balance and dived for Farao's legs. They grappled with one another on the floor, overturning furniture in the process, and, at one stage, *El-Hakim* was surprised to see none other than his brother there, too, shielding Thérèse with his own body. Suddenly everyone's attention was drawn by a gasp from her. One of Farao's henchmen, had lunged out, striking Philip on the head, and another of them, who had been quick to grab hold of Thérèse, was holding her in front of him, his gun to her back, as he slowly began to move towards the door with her.

"Stay where you are," he commanded. "I am taking the princess with me, and if anyone should dare to interfere, I shall shoot her, without hesitation!" It was the tall sheik from the gathering!

A wave of frustration and indecision swept over Hamid Pasha's dumbfounded band. No one moved. They could only stand there transfixed with horror. No one saw the small figure move like lightning, along the wall behind the sheik, until Mamoun raised his arm and his knife flashed. He pointed to the door.

"Run, Highness!" he commanded Thérèse, watching the man crumple to the floor.

After that, the scuffle rapidly came to an end.—Almost! Two of Farao's companions made for the door and one ran to the window, but Rameses and Ali each sorted out one of them, and Little Brother smartly impeded the flight of the third, with a valuable Chippendale chair. Unfortunately however, the loathsome Farao, whom Dominic still had in a clinch in one corner, managed to break free, and also made a run for the window.

"Stop him!" Dominic cried urgently. Farao could not be permitted to go and warn his master.

Ali's foot shot out and Farao stumbled, at which Little Brother, who had remained undecidedly holding the chair aloft, reached down from his great height, and finished the man off with a well-aimed blow. At last it was truly over.

Surveying the wreckage, Dominic rubbed his hands together. "So many less to deal with later," he observed with satisfaction.

He had a good look at his brother, who was sitting up and grinning ruefully. "You seem to be okay....I'm sorry I have to go, *boetie*," he said regretfully to Philip, "but I know of a good nurse who can look after you until I get back. Thank you for watching over her." Then he rushed out, but hesitated at the top of the staircase, from where he beckoned to the rest to follow him.—"Now comes the pay-off!" he promised them.

Downstairs he encountered Sir Humphrey and his houseguests, huddled together in the vestibule. Thérèse was standing alone, apart from the rest of them.

"I sincerely apologize, Sir," Dominic said, addressing Talbot courteously. "We appear to have made a bit of a mess of the princess's bedroom." With that he crossed over to Thérèse, and took her by the arm.

Her reaction was the last thing he would have expected. She stepped back from him as though his fingers scorched her, and her lips curled scornfully. "Go back to your precious Lydia," she snapped.

Dominic laughed out loud, not put off in the least. His put his arms determinedly around her. "I promised that I would return to steal this," he murmured, with his lips very close to her ear and in full view of everyone present, he drew her closer, and kissed her passionately on her adorable mouth, before turning around to take his departure.

"The audacity of the scoundrel" Sir Humphrey spluttered, cursing irately.

"*Oooh*! How romantic!" sighed his daughter, quite beside herself with ecstasy.

From the front door, Hamid Pasha called out to Talbot. "Please take care good care of her, Sir Humphrey. She's very precious!" And then, as an afterthought: "The police will probably be able to help you to get rid of some of the unfortunate people we have had to leave scattered around upstairs!

"Princess," he called over his shoulder, "would you mind attending to the patient in your bedroom?...He's very precious to me, too!"

Dominic had spoken too soon. "You're not going without me!" cried Philip, scrambling down the stairs. "Do you think I'm going miss this?"

And Sir Humphrey could only stand there fuming.

The appearance, behind him on the staircase, of the Englishman from the Bank of England, introduced some light relief, especially as Brent was clad in his pyjamas, dressing gown and slippers—for which he apologized. Blinking, he surveyed the people gathered at the foot of the stairs as though searching for someone, and suddenly his face brightened.

"Oh, there you are Nurse Thérèse!" he exclaimed delightedly. "Am I mistaken or did I hear the voice of my excellent physician, and good friend, Doctor Verwey?—*El-Hakim*," he added, smiling as though he had accomplished something momentous by remembering the name by which the other patients had referred to Dominic. "Young Doctor Philip, asked me to stay quietly in my room, when he ran out so suddenly, but I have not had a chance to thank *El-Hakim*, or..."

"That was no doctor, Christopher!" Sir Humphrey barked. "The voice you heard was that of Hamid Pasha, the brigand who abducted you!...Came here and caused no end of a ruckus, and no one lifted a finger to stop him....Valentine?...Captain Morgan?...Where the devil is my aide when I need him?...My guests have been disgracefully unnerved!"

"You must be mistaken, Humphrey," Brent said, somewhat confused. "Doctor Dominic is the man who *intervened*!... Certainly not one who made off with me!...Been taking dashed good care of me, ever since....Why, I'm here—and alive to tell the tale, aren't I? Excellent little hospital he runs there....Have some good news for him, when next I see him!"

"You are still far from well, dear Christopher," Lady Talbot said, soothingly. "You'll feel better in the morning! That nice young man, Philip is the one who rescued you and brought you here. Do come back to bed!...Thérèse, my dear, since you are a nurse, would you please assist Mr. Brent?"

"Certainly," said Thérèse—and still loyal, in spite of herself, added: "Doctor Verwey *is* Hamid Pasha. He is not, in *my* opinion, a brigand. He *did* rescue Mr. Brent—and Philip is his brother!"

CHAPTER NINETEEN

Beyond the city limits, Dominic and his companions, linked up with the men who had been waiting for him. He did a head count and announced joyfully: "All still here, thank God!—Forty-eight—and then there are the two we sent back to the stockade....In comparison, Abdel Sharia is already short of half a dozen!"

Upon a sign from their leader, the cavalcade set off fearlessly once more. The Bedouin shouted loudly to one another, either carrying on a post-mortem of the tussle at Sir Humphrey's, or describing the course of events for the benefit of those who had not been inside the mansion with them. But the moment they detected a different sound, that of desert sand under hoof beats, the boisterous verbal exchanges became more muted, until all conversation finally ceased. Their thoughts must have turned to what lay ahead, because now every face was deadly serious.

Some of these men had waited ten years for this night. Some not quite so long—but there was not one, except perhaps Philip, who did not have good reason for wanting to settle an old score.

At a short distance from Lydia's house, they dismounted and led their horses closer, in order to avoid unnecessary noise. The animals were carefully tethered because, this time, the leader could not spare a single man to stay with them.

Dominic fortunately knew the way, and he went ahead,

to the gap in the hedge through which he had entered the grounds on his previous visit. The oleanders were reflected in the swimming pool, just as he remembered, but the lawn was dark and deserted.

He lowered his voice to speak to his men, outlining his plan of action.

"Somewhere there should be a window that has been left open especially for me, and I shall aim for that. Most probably we'll find it on the northern side, because as we approached, I noticed that the house was not as brightly lit there.

"The rest of the men from the stockade are underway to support Raschid, and now it's up to us. Abdel Sharia is planning to attack our camp, I know without a doubt, but I also suspect that his preparations cannot yet be complete, because I don't believe he would have had time to send Farao and the rest after the princess earlier this evening, if his troops were already assembled there.

"Our greatest hope has to be pinned on the element of surprise. If we strike unexpectedly and gain the upper hand tonight, we shall make tomorrow's battle easier for Raschid and company.

"I intend to go in alone, and reconnoitre. You must follow later. Now surround the house, watch the windows constantly, and make your entrance the moment you see that it becomes necessary....But just remember this.—Mohammed Ahmed is mine!"

"Please, *Sahbena*," Rameses pleaded, "take my sabre!"

But Dominic shook his head. "Thank, you, my brother, but no! You have taught me well, and I respect your gesture, but you were not in the room with me when El-Bus Mohandess lay dying. In the moments before he died, his the last words to me were: '*Whenever you feel yourself weakening, hold this as a reminder of what I have said to you today.'* His voice was very faint, but he managed to say, 'Finish, *El-Hakim*, what I have begun!'—And tonight, with God's help, Rameses, that is what I plan to do! I do not need any earthly weapon, other than the rapier of El-Bus Mohandess!"

***

The grounds of Lydia's home were like a park, and Dominic could suddenly understand how impressed she must have been if Ahmed had shown this estate to her five years ago. Enough, he thought cynically, to make any self-seeking girl want to drop a newly-qualified young medical specialist like a hot cake, in favour of a wealthy sheik! The house was larger than he had expected. Possibly three times the size of the Talbot mansion, and typical of upper class Egyptian houses, which were usually built on more than one level. As he had noticed earlier, only one light burned on the north side, and when he approached, he was grateful to see, beside the lamp, the open window.

He swung himself over the windowsill, and landed lightly on his feet, on the other side of it, where he found himself in a spacious salon, which was either an art gallery or a museum. Even in the dim light, he could see that the walls were hung with artwork in oils and watercolour, and everywhere he looked there were marble statues that gleamed phantom-like in the gloom.

To find images in a Muslim house seemed strange to him, until he remembered Lydia telling him, when he had been there before, that the house was a treasure trove of antiquities and costly works of art, and for a moment he wished that he had been able to switch on the ceiling lights in order to study the contents of the room more closely. Instead, he tiptoed through the it, and carefully opened the door at the other end.

Ahead of him was a short passage with, no doubt, priceless Persian rugs on the floor, and, at the end of it, he saw a large, rectangular atrium with a fishpond, and also a fountain which, on such a hot evening, made a particularly pleasant, splashing sound.

On his right, a door was slightly ajar, and a narrow beam of light streamed through the crack. The heavy, sweet odour of incense reached him from inside the room, and he slowly pushed the door open wider to look inside. In front of a large wall map, stood Mohammed Ahmed, with a full glass in one hand.

He was standing with his back to Dominic, who thus had a good opportunity to study him unseen. This room, he concluded, was probably the man's private study. Three walls were lined with bookshelves, and against the fourth was a splendid ebony writing desk, across the surface of which a silver lampstand cast a bright light. On this wall, too, was the map that was of such interest to the man.

As though he sensed that he was not alone, Mohammed Ahmed swung around, and an expression of surprise crossed his face when he saw Dominic.

"I was not aware that I had a visitor," he said uncertainly, and set his glass down very carefully, at the same time closely examining Dominic's countenance. "Have we met before, *Effendi*? You seem familiar..."

Dominic stepped closer and his blue eyes narrowed.

"We have met before...aboard a ship from England. Don't you remember?"

Recognition flashed across the sheik's face, but he betrayed no sign of uneasiness. He laughed. "Ah, yes! Doctor Verwey!

One of my wife's former suitors, not so?" he sneered nasally, in a manner that made Dominic's blood boil. "I should let her know that you are here, Doctor. It would be interesting to witness her reaction!"

"I have not come to make a social call," Dominic said quickly, when he saw that the other man was about to ring a bell. "My business is with you, Ahmed, and not with Lydia!" There was something surreal about the fact that he was actually face-to-face at last, with the reprehensible Abdel Sharia!

"So?" Although Sharia seemed weigh his words carefully, there was something insulting in the way he said this. "With me, Doctor Verwey? Are you still smarting because the lady preferred me to you?"

Dominic surveyed him in silence for a moment and then the corners of his own mouth curled up in a smile that was almost mischievous. "My friends know me by another name," he grinned with amusement. He was actually beginning to enjoy himself. "Please permit me, Mohammed Ahmed, to introduce you—to Hamid Pasha!"

The Arab started, but the only signs that he was confounded, were a slight dilation of his pupils and the thin white line that appeared around his mouth. Dominic reluctantly had to admire his self-control. The sheik's hands remained steady, and, when he spoke, his voice was mocking, and as calm as ever.

"That is very interesting," he said. "I have often wondered about this man who has for so long evaded the law. But what is your business with me?" His voice hardened. "I am fast beginning to believe that you are, indeed, seeking revenge for your wounded pride!"

Dominic balled his fists. "Believe me, Mohammed Ahmed, you were unaware, at the time, that you were actually doing me a favour, but what really narks me is that you keep poaching on my preserves! I am, of course, referring to the Princess Thérèse!"

Now the sheik was visibly disconcerted. He gripped the edge of the desk almost convulsively, and his knuckled showed white through the almond skin of his hands.

"What of the princess?" he demanded.

"We-ell," Dominic responded with fierce delight, "it will no doubt be a great disappointment to you, to learn that your attempt to kidnap her tonight, turned out to be a miserable failure! Your men hardly gave what may be described as a brilliant performance!...One is dead, and the others..." He shrugged his shoulders. "You have really gone and done it this time!...I would say that you have tied yourself into a good and proper knot....A bit stupid for a holy one, isn't it—ABDEL SHARIA!"

The Arab made a sharp, hissing sound as he sucked in his breath. With a lightning movement, his hand shot out across the desk, and from behind a pile of books he unexpectedly brought to light a heavy German Luger—of the kind that had been much sought after as a trophy during the war.

"Stay where you are, Hamid Pasha!" he commanded, through clenched teeth...."Don't fool yourself. You'll never get the better of Abdel Sharia!" Without taking his eyes off Dominic for an instant, he pointed over his shoulder, with his thumb, to the map behind him. "Take note of that black circle. That is where your stockade is. While you are still wasting time here, the troops in my camp are making ready to depart for an attack on yours. By this time tomorrow evening, a few smouldering embers will be all that remain of Hamid Pasha's pathetic little efforts!"

For five years Dominic had pictured this moment, and

had often wondered whether, when the time came, he would be afraid. Strangely he was not. It was quite extraordinary how he felt almost outside of himself, which, had he been given the opportunity to do so, he might have rationalized as having the Hamid Pasha persona take over. But it was more than that. While he remained painfully aware of the Luger, a sort of euphoria took over, and he found himself to be completely calm.

"I doubt if that will occur, you fiend!...Fuzad, the *Cadi*, and every other sensible Bedouin in the desert, will prevent that, you may be sure! I surmise that, before sunrise, they will wipe out *your* camp!"

In the passion of their anger, they did not realize how loudly they were shouting at one another, until a light went on in the atrium, and a moment later, Lydia, disregarding Dominic's earlier instruction, came running into the study.

"I heard voices..." she began, but noticing the gun in Ahmed's hand, she took the situation in at glance, and with a smothered cry, she flung herself in front of Dominic.

"Alfit," she screamed. "Don't shoot him—*please!*"

"Stand aside!" His voice cut like the lash of a whip.

"It's all my fault!" she sobbed frantically. "He only came to help me!...Oh, Dominic!"

"Traitress!" the Arab shouted, beside himself with rage. "Christian bitch!"

He raised his arm and Dominic moved to thrust her out of the way, but it was too late. With one shot to the heart, Abdel Sharia killed her, and, with a sigh, she collapsed at Dominic's feet. Because he had moved automatically to catch her before she fell to the floor, a second shot missed its target, striking his left shoulder instead.

As a sharp, burning pain seared through him, all the

hatred he had long cherished rose to the surface. He was like a madman as he sprang forward and hurled the full weight of his large frame at the Arab. They fell over together, and the Luger flew in under the desk, out of reach.

Dominic lashed out with his big, powerful fists, but before he could subdue Sharia, about twenty of the sheik's guards, lured by the sound of gunshots, stormed into the room and made straight for him. At the same time there was a loud crashing noise, and the sound of breaking glass, as Hamid Pasha's men, led by Philip, came through the glass doors and the windows. Sabres aloft, they had to step over the lifeless body of Lydia, where she lay on the floor, in an ever-growing pool of blood.

Instantly crawling with Arabs—Sharia's as well those of *El-Hakim*—the room became a veritable battleground, and it very soon became obvious that the combatants were not evenly matched.

None of Dominic's people owned a handgun, and Dominic refused to carry one. To the desert fighters among them, their mightiest weapons were their God-given wits, their skilled horsemanship and their courage. If you engaged in a skirmish, you went into it prepared to fight with a sabre or a sword, and if you were going to fire at anyone you did so with a rifle, from the back of a horse, and preferably from a galloping one. This was how they had trained Hamid Pasha, who normally possessed the additional attributes of above-average physical strength and stamina. But this was his second brawl of the night, he was seriously sleep deprived, and his left arm was as good as useless.

Tonight, for Dominic and his people, this looked to be a fight to the death, and ill-equipped, they fought with everything in sight. They fought with sabres, scimitars, *nabbuts*, and whatever else was handy, hurling chairs, inkbottles, books and even vases at the Bey's henchmen. Under cover of the tumult, Abdel Sharia took his chance and slipped quickly through the door, but Dominic saw him, and resolutely set off after him. He grabbed a discarded sabre that was lying on the floor, and threw it into the passage for Sharia.

"Now fight, you heathen dog!" Dominic challenged him, and simultaneously drew his rapier from its shield. "Take a good look, Abdel Sharia," he said, with a dangerous glint in his blue eyes. "Perhaps you recognize the rapier of El-Bus Mohandess!"

Sharia was the first to attack. Dominic, now realizing that it was not what he was accustomed to, had to calculate what strategies Sharia might adopt with a sabre, and thinking quickly, he avoided the strike. Swinging his rapier in a wide arc, in an attempt to break through the sheik's defence, he succeeded in tearing his antagonist's sleeve, and a red scratch appeared on Sharia's arm, but the Arab saved himself with a brilliant movement. The clash of steel upon steel echoed through the vast house. Meanwhile, more guards came running in from the direction of the front door. Lydia had no doubt miscalculated, or had perhaps not known how many there actually were. One of them dropped down on one knee and jerked a Persian mat out from under Dominic's feet, so that he fell heavily, but just then, Rameses, who—chiefly because Dominic was his protégée—had been attracted by the sound of a duel, fortunately moved in, blocking the path for the rest of the guards, with his sabre. Dominic's other men, also coming to his aid, plunged through the door, and the main fighting moved from the study into the passage.

Back and forth, and up and down the stairs, *El-Hakim* and Abdel Sharia remained locked in fierce combat. Dominic soon realized that he was in the presence of a master of the art, and, in his heart, he blessed his mentor, Rameses the Turk, for having so mercilessly made him sweat.

"Have you had enough, pig," the Arab panted. "Or shall I bring an end to this, right now?"

"This...will...be...your...last...duel...Sharia!" Dominic emphasized every word with a lunge! But perspiration was now running down into his eyes, and his left shoulder was completely numb. Blood seeped through his clothes, and he felt himself growing weaker every moment. At one stage the Arab had him pinned up against a table on a landing, and stood poised with his sabre, ready to deliver the deathblow.

This was no gentleman's duel. It was becoming a street fight. With as much strength as he could still muster, Dominic succeeded in bringing his knee up, overturning the table, and Sharia temporarily lost his balance, giving Dominic a chance to straighten up. The sheik then dashed down the stairs again, and ducked in behind another table, which he shoved forward to impede Dominic's progress, before darting towards another flight of stairs, opposite the fishpond Dominic had seen earlier, and which led up from the atrium to a small balcony.

Swerving just in time, Dominic managed to avoid the falling table, and, in full pursuit once more, tore up the stairs after Sharia. Upon reaching the top, Sharia swung around unexpectedly, and aimed a kick at Dominic's face, which—when he, Dominic, succeeded in dodging it—caught him on his maimed shoulder. He fell forward onto the steps, hearing his precious rapier clatter as it shot out of his hand.

For a moment he could hardly move, and he slid down, backwards, for a short distance. There was a dark mist before his eyes, and every breath he took was like a knife thrust to his chest. He was worn out, but, as he lay there, a wonderful thing happened. He had fallen in such a way that, as his vision cleared, his eyes rested on the old rapier, lying a few steps above him, and probably because it had for so long been a symbol of strength and encouragement to him, the very sight of it lent him new courage. It was almost as though El-Bus Mohandess were standing next to him, in person, and saying: *"Get up, my son. You cannot give up now!"*

He reached for the rapier, which, in his dazed and exhausted state felt like a living thing in his hand...and, with near superhuman strength, he rose to his feet again and went blindly after Abdel Sharia. In the limited space provided by the balcony, they locked into the duel once more, Dominic carrying out every parry, and every thrust in a daze. To this day, the events of the next few moments are like a dream to him.

He was standing with his back to the iron railings of the balcony, when Sharia suddenly swung at him, and once again, as Dominic tried to ward off the thrust, the rapier flew through the air. There was a single, tense moment as Sharia stood ready to finish him off, and all of a sudden Dominic was wide-awake, and alert enough to jerk himself out of the way. With a bloodcurdling yell, the Arab went over the railing, and there was a dull thud as his body hit the marble tiles in the atrium below.

***

Dominic staggered dizzily down the steps, and when he reached the bottom, he became aware of an unearthly quiet. Lying in tragically abnormal positions, men were spread out all over the floor.—Two of his own, as well as those of Abdel

Sharia. With a catch in his throat, he recognized one of them as Ali, and Haroun's small, deformed body was unmistakable. The battle was over, but at incalculable cost!

He looked about him and noticed the rest of his men, eighteen in all, waiting for him, and as he walked unsteadily over to where Abdel Sharia lay, they watched him in tense silence. Abdel Sharia was stone dead, one leg bent grotesquely under him, and Dominic shuddered. But suddenly he gasped. Somehow, the sheik had landed not three feet away from where the rapier of El-Bus Mohandess had fallen.

Dominic had to step over the body of Abdel Sharia in order to retrieve the rapier, and, as he bent down to pick it up, he saw, with inexpressible dismay, that the blade was cracked from point to hilt!

***

Suddenly a shout went up. At some time during the skirmish, someone had upset the tall and elaborate, Egyptian 'pillar' incense burner in the study where Lydia's body lay, and the room was already totally engulfed in flames. Smoke billowed through the door, into the passage, and through the broken windows to the outside. Gradually the carpets and drapes would begin to smoulder, and soon only a blackened ruin would remain to mark the scene of so much vicious, unconscionable, cruelty and evil...

Dominic swayed on his feet and Philip rushed forward to help his brother. "Thank you, Jesus," he heard *El-Hakim* mutter. "I did not have to kill Lydia's husband!—I did not need to kill *anyone*!"

(ii)

For the first time since he had become a man, Dominic, himself, required the help of a physician. When the bullet had been removed from his shoulder, in Cairo, and everyone else who had been hurt, had received medical attention, the journey back to the stockade was undertaken, in short stretches at a time. The bodies of Ali and Haroun had already been taken back to the camp.

The sun was up by the time the battered warriors arrived. Finally the exhausted children of *Sahbena El-Hakim* could rest. This was one time when the burials would have to be delayed.

Late that afternoon, as they came away from the observances, they were met by a horseman, who came galloping into the stockade. Soon the news swept through the camp like wildfire, and in the midst of sorrow there was jubilation. A loud, exuberant cheer went up.

"The hell of Abdel Sharia is no more! Raschid and Fuzad the *Cadi* have triumphed."—Some cried out: "Allah be praised!" But there were many who like, Dominic, Philip, and Ezra, said: "Praise El-Shaddai, the Almighty God!"

CHAPTER TWENTY

The following day was an eventful one for the Princess Thérèse. She received two visitors—each, for whatever reason, important to her.

She was back in her bedroom, not long after breakfast, when she was informed that a young gentleman awaited her in Sir Humphrey's office, and she went down immediately, wondering whom the visitor could possibly be. And even when she saw him, he looked unfamiliar. Then he rose to his feet with a smile and she hastened towards him with outstretched hands.

"Philip-brother! I hardly recognized you in your posh, city clothes!"

He grinned with embarrassment. "I hardly know myself! After all these years it is torture to wear a collar and tie!"

She was overjoyed to see him and, leading him to the window seat, she asked, "What brings you to the city so early this morning?...You could not have come on horseback in that smart get-up!...I'm going to order tea for you!"

But he restrained her. "No thank you, Thérèse. I really don't have much time....Don't ask why or how, but Dominic and I were brought as far as the city in a British army Jeep!" He spoke lightly, but seemed nervous, and he looked at her solemnly. "I have just come to say goodbye. I'm going home today!"

Thérèse could hardly believe her ears. "What you mean by 'home'? To South Africa?"

He nodded. "Dom is in the city right now, making arrangements, and then he'll take me to Alexandria. It's high time I began to think of a career for myself, and there is nothing more I can do here for him, for the time being."

"What does he think of this?"

"He agrees," Philip told her. "The plan is that, if I go home now, I might be able to begin my medical training right away, so that, when I am ready, I can come back here and take over from him. That should make it possible for him to go home one day. He believes that, with the experience I have gained here, a career in medicine should not be a problem for me."

"I see." But she did not. Thérèse felt as though she were dreaming. She knew that what Philip was saying should have been significant, and she was dying of curiosity, but she was afraid that, if she asked too many questions, he might think that it was in Dominic that she was interested. She ventured only to ask: "Would Dominic ever leave the stockade?...I can't see that happening any time soon!"

Philip looked at her apologetically, and then with rising eagerness. "But of course you don't know! How could you?" he cried. "I did not think to tell you!...Abdel Sharia is dead!...After we left here last night, we launched a raid on his residence, and he and his entire local gang were killed. The house has been totally destroyed!—Not purposely. It caught fire by accident!

"His camp has also successfully been attacked, by about five-hundred Bedouin, led by Raschid, Fuzad—a *Cadi*—and fifteen other sheiks and *cadis*. Every guard who was not killed, has been taken prisoner, and Sharia's captives have been set free. Mustapha, among others, has already arrived in Cairo. Although he's in poor shape, he managed, nevertheless, to arrange for government trucks to bring the rest back to Cairo....It's in all the papers today!"

"But that is marvellous news! Almost unbelievable!" Thérèse was beginning to understand his unrestrained excitement. She, herself, had been rendered almost speechless. "And the people in the stockade?"

"No one knows yet, what will happen to the stockade or to *El-Hakim*, now that his identity is known, but his people will quite possibly all be given unconditional pardons—if Mustapha can swing it. Dominic will not know that until tonight, and then he'll probably come and tell you, himself. I'll have to wait until later to learn the outcome."

"Dominic is coming *here?*" She tried hard to disguise her own excitement, but it was impossible. "He's coming *here?*"

"Of course! He asked me to tell you that he is coming as soon as he gets back from Alex, and has had time to speak to Mustapha....Actually," he confessed, "I am ready to go home, but not today. I am concerned that he is not up to the long trip to Alex and back, but he insists that he wants me out of the way before Pandora's box is opened."

"What's wrong with him, that you should talk about his not being 'up to it', Phil? I've never know him not to be!"

Philip seemed to be uncomfortable. "Please don't ask me to go into details right now, Princess of Hearts. There's too little time. All I will say is that we have had to bury three people about whom we cared very much, we have had a very rough night, and he is a little under the weather as a result.

"As I said, he can tell you everything you want to know, later." Philip rose to his feet. "Now I really must go, little one. It's getting late and my transport has been waiting downstairs for quite some time." He took her hand. "Just be patient, dearest," he said solemnly. "Everything will come right, you'll see. And remember—South Africa awaits you!"

"Goodbye, Phil." His courage and kindness moved her

deeply, and her eyes swam with tears. "I shall remember," she said as clearly as the constriction in her throat permitted. Then she impulsively drew his head down and kissed him on the mouth. "Take good care of yourself, do you hear?"

He put his arms around her and held her very close, burying his face in the silken curls for a moment before letting go of her. Without another word, he went straight to the door.

A few minutes later Thérèse heard a car engine start up downstairs near the gate.

(ii)

Lady Talbot had very kindly placed a small sitting room on the first floor at the princess's disposal, for the duration of her stay, and Thérèse spent most of her time in the pleasant room with its cheerful curtains and rose-patterned, linen-covered, chairs. Late that afternoon, already dressed for dinner, she was sitting there, writing to Gerda, when Sir Humphrey knocked softly and entered.

"Thérèse," he said, with an inscrutable expression on his florid face, "that unmitigated scoundrel, Hamid Pasha, is downstairs, and has the audacity to ask if he might speak with you!" He pursed his lips, meaningfully. "Do you wish to see him?"

She jumped up with such alacrity that she almost upset the inkbottle, and clenched her fists. "Tell him to go away," she said quickly. "Or, no, say I'm out...or..."

"I wonder if he'll accept that," Sir Humphrey responded, with quite uncharacteristic skittishness. "He appears to be quite a determined blighter!"

"I can be just as determined when I choose," she informed him, but he noticed that she was already glancing at the wall mirror and nervously checking her appearance. She brushed a stray curl away from her face and plucked at the wide skirt of her sapphire blue, silk dress as if to make sure that it hung becomingly. "In any case it's far too late for receiving visitors!"

"That is perfectly true," the man said, hiding a smile, "but perhaps he won't stay too long. Besides, Princess, I think you should at least thank him for what he did for you the other evening....What I mean to say is, that it was, when you come to think of it, extremely dangerous for him to come here, and he must have known that!"

Thérèse sighed resignedly as though she were making a great sacrifice, and said with quite regal hauteur: "Very well, then. I shall receive him....But please remember that it was you who talked me into it, Sir Humphrey!"

"I shall remember..."

He moved towards the door, but before he could reach it, a liveried servant appeared in the doorway and bowed.

"Doctor Dominic Verwey!" he announced formally.

Thérèse turned around and stared through the window at the street below, so that her reaction would not be obvious. She was older and wiser than when she had so summarily been removed from the stockade, but unfortunately, it seemed, the presence of *El-Hakim* would forever have this upsetting effect on her.

"Good evening, Doctor," she heard Sir Humphrey say, and to her astonishment he added heartily: "You are most welcome!...I hope you are not in any pain."

She could not see Dominic, of course, but she knew that he would also be surprised at the unexpected warmth of his welcome.

"Good evening, Sir Humphrey," he responded courteously. "That is most kind of you. And, thank you, Sir. The pain is neither too severe, nor too limiting. I am very fortunate not to be left-handed....I am most honoured by your kind reception. You are aware now of who I am, and it is well known that Sir Humphrey Talbot and Hamid Pasha are considered to be sworn enemies."

If the day had not already brought enough shocks, upon hearing the Englishman's rejoinder Thérèse might very well have fainted.

"Hamid Pasha?" he echoed. "Who is that? As far as I know, such a man no longer exists!" He took Dominic's good arm. "Mustapha visited me this afternoon," he kindly elaborated, "and told me the whole story. What that man, and others like him, must have suffered!...*You* are not—as far as the governments of both Britain and Egypt are concerned— Hamid Pasha. That was a legendary being who existed only while there was a critical need for him, but he died two nights ago, along with the Bey, Abdel Sharia. I do not know a Hamid Pasha and nor does Senator Mustapha.—Like my friend, Christopher Brent, we only know a doctor. An extraordinary, selfless man who has done this country a great service."

By this time Dominic could hardly believe his ears, and neither could Thérèse. It was no wonder, she thought, that he diffidently asked for permission to sit down. She knew little about anything to which he referred, but what she heard Sir Humphrey say next, was enough to concern her, and it was difficult to restrain herself from taking a quick look at Dominic.

"Of course, my boy. From all accounts, you have been through a most dreadful ordeal. Is there anything that might help to refresh you?...Perhaps a brandy? I can ring for anything you prefer..."

Dominic, however, politely declined the offer, and Sir

Humphrey, reverting to the third person continued: "Now about this doctor....I am told that he has refused all rewards offered for the return of Christopher Brent, Senator Mustapha and several other prominent citizens, suggesting that the money be used to make restitution for, or pay off any fines that might have been imposed upon the notorious pasha. And"— Sir Humphrey could not restrain his mirth—"he is naturally, and quite understandably, disqualified from receiving the reward for the capture of Hamid Pasha....So that leaves us in something of a predicament...

"Mustapha and his friends in the Senate, have instead, proposed an alternative....They would like to ensure that, whenever the Bedouin tell stories, there will always be one about *Sahbena el-Hakim*, their friend the doctor—for a man is not remembered so much for what he breaks down, as for what he builds up—and a hospital where travellers in the desert may find help, will be your lasting monument! In that, with the help of Christopher's bank, the reward money, and any interest accruing, will be invested!"

The was a long silence during which *El-Hakim* swallowed with difficulty. People who did not know better, might even have thought that they saw tears in his eyes—but that would, of course, only have been a trick of the light!

Sir Humphrey was not unmoved either. He stared fixedly in front of him, but suddenly coughed self-consciously. "I think I hear Lady Talbot's voice. Perhaps my wife needs me." He shook Dominic's hand. "Please excuse me, Doctor. Perhaps you'll invite me to visit your hospital some day."

"Most certainly." Dominic replied sincerely, rising to his feet as Sir Humphrey was about to go. "It would be an honour to have you visit us, and a pleasure to entertain you! It will not be the most comfortable journey you have ever undertaken,

I'm sure, but please bring Lady Talbot and your daughter with you." He grinned wickedly. "I am greatly indebted to Miss Ruth!"

"We have the Jeep at our disposal, if you recall, so a trip into the desert presents no problems..."

"I do recall that, Sir," said Dominic. "In that case I shall look forward to your visit—and thank you for making both the Jeep and a driver available to me, this evening."

"Well, I must leave you now," the man said. "And as we have solved your own transport problem for the moment, I hope the princess will be able to persuade you to stay to dinner!"

Thérèse heard Sir Humphrey's footsteps disappear down the passage. They were alone at last, but still she averted her gaze.

"Thérèse," *El-Hakim* said yearningly.

"Yes?"

"I can't talk to your back!"

"The view is better from the window."

He sighed, "Well then, look at the view if you must! But will you please listen to what I have to say?"

She shrugged her shoulders. "I can't help hearing, of course, but nothing you say will be of the slightest interest to me."

Her behaviour was inexplicable to Dominic. When he had last spoken to her he had thought her to be a little more approachable. Perhaps she was angry because he had kissed her. He wracked his brain for something suitable to say, in order to initiate a conversation.

"Did you hear what Sir Humphrey said about the hospital?"

She nodded.

"Do you know what this means, Princess?" The emotion

in his voice did not escape her. "Mustapha and his friends are going to hand me a massive cheque tomorrow, and, from now on we will be under the protection of the state. My hospital will always be there for as long as the Bedouin have need of it. Furthermore, any of those now living in the stockade, and who wish to do so, may remain there. So far, everyone who assists me in the hospital has agreed to stay.—Perhaps because they know how lost I shall be without Philip!

"It is hard to absorb all this, and I am not sure whether to be glad or sorry, but it seems that I shall no longer be required to be the 'father of the desert', either. Everyone who stays to work, in whatever capacity, will be paid, food and other supplies will be brought in for us, and all will be free to come and go as they please! He chuckled mischievously. "The next time I become a father, it will be of my very own children!"

His enthusiasm was so infectious that she could no longer pretend to be disinterested. She turned away from the window. "That *is* wonderful news, Dominic!" she exclaimed, genuinely happy for him. "All of it! I wish you success, fulfilment and great joy!" That was when she saw the sling and involuntarily cried out: "Oh, Dom…your arm! What happened?"

"Oh, it's nothing. Abdel Sharia just happened to be a bit off his aim!" The concern in her voice and eyes were most encouraging. Perhaps she was not quite as disinterested as she had pretended. "It will be forgotten within a few days", he said.

"Philip did tell me about Sharia's death, but provided none of the details. I know now that that ghastly man was sent here by Abdel Sharia, and I must thank you for what you and your people did. I do appreciate it, Dom."

"That's nothing," he said again, with obvious embarrassment. "There is something I have to ask you, but first I think you would want to know that Ali and my little friend, Haroun, were killed during the skirmish with Sharia."

"Oh no!" She was horrified. "I knew about Sezit, which was bad enough—but not those two as well! Poor Meriam! How dreadful for her and the child!...And Mamoun must be desolate!"

"We all are," he said sorrowfully. "I am so grateful that I can continue to offer them shelter." He looked pleadingly at her. "Thérèse, I said I had something to ask you....A while ago you said that you wanted to help me. Does your offer still stand?"

To his astonishment, and dismay, she shook her head. "I'm sorry, Dominic. The circumstances are different now!"

"But why?" Extreme concern made him move closer to her and across a table they faced each other, in such uncomfortable silence, that Dominic was obliged to inquire: "Have I done something to upset you, or do you now find the sacrifice too great?" In a flash, something she had said two nights before, sprang to mind. "By the way, what did you mean when you told me to go back to 'my' Lydia?"

He looked at her so intently that she blushed, and stammered: "She wrote to you, didn't she? Her husband is out of the way now, and the two of you can look forward to a rosy future together." All of a sudden, the memory of the intense misery she had endured lately, washed over her, and she went on bitterly: "You could not wait to be rid of me, could you? How quickly my offer became of minor importance!"

Before she could say another word, he had come around to her side of the table, confronting her with his face so close to hers that it was unnerving.

"Is *that* how it seemed to you?" He shook his golden head incredulously and comprehension dawned in those blue, blue eyes. His took her wrist in a firm grip. "But, of course—you darling, obstinate little idiot!" He grinned exultantly as the entire misunderstanding began to unravel before him. "Of course! Philip told you all about Lydia and me!" A warm glow spread through his whole being as new hope unfolded in his heart. He began to grin delightedly, but stopped abruptly, and a shadow moved across his face.

"Sit down here with me for a moment, please. We have so much to explain to one another."

Although she was growing more confused by the minute, she obeyed, but even seated beside him, she remained distinctly aloof.

"All of a sudden I can fully understand how you must be feeling," he said earnestly, determined not to be put off by her manner, "but the picture might look very different to you once I have explained.—Thérèse...Lydia is dead!"

This information evidently shook her to the core, because her eyes darkened, and she gasped. She turned to look questioningly at him.

"Yes," he said. "It's true. And this will sound even more unbelievable to you, my dearest. She saved your life, Thérèse, and mine, too!" He saw that he now had her undivided attention, and went on. "Lydia was the wife of Abdel Sharia.—What did you think was in the letter? And how do you think I found out that he was about to have you abducted? Later, in her home, when she saw him about to shoot me, she tried to shield me and he shot her.—She died instantly...!"

Thérèse heaved a deep, shuddering sigh and covered her face with her hands. "I have been so foolish," she murmured with deep regret in her sweet voice.

Dominic leaned over and took her hands away from her eyes. Then he tipped up her firm, rounded chin so that she had no option but to look at him. "Thérèse," he said gently, and his heart was in his eyes, "I have so much ahead of me, but with you at my side, I can do anything. I can make of my hospital all it should be. Won't you reconsider your answer?"

She seemed bewildered for some reason, and still immensely confused. Her lips quivered, and she gestured helplessly, trying to find the right words. "I don't know Dom!...I just don't know! It's not that I don't want to....I do!—But there's so much doubt in my heart. Thus far, every time I have proffered my help, something has unfailingly gone wrong. Each time something has happened to disillusion me, and I don't think I could face that again!"

"Whatever do you mean?" he asked, baffled. "I don't understand!"

As she now found herself totally unable to look at him, she lowered her eyes. "The first time you also sent me away, very suddenly! While I was expecting you to be pleased because I had looked after Philip for you, you could not wait to be rid of me! That hurt, *El-Hakim*....That hurt!"

"I am so sorry!" he exclaimed, contritely, but with immeasurable relief. "The last time it was because I was afraid that Abdel Sharia would attack the stockade and it was too dangerous for you to be there....The previous time..."—His voice betrayed amusement, but, at the same time, there was a cadence to his voice that had her holding her breath.—"The first time it was *I* who was in danger, sweetheart!...Thérèse, I came home from the disastrous meeting in the desert, tired, disappointed and filthy dirty, to find you in my bed..."

She put her hands to her mouth, greatly embarrassed. "You weren't expected back so soon!...Didn't Ali warn you?... He should have!" she exclaimed with concern.

He shook his head, smiling broadly. "No. I walked in and

saw you there, and you looked so clean, so sweet, so utterly adorable, that I panicked....There was no room in my heart for a woman, Thérèse—or so I thought—but I was so far gone that, without your knowledge, I could not resist giving you kiss!" He shrugged his shoulders resignedly. "Princess, my heart was in mortal danger! I *had* to send you away before it was too late..."

While he was speaking, Thérèse had slowly risen to her feet. The violet eyes misted, and her words came haltingly, as she asked: "And the job you are offering me is...?"

Because Dominic was still seated, his face was almost on a level with hers, and he needed only to tilt his head slightly, and hold his beautiful, cool hands to her flaming cheeks, to make her look at him directly. His eyes looked deeply into hers, and the tension between them was like a living thing.

"Thérèse," he said huskily, as though he spoke in a dream...."I am going to call my stockade 'Soravia'. It must be like that wonderful, fairy-tale land of yours, where everyone is made welcome. Where there is room for everyone....I so badly want it to be your place, too....Especially as my hospital is to be named 'The Princess Thérèse'!"

He took her tiny hands in both of his. "My darling, the 'job' I am offering you, is that of the doctor's wife!" He had by then come to his feet, and, looking down at this exquisite, small creature, something he saw in her expression made him short of breath.

Aware of nothing except the inviting red mouth so close to his, he could only continue vaguely:...."There...is...so... much...that we...can achieve...together!"

He had drawn her closer without realizing it, and her pulse raced. She could hear the blood rushing in her ears, and, in the midst of this, she was aware of a longing that was as much fear as bliss. She met his ardent gaze, and as she saw in his eyes the flickering darkness of passion, she felt as though something inside her were fighting to be set free.

He spoke and his voice was thick. "Don't look at me like that, Thérèse, if you don't mean it!"

"Look at you, how" she whispered.

" As though you are beginning to feel as I do ?"

Her rosy lips parted—surprised and utterly lovely—and her hands went out to him shyly.

"Dominic...!"

With his good arm, he held her so close that she could hardly breathe for the wonder and joy of his embrace. This was not just a kiss. It was a casting out of all doubt; an affirmation of all vows; a boundless ecstasy of relief in the acknowledgement of love.

In the distance the dinner gong went, but no one took much notice of it...

EPILOGUE

Between Durban and Pietermaritzburg in South Africa, there is a narrow, sandy path that turns off from the highway, and winds around a hill between an avenue of Jacarandas, Oleanders, Tibouchinas and Flamboyants.

If the traveller should go to the trouble of following the pathway all the way down to the end, he, or she, would find there the gables and thatched roof of a house with whitewashed walls, and also a breathtaking view across the verdant green of the 'Valley of a Thousand Hills'. On the gate, the intriguing wording engraved on a brass nameplate would probably catch the eye, because all it says is—'*El-Hakim*'.

People living in the surrounding area tell that a doctor has come to live there, and that he does much good among the Zulus, whose characteristic beehive-shaped, grass huts are dotted everywhere among the hills, but it is also said that his ménage is very odd. One rumour has it that his wife is a former princess and there is apparently an Indian, as well as a dwarf, who have helped to raise their sons. One of these 'servants', for want of a better word, apparently wears a turban, which everyone finds strange—particularly when he and the Indian follow the family down the aisle at church on Sundays!

They say that the doctor has consulting rooms in Pietermaritzburg, and that people come from far and near to consult him because of his wide knowledge of malaria, Bilharzia and other tropical diseases. They tell of his extraordinary hands, and about a remarkable old rapier that hangs behind his desk. Unfortunately, however, close inspection will reveal that it is badly cracked.

New patients usually kill time—as most sick people do—by discussing the virtues, or otherwise, of their physician, and sometime the old dame with the ostrich feather in her hat, might say to the old chap with the long beard, sitting in the corner: "Actually I don't believe that there can be much of a difference. After all—you know how it is.—One doctor is pretty much the same as any other!"

POSTSCRIPT

The weather forecast has proved to be correct. It has snowed continuously since Christmas, and before that, as the holidays approached, all of us, breathlessly anticipating the arrival of people we love, kept looking up anxiously at the sky. But we need not have worried. Most of my friends in North America seem to be under this misconception that there is no snow in South Africa, but Stephen lives close enough to the Drakensberg mountains for him to have seen snowy peaks before, and the folk from Nelspruit, were ecstatic about experiencing a white Christmas. Especially when, back where they come from, it is mid-summer and very, very hot!

For me, the time has passed too quickly. All too soon, a new year has dawned, and with it, my brother Gregory's birthday. We have spent most of this day sitting in front of a roaring fire in Uncle Ash's drawing room, sipping eggnog, staring at the flames, silent and lost in happy retrospection. Unfortunately this afternoon, my mother, who has this disconcerting way about her, had to go and disrupt it.

"Antoinette!—Get off Stephen's lap this instant!.... I don't care that you two are engaged now. Nice girls just don't do that...engaged or not!"

Fortunately Stephen is not easily disconcerted. He kissed my cheek, quite unselfconsciously, disentangled my arm from around his neck, and shoved me off his knee. "Listen to your mother, Antoinette!" he grinned good-naturedly, winking at

Fallah. "Be a nice girl for her.—I need to stay in her good books!" He then turned and looked meaningfully at my father. "And in yours too, sir, don't I?"

"You won't have to try too hard, my boy!" Fallah smiled back at him. "Just keep her as happy as she is now. After what you told me on Christmas eve, that's all I'll ever ask of you!"

He explained, for the benefit of the others in the room, but mainly addressing Benjamin Ashton: "What Stephen and I talked about, made me think of how, when we lived in the Transvaal, there was a time when you and I were driven to scaring our children with dire, lurid warnings about Schistosomiasis, in order to stop them from swimming in possibly infected rivers. And how concerned you were, Ash, about the possibility of your friend and servant, Phineas, baptizing his flock in them!

"After all these years, I actually believed that, with the development of new medication and treatments, Bilharzia was a thing of the past in Southern Africa. I was pleased, moreover, to read somewhere, not long ago, that vaccines to combat the disease were being developed in Egypt, where the Ministry of Health hoped that with treatment and prevention, they would be able to eradicate Bilharzia within five years.

"Well, I was distressed to hear from Stephen, that the health ministry in Swaziland is having to mount a radio campaign urging people to seek help if they detect suspicious symptoms. Apparently in one school, in the far north region, it was recently found that the entire student body, except for two children, were infected with the Bilharzia parasite. Rural residents are being instructed to bottle snails from the water sources they use and bring them to clinics for parasitic testing.

"This may seem to have little to do with the case, but my prayers have been answered. Stephen went on to tell me, further—and he has, of course, told Tony about this as well—that he has been fortunate enough to purchase the rather lovely colonial house in Pietermaritzburg, that she has much admired, and he can now make a home for her to go to. This has, in turn, come about because of a decision he has reached, that, before it is too late, and while his grandfather is still active and available, he must make the most of the opportunity to involve *El-Hakim* in further research into some of the diseases about which he is so knowledgeable....Particularly Bilharzia, which has long been prevalent in Egypt. Don't the experts maintain that it was carried down the Nile until it finally showed up so far down in sub-Saharan Africa?

"After really seeking God in this issue, Stephen feels he needs to do that research before even thinking of going back into the mission field....I'm not loath to admit that I welcome this respite for both of them, while my little girl has time to settle down, regain her strength, enjoy her new home with Stephen, and be a normal newly-wed!"

This information naturally triggered a buzz of conversation. It was heart-warming that everyone was so pleased for us, and it was Paul Verwey—*El-Hakim's* great-nephew—who went on to ask Stephen about the recently-published paper which he, Stephen, and his grandfather had co-written, on the subject of the mysterious illness that had afflicted Doctor Philip in Egypt.

"I've just had a strange thought," Aunt Amy-Lee said suddenly. "I was wondering why Doctor Philip had never married, and, in thinking of him, it occurred to me that, if he not been sick, *El-Hakim* might never have met and married the princess, they would never have had your father, Stephen, and you would not have been here with us today!"

"By the same token," was Aunt Stella's observation, "would

335

any of us?...Doctor Philip might not have brought you and Doctor Dick Evans into the world, Father Peter."

"That's right!" Zhaynie Ashton picked up the thread eagerly. "Uncle Dick, might not have wanted to be a doctor if he had not admired the Verwey brothers so much, and would not have brought you, Izzie, and Benjamin into the world, Tony. You would not be engaged to Stephen, and Father Peter would never have become friendly with my dad, and so on...and so on...and so on...!"

"The Lord certainly moves in wondrous ways," commented Aunt Amy-Lee. "But, as my dear Ash always insists, there is no such thing as coincidence!...This also leads one to speculate on why the rapier cracked, right when it did. According to Tony's record, it had fallen before..."

This was certainly food for thought, and it sent me off on a mental excursion of my own...

I had been in a constant daze since Stephen had put my ring on my finger, and, looking across to where Zhaynie (Eugenie) Ashton sat with her fiancé, Dominic, and his parents, Doctor Paul Verwey, his wife, Aunt Stella, who had come all the way from Nelspruit to be here with us at this time, I could identify with her. She has that same glow on her lovely little face, that I feel sure there is on mine, and also the bemused smile that neither of us has been able to wipe off our faces since Christmas day. We have both acquired the habit of periodically having to hold our hands up to the light, in order to admire our sparkling new rings, as though needing to check that they are really still there....And I have an additional cause for celebration.—They all seem to like my book!

My thoughts then went off at a different tangent, as I relived some of the tense weeks before I finished it. What lay ahead for us? I had wondered…For Stephen and me?…I was hardly able to wait for Christmas so that he could be with me. It was wonderful to know that I was completely well again, and gradually, over the months I had finally come to appreciate that it was not due to any antipathy towards him, or disapproval of *El-Hakim* on Fallah's part, that he had seemed so reluctant to accept my impending marriage.

Many of these, very same thoughts often went through my head while I was writing, and especially as I waited for the final pages of my manuscript to shoot out of the printer. How breathlessly I collated the pages and tied a ribbon around them, ready for Uncle Ash to take into the city with him.

He has been such an inestimable blessing to me. At the end of each week, as the work progressed, he saw to it that what I had written was photocopied, and both my parents, as well as Aunt Amy-Lee, were given a few chapters at a time, to edit and discuss. I'm sure that the rising excitement I felt, as the story went on, greatly contributed to the restoration of my health, but the gratitude I already felt for Benjamin Ashton was about to exceed anything I could have imagined thus far.

He personally—and very carefully—put the manuscript into his briefcase, before giving it to Ferguson, the chauffeur, to take out to the car, and then he put an arm around my shoulders and kissed my cheek. "Amy-Lee and I have been debating the question of whether to tell you this now, or not, Tony," he said, "because, while we are reluctant to spoil our surprise, she feels that you should have a share in making the decision…

"This will probably be the last Christmas we'll have you with us here at *Bentleigh*, for some time, so we have had many a discussion on the subject of a suitable present for you.…What we have decided to do—and please keep this a secret until it's done—is to have a hundred copies of your book printed for you, to give to whomever you please—although we know very well who the first recipient will be!" His eyes were twinkling and he smiled that wonderful smile I had known since I was a toddler. "Stephen should get here in good time for Christmas, not so?...Well, we will also gladly cover the cost for shipping any others you want to send away, and we think they should be bound in leather so that they will endure.—Now, what colour would you like?"

For a moment I was speechless (a rare condition for me, I tell you!) Then I had to stand on tiptoe in order to throw my arms around his neck. "Oh, Uncle Ash, you and Aunt Amy-Lee grant more than wishes! You help to answer prayers! I was wondering what sort of Christmas presents I could give to Stephen and his family, that would be remotely special enough!"

"Ash?...Benjamin...where are you?" I remember Fallah, who had been on hospital visiting rounds, calling out just then.

"We're here in the library, Pete!" Uncle Ash responded. "I'm just about to leave for the city, and I'm taking Tony's manuscript with me..."

"Great!" Fallah remarked, beaming at us as he came into the room, still in his cassock. "I was hoping to catch you before you left. If you're going to make Tony a copy of the finished article, is there any hope that you can make one for Marina and me, too?"

I'm sure he did not see Benjamin Ashton grin conspiratorially at me as he, Uncle Ash, said cheerfully: "Certainly, Padre. I'll do that with pleasure, but unfortunately I shan't be able to bring it home with me right away. Everyone in the downtown office, is so busy at this time of the year that I shall have to leave it there for Ferguson to pick up later, when it's ready!"

They walked out together, chatting animatedly as they always did when they were together, and as I put away the scissors, picked up a few scraps of ribbon, and cleared the top of the desk where I had spent so many happy hours, my heart was suddenly very full. Even now I still bask in the warm glow of Fallah's approval, when after he had finished reading my story, he said: "Tony, my dearest little girl, you have done your Stephen and his entire family proud. I have heard many urban legends over the years, and have read news clippings and numerous other, very unreliable reports about *El-Hakim*, but I believe that, while you have told his story accurately, truthfully—and with the impartiality which you owed to your readers, among whom I now have the privilege of counting myself—you have made it as readable as you possibly could for anyone interested in the legendary 'Samaritan of the Sahara'. And as for me?...Well, a boyhood hero has been restored to me, and I thank you for that!"

I know he is biased, but can there be anything sweeter than praise from one of the two people you love best in the entire world?

Once again it was my mother's voice that brought me back to reality. I'm sure Marina Crawford must be the most outspoken, direct woman in the world.—Hardly what one would have expected of the rector's wife, back in Nelspruit. It is a good thing that Fallah loves her so dearly, and it was a *very* good thing that most of the older members of the congregation could still remember the day she was born!

She was talking to Aunt Stella Verwey, the mother of

Zhaynie's fiancé, Dominic, and they were teasing Uncle Ash because of the way he would borrow magazines from Aunt Stella's mother, and then tear out any page that had a picture of Aunt Amy-Lee on it.

"By the way, Stella," my mother remarked bluntly, "you were a Morgan before you were married, now I come to think of it....Wasn't your father's name Valentine? And wasn't he old Talbot's *aide-de-camp*?...I seem to remember that the main reason he didn't want you to marry Paul, was because of his antipathy towards Dominic Verwey."

"Marina!" Fallah remonstrated.

"Well," my mother persisted, "I hope my daughter has not hurt your feelings by appearing to criticize him in her story—but what I can't understand is, why, if Hamid Pasha was exonerated, and Sir Humphrey Talbot, and all those other people, found it in their hearts to forgive him, your father could not do the same?"

Because it was well known that the Nelspruit people used to refer to Captain Val Morgan as an 'irascible, difficult old coot', I could not help admiring Aunt Stella at that moment. She looked directly at my mother, and said levelly: "He must have resented him for a different reason, Marina....The tragedy of his life was, I think, that the only two women he ever loved, were both in love with *El-Hakim*! One of them married the legendary doctor—and the other...was my mother!"

"What was your mother's name, Aunt Stella?" Zhaynie Ashton asked gently, riveted by the drama of the situation.

Stella affectionately stroked the silky, raven hair of her son's wife-to-be. "My mother's name was 'Ruth', sweetheart," she told her. "Ruth Talbot!...After all this time she still maintains that *El-Hakim* has the bluest eyes she has ever seen!"

ABOUT THE AUTHOR

Until her husband became seriously ill at the age of 42, Marie Warder was listed by a South African Book Club, among South Africa's top seven 'favourite novelists'. She was certainly one of the most prolific. Mary Morrison Webster, book critic of the widely read *Sunday Times*, once recorded among her recommendations, two books written 'in time for Christmas—in two different languages.' Considered one of the country's favourite public speakers at that time, Mrs. Warder's biography is included in the Archives of the National Council of Women among 'Notable Women of Johannesburg'. Few know that she was also the founder of 'Windsor House Academy', a prestigious private school of which she was the principal for many years until she and her family immigrated to Canada in the late 1970s.

Locally, where she lives in South Delta, British Columbia, she was familiar for many years as a chaplain at the Delta Hospital, while, to most people in the rest of the world, she is known chiefly as the Founder and President Emerita of both the Canadian and South African Hemochromatosis Societies, and the Founder and former President of the International Association of Haemochromatosis Societies.

Before embarking on her two ground-breaking books on Hemochromatosis, made available together, since 2000, in the 'new edition' of *The Bronze Killer*—which contributed to her being awarded a medal of honour and certificate of honour in Canada—she was already the author of 15 very successful novels. All were chosen 'Books of the month', and three were used in South African schools.

Not surprisingly, many of her stories take place in and around newspaper offices for, according to "The Journalist", she became, at the age of seventeen, the youngest chief reporter in the world, having sold her first newspaper article at the age of 11 and her first short story at 17. During her career as a journalist she interviewed some the world's most famous people.

All in all, it seemed that she had a good career ahead of her in her native South Africa, but when—just before her 17th birthday—Frederick Abinger (Tom) Warder, a handsome, tanned young man in an Air Force uniform walked into the newspaper office one day, her life changed radically. It was a clear case of 'love at first sight' and, after that meeting, her life would revolve about him. She played the piano in Tom's very popular dance band....He was wholeheartedly supportive of her writing.

Unfortunately, when he suddenly became ill, they had come to the end of the good times, as she tells in the book, *The Bronze Killer,* an 'internationally acclaimed best-seller'. (The *Delta Optimist*). After nearly eight years of steadily deteriorating health, he was finally diagnosed with Hemochromatosis (iron overload), and until recently, except for a series of travel articles for a magazine she has, for more than 28 years, devoted her literary efforts entirely to the writing of more than 200 articles on the subject of hemochromatosis, and to the production of patient literature for individuals, hospitals and other medical facilities. Her newsletters and brochures have gone out to more than 16 countries. Now, believing that she has done all in her power to promote awareness of the world's most common

genetic disorder, she is back to doing what she likes best....
writing stories.

Published in 2004, '*Storm Water*' and '*With no remorse...*'
were the first in the new Dromedaris series, followed, in 2005,
by: '*When you know that you know that you know!*' and '*Tarnished
Idols*'. '*Dominic Verwey: The Samaritan of the Sahara*' is her eighth
book to be written in Canada.

'*When you know that you know that you know!: or The
redemption of Benjamin Ashton*' (April 2005) caused a sensation.
The response has been phenomenal. One reader describes it as
'The best novel I have ever read!' Another reports that she read
it 'four times in less than a month', and wished that it were
'twice as long!' This about a book that contains 576 pages!

Now we bring you the fifth title in the Dromedaris 'Stories
from South Africa' series. About this book, a reviewer writes:
"After the success of '*Tarnished Idols*', Marie Warder has gone to
the other end of Africa for the setting of her new novel, '*Dominic
Verwey—Samaritan of the Sahara*'. Mrs. Warder's romantic
imagination and facile pen provide plenty of local colour, and
she captures the reader's attention from start to finish. The
very unusual theme concerns the adventures of a doctor in the
Sahara who, besides being skilled with the scalpel, is also a
dashing figure of the Robin Hood type. Well worth reading
and highly recommended." (*Publisher's review.*)

In it we recognize some of the well-loved characters from
'*When you know that you know that you know*', as the *Beauclaire*
saga continues...

BY THE SAME AUTHOR
Non-Fiction
The Bronze Killer: New Edition: Imperani Publishers,
2000
The story of a family's fight against Hemochromatosis—

the most common Genetic disorder—including the first-ever 'layman's' reference: *"Iron...the other side of the story!"*

THE BOOK THAT GAVE A DISEASE A NEW NAME, evolved from *'Iron...the other side of the story!'* (1984) which was the first book ever to be devoted entirely to the subject of Hemochromatosis—iron overload. (Please note alternative spelling, outside of North America, where the disorder is known as 'Haemochromatosis'.)

Since this book was first published in 1989, thousands of families around the world have found it to be a valuable resource. More than just the personal account of a family who have suffered through the ravages of this terrible disease, it has been a source of information, encouragement and enlightenment to many. Included is *'IRON...the other side of the story!'* which provided the world with first 'layperson's reference to the genetic disorder that, if untreated, can lead to a destructive overload of iron in the body; far too often with fatal results. Recommended by physicians and clinics in Canada and further afield, *'The Bronze Killer'* earned high praise for the author in her 1991 citation for the Canada Volunteer Medal of Honour and Certificate of Honour, which read in part: *"Through Marie's research and most noted book, 'The Bronze Killer', she has educated doctors and the general public about the disease. As a result, Hemochromatosis is now recognised as Canada's most common genetic disorder and routine blood tests for the disease may soon become standard diagnostic procedure."*

This from the former Director-General of Genetic Services in South Africa:

"We are highly impressed by the evidence you have

collected and summarised, regarding the importance of Haemochromatosis as a genetic disease in South Africa and on the potentials for preventing its consequences. Your efforts, as outlined, fully coincide with our objectives, i.e. to promote the prevention of inherited diseases and/or their consequences by the means at our disposal."

A valuable and highly recommended resource.
Toronto Star